ODDJOBS 5: THE LONG BAD FRIDAY

HEIDE GOODY

IAIN GRANT

Copyright © 2021 by Heide Goody and Iain Grant

All rights reserved.

No part of this book may be reproduced in any form or by any electronic or mechanical means, including information storage and retrieval systems, without written permission from the author, except for the use of brief quotations in a book review.

PART I

HELL

Yoth-Kreylah ap Shallas – the living black and white – bent over the latest pages of the Bloody Big Book and wrote.

"Life is strange, isn't it?" *said Morag Murray.*

"*Compared to what?*" *asked Vivian Grey.*

From the edge of the canal towpath a family of five ducks watched the two women. Ahead of them was the Cube building and the Court of Yo-Morgantus, temporal ruler of Birmingham. In the Cube, in twelve minutes time, Morag would meet the man with whom she would conceive the kaatbari and bring about the end of the world.

Morag sighed. "*Do you ever wonder what it all means?*"

Vivian Grey despised such vague and whimsical questions.

"*No,*" *she said. This bluntness caused Morag to stop walking and turn to her new colleague.* "*Meaning is created in the minds of intelligent beings,*" *continued Vivian.* "*The 'it' you are referring to is the universe including those self-same minds. It is logically impossible, like trying to fit a gallon into a pint glass.*"

. . .

AP SHALLAS PAUSED in her writings. She was disquieted, but could not quite pinpoint the reason.

Ap Shallas occupied much of the floor space of the scriptorium of *Hath-No*. In an earlier existence, when *ap Shallas* had fewer limbs, there had been desks and seats and even other scribes. They were gone now. As the task of writing the Bloody Big Book had grown, so had *ap Shallas*. Articulated mechanical arms had been gifted to her and grafted onto her by *Sha-Datsei*, regent of *Hath-No*. Blood-ink flowed through those limbs to pen nib fingertips and produced the incalculable number of words that went into the production of the largest book in existence. As *ap Shallas* grew, she became more machine than living thing – ah, there was that feeling of momentary unease again! – as she grew, seats and desks became unnecessary. All *ap Shallas* needed was *ap Shallas*. And a constant supply of paper.

The scriptorium sat in the bowels of the fortress of *Hath-No*. The fortress was an imperfect sphere of fortifications, tunnels and chambers floating in the non-geography of *Leng* space. In truth, it was no fortress at all, but the body and shell of the titanic god *Hath-No* whose eyes saw all and who permitted *ap Shallas* a view of all existence.

The task *ap Shallas* had set herself was the completion of the infinite Book of *Sand*, the Bloody Big Book, a volume which would describe all that had been, all that was and all that would ever be, in precise and complete detail. The woman whose life she was currently detailing in the book, Mrs Vivian Grey, would have said such a thing was a logical impossibility— There! Again! The sense of disquiet! *Kreylah ap Shallas*, a being who had glimpsed all things, felt she was overlooking something vital and obvious.

Ap Shallas straightened and stretched. Several dozen writing arms clicked and unfurled. In the rafters of the scriptorium, sheets of paper dried. On the walls were the thousands of books that made up the library of *Hath-No*. Before *ap Shallas's* arrival, the books had been composed of vellum made from human skin. But since there was no death in hell, those dried skins were still very much alive and rustled and whispered to each other through the aeons.

Unable to focus, *ap Shallas* raised her voice above the whisper of the books.

"*Tea! Barry! Bring me tea!*"

There was the slap of damp flipper feet on stone and Barry the *Thoggan* ran into the scriptorium. He paused at the entrance to bang a gong to announce his own arrival before scurrying to *ap Shallas's* side. At some point in the immeasurable time they had been together, Barry had either found or made himself a gong. It went *donk*! when struck with his little hammer. He used it to announce the arrival of visitors but since *ap Shallas* had very few, he mostly used it to announce himself. It was a frivolous item, but it appeared to make him inordinately happy.

He scurried to her side and smiled up at her, gong clutched pensively in amphibian hands. Barry smiled a lot. With a mouth like his, it was possible he didn't have a choice.

"*Bring me tea,*" said ap Shallas.

"*I'm thorry, mithtreth but I can't,*" said Barry, lisping through a mouth overfilled with pearly-white molars.

"*We have not run out of tea leaves,*" said *ap Shallas*.

"*No, mithtreth but—*"

"*That last consignment from the* bodu-papa *was of dubious quality and certainly not very tea-like, but there was enough to service an army.*"

"*Yeth, mithtreth, but we can't have—*"

"*And milk? You're not afraid of the* shokosz *beast still? They only tried to eat you once.*"

"*No, although getting their glandular thecretionth remainth a daunting tathk. It'th thimply that I cannot—*"

"Do I need you show you once again the five steps to making a perfect cup of tea?"

"*No, mithtreth. I mathtered it long ago.*"

A claw hand reached out blindly and found the teapot on a bookshelf. "Here is the teapot. Here is ... the coaster. Must always have a coaster. Tea without a coaster—"

"*Ith the thin end of the edge, yeth,*" nodded Barry. "*But we cannot have tea now. There ith no time.*"

"No time?" Ap Shallas scoffed. "This is hell. There is no time here at all. Apart, possibly, from tea time."

"*No time,*" said Barry and pointed upwards.

Ap Shallas began to look upwards before realising he was referring to a sound, not a sight. The fortress around them reverberated with the voices of a hundred cracked horns. *Ap Shallas* was momentarily nonplussed.

"*The Soulgate?*" she said in disbelief.

Barry nodded. "*It clotheth around the world of humanth. It ith the end of dayth.*"

"*The end of the world?*" Ap Shallas found herself to be irritated rather than shocked. "*But my work is not yet completed. I am so close, but I am not done. A few thousand pages left, maybe less.*"

"*Her Majethty* Thya-Datsei *hath decreed that her fortheth are to be in the vanguard.*"

"But why?"

Barry shrugged. "*Becauthe* Hath-No *told her and hith thecret godth told him and thye told me and now I'm telling you. All the Venithlarn, conthuming the world together.*" He smiled merrily like it was going to be a swell party.

Ap Shallas could not get over the injustice of this news. "*Tell* Sha-Datsei *I shan't be coming. My work here is far too important. I* have to catalogue everything. Does she comprehend how big 'everything' is?"

"Her Majethty will inthitht. You carry her thord. You are her truthted advithor."

Ap Shallas drew the *Menscuzo* wordblade. As *ap Shallas* had expanded and augmented herself over the uncountable ages, the wordblade had ceased to be something she carried at her side and become simply another component of her increasingly mechanised body.

"*If she wants my sword, she can have it back,*" she said.

"*Pointy end firtht?*" asked Barry fretfully.

A grunt rose from deep within ap Shallas's decrepit chest. "*Just tell her that she will have to contend with the end of the world without me. I have a book to finish.*"

"Yeth, mithtreth," he said, bowed deeply, and fled.

"And bring me tea!"

"Yeth, mithreth!" came the fading reply.

Kreylah ap Shallas bent to her work once more. She frowned. There was something about the two women in this narrative that seemed achingly familiar, but she could not recall what. Pen-fingers descended onto the waiting page

VIVIAN GREY GAVE Morag Murray a look, one that conveyed no empathy or interest in Morag's search for universal meaning.

"Is this to do with you dying?" Vivian asked.

"Yes," said Morag.

"And why do you think you are going to die today?"

"I've been told. I have enemies."

"We all do," laughed Vivian. "Do you want the truth? A lot of things in this world hurt us and cause us pain. A small number of things do not. The only meaning to life involves avoiding the former and finding the latter. Death is the end of all of them, the good things and the bad ones. There is no more meaning than that."

She did not speak again until they had walked a further twenty yards down the towpath at which point she asked, "Do you know we have the Wittgenstein Volume in the Vault?"

"The Bloody Big Book?" said Morag. "Yes."

"You should read it sometime. Then you will understand."

"I'm going to die today," said Morag.

"True," Vivian conceded. "Then don't read it. You have probably got better things to do with your final hours."

The women walked on.

BIRMINGHAM - 12:15AM

It was a quarter past midnight.

Morag Murray had just given birth to a baby girl. She was currently trying to hobble down stairs from the room in which she'd recently been imprisoned to the waiting police vehicles outside. Rod Campbell carried the bundled-up baby in his arms and walked ahead. Nina Seth was beside Morag, holding her elbow. Nina probably thought she was being helpful, but the way she was holding Morag's arm simply meant Morag had one less free hand to use as she navigated the stairs.

Some distance above there was a holler and yell from Steve the Destroyer as he battled with the warbling squid creature that had appeared in her makeshift delivery room not half an hour ago.

"Down! Down! You will bend to my will, puny creature!" Steve commanded, seemingly without much success.

Morag had felt nothing but relief since the baby emerged. Relief that the searing agony consuming her entire being had stopped, and also relief that she was no longer the most vulnerable being in a five-mile radius, given her situation. The relief was tempered with the unsettling realisation that her body was a different shape to the one she was used to. The most worrying part was an ominous sense that her vagina was something like a door that had been left unintentionally open. It was flapping around, loose, bloody and weird, and she wasn't happy about it. And she was tired. Not the sort of tired which spoke of a busy day, or a long run, this was something else. Her body demanded rest and the chance to repair itself.

At the sound of heavy boots on the stairs, Rod held back and readied his pistol. Two police officers appeared at the turn of the stairs. They wore body armour and carried big guns (Morag didn't give a damn about weapon details, even when she hadn't just pushed a baby out through her uterus). Chief Inspector Ricky Lee, unarmed and unarmoured, was right behind them.

"They're with us," barked Ricky to forestall any trigger-happy stairwell firefights. "Building's clear to the ground floor, Rod. Safe to go down."

"Could everyone—" said Morag and then had to pause for breath. "Could everyone stop waving guns around near my baby?"

The coppers lowered their weapons instantly. Morag looked to Rod.

"Aye, sorry," he said.

"And let's just take this a little slower, eh?" she said. "You know those Italian pizza chefs who take a piece of dough and spin it out so it's ridiculously thin and bigger than you'd ever think possible?"

"Yes…?" said Rod, his face telling her he was way ahead of her with this metaphor.

She pointed between her legs. "That. I haven't even looked. I'm afraid to, but it's … delicate."

"We're kind of on the clock here," said Rod. "End of the world and that."

Morag glared at him. Sweat trickled down her brow. "Have you just given birth to a baby, Rod?"

"No."

"No, you have not. So shut your hole and let's take it slow."

"Yeah," said Nina. "Have some consideration, Rod."

Morag threw her a glance too. "Have you just given birth to a baby, Nina?"

"Hey, just offering some sisterly solidarity."

Morag sneered. "You... You and your pert wee fanny. I bet yours doesn't look like pizza dough after some celebrity chef's been—"

"—So-rry."

"We could get a stretcher?" suggested Ricky Lee.

"Did I say I needed a bloody stretcher?" Morag snarled, knowing she was sounding unreasonable and not caring one damned bit.

She grunted with exhaustion as she continued slowly down the stairs. "This is not how I wanted to spend my last day on earth. Limping about with my genitals strung out like bunting, in an evil mansion wearing nothing but a doctor's coat to hide my indignity." She laughed at that. "Damned dictionary definition of indignity, this."

Somehow they made it down to the ground floor and out into the night. Blue police vehicle lights strobed the scene. Morag could now properly see the building where she'd been captive for the last twelve hours. The Maccabees – Kathy Kaur's deluded band of anti-Venislarn terrorists – had made their base in the carcass of a stately home, refurbishing the inside and maintaining the ruined exterior as camouflage. Morag did not know where Kathy and the remnants of her group had gone, but judging by the glowing red rent in the sky, they were either gearing up for some sort of 'Plan B' or generally regretting their poor life choices.

The rip in the night sky was a wound, glowing red and raw. It made Morag involuntarily think of her own unfortunate undercarriage. She'd just given birth to the *kaatbari*, the Venislarn anti-Christ. The things pouring out of that hellhole and bubbling across the stratosphere were numerous, multi-limbed and thankfully too distant to be easily viewed.

"So, is that it?" said Ricky, staring up like so many of the police officers on the scene.

"Fasho," said the *samakha* next to him. Morag had no idea why teen gangster Pupfish was here but it was testament to the horrifying spectacle above that none of the police officers around them were freaked out about the presence of a walking fishman among them. "It's the – *ggh!* – end of the world, cop-man."

"Beginning of the end," said Nina. "The Venislarn will rise up to torture us for eternity." She looked at the sky. "Rise. Descend. Those *bhul-tamade* are gonna come at us from all angles."

"We need to do something," said Rod.

"Car," said Morag and made for the open rear door of a police vehicle.

"Where we going?"

"I'm just looking for somewhere to sit," she grunted. She lowered herself carefully, winced at the thought of actually putting her weight on whatever remained of her sitting-down equipment. She was also going to leave blood wherever she sat, but given it was the end of the world, she wasn't all that bothered. She gestured to Rod. "Baby."

He handed her over. It was an awkward exchange, composed primarily of elbows, but Morag soon had her bundle in the crook of her arm. She pushed the swaddling sheet aside. A round puffy face, eyes screwed shut, wisps of ginger hair poking over her brow.

"Hey, baby," she whispered. Tiny delicate lips, terrifyingly delicate, mushed together and big brown eyes opened a crack. "Baby. It's mum. Can you hear me?"

"You expecting a reply?" said Rod gently.

Morag blinked tears, not willing to tell him that up until the moment of birth, she could hear her child's voice, loud and clear in her head. Now, nothing.

"You think the general public are seeing this?" said Ricky.

"They'll be hearing it at their door soon," said Pupfish.

Even from within the car, Morag could see the edges of the expanding sky horror curving down to touch the earth.

"I've got to find my parents," said Nina.

"We've got a job to do," Rod pointed out.

"You don't have any family. Morag has no family apart from poopy-pants there. I've got a mom and dad who are going to be terrified when they wake up. Ricky, you're driving me. Pupfish?"

"Sho thing," nodded Pupfish.

Ricky was momentarily torn. "You need a ride somewhere?" he asked Rod.

Rod looked helplessly to Morag.

"Kathy said that the Soulgate wouldn't finally close until the arrival of *Yoth-Bilau*," she said.

"Who's that?"

"I don't know. I wasn't paying attention – having contractions at the time."

"The consular mission then." Rod looked to Ricky.

Ricky called a police officer over. "Take these two to the Library of Birmingham."

The man nodded, even though his attention was still fixated on the hellhole overhead.

There were shouts of alarm from near the mansion house. A sinuous shape flowed out of the door on a mat of tentacles.

"Giddy up, my mount-slave!" squeaked the demon-possessed voodoo doll riding on its back, poking the creature with his pencil spear.

"That'll be three of us going to the Library," corrected Morag.

"Three and a *dnebian* land-squid," said Rod.

"Is that what that is?" said Morag.

12:20AM

Ricky kept glancing up at the sky as they drove down the dual carriageway from Great Barr to Nina's home in Handsworth.

"You keep your eye on the road," Nina told him. "I'll keep watching the skies."

The midnight traffic on the road into the city had mostly come to a halt. Cars and vans had stopped here and there. Drivers came out of their vehicles to gawp, to exclaim wildly at each other and, naturally, to video the end of the world on their phones.

"I can't believe this is really it," muttered Ricky as he wove speedily through the staggered vehicles.

"You don't think that this is the end of the world?" said Nina.

"I expected something more... More than distant monsters in the sky."

"Oh, there will be more."

"Yeah but—" He paused to chicane between two taxis whose drivers were arguing in the middle of the road. "I expected more fanfare."

"You want trumpets?"

"I ... I don't want anything. I just expected, you know, space cannons blowing up the White House, volcanoes rising up, tsunamis."

"Give it time," said Nina. "I'd rather we get to my parents before any of that stuff kicks off." She realised something for the first time. "Your wife..."

"I texted her," said Ricky. "She's working in Manchester today."

"You think they've got – *ggh!* – the end of the world there too?" asked Pupfish from the back seat.

"It's kind of a global thing," said Nina. She swivelled in her seat to look back at him. "You need to find your mom and Allana?"

He waved her concerns away. "They're fine. They're with me. They're on *our* side." He flicked a blue fishy finger between himself and the horrors above.

"Oh, is that how this works?" said Nina, unconvinced.

On a slip road, two cars had collided and one had wrapped its front end round a lamppost. A woman was helping an injured man from the vehicle. Ricky radioed it in to the police control centre. The clipped manner of the operator suggested that a prang on the A34 was the least of her concerns.

"They're going to be overwhelmed," said Ricky.

"And it's not even morning," agreed Nina.

Nina's mom and dad lived on a long road of tightly packed terraced houses, directly off Handsworth's main high street. As Ricky pulled up, neighbours Nina had known all her life were out in the street, pointing and fretting at the unfolding sky show.

"Hello, Mr Chowdhry," said Nina, trying to get past him to her own front door.

"What's all this about then, eh?" said her neighbour but one. Mr Chowdhry owned the Freakshake Shack on the high street and Nina reckoned he consumed half the product all by himself.

"It's the end of the world, Mr Chowdhry."

He screwed up his fat face and shook his head. "Nah. I think it's an advert for something."

That was sufficiently stupid to stop her in her tracks. "An advert?"

"You know, a trailer for a movie or something."

She pointed up without looking. "The great gaping hole in the sky?"

"Done with lasers, innit? Looks like one of them adverts for heartburn."

It'll take more than a dose of Gaviscon to fix that quantity of heartburn, Nina thought as she reached her own front door. It opened as she raised her key to the lock.

"And now she turns up," said her mom fiercely, as though everything was entirely Nina's fault. Behind her in the narrow hallway stood her dad and, behind him, Mrs Fiddler.

"What are you doing here?" Nina said to her former primary school teacher.

"What are you wearing?" said Mrs Seth with a disdainful look at Nina's attire.

Nina had spent much of the previous day in eighteenth century England. In fact, she'd spent several months in Industrial Revolution Birmingham and returned before she had even left. She'd not had time to check with payroll if she could claim overtime for those months. She'd also not had time to change out of the long coat and tricorn hat she'd taken to wearing in the past. She had been kind of enjoying the look up until the moment her mom clapped eyes on it.

She touched the brim of her hat. "This is a long story. Right now, we need to get you two out of here."

"You look ridiculous," said Mrs Seth.

"Mrs Fiddler says you can explain all of this," said Mr Seth.

"Is this something to do with you?" asked Julie Fiddler, trying to look at Nina through her parents. "I saw it happening and thought of you."

"I don't, I can, and yes it is," said Nina. "I need you all to come with me. We're going to get you to a place of safety."

"Is there are a safe place from this?" said Mrs Fiddler.

Julie Fiddler had been Nina's year six primary school teacher and had remained completely absent from Nina's life until earlier that week, when Nina had cause to poke around Soho House museum in search of Venislarn weirdness. Nina had given Mrs Fiddler more of an insight into the Venislarn situation than was strictly permitted for members of the public. Her ex-teacher had taken it all rather well, despite being a cardigan wearing, bead twirling fuddy-duddy.

"No," said Nina. "There's no safe place from this, but I can take you to the Library. It will be ... well, maybe a bit safer."

"No library is open at this hour," tutted Mrs Seth.

"Are we going somewhere?" said Mr Seth.

"I have not got my shoes on, for one."

"You have time to put shoes on, mom," said Nina.

"Do I need to pack a bag?"

"We're not packing bags."

"Food!"

"We don't need to take food."

"Do they serve food at the Library? No. No, I don't think so."

Mrs Seth did a U-turn in the hallway and pushed past the others to get to the kitchen. This was quite a manoeuvre in a narrow hall. Nina's parents were round folk. They carried it on their bellies, their chins and their jowls. Her dad had the height to carry it off, but Nina's mom was no taller than Nina herself and did not. Nina had always told herself that one perk of the impending apocalypse was the world would be over before Nina's youthful metabolism slowed and she became spherical overnight.

"No time for food, mom!" Nina shouted. She looked along the

road and could see Ricky standing in his open car door. She gave him a helpless gesture and plunged in after her mother.

Mrs Seth stood at the fridge, pawing through sealed plastic boxes of cooking. She opened one, nodded and put it to one side.

"We don't have time!" said Nina.

Mrs Seth lifted a corner of a box and held it up to Nina. "Sniff that."

"I don't want to sniff that."

Mrs Seth sniffed it, judged it passable and added it to the pile.

12:26AM

s the police car drove along the motorway flyover to descend into the city centre, the whole roadway bucked and shook.

"What the hell was that?" gasped the driver.

"Not rightly sure," said Rod.

"The inevitable destruction of your earth, gobbet!" declared Steve the Destroyer, still riding the *dnebian* land-squid despite the fact it had suckered itself to the rear passenger window.

"Aye, something like that," said Rod.

The roads were a mess of abandoned vehicles and those trying to flee at speed. In the rear of the police car, Morag held her baby tightly and stared at her face.

Birth was a surprise. After the pain and exhaustion, there was bewilderment and a strange euphoria. Morag had made this thing. Morag and poor dead Drew. They had cooked up this creature, and despite her own insistence that she was not the maternal type, Morag was enthralled by this wonderful little person.

The traffic became impossibly snarled closer to the city centre and the police officer took the unilateral decision to drive directly through some roadworks, go the wrong way up a one-way slip road and drive straight across the pedestrianised Centenary Square, narrowly squeezing between the Forward Management building site and the Hall of Memory war memorial. He pulled up directly outside the revolving doors of the Library.

Morag opened the door and cautiously swung her legs out, knowing the coat she was wearing was now soaked with blood. She waited to see which parts of her would cause her the most discomfort when she stood up again. She tried it. There was some residual pain, but the unfamiliar wrongness of her body, along with its enthusiastic leakages, was more disturbing.

"Are you guys going to solve this problem?" the policeman asked.

"Inconceivable!" yelled Steve as the land-squid leapt from the open door.

"Well, not likely," said Rod.

"*Yoth-Bilau*," Morag grunted.

Rod offered to take the child, and when Morag insisted she was fine, supported her back as they walked to the door.

"Big bonny baby you've got there," he noted.

Morag smiled automatically and then judged the weight of her daughter. Were her arms getting tired or had the baby – impossible though it was – actually put on some weight since birth?

Steve and his mount slammed into the glass doors with a wet slap, startling the security guard inside.

"Bob, open up!" called Rod.

Security Bob tore his eyes from the creature smooching slimily against the glass to look at Rod.

"Identification," he said.

"Bob, it's us."

"Identification," the man repeated.

"Have you not noticed the world's ending, mate?"

"All the more reason to follow protocols."

"When we're inside, I'm gonna kill him," muttered Morag.

Without letting go of Morag, Rod found his ID and flipped it open.

"Miss Murray?" said Bob.

"Do I look like I'm carrying *adn-bhul* ID, Bob?" she snarled. "You know it's me."

"And who's that?"

Morag thought for a moment he was referring to Steve, who was now – with a "Hi ho! Steve away!" – riding his cephalopod pet up the vertical wall of the building, but, no, Bob was pointing at her daughter.

"It's a baby, Bob."

"Does it have a name? For the security log?"

Rod thumped the glass and Bob relented. He unlocked the door and allowed them in.

"Seriously, mate," said Rod with as much menace as the gentle man could ever produce, "you need to sort out your priorities."

Morag and Rod moved to the bank of lifts, across a lobby busy with consular mission office staff hurrying to and fro, as though utterly surprised by the arrival of the day they'd always prepared for. A dual bell and klaxon was sounding throughout the building just in case people didn't realise that the end of the world was here.

They crossed paths with Lois Wheeler, the mission receptionist. She smiled out of habit.

"Well, this is horrible, isn't it, bab?" she said. "They're convening in the sub-sub-basement. Vaughn's expecting you. Don't let him near any sharp objects."

"Er, okay," said Rod, pressing for the lift.

"I didn't know we had a sub-sub-basement," said Morag.

"What do you think she meant about Vaughn?" said Rod.

The lift announced its arrival. Morag was glad to get inside and lean against the support rail. The doors closed and muffled the alarms.

"Prudence," she said.

"What's that?" said Rod.

Morag nodded downward. "My Uncle Ramsay said that if he ever had a daughter, he'd have called her Prudence."

"Prudence Murray. Nice name."

"You think so?"

Rod shrugged. "Most kids grow up to hate their name at some point."

Morag exhaled long and slow, feeling the ache in her body. "At least that's one problem she won't have, hmmm?"

12:30AM

Six people into one policeman's car did not go easily. Mrs and Mrs Seth stared with wild-eyed distrust at the fish-headed *samakha,* so Nina put Pupfish in the front and her parents in the back. Ricky Lee threw out the parcel shelf and, since Nina was by far the tiniest and Mrs Fiddler by far the oldest, Nina inserted herself in the boot and let her ex-teacher squash up in the back seat with her parents. Ricky gently shut the boot and drove them all towards the city centre via the Soho Road.

In the confines of the back seat, Mrs Seth tried to off-load the carrier bag of food supplies on her knees onto Mr Seth's equally occupied lap. "You will have to take them so I can get my phone," she said.

"I have no room!" her husband argued.

"Nina, what is the address? I need to tell your sister where to meet us."

"Priya's in Coventry," said Nina. "It's too dangerous a journey."

"Where should she go? Take the Tupperware, man. I only want you to hold it for a second!"

"Tell her to stay at home." Nina swallowed any emotion in her voice. There was little love lost between the sisters. The first twenty years of their lives had been a constant battle of one-upmanship, but Nina realised she had just acknowledged she would never see her sister again. "Tell her to stay inside. Stay safe. The cousins. Tell them the same."

It was not the right advice. The right advice would be to tell them to kill themselves immediately, in the faint hope they could escape the closing Soulgate, be dead and out of this place before hell wrapped itself around the world – after which even death would be no escape from the eternity of tortures to come.

As the weight of this truth settled on Nina, her parents squabbled over who should carry what on their knees. Outside, a streak of sickly yellow lightning ripped across the sky, illuminating a vast serpentine shape within the clouds.

"Hey you, mister sir," said Mr Seth to Pupfish. "Could you hold some of these?"

"Do not speak to it!" whispered Mrs Seth harshly, fearfully.

"Sho thing, Mr Nina's dad," said Pupfish.

"Mom, dad," said Nina. "That's Pupfish. He's a friend of mine. And that's Chief Inspector Ricky Lee driving us."

"Oh, we know all about *him*!" said Mrs Seth loudly.

"Er, nice to meet you," said Ricky.

"Don't think I don't know what you two get up to. Filthy! And you a police officer too, young man."

"Mom!" moaned Nina and wished she could sink further into the boot, away from the embarrassment.

"These smell —*ggh!* – really nice, Mrs Nina's mom," said Pupfish.

"You should try one of these," said Mrs Seth. There was the creak-pop of a plastic lid coming off. "Pakora. I made these yesterday. I make a lovely spice cake too."

As snacks were passed about, Mrs Fiddler tried to shift around in her seat to look over the chair back at Nina. There was an unexpected twinkle in her eye, and the faintest of smiles on her lips.

"I'm glad someone's enjoying this," said Nina.

Mrs Fiddler tapped a point on Nina's tricorn hat. "So you did it? You went back in time. Last I saw you, you were climbing through the oculus. But you did it."

Nina nodded. "Georgian England. Seventeen seventy-three."

"And you stayed long enough to pick up some clothes. Look at the stitching on these." She ran a finger along Nina's shoulder seam.

"Three months," said Nina. "I was stuck there for three months."

"You smell it."

"Oi," said Nina, smiling. "They don't have deodorant. Or washing machines. Rod gave me a bottle of anti-wolf pheromone spray to cover the smell."

"Not sure it worked. And did you ... did you explore?"

"I stayed at the Old Crown in Digbeth. I ate oyster pie. I learned to ride a horse. Sort of. I met Matthew Boulton."

Mrs Fiddler's eyes sparkled. "What was he like?"

"Nice guy. Kind of intense. And I met Darwin and Wedgwood. We got off on the wrong foot. They took exception to my knees. There was a mad woman – Isabella – who was trying to start the end of the world two hundred years early. She had a *Gellik* orb that she got from my friend, Vivian Grey. She used it to summon these *kobashi*."

"The ones we saw through the oculus."

"Exactly. They were the ones who trashed Soho House. We chased her to Hagley Wood where she was opening a gateway to the end of the world. We stopped her. Just. Then she tried to escape through time with the oculus, but I think she just telefragged herself into a tree she wasn't expecting to be there, in the future. If I had been able to get the orb off her, I could have used it to rescue Vivian."

Nina remembered what she had seen through the window to the future Isabella had opened up. The armies of the Venislarn pouring across the landscape, a tidal wave of gore carried in the mouths and on the talons of *dhius* and *dendooshi* and *Voor-D'yoi Lak*. "*Bhul*, it's going to be horrible," she murmured.

"Hang on," said Ricky, swerving to cut between a traffic island and an abandoned lorry.

"These are lovely pakora, Mrs Nina's mom," said Pupfish, munching happily.

"Bella in the Wych Elm," said Mrs Fiddler out of nowhere.

"What's that?" said Nina.

"Who put Bella in the Wych Elm?"

"I didn't say anything about a … wych elm?"

"No," said Mrs Fiddler. "It's an urban legend. Except it's not, because it's true."

Nina's dad was nodding. "I saw the graffiti once."

"It pops up sporadically, even now," agreed Mrs Fiddler.

Nina had no idea what they were on about and said as much.

"Nineteen forty-three," said Mrs Fiddler, settling into teacherly story-telling mode. "Four boys found a human skeleton wedged inside an elm tree in Hagley Wood. A skeleton. The woman had been dead for some time. The body was taken away and there was an autopsy but the police investigation didn't get very far. There was a war on at the time."

Nina wasn't going to ask which war. Mrs Fiddler would only give her a disappointed look.

"Graffiti started appearing on walls in Birmingham. 'Who put Bella in the Wych Elm?' In the city centre, in Hagley. From the Forties right through to present day. This graffiti keeps popping up. If you go to the Wychbury Obelisk, it's probably on there right now."

"Vandals," nodded Mr Seth.

"If you say so," said Mrs Fiddler. "But someone clearly knew something about her."

"And the body?" said Nina. "The orb around her neck?"

"Well, that's another interesting part of the mystery. The skeleton was taken away. There was an autopsy and then…"

"Then?"

"They vanished. Skeleton. Autopsy. All evidence relating to the woman. Bella vanished."

Nina huffed. "Someone stole it."

"There was a war on. Things went missing."

"Mmm – *ggh!* – delicious!" said Pupfish up front.

"He's eaten them all!" said Mr Seth.

"The boy has an appetite." Mrs Seth, unfazed, cracked the lid on another container.

12:34AM

The Venislarn were always going to destroy the earth. But still, the *actual* arrival of the end of the world was a surprise.

For decades, consular missions to the Venislarn had been working behind the scenes, keeping the public safe and in the dark. The Venislarn were here on earth, had perhaps always been here, had written themselves into human history and inserted themselves into human society. They slumbered and loitered and played games in the affairs of humanity, waiting for the moment when the Soulgate would snap its jaws around the world and begin an eternity of endless tortures.

In Birmingham, most of the Venislarn had been under the sway of *Yo-Morgantus*, a mere prince among the great, terrible and unknowable gods who were yet to descend upon the earth. Until now, *Yo-Morgantus* had confined himself to the top floors of the Cube office building. The consular mission had built its local headquarters less than half a mile away, nine storeys of offices, research and storage facilities, all masquerading as a shiny new city library that the public rarely had the opportunity to use. The outside of the building was covered in an overtly decorative pattern of interlocking rings. Rod had been told that the rings, of a tungsten-magnesium alloy with a selenium core, were some form of protective ward against any Venislarn that might try to breach the mission's walls. Rod suspected that assertion would be put to the test today and be revealed to be absolute codswallop.

Rod put more faith in the layers of concrete now placed between the Library's sub-sub-basement and the world above. This level, even deeper than the mission's storage Vault, had corridors of white concrete and the simplest of strip lighting. It had a definite 'bunker' vibe and Rod had no issue with that.

It appeared that most of the mission staff who had managed to get into the city centre were down here. Rod wasn't entirely sure what value the PR and marketing team were going to bring to proceedings on this final day (did anyone care about colour or font choice now?) However, he did spot the marketing guys in a side-room kitchenette, apparently giving each other tearful, comforting head massages as Rod and Morag walked past.

A leather swivel chair came down the corridor towards them.

It was being propelled by the mission chief, Vaughn Sitterson. He peered round the bulky headrest as he steered himself backwards. He caught Rod's gaze.

"Don't mind me," he said in a jolly whisper. "Just heading to the lift. You wouldn't press the call button for me, would you?"

Rod could not recall Vaughn ever speaking to him so directly and convivially before. Vaughn's usual manner was to treat human interaction as a painful burden.

"Er, sure," said Rod.

As Vaughn wheeled past, Rod saw his hands were bound to the chair arms with cable ties and, furthermore, below his rolled-up sleeves his forearms were wrapped in bandages. Dried blood had seeped under the edge of one of them.

Down the corridor, a mission security guard stepped out of a door and waved. "Mr Sitterson, sir. Can you come back down here, please?"

Vaughn gave Rod an imploring look. "Just take me to the roof. I don't need any help. I'll wheel myself off."

Rod looked to the guard. "You want me to push him back to you, Andy?"

"Thanks, mate." Andy gave him the thumbs up.

Vaughn obligingly tucked up his feet as Rod pushed him. "There's still time," he whispered to no one. "Death is still a way out. For a time."

"That's right," said Rod, deliberately ignoring him. "You keep thinking cheery thoughts."

Security Bob chased Nina and her entourage across the Library lobby. "But they can't all come with you," he argued as he tried to keep up. Nina's legs were short, but Bob wasn't used to moving any faster than a rolling waddle.

"They're coming with me," said Nina, unwilling to consider any arguments.

"It's only key personnel allowed in the sub-sub-basement."

"You just make rules up."

"I have the authority to taser you if you don't comply," he said in a darker tone.

Nina, who knew first-hand what it was like to get tasered in the back by consular security staff, whirled on the man. "Just because you've got a beret and those silly shoulder things—"

"Epaulettes," said Ricky helpfully.

"—doesn't mean you're bloody important." She stabbed a finger at Ricky. "This is the police Venislarn liaison officer for Birmingham." She pointed at her mom. "She's in charge of catering."

Mrs Seth raised the bags and boxes that filled her arms. "Food."

Nina pointed at Mrs Fiddler. "This is the best school teacher I ever had and might even be able to help us find Vivian Grey."

Bob gestured in exasperation at Pupfish. "And him? He's a bloody Venislarn fishman!"

"You 'bout to get – *ggh!* – racist on me, pig?" sniffed Pupfish.

"He's fine," said Nina. "He's even been here before."

"At a time of war?" said Bob, squeaking with emotion.

"This isn't a war, you stupid man," said Nina. "This is us ... *messing about* while the world ends."

Pupfish had his hand in his trouser waistband. "You wanna go, old man?" he said, rummaging around in his codpiece for a pistol. On reflection, Nina should not have let him take the gun from the Maccabees man who'd tried to kill them in Dudley. "I'm ready when you are, dog."

"Enough of this *muda*," said Nina. "Pupfish is our personal Venislarn expert. Pup, take your hand out your pants."

Bob did not follow them as they backed off towards the lifts, but he did gesture at Mr Seth. "And him?"

"Oh, I just stay in the background and try to make sure everyone stays happy," said Mr Seth. "Anything for a quiet life."

Nina called the lift.

As they rode down, Ricky leaned in close to her. "The phrase you were looking for back there was rearranging the deck chairs on the Titanic."

"Right," said Nina. "I don't remember that scene. Was it in the director's cut?"

"I liked that film," said Mrs Seth. She made sure she caught Ricky's eye. "The boyfriend drowned."

12:45AM

Someone had managed to find Morag a pair of trousers among the office uniform supplies so that when she sat down in the sub-sub-basement conference room she might have looked like crap in a blood and fluid-stained doctor's coat with a heavy new-born baby clutched to her chest but – by the gods! – at least she had her legs covered.

The conference room designers had definitely opted for Cold War chic when decorating the place. Bare concrete walls contrasted with stark strip lighting overhead. A bank of monitors on one wall showed various live maps of the city, plus a few rolling news channels. Even on mute, the BBC newsreader did not look as if he was having a good night.

The round conference table was large but only half of its twenty-something seats were occupied.

"The Fifth Fusiliers A Company have already been mobilised," said a grey-templed soldier who had curtly introduced himself to the table as Major Sanders. "Six hundred and fifty soldiers moving out from their barracks in Sheldon, supported by Warrior fighting vehicles."

"And doing what?" asked the middle-aged man in a lilac tracksuit who looked like he had literally been dragged from his bed in the last half hour.

Major Sanders sorted through his papers. "Forgive me, councillor. It should have been Lieutenant-Colonel Ambrose here today. We don't know where he is at the moment. I'm filling in for him. Our sealed orders direct us to initially undertake urban pacification."

The councillor was Sajid Rahman, the deputy leader of Birmingham City Council. Morag guessed that day-to-day meetings for him leaned more towards the book-balancing, planning approval and library closures variety. Right now he looked seriously and fearfully out of his depth. He kept himself close to the equally bewildered Chief Executive Officer of the council, who at least had managed to throw on a suit and a tie before being dragged here. Morag judged that the tie, with its lurid SpongeBob SquarePants design, was a little too jolly for the situation they were in, but she couldn't blame a guy who had been forced to oversee the end of the world (or at least the localised aspects of it) at a moment's notice.

"'Urban pacification,'" said the Council CEO. "Sounds a bit euphemistic."

"The British Army does not do euphemisms," said Major Sanders. "Clear communication avoids cock ups."

"So, it doesn't mean shooting people in the street?"

"No, Mr Groves," said the major. "That comes later."

Councillor Rahman made an apoplectic peep of alarm.

"The consular mission to the Venislarn has a clear set of procedures detailing our response to the Soulgate," said Vaughn smoothly, without addressing anyone in particular. "This policy here—" His bound hand flailed as he tried to reach for the printed document in front of him. "This one here – that one—" He gave up and pointed. "—details the army, police and civil response to this emergency."

Holding her squirming but still sleeping baby close, Morag flipped open the policy document. It was still warm, fresh off the printer.

"Is this really happening?" said Councillor Rahman. "Is this —" he spread his fingers, 'hey presto'-style over the document, and figuratively everything else "—is this a real thing that's actually happening? I mean, I'm only the deputy council leader. The major here is standing in for a colonel—"

"Lieutenant-colonel," said Sanders.

"Right. The lieutenant-colonel's gone AWOL."

"And we are definitely not quorate," said the CEO. "Surely, this can't be enough people to handle…" He looked round the table. Two representatives from the local council, an army officer and a handful of consular mission office staff including Vaughn, Rod, Morag and, for some reason that Morag could not fathom, Chad from marketing. Down by the screen end of the table in the half shadows sat Professor Sheikh Omar and his companion Maurice. Omar was in a wheelchair, and had an unhealthy pale sheen to his face.

"What's up with Omar?" Morag whispered to Rod. "He doesn't look well."

Rod leaned in. "Better than I expected, truth be told. He took a bullet to the right lung yesterday. Flamin' Maccabees."

"He should be in hospital."

"I hear the hospitals are already euthanising their patients," Rod said.

Omar caught Morag looking at him. He raised his eyebrows above his black-rimmed specs, silently expressing his surprise at the Venislarn anti-Christ in her lap. Morag tilted her head, a 'hey, what can you do, eh?' gesture. She frowned at his chest which, now that she looked at it, bulged oddly, and seemed to be shifting and pulsating. Omar's face took on a familiar superciliously amused expression, an admission he was perhaps doing something a little naughty and was, as always, playing by his own rules.

"I don't know if I can even make any decisions on any of this," the CEO continued. "I'm only the *interim* CEO. Holding the tiller for Mr Jordan until the nasty business with the waste collection dispute can be resolved."

"I think we've moved beyond striking binmen now," said Rod.

"But is this *real*?" said Councillor Rahman, stretching his face as though everything was a nightmare he was still hoping to wake from. "Like, really real? Is it one of those war game scenarios? Shouldn't we be in the Anchor Exchange bunker?"

"It's flooded," said Morag.

"And it's got a spider infestation," added Rod.

"Everything is in order and as it should be," said Vaughn. "We have policies in place and wheels in motion. Euthanasia packs are being delivered to as many residents as possible, the Prime Minister is going to appear on television in the next half hour to address the nation—"

"A live broadcast?" said Morag, who had a low opinion of the national leader's ability to deliver any kind of coherent message on the first attempt.

"A recording," said Vaughn.

"A *live* recording," said Chad from marketing.

"What does that even mean?" said Morag.

"Recorded as though live," said Chad. "At the moment it was recorded, it was live. The Prime Minister was live at that time."

"That makes no sense," said Rod.

"The PM will address the nation," said Vaughn firmly. "A clear message will be given to the people of the country. We can rely on their common sense to do as requested at this time. The public will remain calm and through a combined military and medical operation, as many of the population will be euthanised as possible."

"We prefer the word 'kill'," said Major Sanders, looking aside as an aide entered the room and passed him a slip of paper.

"The medics will euthanise," Vaughn corrected himself. "The army will just kill people. The point is, we all have a role to play and as long as we do that—"

Major Sanders had his hand up. "Lieutenant-Colonel Ambrose is currently on the M54, heading to North Wales."

"What's he doing there?" said Vaughn.

Sanders looked at the slip of paper but finding no answers there, put it down. "I believe he has a holiday home in Snowdonia. Perhaps he intends to co-ordinate matters remotely from there."

"Everyone playing their role, eh?" said Rod quietly.

"This is all falling apart," said Councillor Rahman.

Chad leaned forward. "I think what we all need to do in this instance is take a deep cleansing breath—" He did just that, in case anyone didn't know how. "I use the Buteyko technique. Works wonders with a bit of barefoot grounding therapy, although that's hard to do in this environment. We all take a deep breath, think about where we are now and then collectively visualise – we can all visualise, can't we? – where we want to be in the future."

"Where we are now..." said Major Sanders. "It's the last day of planet Earth."

"And yet the pubs are open," said Chad brightly. He held up his phone to show his Twitter feed. "Landlords are opening up in the middle of the night for those who can't cope with the end of the world sober. We really must gauge all of our actions through the lens of the media."

"We do not need to know how this is going to play out in the media," said Vaughn. "Our policies on the matter are—"

"I'm sorry, Vaughn," said Chad. "I can't allow that. It is through the media that we perceive ourselves. YouTube, social media, television, radio, recherché arts periodicals. And by perceiving, so we become."

"Does this man need to be here?" asked Major Sanders.

The council CEO put up his hand. "I just think that if this is happening—"

"Really happening," added Councillor Rahman.

"— then someone should have planned for it."

"We *have* planned for it," said Vaughn. "If you look at the policy here … please, can someone move it closer to my hand?"

"I think," Morag whispered to Rod, "I wish I was in one of those pubs."

"Aye," Rod nodded.

Whether it was in response to her movements or some faint telepathic connection to Morag's thoughts of drink, the baby stirred. Prudence Murray squeaked, blinked and then cried, if only faintly.

"You hungry?" said Morag. She had no idea. During the pregnancy she'd accidentally unlocked a telepathic link between her and her unborn. Her foetus's wants and needs were clearly expressed. Now, she didn't know if Prudence was hungry, had pooped herself or was just angry with the state of the world.

Morag unbuttoned the doctor's coat awkwardly.

"You need a hand there?" said Rod.

She gave him a look. He shrank back.

Morag pulled aside the coat and shifted Prudence in her arms to bring her in line with her exposed nipple. She had no clue what to do next, but Prudence clearly did. Her mouth opened and her face twisted around with urgent focus. Before Morag knew what was happening, her tiny mouth was clamped on like a limpet mine.

"Hey, you missed! Ow!"

Morag prised her breast away, slightly aghast at the force it took, and relocated Prudence's mouth onto her nipple. Morag had never taken the time to picture what it would be like to breastfeed a baby, but if she had, the picture would have involved rosebud lips daintily suckling. The reality was much more earthy, and involved Prudence swallowing down an improbable amount of breast.

"Do you need to go somewhere to do that?" asked Vaughn, trying to conceal his disgust at the sight of a breastfeeding woman.

"Go somewhere?" said Morag, glaring.

"Somewhere more comfortable?"

"Oh, I am fine right here, Mr Sitterson," she said with fierce sincerity.

Vaughn looked away, muttering, "I'm not entirely sure where that baby came from…"

"The media is providing us with startling and constant updates on the local situation," Chad was telling the table. He flicked his phone and cast his social media feed to the screen. "Lots of photos and videos of the … thing that landed on the QE Hospital."

Omar turned round awkwardly to look and adjusted his specs. "A *bezu'akh* annihilator."

"God, it's ginormous," said Major Sanders as, on the screen, a giant apparently composed of butcher's off-cuts slowly but thoroughly pounded the hospital's multi-storey car park into rubble.

"And that's not even one of the true gods, dear boy," said Omar. "We've been too loose with the terms we have. There are soul-sucking, mind-robbing, country-flattening gods which we've not even glimpsed yet. They are all coming, and they'll rush in like it's the first day of the January sales."

"And you knew about this?" said the deputy council leader, aghast.

"Need to know basis," said the major, which was rich from someone who had only needed to know in the last hour.

"Best to keep these things under wraps," Omar assured the councillor. "Knowledge generates a level of complicity. Whereas there's something honest about complete ignorance."

Major Sanders pointed at the screen in outrage and the dark shadows at the base of the footage. "And why in hell are there people standing around watching the thing? Look, they're actually take photos! Selfies!"

"I know I would," said Chad.

"Those people are putting themselves in terrible danger."

"I propose that something is done about it immediately," said Councillor Rahman.

"I second that," said his chief executive.

"A Company are en route," said Major Sanders.

"Oh, dear," said Chad, looking at his phone. He cast it to the screen for all to see. "This is in Edgbaston."

The selfie-taker had performed the tricky act of taking a selfie at the very instant a *Croyi-Takk* had swooped down to snip his head from his shoulders with its fearsome front claws. It was a feat that the selfie-taker would never get to repeat.

"Perhaps we should put out some kind of warning," Chad conceded.

"We need to tell people that trying to get a selfie with an unspeakable horror is a bad thing?" said Morag, then winced at a sudden pain. She pulled Prudence away and looked at her angrily pink nipple, then her little girl. Prudence opened her mouth, showing off six tiny white baby teeth.

"Teething? Already?"

Morag had suffered a supernaturally accelerated pregnancy, galloping through the second and third trimesters in less than a day. The thought that her girl might grow up at an equally speedy rate was alarming. Prudence, unmistakeably larger than at her moment of birth, pressed her lips together and blew bubbles of spittle while producing a grizzling 'mmmmm' noise.

"Okay, girl," said Morag and rocked her teething child. Prudence Murray wriggled powerfully in Morag's lap. "What do you want, eh?"

Prudence gave an irritated 'ngh' and tried to slide off Morag's lap. Morag let her so. As her pinky chubby feet touched the ground, the little girl sought out a stance that would maintain her balance. Trying to walk at less than two hours old? Despite the insanity of it, Morag couldn't help but feel a ridiculous sense of pride.

Grunting at the aches brought on by fresh movement, Morag held Prudence's hands high and helped her toddle to the door. Rod looked round at her in shock.

"Just going for a little wander," she told him and gave a crazy grin.

12:51AM

For Nina, getting her parents into the relative safety of the basement under the Library was one thing. Getting them to stay safely out of harm's way while she got on with her actual *adn-bhul* job was something else entirely.

"So this is where you work then, is it?" said Mrs Seth, touching the concrete wall disdainfully as the group moved along the corridor, seemingly against the flow of people who had real and important jobs to do. "No wonder you weren't keen to talk about it."

"I have an office on the seventh floor, mom. An office and a swivel chair and a view across the city."

"But you bring us down here, eh?" Mrs Seth tutted.

"I think it's lovely," said Mr Seth automatically.

"Here. In here." Nina steered them into an alcove area. "Right, this is you."

"This is a kitchen."

"Exactly."

"Listen," said Ricky. "There's got to be some sort of operations room down here. As police liaison, I really need to be there…"

"Yeah, yeah. One minute," said Nina.

"And what are we supposed to do here, hmm?" said Mrs Seth.

Nina pointed. "Fridge. Put the food in it. Kettle. Make everyone a decent cuppa. If you've got time, I dunno, bake some cakes."

"This will be fine," said Nina's dad. Her mom's face told a different story.

"Right. You three," said Nina to the others, "let's find out who's making the decisions right now."

"Oh, I see how it is. The young fishboy gets to go, but mom and dad are told to stay in the kitchen," Mrs Seth continued.

Nina wanted to keep Pupfish close. In the heart of the consular mission, she didn't want the young *samakha* detained or even killed by jumpy, over-zealous staff. Scouting around the nearby corridors, Nina found Morag crouched in one, supporting a ginger-haired toddler as it wobbled about on unsteady feet, making constant 'ma ma ma ma' noises.

"This..." Nina stared at the kid. "This isn't your child?"

Morag looked up and smiled. "It's been a strange day already." She jerked a thumb at the door nearby. "They're still squabbling about who should be doing what to handle the apocalypse."

"Thanks." Nina pushed through the door with Ricky, Mrs Fiddler and Pupfish in tow. She saw Omar, a man who looked as well as a man who'd been shot in the chest should look.

Nina tipped her tricorn hat to the assembled people. "Sorry, I'm late, Vaughn. We got a little tied up. Ah, I see you did too."

"Chief Inspector Ricky Lee, police Venislarn liaison," said Ricky, gravitating towards a free seat near the po-faced army guy.

"Julie Fiddler. Er, Birmingham Museum Service," said Mrs Fiddler.

"Yo, I'm Pupfish," declared Pupfish.

"Oh, God. It's one of them," said the tracksuit wearing guy at the far end.

"Pupfish is cool," Nina insisted. "One of us."

"And a sterling young actor," said Chad. He patted the seat next to him for the *samakha* to sit.

An army officer had his phone on the table in speaker mode and was struggling to communicate with whoever was on the other end.

"Say again, sir," he said. "We didn't quite catch the last bit."

"You are to proceed as ... ... Major Sanders. We are working on a co-ordinated ... ... other military forces, although the Americans ... ... from the general plan vis-à-vis nuclear deployment."

"Sir, I didn't quite catch that," said the major. "Say again?" He looked at his phone. "The lieutenant-colonel has gone again," he told the table.

"The reception in Snowdonia, huh?" said Rod. "Does he reckon he can sit out the end of the world there?"

"It's clear – relatively clear – we are still proceeding with a worldwide co-ordinated military plan."

"A lot of social media comments are suggesting this is all a Russia ploy," said Chad.

Nina slipped into a chair next to Rod. "The Russians created the Venislarn apocalypse?"

"The main suggestions are that it's all down to nerve agents and mind control signals broadcast from mobile phone masts," said Chad.

"Normally, I would not discount any theory regarding hostile enemy action," said Major Sanders, "but no. Let's cut to the chase. Apart from our immediate orders, what are the next steps?"

"The electorate will want to see decisive action from us," nodded the guy in a tracksuit.

"Action, councillor?" said Omar with quiet disdain. "Human action plays no part in what's to come. Maurice, now might be the time to bring out the map."

As Maurice (who wore a golfing jumper with pink and lilac diamonds to greet the end of the world) went off into the shadows,

Omar struggled to his feet. "Let me outline what will happen, if I may."

"Professor Omar, please," said Vaughn with a gracious half-wave of his restrained hand.

"Some background," said Omar. He leaned against the back of a chair for support as he began his lecture. The bulging mass at his chest squirmed and clicked. "Nineteen forty-nine, a mysterious skull was discovered in a shop doorway on Broad Street, a skull so massive that it damaged the back door of the police car they took it away in. The official story was that it was an elephant skull and the whole thing was a surrealist joke, left there by the artist Desmond Morris.

"This was a variation on the truth. It was the skull of a *caliturn* ogre which had been released in the city following an occult ritual during a party in Varna Street in Balsall Heath, before being destroyed by the consular mission of the time. A wild party by all accounts: students, nuns, gypsies, jazz musicians. I believe George Melly was there. Birmingham had a thriving surrealist scene at the time. The ritual left three people dead – poets, I believe, so no great loss – and had a lasting impact on the survivors, including Desmond Morris and Conroy Maddox."

Maurice wheeled in a large picture, as big as a school blackboard and held between two sheets of Perspex. It was a violently colourful, indeed almost jaunty, painting featuring abstract animal shapes in primary colours against a background of lines, dots and squiggles.

"Conroy Maddox, the surrealist painter and collage maker, who had been making uncannily accurate images of the Venislarn apocalypse since the beginning of the decade, produced this monstrosity in response to what he had seen during the ritual. The fact that he managed to retain his sanity after committing this horror to canvas is testament to the man's willpower."

The collected group around the table stared at the painting.

There was something utterly arresting about it. The titanic creatures that marched along the landscape were all trumpet mouths, spindle legs and bulbous bodies, executed in bright primary colours. They did not look like any Venislarn Nina had met, yet it was unpleasantly compelling and somehow felt instinctively 'true'.

"It's a map of the final days of planet earth," said Omar. "It is, in short, an utterly perfect representation of what is about to happen to us all." He shuffled to one end. "Following the birth of the *kaatbari*, the Venislarn hordes will make themselves known in all their bloody glory. The annihilators and Handmaidens and sprouting *girr'xod* that we're already seeing on the streets are the leading edge only. What we are presently witnessing are the monsters, things that we can at least physically comprehend. Within hours, the lesser gods will make themselves known. *Daganau-Pysh* will rise from his slumbers in the Warwick and Birmingham canal and—"

"There's a god … thing currently sleeping in the local canal?" said the councillor.

"As council CEO, I should have been made aware," said the suit next to him.

"Even as deputy leader—"

"Was planning permission sought?" The council executive gave a distraught shake of his head. "Surely, someone should have foreseen this!"

Omar frowned and waved at the map painting. "Someone literally did."

"But could we not have put plans into place?"

"We *have* plans," said Vaughn.

"Contingency planning of some sort…"

Vaughn waved about the policy document in his hand. "So much planning. So many pieces. Right now there are stockpiles of euthanasia drugs in warehouses around the country and—" He looked around. "Lois? Lois! Bring in the Tranquill! We have a force of a quarter of a million volunteers who will be taking them door-to-door in their local area."

"Volunteers?" said the deputy council leader.

"We ran a very effective but ambiguously worded social media campaign," said Chad. "Lots of young people wanting to do their bit for the world. Targeted ads for climate strikers, people who give to Just Giving campaigns. We even got a celebrity endorsement."

"That one who used to be in a boy band," said Vaughn.

"They all downloaded the app and are now mobilised to hand out boxes of euthanasia pills."

Lois entered with a cardboard box. It was small, white with a perforated lift away lid with the word *Tranquill* printed in a calm, flowing blue font. She placed it in the centre of the table for all to see.

"Looks like a box of tampons," said Nina.

"*Thank* you," said Chad. "That was exactly the vibe we were going for. Personal, feminine, caring."

"The government target is to have these in half a million homes before three a.m.," said Vaughn.

"We predict a seventy percent customer conversion rate," said Chad and then, aside to Nina, "I picked the font."

"Customer conversion rate," said the council suit numbly.

"A lot of gentle deaths," said Vaughn.

"A lot of our voters," said the deputy council leader. "I wouldn't put it past central government to try to kill off the competition."

"Oh, look on the bright side," said Omar. "You'll never see your political opponents win an election ever again."

12:54AM

"Mu-mu-mu-mu-mummy."

Morag held her girl by the shoulders and stared into her eyes. "Did you just say 'mummy'?"

"Mummy," said Prudence and giggled.

It was very clearly said, particularly for a first word, particularly only an hour or so after birth. And – Morag would have to listen again to be sure – was that a highland accent the wee lass had?

"Well, aren't you the cleverest thing?"

"Mummy!" agreed Prudence and clapped her hands. A passing consular staff member glanced at the little girl but said nothing. Just an ordinary toddler. And the woman probably had more pressing matters on her mind.

"And if you're old enough to be speaking. I really think we need to find you something like proper clothes," Morag told her daughter.

Prudence wrapped the sheet she wore more tightly around her neck and waddled about making a noise with her lips like an idling tractor.

"Yes, let's see what we can find you."

There were clothing supplies down here, overalls and uniform spares. From a storage room, Morag took the smallest T-shirt she could find, and the smallest trousers. A pair of scissors turned the cheap trousers into short shorts which, with a length of string for the belt provided Prudence with a wildly flared pair of trousers that looked more like a Georgian ball gown than anything else. The shirt, knotted and tucked into the huge trousers, just about managed to stay on the tot's shoulders.

"That okay?" said Morag.

Prudence nodded and smiled, and raised her arms to be picked up.

"Hungry again?"

Prudence made approving sounds.

"Okay," said Morag, slinging her girl into her arms. "Let's take this back inside the meeting room and see how many males we can freak out with the sight of your mum's tits."

She opened the meeting room door with her shoulder and found her seat while the deputy council leader and his CEO bickered about some detail. When Morag sat, Prudence immediately began to wriggle free. Morag lowered her to the floor and let her crawl around under the big table.

"Sorry, professor," said Major Sanders, "you were telling us something about *Yo Thothothoth*-something, the time-eater?"

"*Yo Khazpapalanaka*," said Omar, gesturing to a convoluted ball of shapes on the painting. "As best we understand it, he – it – is the manifestation of time within our universe. Ever wondered why everything doesn't happen at once? *Yo Khazpapalanaka*. He will arrive, accompanied by the *Cha'dhu Forrikler,* who are the maintainers of objective reality."

"They're what?" said the council CEO.

"You think this is real?" said Omar withering. "You think that anything in this universe is real? These gods – and these are the ones which we can just about conceptualise – they are the true foundations of the universe and will be the undoing of our world. The end of the world isn't going to be monsters and rivers of blood and volcanoes – although we will have all these things soon enough. What we're going to endure is the deconstruction of our entire reality. You, sir, might spend an eternity as a super-taut violin string of high-pitched pain. Imagine feeling nothing. Or everything. Imagine you are not you, but an infinite number of copies and all of them having the worst possible wet Sunday afternoon in Cardiff. And it's always Sunday afternoon and it's an infinite Cardiff."

"A bit unfair on Cardiff," said a middle-aged woman in a chunky bead necklace.

"Omar's gone a bit hellfire preacher crazy, hasn't he?" said Morag to Rod.

"I think he's trying to stamp out any unrealistic optimism in the room," Rod replied. "The city councillors there are having a hard time getting their heads around it."

"So, we need to effectively kill the entire civilian population before physics itself comes apart at the seams," said the major, clearly trying to keep up.

"It's madness," said Councillor Rahman.

Major Sanders shook his head. "Fighter jets have already been scrambled from all available bases. Once the codes have come through, the Trident submarines and our other bases will launch their entire complement of nuclear missiles at large urban centres."

The city council dude in the tracksuit seemed most upset. "This … this whole thing strikes me as … very bad."

"Very bad," nodded the suited man next to him.

The deputy council leader quivered with fearful horror. "It's not going to be popular with the electorate. I mean, I am voting against it. I propose we just back out of this thing straight away."

"We're not even quorate anyway," said the suit.

"Oh!" said Chad, looking at his phone and standing up. "Time for the Prime Minister's address to the nation." He swiped with his phone.

The wall screens changed to show the wood-panelled walls of a ministerial conference room. The Prime Minister stood at a lectern. A banner hung from it, bearing the slogan *Stay at Home – Follow Instructions – Be at Peace*.

"We had a lot of discussions about the colour of the border," said Chad. "I was all for green or blue, something calm – with perhaps the reassurance of a slight medical feel. But they went with the attention-grabbing red." He shook his head.

The Prime Minister, without expression or tone, addressed the camera directly. "We are facing the biggest threat this country has faced for decades. All over the world we are seeing the devastating impact of this threat. And so tonight I want to update you on the steps that all of us must take in the coming hours."

The PM paused. For a good few seconds, Morag assumed this was for rhetorical effect; but no, the screen had frozen.

"Technical problems?" said Rod.

The screen juddered, went to static for half a second, then the image resumed. The Prime Minister was no longer at the lectern. A change in light suggested a change in time.

"Is this now live?" said Morag.

On the carpeted space behind the lectern, a woman's leg could be seen. A trail of blood stretched from one side to the other. Morag realised there was sound too: a continuous *'schlup schlup schlup'*. A half-drinking, half-eating sound. A few seconds later the video feed disappeared completely.

Councillor Rahman broke the stunned silence. "I don't think that will play well with the electorate at all," he said.

"I strongly argued for a green or blue border," said Chad.

"That was terrifying," whispered the council CEO.

"We might need to try and put a positive spin on that," agreed Chad thoughtfully.

"Surely, it is better to fight back," said Councillor Rahman suddenly. "Those things... You!" he said to the major. "You've just been bragging about – what was it? – six hundred men? Tanks?"

"Armoured fighting vehicles," said Major Sanders.

"Has no one thought about fighting back?"

"The Maccabees," said Nina. She leaned forward and placed her hat on the table in front of her. "We've just spent the last day trying to undo the damage caused by nutjobs who believed it would be possible to fight the Venislarn."

"It's arguably their fault that the world is ending today," said Rod, glancing at Morag and Prudence. "And not in six months' time, if things had been allowed to take their natural course."

"Then can we not at least come to some accommodation with these things?" said Councillor Rahman.

"Have you not listened to anything I've said?" said Omar. The pulsating mass covering his chest wound shifted and something rolled out onto the floor.

The councilman batted away Omar's negativity. "There's always compromise, always a way forward. You think Birmingham got the Commonwealth Games by sheer luck? Compromise, discussion, negotiation."

"I think there's something in this," said Chad enthusiastically. "Yes, yes, yes, Professor Omar has painted a clear and definitive picture of how the world is going to end. But is it really all that bad?"

"Yes, it is," said Omar.

"Is there not a glimmer of hope?" Chad asked rhetorically.

"No, there is not."

"Isn't there a means by which we and the *em-shadt* Venislarn can sit round a table and thrash something out?"

"Have you not seen what's going on?"

Omar gestured (wincing as he raised his arm) to the screens. Spindly creatures galloped through a city centre park. A hulking shape, bigger than a cargo ship, was surging up the Bristol Channel. On another screen, what looked like a southern European city was wrapped in an all-consuming firestorm.

"Even if the world is ending," said Councillor Rahman, his voice a ghostly autopilot, "surely we must make plans for continuity government."

"Oh, someone wants to reign in hell," muttered Omar bitterly.

"Cos even in hell, someone needs to run the libraries," said Ricky Lee and cracked a smile.

"And the museums," said the bead-wearing woman.

"Just don't mention the bins," said the councillor.

"I mean, there's going to be some pretty unhappy tortured souls if their buses aren't running on time," said Ricky.

"If we can perhaps move beyond such facetious comments and get back to the simple business of overseeing the final hours of human life, *please*," said Vaughn.

The door banged loudly and a rotund woman backed in with a wonky-wheeled trolley. "Now, who is wanting a nice hot cup of tea and some digestives, eh?" she said cheerily.

From the way Nina buried her face in her hat, Morag surmised this was the fearsome Mrs Seth. Morag also realised that she was thoroughly parched.

"Tea here, please," she said loudly. "And are those Tunnock's wafers I see on your second shelf?"

01:00AM

The space under the big table was dark and empty except for the forest of legs around its edges. Prudence Murray crawled into the centre, rolled onto her back and gazed up at the slices of light appearing through the gaps in the table sections. Prudence had never seen stars, but had heard her mother talk about them. She wondered if they looked something like these lines of light.

The adults talked on and on and on in droning voices. If she let them wash over her, the muffled talk and the darkness of the under-table were comforting, although the floor was hard and cold. When something dropped between Professor Omar's feet and landed on the floor with a tiny, hard 'clack', Prudence rolled back onto her knees and went to investigate.

It was a small silvery object with a hinged shell that was half ajar. Inside its shell mouth was a glistening wet creature, slimy like a tongue. Its shell mouth was crusted with blood.

"Hello," said Prudence.

The shell creature did not respond. Prudence poked it with

her finger. The shell mouth clacked viciously as it tried to grab her.

"You are a very angry shell," she told it.

The angry shell had nothing to say on the matter.

"I will pick you up and you will not bite me," she told it, and did just that. The shell flexed its sharp mouth but behaved. "You will be my friend and you will come with me."

Beyond the angry shell and the (slightly smelly) forest of legs, there was not much to entertain Prudence under the table, so when the door swung open and was held in place by a noisy trolley, Prudence made towards it. As the trolley trundled inside the door began to swing shut. Prudence did a turbo crawl and slipped out, shell in hand.

In the corridor she got to her feet, adjusted her string belt – which was far too tight – and went exploring. The grownups stared at her when they passed but most were far too anxious and busy to stare for long. When they asked her if she was all right or okay, she said, "Yes, thank you." When they asked her where she was going, she said, "Exploring." No one ever asked more than one question.

There was a lot of corridor and many rooms. People were busy at desks in many of them. Most of them were talking; a few were shouting. Some of them were weeping. In a glass fronted office, Prudence patted the leg of a man who was sobbing gently to himself and showed him her angry shell. She wasn't sure if it cheered him up, but he stopped crying for a bit.

As Prudence continued her explorations, she heard a thumping clatter from a metal panel in the wall. The panel had slats in it to let air pass and Prudence peered through. Something shifted and moved in the darkness.

"Hello," she said. "Would you like to come out and see my angry shell?"

"You can't see me! I'm incognito," squeaked a furious, high-pitched voice from within.

"Hello. I'm Prudence," said Prudence and pulled at the panel. It popped away in her hands and fell heavily to the floor. Inside the square space within was a little cloth man riding on a creature with many wriggling arms.

"How dare you disturb me while I'm incognito, fleshling!" snarled the cloth man.

Prudence poked her head inside. The square space was narrow and ran up past the height of the ceiling and away into the distance. "Do you live in here?" she asked.

The creature with many arms patted her face with its suckered tentacle. Prudence laughed at its peculiar touch.

"Foolish question, tiny human!" said the cloth man. "I do not live in this chimney! Steve the Destroyer roams where he wishes and calls no place home!"

Prudence abruptly remembered where she had heard the voice before, even if it had been in utero. "Uncle Steve!"

"I am no human's uncle," he said.

"It's me, Uncle Steve. Prudence Murray."

"Who?" demanded Steve.

"I'm the *kaatbari*!" she said, grinning.

Steve looked her up and down. "But you are massive," he declared. "I did not realise you were so large. Your mother must have a cavernous uterus! I must compliment her on the size of her womb when I next see her." He struggled to control his squid creature as he spoke.

"What is that?" asked Prudence.

"This is my *dnebian* land squid mount."

"And what is her name?"

"I do not have the time to give names to dumb creatures, gobbet."

Prudence held out her pet shell. "This is Mr Angry Shell," she said. "You should give your squid a name."

Steve considered this. "It should be a bold name," he said, thinking it through. "It should strike fear into the hearts of my enemies. It should be a name suited to a battle charger, one on which Steve the Destroyer might ride into the final conflict which is to come."

"Mrs Squiggly," said Prudence.

"Pah! Idiotic suggestion!" spat Steve.

"She is very squiggly, though."

Steve shook his head in disgust and disappointment. "So, you're the *kaatbari* then," he said.

"I am," said Prudence.

"I expected you to be a bit more—" he waved a cloth hand about "—fearsome. Have you got any powers?"

Prudence considered this. "I made friends with Mr Angry Shell."

Steve moved closer to inspect the shell and poked it. The shell snapped viciously at his pudgy little hand. Steve yelped and waved his hand about until he was sure it hadn't been bitten off. His land squid joined in with an alarmed "*Mwwa-waa!*"

"I meant stuff like making people's brains melt with the power of your mind. Or scalpel fingers. Or laser eyes."

"I might have laser eyes," said Prudence and stared at him very hard. "Are they working?"

"Not at all," said Steve.

"Maybe I need to try harder."

"You're far less puissant than I'd imagined."

"What's puissant?"

"Never you mind, fleshling. Seems like you need a mentor to show you around and guide your powers."

"Do you know where I can find one?"

"None would do a finer job than Steve the Destroyer. *If* I

choose to take you on." He stroked his rough cloth chin. "I think you should come with me. I have such sights to show you."

"Like what?"

"You'll see." His land squid angled itself and began to climb the wall of the shaft.

"Do you want me to come with you?" said Prudence.

"I did say," snapped Steve. "You should listen more."

Prudence clambered into the space beyond the hole. The shaft above was ringed by lips where sections of the shaft had been bolted together.

"Can I have a ride on Mrs Squiggly?" she asked.

"Of course not!" said Steve from above. "And her name's not Mrs Squiggly!"

Prudence began to climb.

01:04AM

Judging by the faces around the table, some were clearly not happy to have the meeting interrupted by Mrs Seth the tea lady, but Rod for one thought the end of the world ought to be faced with a cup of strong builder's tea. Actually, he thought it would be better faced with a pint of craft beer but, at times of crisis, one took solace where one could.

Across the table, Chad turned to Mrs Seth. "Is there any chance you could rustle me up a cruelty-free soy latte?"

"Don't be ridiculous," she said. "There is tea. And a macaroon."

Rod untied one of Vaughn's hands so the man could reach his own fresh cuppa.

"So, there is no avoiding the destruction of our world," said Councillor Rahman, who seemed to be finally getting the point.

"And the eternal hell that awaits us all," added Omar.

"What about *Yoth-Bilau*?" said Morag. "Kathy said..."

Omar chuckled, although it was clearly an affectation, as the pain his wound was causing him was writ large on his face. "Don't be so quick to take the word of our treacherous doctor," he said.

"But is it true?"

Omar addressed the whole table. "There is an apocryphal story that the Soulgate will not truly close around our world, that the Venislarn apocalypse won't be an inevitability until the arrival of the god *Yoth-Bilau*." He searched around on the map and located a mass of writhing red tentacles in one corner. "As the *kaatbari* is the herald, so *Yoth-Bilau* is the rear guard. The one who shuts the door behind the horde and seals our doom."

"So there *is* hope?" said the council CEO.

"I think the electorate would be interested in some hope," said Councillor Rahman.

"That's certainly something we can sell," nodded Chad enthusiastically.

"There is no hope," said Omar with quiet certainty. "For one thing, all it gives us is time."

"Time is good," said Mrs Fiddler, and Major Sanders nodded.

"If we had a remarkable plan, a way out of this, but no. An impossibly powerful and generally incomprehensible army is descending on us. We are animals in the abattoir. This business with *Yoth-Bilau* is just the slaughterman stopping to tie his laces. Furthermore, it's really quite doubtful *Yoth-Bilau* even exists. Mentions of her are scant and sparse and frankly unbelievable."

"But if she existed…" said Nina. "Prof, prof, look at me. What *if* she existed?"

Omar shrugged wearily. "Then – huzzah! Put up the bunting! – you've got an extra few minutes, hours or days in which to put a bullet in your head."

"We should starting killing civilians at once," said Major Sanders with grim conviction.

Vaughn pushed himself forward, grunting as he stretched across the table with his free hand.

"What are you doing, Mr Sitterson?" said Rod.

With a victorious gasp, Vaughn snagged the edge of the box of

Tranquill suicide tablets and dragged it across the table. He tore it open with his one free hand and brought his face down to devour the contents.

Rod grabbed his shoulder to pull him back. In the scrappy struggle over suicide pills, the box was shredded.

Vaughn paused, staring in despair. "Lois!" he yelled. "You brought an empty one!"

Rod gathered the scraps, to be sure there really was no poison.

"Wise of her not to bring an actual box of them in here," said Morag.

"Most of the boxes *are* empty," said Vaughn, wearily.

"Huh?"

He tidied his scattered papers. "A lot of countries signed up to the Tranquill programme," he muttered.

"Agreed to dish out suicide pills to their citizens?" said Councillor Rahman, appalled.

"But it turns out there were a limited number of companies who could be trusted to mass produce potassium cyanide capsules. There's the tendering process, plus the matter of secrecy."

"You didn't make enough pills," said Rod.

"Some countries unfairly stockpiled what they'd manufactured." Vaughn turned and grabbed Rod's lapel. "You've got a gun! You could kill me!"

Rod pushed his clawing hand away. "You've got a job to do, sir. We all have."

"I'll pay you. A pay rise."

Rod gave him a patient look.

"Or whatever else it is you want," added Vaughn. "Even now, I —" He faltered at the pronoun. Vaughn had always been a man who took exception to his own existence. He tittered madly. "I can grease any number of wheels for you."

"Are you going to drink your tea there, Mr Sitterson?"

"Who gives a fig about tea at a time like this?" Vaughn spat the words with quiet, miserable fury.

Rod took the man's hand and, meeting ineffectual resistance all the way, once more tied it to the arm of the chair.

"So, this team of volunteers handing out door to door suicide pills is going to run out of boxes very soon," said Nina.

"Shame," said Chad. "It's a lovely design."

Major Sanders put his hands on the table in a solemn and significant gesture. "If we can't provide a ... an easier death for the population, and I can't get through to my commanding officer— If the nuclear warheads aren't yet in the air to put us all out of our misery, then I should order my troops to begin killing people on sight."

He looked from person to person for some form of confirmation. Rod gave him a firm nod of agreement.

"But if we have time..." said Councillor Rahman.

"This *Yoth-Bilau* character..." said the CEO.

"If we have time, then we can negotiate an end to hostilities," said Chad brightly.

"You can't win them over," said Nina.

"You have not seen my PowerPoint skills," said Chad. "I can be quite persuasive. And we have one of the Venislarn here."

Rod looked wildly about as though expecting *Yo-Morgantus* or *Zildrohar-Cqulu* to be lurking in the shadows, before realising Chad was referring to Pupfish. Morag too had started to look around, on the floor behind her and under the table.

"Mr Pupfish," said Chad. "Perhaps you can tell us what you, the Venislarn, want."

"Me?" said the *samakha*, wide-eyed with the sudden attention on him (although, being a fish-headed creature made him generally wide-eyed all the time). "Uh, well – *ggh!* – me, I've always wanted a bit of respect."

"Respect," said Chad, as though that was the most profound

thing ever. He clicked his fingers at Maurice. "You. You rustle us up a flipchart or whiteboard from somewhere. What else, Pupfish? What do the Venislarn want?"

"My girl, Allana – she's human – I always wanted to treat her right."

"Want to treat her right." Chad nodded. "Flipchart, now," he said to Maurice who hadn't moved anywhere.

Morag was looking under the table. "Prudence!" She stood up.

"What?" said Chad.

Morag glanced at Rod. "She's gone missing."

01:11AM

The tiled floor was cool under Prudence's bare feet. She made no noise as she walked but could feel the slight, sticky tension between her soles and the white tiles. Steve's land squid made a rhythmic *slurp-slap slurp-slap* as he rode beside her.

This place was very different to the level below. Prudence had been born into a world of rough concrete and harsh lighting. Here the lighting was no friendlier, but the walls and floor were a smooth white. The shiny white floor tiles were squares; Prudence tried to walk without putting her feet on any of the cracks.

She looked at the shelves they passed. Cups, crowns, bones, plants, books. There were lots of books. There was a different smell in here as well. This place smelled of old things rather than people.

"I suppose you think you're a big deal, morsel?" said Steve.

"Am I?" said Prudence, taking a mask from a shelf to look at it closer. It had a very long oblong face, painted with a few blood red lines. The eyeballs in its wooden sockets swivelled to fix Prudence with its gaze. The voice of the *Shus'vinah* mask (which was no voice at all and rose from a place as deep as centuries) told her that she must wear it and join in the dance of ecstatic slaughter.

"No, thank you," she told it, showed it Mr Angry Shell and put it back on the shelf.

"I'm a big deal," said Steve.

"Are you?"

"You doubt me?" he sneered. "I was an outrider of the entourage of *Prein*, an emissary of—"

"What's an outrider?" asked Prudence.

"Someone who rides out, foolish child. An emissary of the shattered realms—"

"And what's one of them?"

"Must you always interrupt? Do you know what I do to prattling mortals who interrupt me?"

"No, what?"

The land squid paused in its slurp-slapping and Steve turned in his seat to waggle a pencil spear at Prudence. He didn't seem sure what to do next. "An emissary is a very important person sent with messages to other important people," he told her.

"Oh," said Prudence and walked on. "Sort of like a postman?"

Steve made a grumbling noise. "What is this *post man*?"

"I think it's someone who rides out and delivers messages to people."

"And does the post man impale people on this post of his?"

"Perhaps," said Prudence.

"Then I was a post man of *Prein*."

"That is a big deal," she said seriously.

"A very important individual," Steve agreed. "I am the hero of *Hath-No*. My actions secured the throne for *Sha Datsei* and my unparalleled impression of a *tito* fruit saved the day."

"What is this place?" asked Prudence, pointing at the shelves.

"The people here call it the Vault. It is where they store all the objects that frighten them, or which their pathetic human minds cannot comprehend. This body of mine came from here. Apart from my legs, which were replacements stitched for me by human servants. Note well the explosions of red blood. Note them well."

If he had stood on the floor, Steve would have not quite reached Prudence's knees. His head, upper body and arms were made from two pieces of scratchy beige cloth, one for front and one for back. If not for his stitched-on face, it would not be possible to distinguish front from back. His legs were made of finer cloth and covered with a pattern she would have mistaken for pretty flowers if Steve hadn't told her otherwise.

"What happened to your legs?" she asked.

"I lost them in battle against a giant *kobashi*," he said.

"Did you lose the battle?"

He laughed derisively. "Steve never loses battles."

"You beat it even though you had lost your legs?"

"Ha! You have no imagination, snotling! Steve could beat any enemy without his legs! Or his arms! Or his head! Probably."

"And why were you here?" she asked, idly picking up a mirror with a black twisted frame. A silver hand reached from within the mirror, long talon fingers groping for her eyes. Prudence slapped the silly hand away and put the mirror back.

"I was summoned here by your mother, Morag Murray, through a powerful puzzle box," said Steve. He stood up in his seat and made a show of scouting his surroundings. "I suppose it must still be here somewhere. In a big impressive display case to show how important it is."

There was a slow repetitive thumping sound which grew louder. A vaguely head-shaped blob appeared above the shelves to one side, then the whole creature moved into view. It was taller than any adult and made from concrete like the walls and floors of the level below. However, it moved in a very un-concretey, fluid manner. Prudence suspected it was meant to be a horse (even though she had never actually seen one) although it only had two paddle-like legs, one forward, one back, and a head that was more fist than face. It moved in a back-arching motion, stretching its front leg out then pulling the back one behind it.

"Hello," said Prudence.

The concrete horse twisted its long neck and bent its head to hers. Prudence patted its face. There was a tingling sensation, a million tiny pinpricks as it tried to drink her blood through her skin.

"No, don't do that," she told it and gently pushed its head away. The concrete horse turned slowly and moved on ahead of them.

At a large chamber-like box, Steve swung himself up by the metal struts on its outer door and looked through the round window. "Ah ha!" he declared victoriously.

Prudence peered over his head.

Inside the chamber, on a square pedestal, was a large book. It looked old to Prudence's eyes. Its pages were a light mottled brown, the edges of its heavy covers frayed and battered. Its pages were covered in tightly packed but neat writing. Prudence tried to read them. She'd never read anything before but thought it was worth a try.

"What is it?" she asked when the meaning of the words weren't forthcoming.

"It's the Bloody Big Book," said Steve. "Don't you know anything?"

Prudence decided he was being rude so she stuck Mr Angry Shell on Steve's head. Steve squealed in alarm, lost his footing and fell to the floor where he flapped and rolled about.

On the ceiling, a camera lens had turned to watch them. Not much further along, a big red light had started to flash alarmingly.

"My mum told me about the Bloody Big Book," said Prudence. "When I was smaller and inside her."

"Pah," said Steve, rolling free of the angry shell and leaping hurriedly to his feet as though nothing had happened at all. "I saw it being written."

"All of it?" said Prudence.

"Of course not all of it. I saw the three-limbed fury Mrs Grey start to write it." He picked up his pencil spear and proceeded to jab at Mr Angry Shell with it. The silvery shell creature fought back with its snapping mouth.

"My mum told me about Mrs Grey," said Prudence. She watched Steve try to stab Mr Angry Shell. He wasn't having much success. "Where is she now?"

"In hell," grunted Steve as he fought.

"Where's that?"

"Look around you, fleshing!" he said.

HELL

The many pens of *Yoth-Kreylah ap Shallas* swirled across the page.

Morag Murray tried to explain it to Cattress, attempting to hold back her utter disdain for the man from the Foreign Office.

"Well, the Venislarn are not from another galaxy or another dimension," she said. "They're from somewhere else entirely. Yes, they're not actually gods. There are no gods, but it's the best word we've got to describe them. Their power is limitless and their plans utterly unknowable. They are here. They have been here a long time." She tilted her head. "We think. They've certainly inserted themselves into our history, but they're not restricted by time in the way we are. They might have arrived fifty years ago, ten years ago. Maybe they will come here for the first time next week and then just insinuate themselves back in time to the present day. We don't know. What we don't know about them would fill a bloody big book."

Inspired, she took hold of him and dragged him to the chamber that had been built to house the Bloody Big Book.

"That is the Bloody Big Book," she said, "AKA the Wittgenstein Volume AKA the Book of Sand. It is a book with an infinite number of pages."

"That's ridiculous," said Cattress.

"Isn't it? But it's real. It details everything that ever has happened, is happening and will happen. It contains every other book ever written and translations of them all into every language known and unknown."

A SOUND DREW her back to the here and now of the scriptorium. It was not the sound of the horns and bells and the general preparations for war that filled all of *Hath-No*. It was something nearer – speech. Someone had spoken to her.

Ap Shallas turned to the scriptorium entrance. This involved disengaging from her great work and wheeling round her mechanical body. Limbs, extensions and extrusions had accumulated on her like tumours over the ages, and controlling her own body was a feat of effort and memory. Two of her hands continued to write until she physically pulled them away.

Fifteen spiderous *zhadan* warriors lined the entrance. Before them stood *Sha Datsei*, Regent of *Hath-No*, guardian of the scriptorium and patron of *ap Shallas*'s work. Beside her, crouched in subservient worry, Barry held up his gong.

"*I did announce her, mithreth*," he said.

Sha Datsei stalked forward. Today, she wore the body of a combat general, tall, noble and covered in jutting plates of armour. Beneath the milky white skin she had woven for herself, her many-jointed skeleton, her true body, shifted and gave life to the puppet costume she wore.

"*The horn sounds a call to arms and you do not come*," she said.

This was fact and *ap Shallas* saw no need to comment on it.

"*I send a personal summons and still you do not come.*"

This was also true.

"*The pathway to Earth is open and we will take it. Are you not one of my subjects?*" asked *Sha Datsei*.

"*We are both subjects of Hath-No,*" said *ap Shallas*.

"*Whose will I interpret.*"

"*Incorrectly.*"

Sha Datsei's battle face twisted in amused surprise. Even though this outer body of hers was a sock puppet she controlled, *Sha Datsei* was an honest and open individual. She walked round *ap Shallas* and gazed up at the unquiet shelves.

"*Do you remember when you first came here?*" she said. "*What you were like?*"

Ap Shallas struggled. Through the eyes of *Hath-No*, she had observed all reality, at the microscopic, macroscopic and the cosmic, but it was reality observed through a narrow singularity, a fragment at a time. She was not omniscient, and recalling her own existence, down the uncountable ages, was near to impossible.

"*You were a pathetic human being with only one arm.*"

"*Human...*" said *ap Shallas*, who did not remember and could barely believe. She looked up at the books of human vellum skin around her and wondered why she had always felt a kinship with them.

"*Only your will kept you going,*" said Sha Datsei. "*I rebuilt you. I replaced the missing limb. I gave you others. There is barely a single part of you that I did not construct.*"

With difficulty *Yoth-Kreylah ap Shallas* sought out her flesh and blood hand, the odd appendage among the greater and finer limbs that had been grafted onto her.

"*What I have given you, I can easily take away,*" said *Sha Datsei*.

At a flick of a claw, the *zhadan* warriors came for *ap Shallas*. Her body might have been a loose confederacy of parts, but the threat galvanised them into unified action. *Ap Shallas* lifted herself up on legs new and old that she had almost forgotten were there. As the lead warrior came chittering at her, she met it with the *menscuzo* wordblade. She dissected the creature before it could even bring its weapon to bear. The warriors fanned around her, but she had a limb for each of them. A thorax crushing grip for that one. A pen nib plunged into the compound eye of another.

Sha Datsei roared and, drawing wordblades of her own, joined the attack.

Ap Shallas also responded with a cry, a call to arms of her own.

Books leapt from the shelves. Tomes, pamphlets, scrolls and loose sheets. Human beings who had long been butchered, mangled and transformed into something entirely other, yet who had not been granted the clemency of death. An army of a thousand tortured humans flew to *ap Shallas*'s defence. They wrapped themselves in suffocating numbers around warriors' heads. They battered them with sharp spines and heavy volumes.

Sha Datsei batted away a vellum swarm that could not die. The more she slashed them into confetti, the more numerous they became. "*Enough! Enough!*" she yelled.

The fight stuttered to a halt in an instant. A band of airborne sheets fluttered up into the heights to roost.

There was a deep tear in the face piece *Sha Datsei* wore. She regarded *ap Shallas* with wonky, malevolent eyes. "*What makes you think you can resist me?*" she said in cold disbelief.

"I have written this scene already," said *ap Shallas* simply. "I have written this one and I know I shall write them all."

Sha Datsei shook her head. As the mask fell apart further, she ripped it from her naked face entirely. "*We are nearly upon the Earth. You will fight. With me or against me. You will fight.*"

Ap Shallas watched *Sha Datsei* and her remaining warriors leave the scriptorium chamber. She regarded the floor, strewn with bits of *zhadan* warrior and fragments of paper.

"*This is a mess*," she said. She sought out Barry, who had wisely decided to cower in a corner. "*Tidy this up.*"

"*Of courthe, mithreth,*" he said.

She turned back to her writing position. There was a teapot nearby, a cup, a saucer and a coaster. She reached out with her human hand – human, eh? she thought – and found the teapot to be cold.

"*I thought I asked for tea,*" she said.

"*You did,*" said Barry. "*Ageth and ageth ago.*"

"*Oh.*" There was an ancient brown stain in the bottom of the cup. "*Did I enjoy it?*"

"*I made it jutht like you athked,*" he said and smiled encouraging.

"*More tea then,*" she said and bent to her work. She looked at where she had just left off and continued writing.

BIRMINGHAM - 01:20AM

"It's just not acceptable," said Security Bob for at least the fourth time.

"Yes, I understand," said Morag kneeling before Prudence by the entrance to the Vault. She was about to give her girl her very first heart-to-heart telling off. She hesitated. Morag had not been a well-behaved girl herself. She had ended up in many scrapes and pickles. That business with the teddy bear and the seagull leapt immediately to mind. And the time she'd stolen the neighbour's tortoise and tried to put it in the Moray Firth. True, she'd not triggered the security alarms in a restricted area within two hours of being born; that was a special achievement. Kneeling besides Prudence, she realised that the girl had continued to grow at an unnatural rate. What physiological age had Prudence reached now? Six? Seven? Hair sprouted in unruly curls around her face. She had freckles and a full set of baby teeth.

"Prudence, you can't just come in here," she said. "This place is dangerous."

"Uncle Steve was with me," said Prudence.

Steve the Destroyer, hearing his name, struck a macho pose.

"Yes, but Steve's a moron, sweetie," said Morag. "You need to stay safe. You need to stay with me."

"It's just not acceptable," said Security Bob again and rearranged the belt around his broad middle.

"What more do you want from me, eh?" Morag said to him.

"There should be consequences," he said sniffily.

"You want me to put the anti-Christ on the naughty step, do you?"

"I'm just saying…"

"Yeah, well go say it somewhere else."

Bob made a number of disgruntled and affronted gestures but Morag ignored them, and the irritating jobsworth moved off. Rod and Nina passed him in the aisle. Professor Omar, wheeled along by Maurice, was not far behind.

"Found her then?" said Nina. "The ginger menace."

"She's grown," said Rod. "Blummin' heck, she's the spit of you, isn't she?"

He was possibly right but when she was young, did her hair look quite so wild, was her demeanour so feral? Probably. Morag felt a weird momentary embarrassment that her daughter had no shoes.

"You didn't all need to come and help look," she said to her colleagues.

"Anything to get out of that meeting," said Rod with feeling.

"This is Mr Angry Shell," said Prudence, holding up her find for all to see.

"She's talking," said Rod, astounded.

"That's one of the angry whelks," said Nina.

"I thought I had lost one somewhere," said Omar.

Rod and Nina parted to let him be wheeled through: a frail and venerable elder being brought before the god child. Morag had never thought of Omar as old, but he wore his injury poorly. The pulsating mass beneath his shirt, shifted and clicked.

"They're vampiric," he explained. "They consume flesh and excrete certain arcane energies that I can use to keep this body going."

Prudence offered the whelk up to him. Omar waved it away with a limp hand.

"I think forty-eight nibbling at my breast is sufficient."

Morag made to take the whelk from Prudence. The shell snapped frenziedly at her fingers as they neared. "Oh, that's a feisty one." She took what looked like an old tobacco tin down from a shelf and opened it. "Let's pop the nasty thing back in the box."

"But mum..."

"Now!" said Morag, surprised when her little girl complied.

"Back in the box," said Prudence.

As Morag closed the lid, the whelk bounced and threw itself around furiously, tapping out a tinny Morse code.

"And you've got those things eating you?" said Nina, impressed.

"As life-support systems go, it has its drawbacks, dear Nina," said Omar. "It can't sustain me for long." He smiled wryly. "But maybe for just long enough. *Croyi-Takk* have overrun Edgbaston. A *bezu'akh* annihilator is trampling through south Birmingham. *Daganau-Pysh* is on the hunt. Anytime now, our own soldiers will receive orders to shoot all humans on sight. I wouldn't be surprised if the nukes aren't in the air at this very instant, flying to put us all out of our misery." He looked from Nina to Rod to Morag. "And you three would like to do something to stop it even though you've been told it's quite impossible."

"If the Soulgate doesn't close until the arrival of *Yoth-Bilau*..." said Morag.

"Oh, I do love that look of hope when all hope has gone," he said. "Something in the eyes. I can never be sure if that's because I'm a sentimentalist or a deeply cruel man."

Maurice made a wordless noise to indicate his thoughts on the matter.

"Oh, shush, you. You can go prepare a flask of green tea. Some of us have journeys to make."

Morag, who had been instinctively trying to untangle the worst knots from Prudence's hair despite her daughter's silent protests, frowned at Omar. He winked in reply.

"There are theories regarding the Soulgate," he said slowly. "Rituals which could be enacted, even at this dire moment, to turn back the tide and save at least some fragment of this world."

"I knew it," said Nina. "There's always something."

"Theoretical rituals," said Omar. "And they weren't my theories. The expert in question was Mr Giles Grey."

"Mr Grey?" said Nina. "As in Mr and Mrs Grey?"

"As in the *late* Mr Grey?" said Rod.

"Well, quite," said Omar.

"Did Vivian know anything about his work?" said Morag. "Did they write anything down?"

Prudence had run out of tolerance for Morag's hair tidying and twisted out of her grip. Prudence took the rattling tobacco tin from the shelf and went over to Steve the Destroyer who appeared to be trying to teach his land squid command words.

"Do not wander far, you hear me?" said Morag. "And no poking things from other dimensions."

"Do you know anything about Bella in the Wych Elm?" asked Nina, which to Morag's ears sounded like a nonsensical non-sequitur.

"Anyone with an ounce of local knowledge knows the legend," said Omar.

"Bella – Isabella – grew up in hell. *Hath-No*. She knew Vivian. Then the bitch tangled with me in seventeen seventy-three and ended up being blasted forward to World War Two and into the trunk of a tree." She caught Morag's puzzled gaze. "It's been a busy few months. She had a *Gellik* orb on a necklace."

"A tunnelling device?" said Morag.

"Between *Hath-No* and here," said Nina. "Except her body went missing."

"A lot of things go missing during wartime," said Omar.

"That's what Mrs Fiddler said," said Nina. She hadn't noticed the tone in Omar's voice.

"And some things don't go missing but are stolen," said Morag.

Omar nodded. "An officer from Special Branch was responsible for the original theft. That *Gellik* orb has passed between a number of paddlers in the lake of darkness over the decades, before ending up in the hands of a thoroughly disreputable occultist."

"Where is it now?" said Rod.

"In my private stash, Rodney. At Birmingham University."

"You have it!" said Nina. "We can summon Vivian back from hell! I'll go and fetch it."

"This being the part of the city currently being stomped on by a bazooka annihilator," pointed out Rod. "We'd have to fight our way there."

"*Bezu'akh* annihilator," corrected Omar. "And, yes. Rod, you should go."

"I can go," insisted Nina.

"Rodney will go," said Omar. "And Maurice with him. Maurice!" He called out to the kitchenette Maurice had gone to. "Have you made that flask of tea yet?"

"Why not me?" said Nina. "Don't you trust me?"

"You have other tasks. Rod is to go to the university. He'll need Maurice to help him circumvent the riddles and traps."

"Riddles?" said Rod.

"Morag already has her hands full with the *kaatbari*." Omar raised his eyebrows. Morag looked back down the aisle to Prudence who was playfully wrestling the land squid.

"And me?" demanded Nina.

"You're going to fetch Mr Grey."

"I thought he was dead."

"He possibly wishes he was," said Omar. "And it's a fiction that Mrs Grey was keen to maintain. He was put under a curse, one that only the caster can lift."

"Aye, I knew there was something amiss," said Rod. "I saw on your office planner the other day. You meet him in Sutton Park every week or so."

Nina's face took on a shocked expression, like she'd swallowed a fly. "Sutton Park...? Um." She raised a hand tentatively. "You know that thing where I say something and everyone looks at me like I'm a moron?"

"Not a moron exactly," said Rod.

"Was Mr Grey turned into a donkey?" she asked.

Morag snorted with laughter.

"He was," said Omar.

"What?" said Morag.

"Knew it," said Nina and threw a finger snap of victory. "The picture in Mrs Grey's house. The fact that she left everything in her will to the donkey sanctuary in Sutton Park." She stared at nothing for a full second. "Dang. Mr Grey's a *donkey*?"

"This is nonsense," said Morag.

"You wanted your one last ditch chance to stop the end of the world," said Omar. "This is it."

"A magic donkey who may or may not know some ritual to undo all of this?" said Nina.

"Have you got anything better to occupy your last few hours, Nina?"

Nina clapped her hands, enthused. If this is what was on offer, she was going to seize it. "Let's do it! I'll go grab my driver. Rod gets the *Gellik* orb. I'll get Mr Grey. We'll be back by breakfast and the world will be saved."

Maurice appeared, a tartan thermos in one hand, a small lunch pail in the other. "Now, who's going on a journey?" he asked.

Prudence squealed with laughter as the land squid tried to bind her legs together with its own. It was hard to say who was winning.

FAREWELLS WERE SAID in the Vault. Whatever tenderness passed between Omar and Maurice was said in hushed whispers and held hands. Maurice's hands were tiny in Omar's bronzed fingers.

Morag watched Rod do a mental pat down of his weapons and array of concealed gadgets. "You come back in one piece," she told him.

"I'm not going back in time to save you again," said Nina. "I can't."

"This'll be a breeze," said Rod. "I've been in worse scrapes."

"Like that time in the Syrian Desert?" said Morag.

"Aye, did I ever properly tell you about that?"

"No," she said.

"Well, you see, this was just before the battle of Al-Qa'im. I'd got separated from my men and lost the anti-tank mortar I was carrying. Night was falling and—"

"You will tell me," said Morag, interrupting him firmly. "*When you get back.*"

He was silent for a long moment. "Aye," he said, sincerely, in the voice of someone who could not promise he would ever return. Rod gave a nod to Maurice.

"Lay on, Macduff," said the smaller man and they made to the lifts.

"Time to get Ricky and fetch us a donkey," said Nina, and then frowned. "Omar, how will I know which donkey is Mr Grey. There are lots of donkeys there, aren't there?"

"The donkeys have their names on their bridles and stable doors."

"And Mr Grey is…?"

"Mr Grey," said Omar.

"There is a donkey called Mr Grey?"

"Kinda works," said Morag.

There was a rap at the door separating this section of the Vault from the lobby area and lifts. Morag assumed it would be Rod or Maurice having forgotten something or other, but it was Lois the receptionist. Security Bob on her heels swiped and tapped to open the sliding doors.

"There's an August Handmaiden of *Prein* outside," she said.

"There's lots of things outside, Lois," said Nina. "It's the big 'come out and play day' for monsters."

"Yes, bab, but there's an actual August Handmaiden of *Prein* on the doorstep. She says she's come to collect the *kaatbari*."

Morag felt a cold weight descending inside her chest. In a night of pain and unpleasant bodily sensations this was the worst.

"You can tell that *teglau* bitch to—"

"Have they come for me, mum?" said Prudence, pausing mid-wrestle with the land squid.

Security Bob was surprised. "What? The girl? Is she the…"? He waved his hand, unable to pronounce the word. "She's one of them, then?" This was said with a certain tone of judgement, as though Prudence Murray should never have been allowed in the building.

"Who wants to take me away?" asked Prudence.

"No one," said Morag firmly. "You play with Steve."

"But…" said Security Bob.

"I will go talk to the Handmaiden," said Morag firmly.

"You sure?" said Nina.

"You've got a magic donkey quest to go on."

"But are you sure you're the right person to speak with the August Handmaidens?" asked Omar, adding, "You do have form for antagonising them."

Morag could have smiled. "You think I'd start a fight with the Handmaidens? In my state?"

"Yes, my dear. I believe you would."

"Too bloody right," she said. She hesitated, her eyes on Prudence.

"I can supervise the young and the reckless here," said Omar.

"Really?" said Morag. "You're hardly the paternal type."

"I tended to let Maurice deal with such things," he conceded. There was a weary honesty to his voice, some sense of his true self riding through the smooth façade. "However, I have always felt I had a certain avuncular charm."

"Oh, I can see that," she said. "Creepy uncle."

"The best kind of creepy," said Omar.

Morag waddled over to where her daughter played. She had to say her daughter's name twice before Prudence sat up.

"What, mum?"

"Come here."

"I am here."

"She is here, fool!" crowed Steve.

"Keep your nose out of family business, fuzzy felt." She tapped Prudence's leg. "Come. Here."

Prudence disentangled herself from the clutches of Steve and the land squid. Morag took her in her arms. "*Muda.* You get bigger every minute."

"I know," said Prudence.

The makeshift shorts which had reached toddler Prudence's ankles were now knee-length baggy culottes. Morag untied the knot in Prudence's T-shirt and it dropped to become a short dress.

"You hungry?" asked Morag. "You must be hungry."

"I believe there still might be some pink wafers somewhere," said Omar.

Morag looked towards the entrance, at all the eyes on her, and then back at Prudence. "Mummy's got to go work."

"Does someone want to take me away?"

"I won't let them."

Prudence glanced sideways at Security Bob. "He doesn't like me."

"He doesn't like anyone."

"But I don't belong here, do I?"

Morag had no answer for that. "How can you be so clever?" she said softly, amazed. "How can you even speak?"

"I don't know, mum. Some things I just know. They pop up inside me. Some things you told me."

Morag felt a wrench inside her. "I would be an awful mum, you know."

The hug Prudence gave her near broke Morag's heart. Prudence put a mushy kiss on Morag's cheek. "You're the best."

"Aw, now you're just mocking me." She pointed at Omar. "You do what Omar tells you. Unless it seems evil or devious. In which case..." She rocked her head. "Make a judgement call. Do *not* ask Steve's advice."

"My advice is golden!" insisted Steve.

Morag rolled her eyes and Prudence laughed.

"I'm only upstairs," said Morag. "I..." She turned and called out. "Bob! You got a walkie-talkie?"

"I have," he replied.

"Give it to me."

"I cannot give out personal equipment—"

"Do not make me come over there and take it from you, man," Morag growled.

The walkie-talkie was soon forthcoming. Morag presented it to Prudence. "You need me, you press this button here. This button, right, Bob? Press it and tell the person you need me. I will come to you."

"This button," said Prudence and pressed it. The walkie-talkie gave a squawk.

"Fine."

Morag stood. As she made to go, she looked at Steve. "You look after her or you are in for a world of pain."

"I fear no world of pain!" he retorted. "Steve the Destroyer was born in a world of pain! Pain is the sea in which he swims, morsel!"

"I'll replace your stuffing with rocks and dress you in wee doll's clothes if anything happens to her."

She made her exit with a minimum of post-natal hobbling.

01:24AM

Rod had his Glock pistol drawn all the way from the rear doors of the Library building, across the road to the multi-storey on Cambridge Street. He watched the night sky, prepared to put a bullet in anything that came within range. Maurice's bright pastel jumper made him a target for any demonic creatures passing by. Once beneath the illusory but nonetheless comforting shelter of the car park structure, Rod stepped down from hyper-vigilance to regular vigilance.

"My car's this way," he said.

"Ours is just there," said Maurice, gesturing to a car in a nearby bay.

Rod looked at its stark and unlovely lines in the diffuse orange streetlight. "That's a British Leyland car."

"A Princess," said Maurice.

Rod felt the touch of ancient memories – childhood journeys in the back of Leyland cars. Hot slippery vinyl seats, rolling suspension, clunky dashboards and shoddy engineering. It might have been the magnifying lens of nostalgia but, as far as he was concerned, the Leyland cars of the nineteen-seventies were the nadir of British engineering. As though the designers had looked at the appalling vehicles produced by soviet Eastern Europe and taken it as a challenge.

"Aye," said Rod, trying to break it gently. "I'd rather we went in a car that won't break down on the way."

"It's a three-mile drive to the university."

"Exactly." Rod gestured to the up ramp. "BMW. One year old. Fully serviced. Nought to sixty in five seconds."

Maurice pointed to the Princess with his thermos flask. "Sturdy. Reliable. Meticulously maintained. They don't make them like this anymore."

"There's a reason for that," agreed Rod. This was building up to be the longest conversation he'd ever had with the man. Maurice was the silent and diligent partner in the Omar and Maurice franchise. Behind every great man there was a great woman. Or a Maurice. There was also a new and belligerent look in Maurice's eyes, as though this was a matter of principle and worth fighting for even on the day of judgement.

"Listen, I'm sure it's a lovely car—" began Rod.

"It's also been marked with various protective wards that will guarantee our safety," said Maurice.

Rod tried to read the man. "Is that true, or are you just saying that to win the argument?"

Maurice said nothing.

Rod sighed. "I'm going to die. And I'm going to die in a bloody awful car."

"They'll be no dying in my car," said Maurice. "I've just had it cleaned."

Maurice unlocked the car, leaning inside to unlock the passenger side. Rod climbed in. There was a lemony fresh smell that spoke of careful and regular polishing of the dreadful vinyl interior. He nearly sat on a bundle of crochet needles and yellow wool. Maurice scooped them out of the way.

"Never got to finish the baby's booties," he said mournfully, passing them to Rod. "Pop them in the glove compartment."

The glove compartment door in the huge ugly dashboard creaked. The compartment was mostly taken up by a chunky Tupperware box.

"Oh, get that out," said Maurice. "We might need those."

Rod exchanged the half-finished woollen booties for the plastic box. "Nice booties," he said.

"She's probably outgrown them already," said Maurice.

"She'd have loved them," said Rod charitably.

"You think so?"

"Aye."

Maurice turned the ignition. It caught on the third attempt. Rod swore under his breath and wished he had the solace of religion to turn to at times like these.

The lobby of the Library was quieter now, but not yet empty. Most but not all staff had gone below ground. As Morag slowly walked to the doors, she listened to the sound of the city: the sirens, the thunder rumbles, the thousand creaks of reality being torn apart at the seams.

"There," said Security Bob, pointing to the August Handmaiden of *Prein* waiting outside the glass security doors.

"Yes, I can see," said Morag. August Handmaidens were hardly difficult to spot.

The Handmaiden was slowly gouging the glass with the spear tip of one of its thin, armoured legs. Its exo-skeletons were white, as though bleached by a harsh sun. Barbs and horns of chitin sprouted from its shell-like aborted growths. The plates of its massive carapace shifted and slid over one another with the scrape of someone shuffling crockery.

Morag nodded for Bob to unlock the door. He only hesitated briefly.

The night air was warm. There was the smell of smoke on the air.

The Handmaiden angled its massive body forward so that Morag was not faced with its soft underside, but one of its sightless armour plates. The August Handmaidens of *Prein* had no faces of their own, so created some for themselves. This Handmaiden's powder-white plates were distended into the shapes of babies' faces. Screaming babies' faces.

Morag looked at the bawling mouth and screwed up eyes of the face before her, She felt an involuntary rush of emotion, a desire to reach out and console that tortured infant. She had never felt a response like that before. Blasted post-natal hormones.

"Who are you and what do you want?" she said bluntly.

A segmented claw came round to within inches of Morag's face. The claw was longer than Morag's arm. It could have snipped her head from her shoulders with minimal effort.

"I am *Shara'naak Kye* and we have come to collect the *kaatbari*." The Handmaiden's mouths were not equipped for speech. Her voice came from nowhere, unaccented and smoothy delivered.

At the mention of 'we', Morag realised this Handmaiden was not alone. In the dark space between the Library and the construction site that filled most of Centenary Square there were other Handmaidens. They waited, patient and still.

Morag attempted a quick count. There were nine, or somewhere near to nine. There had been twelve once, but three had been killed. Morag had been present at all three deaths, and the August Handmaidens seemed to have taken that personally.

"A little family outing, is it, Sharon?" asked Morag.

"The *kaatbari*," repeated *Shara'naak Kye*.

"What do you want her for?"

"It is owed to us."

"Uh-huh." She looked along the square in the general direction of the Cube building, even though it was hidden from sight by the conference centre and buildings beyond. "Were you sent here by *Yo Morgantus*?"

Shara'naak Kye didn't seem to like that. Her plates ground together. "We are here on official business."

It was an odd phrase, and ridiculous enough in the circumstances to make Morag laugh. "Official…? Right. I don't think there's official anything anymore. We're in an end of the world closing down sale at the moment."

"The child!"

Bob stepped away, his flabby face pale with fear and gestured to the lifts. "I could go down and get it."

"Her!" breathed Morag savagely. "She is a person and she is going nowhere!"

"A female!" said *Shara'naak Kye* with the delight of someone finding an unexpected treat on a menu.

"That's right, Sharon."

"Bring her to us. You are still beholden to the *em-shadt* Venislarn."

"*Bhul-zhu, shaska*. You want her, you try come and get her."

The Handmaiden shifted. Claws clicked on concrete. She waved a pincer claw but came no closer. There was something peculiarly restrained about her movements. Morag considered the great interlocking rings that decorated the façade of the Library.

"That's Thingy's Ward of Perfect Something or other," said Morag.

"Dee's Ward of Perfect Intersection," said Bob.

"They said it would stop Venislarn getting in." She pulled a face. "I didn't believe them."

"You think it will stop Lord *Morgantus*?" said the Handmaiden, light laughter in her voice.

"Then you go tell him if he wants to see his daughter – step-daughter, whatever – then he needs to come down here and ask. And pay child maintenance."

Shara'naak Kye was still. Here was the moment when having a face would have allowed her to pout scathingly, but *Shara'naak* had to make do with a tortured baby face.

Slowly, the Handmaidens moved off.

"That's it. Piss off back to the hole you came from," Morag shouted.

"Terrible agonies await you," said *Shara'naak Kye*.

"Yeah, been there, done that, left nasty stains on the bed sheets."

When the door was shut again, Morag let out a ragged sigh. "They will come back," she said softly. "For Prudence and for me." She snatched the beret off Bob's head and slapped him with it. "And what the hell was that about?"

"What?"

"Offering to fetch her!"

"Just trying to do my job," he said. "We do have an official job to do."

She was debating whether to slap him again or throw his beret back at him when Lois came over from the lifts.

"They've gone? Good. Have any of you seen Vaughn?"

"He was in the meeting," said Morag.

"Was," said Lois tersely. "It appears he's gone walkabouts."

"Wheelabouts," said Morag. "He can't have gone far. He's not up here."

"I think if he puts his mind to it..." said Lois and shook her head. "We need someone downstairs."

"To chair that chaos?" Morag grunted.

"Listen, bab. Currently the big idea circling the table is Chad's suggestion that we all go outside and clap in support of our brave soldiers and emergency services. I for one—" She stopped, sniffed and wiped her eyes. Heavy mascara smeared with tears. "I for one would like to get on with things and be vaporised by a nuclear bomb before the elder gods of *Ur-la*-wossname get here and transmogrify us all into pain-lizards, or whatever it is they intend to do to us."

Morag groaned. "Has no one heard of maternity leave? I'd just like a sit down and maybe have someone rub my aching feet."

"I will massage your feet to heaven and back if I can do it in the meeting room," said Lois.

01:35AM

Nina returned to the sub-sub-basement meeting room to find her mum outside engaged in deep conversation with the city councillor. Deep conversation in this instance meant having him virtually pinned against the corridor with the joint forces of her personality and physical bulk.

"And they did not come and collect because it was a bank holiday," said Mrs Seth. "So next week, I put out the extra rubbish in bin bags, and the binmen, they refused to take it."

"Indeed, Mrs Seth – or can I call you Sheetal?"

"You can *not*!" she said, not letting go of the reins of the conversation. "So then I phoned the council to report the missed rubbish collection— But, oh no, you have to do everything 'on line' these days. No phoning people. Can no one pick up a phone anymore?"

Nina smiled at Councillor Rahman's terrified face as she and Morag walked past and into the meeting room. He might have been subjected to the full blast of Mrs Seth for the last five minutes, but Nina had been subjected to it for over twenty years. He should regard it as a character forming experience.

In the room, the meeting had broken down into chatting sub-groups. Vaughn's chair had indeed disappeared, and Vaughn with it. Nina didn't have strong opinions on that, one way or another.

"It would be ideal if all residents stayed in their homes," said Major Sanders.

"And all I'm saying," said Chad – Nina couldn't believe there was such a thing as 'all Chad was saying'. Chad's brain didn't have so much a train of thought as a wildly uncontrolled epidemic of thoughts, spreading out at random and latching onto anything they could. "*All* I'm saying is that it would be great if, at this difficult time, we could have a moment of national unity. Everybody out in the streets, flags, street parties, celebrating the good that unites us and sending out positive thoughts to our emergency workers."

"Your response to this situation is thoughts and prayers?" said Mrs Fiddler.

"Do not underestimate the power of positive thinking," said Chad. "The law of attraction states that if we focus on good things then those things will come to us. That's physics. You can't argue with that."

Nina tapped Ricky Lee on the shoulder. "I need you."

"Now?" he whispered. "The end of the world and you think this is an ideal time for you and me to—"

"I need you to drive me to Sutton Coldfield."

"You going somewhere?" said Pupfish, leaning in. "I'm coming too. *Ggh!* These people are *adn-bhul* crazy."

Morag had shifted a chair to replace Vaughn's and now, at the notional head of the table, rapped a glass on the table top to draw everyone's attention. "Let's get back to business," she said. "We have things to do before the night is through."

"I have some marvellous suggestions," said Chad.

"Yes," said Morag firmly. "We are clearly going to need to communicate our needs and wishes to the general population.

This will require a multi-platform approach. Chad, I want you to find an office and work up a mood board for this campaign. Colour schemes, fonts, images, key phrases."

"Oh, indeed," said Chad, delighted.

"Report back here in six hours with your ideas."

Chad gathered his papers, gave a cheery and triumphant smile to all and left.

"Oh, she's good," murmured Ricky.

Nina gave Morag a good luck thumbs up as she left.

"And *then*," Mrs Seth was saying to the still-trapped councillor in the corridor, "I get a letter telling me that if I leave rubbish out on the street I will be given a fine! What the hell is that supposed to mean, eh?"

Lightning strikes over the Edgbaston cricket ground silhouetted something gently descending on stick legs the height of mountains. It was accompanied by miniature versions of itself – Offspring? Disciples? – that were merely the size of tower blocks.

A car was on fire at the crossroads on the dual carriageway. Maurice checked his mirrors and indicated to go around it.

"So this orb we're going to collect," said Rod. "It's in Omar's office."

"The *Gellik* orb. Big pink jewel. It's in the mine," said Maurice. "Are you familiar with the mine under Birmingham University?"

"Er, no," said Rod.

He watched the speedometer as Maurice drove. The man was sticking to the speed limit on the almost empty road. Rod clenched his fists and tried not to comment.

"They excavated it in nineteen-oh-five as a teaching aid to the mining course that ran there," said Maurice. "It's almost a mile in length."

"And Omar keeps his juiciest treasures down there?"

"His Aladdin's cave. There are some quite rare pieces, hence the security."

"Right," said Rod. He adjusted his head to look in the passenger wing mirror. Something huge and covered with glistening quills had lolloped onto the A38 behind them. Rod tried to wind down his window to get a better look but the handle wouldn't turn.

"You have to jiggle it," said Maurice. "Backwards and then forwards. But not too hard or the mechanism breaks."

Rod jiggled the window winder as instructed. By the time he had it down, the lolloping quilled thing had disappeared from sight. He was not reassured by this. A warm, unnatural wind blew a smell like charred wood into the car as it carried on.

"So, this security," said Rod. "We're not just talking locked doors, are we?"

"There are certain enchantments and protective wards," said Maurice.

"Omar mentioned riddles."

Maurice hummed in amusement and drummed his fingers on the steering wheel. "That's more for ... decorative effect."

Maurice indicated to turn into the university campus. At the corner, in front of the new leisure centre, a dozen figures cavorted about. They looked like students, dancing to unheard music, ridiculous novelty hats on their heads. Then Rod saw they weren't hats, but creatures riding on the figure's heads. Juices dribbled down blinded faces.

"How far now?" said Rod.

"Just here." Maurice pulled over at the roadside. "Through the fence." He prodded the Tupperware box in Rod's lap. "Bring that."

Rod climbed out. By chance or design, some of the creature-wearers wobbled in their general direction. The earth trembled beneath Rod's feet. Two of the blind figures staggered and fell down. Further into the campus, a black cloud shifted and mindlessly toppled the university's clock tower.

"Old Joe," said Maurice, shocked.

"Bugger Old Joe," said Rod, running round the car. "Let's get into this mine o' yours."

Rod propelled the smaller man ahead of him. Through the fence, across a short lawn, he could just make out a brick hut. Keys rattled in Maurice's hands.

"Just got to find the right one."

Rod looked back. Something rustled at the edge of the lawn, struggling to navigate the gap in the fence.

"Quickly now."

"Here," said Maurice. Rod heard the clunk of a key in a heavy lock. As a shadow crossed the lawn, the door swung open. Rod pushed Maurice inside.

"Careful!" said Maurice. "Or you'll fall in!"

The door closed. The sound of it being locked once more was a lovely sound. Maurice found a light switch.

Rod looked at the shaft bored into the ground by his feet. The smell of damp rose up from the darkness. A short railing that would only have served to trip him over the edge if he'd gone any nearer ran around the shaft. There was a stout, caged access ladder.

"Shall I go down first?" said Rod.

"So, eager," said Maurice, taking out a pair of fine leather gloves to wear for the descent.

Something scratched at the door.

"Come and share with us," said a reedy voice. The building shook as the titan demolishing the university took another step.

01:45AM

"And that is the last of the pink wafers," said Professor Omar, presenting the almost demolished packet of biscuits to Prudence.

Prudence took the biscuit. Pink wafers, she decided, tasted of sweetness and air and not much else.

"Is there nothing for me?" said Steve, rocking back and forth on his land squid.

"You have no mouth," the professor pointed out.

"What's this, you blind degenerate?" Steve punched himself in his stitched-on face.

"Mouth with which to eat," sighed the professor.

The professor struck Prudence as someone who needed to sigh a lot. She could see he was in pain and he looked very, very old. Even older than her mum.

"Let's go play," she said to Steve.

Steve grabbed the foil packet from the professor and smeared it across his own face, leaving fragments of biscuit all over it like little pink flecks of stubble. "See?"

The professor threw his hands into a complex configuration.

"*Yhorr ves'nh!*" The lights in the ceiling flickered in a concentric wave emanating from the point directly above the professor's head. "To stop you wandering too far," he said, giving Prudence what she suspected was supposed to be a conspiratorial wink.

He waved a hand at the concrete horse as it loomed over. "I'll have the Bridgeman sculpture stay here. It does tend to eat people when it's hungry. There's one still out there in the wild, you know."

Prudence headed down the nearest aisle.

"I shall lead the way, pipsqueak!" said Steve and tried to gallop ahead. "I am the expert!"

Prudence prodded and examined objects on the shelves as they made their aimless way through the storage space.

"What's this, then?" she said, holding up an irregularly shaped white token.

"It's not important," said Steve.

"What's this?" she said, gesturing to the collected fragments of a broken vase.

"It's not important."

"And this?"

Steve sneered at a configuration of golden wire and jewels that might have been a headdress or might have been a statue of an insect. "Not important," he said, and rode on.

"I thought you said you were an expert," she said, mildly miffed.

"An expert in important things," he said haughtily. "When I see something important, I shall point it out to you."

"Sounds like you don't know."

"If you're to be my apprentice, you must learn to show me proper respect."

Prudence gave him a good hard frown, which was of no use because he was riding ahead of her. "Who says I'm your apprentice?"

He tossed his head back. "We agreed. You said you needed a mentor."

"Did I?"

"And if I am your mentor then you must be my mentee which is much like an apprentice. Now, keep up."

As they explored, Prudence concluded that many of the objects in the Vault were here because they were annoying and refused to behave as objects should. There were some blue gemstones that refused to be counted. There was a heavy gold coin that only had one side. There was a pottery statue of a woman, the face of which, when she turned it, took on a different expression – a trick of the light. However, as Prudence turned it, the woman's face did not return to the earlier expression. Each turn of the statue made the woman's face more vicious and strange than before. The features did not move at all, but within a handful of turns, the woman had a face that was contorted by rage and madness into something utterly inhuman.

After putting the increasingly-angry woman back on the shelf and carrying on, Prudence soon found the air became fuzzy and thick and too difficult to push through.

"Not too far!" came the professor's distant voice.

"No mortal is the master of me," said Steve. He urged the land squid onwards, but it could do no better. Its tentacles wobbled uncontrollably in the fuzzy air, like flags in the wind.

"We'll go this way," said Prudence, and headed down a side aisle.

"That's where we wanted to go anyway," said Steve.

After twists and turns along the boundaries the professor had set them, Steve found nothing important enough to be an expert on. They came upon something that was certainly different, even if only in terms of its scale. In an open area surrounded by shelves, sat a thing of stone or cement, covered in powdery dust. From the central mass, curling tendrils and tentacles sprouted in wild, crazed loops which touched the ceiling and stretched outward in a rough circle five times wider than Prudence was tall.

Prudence looked around. "How did they get this in here?" It was bigger than any door she had seen and couldn't even be moved around in this space without taking down most of the nearby shelves.

"Through clever means and artifice," said Steve.

"But how?"

"I don't have to tell you everything," he sniffed.

Prudence tapped a tentacle to see if it might move like the concrete horse. It didn't.

She placed a hand on the rough surface. It didn't feel like a made thing. There was an unevenness to its shape that wasn't just down to poor construction. It felt like an explosion frozen in time, a single terrible moment captured in this form. She instinctively knew it was alive.

"Hello," she said.

"Do not talk to the rock thing," said Steve. "Ah. Now *that* does look important." He headed off towards whatever had caught his attention.

Prudence ignored him, closed her eyes and flattened her hand on the stone. She could feel the being within. With senses she had not used since birth, she felt out beyond her own body and touched a mind encased in the cement.

"His name's *Crippen-Ai*," she said, to Steve, to no one. "His name's *Crippen-Ai*. And he's screaming."

01:50AM

"There are three security points between the entrance and the store room," said Maurice as they came to a sturdy hatch door.

The tunnel beneath Birmingham University was not what Rod had expected. He considered himself to be something of a tunnel connoisseur. Sometimes it felt as if all the key moments of his life had occurred in tunnels. Sandy ancient tunnels leading to the lair of the King in Crimson. The vast concrete tunnels of the nuclear bunker under the city centre. The abandoned railway under the Mailbox building. Cramped or cavernous, damp or dusty, every tunnel had its own character.

This was the first tunnel Rod had been in with mood lighting. The floor was bare earth. The rough walls had been given a layer of plaster and painted with white emulsion. The intermittent wall and ceiling props – surely not the century old originals, Rod thought – were painted in a contrasting glossy cream. Rod had to duck his head to pass under each beam; Maurice had no such issues. And then there were the wall lights.

Strung along a length of cable tacked to the wall, each light was a feature all by itself. There were luxury pleated silk shades, mounted on chunky wooden brackets so that they resembled a Seventies bistro. Some of the shades were edged with fringing or pom-poms. There were even some tattered vintage paper shades which looked very much as if they had real butterflies squished into their composition. Rod, who had no eye for interior design, suspected someone (almost certainly Maurice rather than Omar) had spent many a happy weekend at antiques fairs, selecting the most kitsch and outrageous lampshades for this unique collection.

Maurice ran his hand over the door in front of him and intoned a short Venislarn phrase. Nothing noticeable happened. Maurice opened the door onto the next section.

"And if you hadn't said the magic words?" asked Rod.

Maurice thought. "I would have exploded. Or gone blind. One or the other. It's been so long since we put this in."

There was rumbling from back along the tunnel. Maybe the leisure centre had been sat on by a god. Maybe a careless foot had swept the entrance building to the tunnel aside.

"Shall we close the door behind us, just to be on the safe side?" suggested Rod.

Maurice nodded and continued. "Three security points," he said. "The second door has a combination lock. The third is a riddle door."

"Right. A riddle door. As in 'My first is in apple but not in pear...'? That kind of codswallop?"

Maurice chuckled. "Do I detect a certain disdain?"

Rod shrugged. "As a form of security, it makes no sense. Passwords and passkeys are fine. But if the 'key' you're being asked for is something you can work out from the question then it's not security; it's a general knowledge quiz."

"You sound like Omar. He has no sense of fun either."

"I'm just saying—" Rod had to duck hurriedly to avoid the next beam. "It's the kind of thing you only find in computer adventure games, or that *Dungeons and Dragons* malarkey."

"Ah, there speaks a man who never knew the thrill of defeating a gelatinous cube with a lucky D20."

"Aye, you're not wrong there," agreed Rod, readily.

The next door had a keypad set into the wall next to it. Maurice tapped in five digits.

There was another rumble, maybe no louder than the last one but deeper in tone. A brutalist chandelier swung on its fixing. Dust motes drifted in the air.

Maurice looked up in momentary trepidation.

"What are these for?" asked Rod, holding up the plastic box.

"Ah," said Maurice with notable cheer. "Very important." He took the box and opened it. "Sandwiches and macaroons."

Rod picked one of the biscuity cakes.

"Vital in an emergency," said Maurice. "If I'd left them in the car, who knows what might have happened to them."

"You never know," said Rod. "When we're done here, it might still be there."

"It?"

"The car."

Maurice whipped out a pocket-sized packet of napkins and passed them to Rod. "Crumbs."

"Quite," said Rod.

Another ground-shaking rumble. Rod tried not to think about the structural integrity of a mine tunnel which predated World War One.

Maurice went back to close the door behind them. Rod put both macaroon and tissues in his pocket. He hardly felt it was time for a dainty repast.

"The sandwiches are ham and piccalilli," said Maurice. "You can't go wrong with a decent piccalilli."

Another crash, louder than thunder, as deep as any explosion.

Rod's knees buckled as the ground wobbled. A ceiling beam silently gave way and wood and earth tumbled into the space between him and Maurice. Earth fell in hard unforgiving clods. Through the cascade of soil, Rod saw Maurice's shocked face, hands raised as he stepped back.

Rod shouted to him, didn't even know what it was he was shouting, and then the cave-in spread. A half tonne of earth clipped Rod's shoulder. He fell into a stumbling run, deeper into the mine. Even when the dull roar had been replaced by the fizz of settling earth, he did not stop. Only in the silence did he slow, now on hands and knees, and look back.

The lights, ripped off the wall in places, were still on. The air was filled with a brown haze.

Earth, rich loamy soil, filled the tunnel some distance back in a solid uninterrupted wall. His mouth was gritty with the dust from it. How much of the tunnel had caved in? Five feet? Ten feet? Thirty?

"Maurice!" he shouted.

There was no reply from beyond the cave in. However, behind him, a melodic baritone spoke. "Greetings, weary traveller. Riddles have I if you wish to pass…"

Rod closed his eyes.

Ricky Lee stopped in the Library lobby to make sure he understood what Nina had said. "You need me to drive you to Sutton Park."

"Yes."

"To the donkey sanctuary."

"Yes."

"Because Vivian Grey's husband is there."

"Mr Grey, yes."

"Because he's been magically turned into a donkey."

"Yes."

"And he knows a magic spell that can undo all of this."

She winced. "It's not as simple as that. And I really don't like the 'm' word. It makes it all sound stupid."

Ricky Lee stepped back and put his hands on his hips. "We're driving to the suburbs to collect a donkey and you think the 'm' word makes it sound stupid?"

"Everything thing you —*ggh!* – *adn-bhul* humans do sounds stupid," said Pupfish.

"And are all the other donkeys magically transformed people?"

"What? No. I don't think so," said Nina.

"Didn't know if it was like that thing in *Pinocchio*."

"I have no idea what you're on about," she said.

"*Pinocchio*. The film. The island." He looked to Pupfish to back him up.

"I seen a version of *Pinocchio*," Pupfish conceded. "Straight to DVD type. Weren't no – *ggh!* – donkeys, although some of the guys were hung like donkeys. There was this one scene where the girl sits on Pinocchio's face and—"

"Getting off topic," said Ricky. "So, we're going to Sutton Park, finding the donkey and ... bringing it back?"

"Naturally," said Nina.

"In my car?"

Nina thought on that. "Can we take out the parcel shelf in the boot?"

Ricky rolled his eyes at her. He spoke into his police radio. "Control. I need a police van in the location of the city centre. Priority."

Lights shifted in the sky outside. The world looked sick.

02:00AM

Rod could not take his eyes off the face in the door. Superficially it could be mistaken for a number of distended knots in the wood, with a warped nub for a nose. On further inspection it was very clearly a face. What Rod found fascinating and disturbing in equal measure was that on even closer inspection, it was really very cartoonish, and spoke as though it was composed of latex foam and was being operated from behind by a Sesame Street puppeteer.

"What the heck are you?" said Rod.

"Is that your answer, weary traveller?" said the door.

"What? No," said Rod. "I'm asking what you are. Are you like a person trapped in a door or are you a magic door?"

"I have a riddle for you," said the door. It even had little rosy cheeks of polished wood. "I'm always old, sometimes new, never sad but sometimes blue—"

"Yeah, yeah. Forget that," said Rod who didn't have time for such things. He grabbed the door handle, twisted and pulled.

"To get through my door, weary traveller, you must answer my riddle."

"Shut up."

Although the cave-in had only been a minute before, Rod could feel the heat and heaviness of the air. There were no ventilation shafts in this section. Whether Maurice had survived the cave-in or not, Rod needed to press on, find the orb and get out of here or he would suffocate. A thought occurred to him.

"Say something, door."

"You would like to hear the riddle again?" it asked. "I'm always old, sometimes new—"

Rod put his hand to the speaking mouth and felt the flow of air. "You breathe?"

"Is that your answer?"

"You're a door with lungs?"

"Is that your answer?"

"Using up my flamin' oxygen." He drew his pistol and pointed it between the face's knotty eyes. The mouth dropped open in alarm.

"Weary traveller! I am but a simple door!"

"I need you to 'a' stop using up my air and 'b' let me through."

"All you need to do is answer my riddle."

"I don't do any of that twaddle," said Rod. "Now, open up."

"But if you would but listen!"

In the cloudy light and the increasingly hot air of the tunnel, Rod did not harbour much patience but he was an inherently polite man.

"Fine!" he hissed. "But be quick about it."

"I have a riddle for you—"

"I know that."

"That was by way of being my preamble, weary traveller," said the door and cleared its throat. "I'm always old but sometimes new, never sad but sometimes blue. I'm never empty but sometimes full. I never push but always pull."

"No idea," said Rod and took aim again.

"Wait! Wait!" said the door. "You've barely thought about it."

"I've thought about it enough," said Rod. "Now, open up or I will shoot my way through."

"But it's not that difficult a riddle if you put your mind to it, weary traveller."

"No time."

"Sometimes new, sometimes blue, sometimes full, always pull..."

Rod shrugged. "A car?"

"A car?"

"A car."

"That doesn't work," said the door.

"Yes, it does. It's a car. Open up."

"But that's not the answer to the riddle."

"Why not?"

"Always old?"

"Been around for ages, haven't they, cars?"

"Never empty?"

"They've got seats in them."

"Sometimes blue?"

"Some cars are blue."

"No, no," said door, waggling its cheeks as though trying to shake its head. "The correct answer to a riddle should feel inherently truthful. There's an element of poetry to it. The answer can't be something that merely fits the criteria."

"It's a car," said Rod. He placed the barrel of the gun against the face's forehead. "It's a blue bloody car. Tell me I'm wrong."

The door looked panicked. "Weary traveller, please—"

"I will reduce you to matchwood. It doesn't matter to me."

"But this is my one sole purpose. I exist to ask the riddle! If I give in to threats, then what is my purpose? Where is my raison d'être?"

"And then I'll burn that matchwood."

"Please, just think on. New something, blue something, full something. Common phrases. You just have to find the word that fits, weary traveller!"

Rod didn't waver. "It's a car. Final answer. Locked in. And I dare you to call me 'weary traveller' again. I double dare you."

The door squeaked in fear, tried to screw up its knothole eyes and then the lock went *click*.

"Well done," it said, in a trembling, sullied whimper. "You have solved my riddle, weary – dear sir."

"That's more like it," said Rod and pushed through into the next section of tunnel.

There was another identical face on the other side of the door.

"Would you like to know the answer?" it asked.

"Not particularly," said Rod.

"You'll kick yourself when you hear it."

"Not interested."

He closed the door rather than leave it ajar, hoping it would lend some minor structural support to the unstable tunnel.

"I've got one for you though," he said. "A riddle."

"Have you?" said the door eagerly.

"Aye. When is a door not a door?"

The weird squishy wood face did its best thinking impression. "I do not know, sir."

Rod holstered his pistol and carried on down the tunnel.

"What is the answer?" the door called after him. Rod ignored it. "When is a door not a door, sir?"

As he walked on, it shouted out to him. "Tell me! I must know! When *is* a door not a door? Please! Tell me!"

Rod wasn't in the habit of causing mental anguish to woodwork, but riddle-spouting gits deserved to suffer.

02:04AM

Prudence leaned her weight against the twisted cement-coated body of *Crippen Ai*. She could feel the mind of the creature within the stone casing, and by physically pressing on it she hoped to mirror her mental efforts and push through to its inner thoughts.

She was only peripherally aware of Steve the Destroyer, wittering to no one about something he had found down the aisle, but his voice faded as Prudence slipped inward...

......

......

......

...Her feet touched down in a hall of monsters. She knew this place. She had been here in her mother's womb.

Human furniture – metal chairs and metal tables – cluttered portions of the floor, scattered about as an afterthought by the Venislarn inhabitants of this unnatural and geometrically inconsistent space. Huge wall mirrors reflected this reality, and others.

This was a place where the local Venislarn waited. *Royogthraps* would wetly toy with their food in dark corners. *Draybbea* would slouch in oozing puddles, or hang like damp washing from ceiling roosts. *Uriye Inai'e* would wrap themselves around their slowly-digesting dinners and their plots of conquest. This was normally a place of waiting, a departure lounge, but there was now (and Prudence could sense that this was *now*, occurring at this moment, a short distance across the city), there was now a sense of action and urgency, a readiness to move.

Some of the human slaves of *Yo-Morgantus* hurried on errands. Others were snatched up by trailing limbs and put to other uses that Prudence could not quite see or comprehend. The August Handmaidens of *Prein*, the nine which were left, arrayed themselves in military formation. A stone *Skrendul,* standing in nightmarish stillness in the corner, was drawing out of its hibernation. Patterns etched into its moss-encrusted flesh shifted and locked into formations that would drive mortals insane.

Through all of this, Prudence walked unnoticed. She could smell the rotting heat rising from a nearby pool. She could hear the rustle of stick-dry *Presz'lings* legs. But none saw her.

An August Handmaiden of *Prein* presented itself to a naked woman on a slightly raised dais. The Handmaiden was called *Shara'naak Kye*. The woman was named Brigit and was the mouthpiece of the god *Yo-Morgantus*. Prudence found she simply knew these things. Knowledge wasn't something to be learned, but unlocked from where it already existed in her mind.

"We seek your authority to seize the *kaatbari* child," said *Shara'naak Kye.*

"To what end?" said Brigit. She slinked around the Handmaiden's legs, stroking them slowly with her fingertip.

"We demand vengeance," said the Handmaiden. "Morag Murray killed our sister in Edinburgh. She killed our sister in Bournville. She killed our sister at Millennium Point."

"She only killed one of them."

"She was the cause!" said *Shara'naak Kye* bitterly.

Brigit sighed, bored, and walked away. Prudence noticed that as she moved, she did this slow swaying, wobbling thing with her hips and bum. Prudence wondered if it was deliberate or if there was something wrong with her.

"Is there any reason I should acquiesce?" said Brigit.

"There has always been amity between yourself and the entourage of *Prein*," said the Handmaiden. "*Hath-No* approaches and brings our armies with it. Even now, an alliance between us would be beneficial."

Brigit laughed but Prudence didn't really understand why.

In the shadows behind a mirrored pillar, Prudence saw something move. It was dark, the dark of charred flesh. Blue-white slime steamed in the cracks of its baking skin. Its many irregular limbs spasmed in agony, desperate to move but trapped in this one pose.

"*Crippen Ai*," said Prudence.

She was abruptly thrown upwards, through the ceiling of this place, and up into the night sky above the city. There were the glows of fires and other things in the distance. Cars piled up in twisted wreckage on the streets directly below. A police van, its blue lights silently twirling, drove at speed to the north of the city. Something shimmered on the horizon in that direction but Prudence could not make it out in the dark.

Crippen Ai, quivering in burning agony, hung in the sky behind her. As he pulsated, flakes of his crisped flesh fell away.

"You can see everything that's happening?" said Prudence.

Perhaps in response, Prudence was yanked across the sky, away from the Cube and the Library. Prudence tumbled end over end, passing through a swarm of fiery mouthed *Tud-burzu* and over a parade of paper-thin *hort'ech* dolls that asked nothing of their human audience but their eyes.

Below her now was a village or a workplace, clusters of

buildings dotted with lawns and parkland. The *bezu'akh* annihilator kicked through buildings and stomped on the ground. Its scale dizzied Prudence. Even up here, she was only level with its pustulated shoulders. Joints that had not yet decided where to settle rotated and ground against one another. It breathed as it danced – and it was dancing – and its breath, sweet and oaty and sour, was both of something new-born and already rotting. The annihilator had come into this world already dying.

"*Crippen Ai,*" she called out, twirling in the air to seek him out. "Is this happening now? Is this already happening?"

She could not see him, but wherever he was, he pulled her back down. She did not cover her eyes as they passed through the ground; she knew she was here only as an observer, not physically present.

She stepped onto a solid floor. Impossibly, there was light. Little lamps hung along the wall of the tunnel. Dust and earth filled the air. The ground rumbled under the annihilator's foot and more earth fell into the tunnel. Coughing as he ran ahead of the collapse, her mum's friend Rod stumbled past, bounced off a wall and through a doorway.

Prudence followed.

She was in a treasure house, not unlike the Vault at the Library, but very unlike the Vault. Where the Vault had dull books and rows of objects that looked mundane but which were dangerously magical, here there was nothing but glitz and sparkle and shine. Jewelled daggers, crystal lanterns, statues of brilliant amber, intricately painted clay, shimmering insect cases. In tiered shelves like in a shop display, candles burned eternally. Music box dancers turned: brightly painted but nonetheless sinister marionettes lolled with only temporary lifelessness. This place was exciting and beautiful, and Prudence could feel the raw danger radiating off it all.

Rod ignored all the treasures and went to the far wall. He slapped it. He thumped it with his fist.

"Would it hurt to have put in another exit?" he panted.

Prudence studied his face. His eyes flicked to the doorway, to the unseen carnage going on above, to the side. It was a fascinating expression on his face. There was sheer exhaustion and defeat – she could tell that he was trapped, doomed – but there was an unstoppable air about him. He was a car that had run out of road but the wheels were still spinning, the engine unable to slow.

"Is this where he's going to die?" she asked.

02:09AM

If he was going to be killed by a cave-in, Rod wanted to meet that death on his feet.

He couldn't clearly express why an upright death was any better than a prone death, but he supposed if he was going to be buried alive, he wasn't going to obligingly lie down and wait for it. After several long minutes of standing like a wrestling action figure prepared for the roof to fall in, Rod quietly considered the possibility that the earth-shaking giant had passed by and there would be no more cave-ins for the time being.

He kept such thoughts quiet, barely acknowledging them. Rod did not believe in coincidences, or fate as such, but he believed that the universe had certain rhythms. What went up had to come down. For every drum roll there was a cymbal crash. For every idiot who declared, "It's okay. It's stopped now," there was a horrible final surprise.

So, whilst clearly broadcasting the silent opinion that, yes, this one surviving space in the mine might be obliterated at any moment, Rod forced his body to adopt a more relaxed pose and inspect his surroundings.

Beyond the doorway, the tunnel had vanished. There was a minimum twenty feet of caved in tunnel between his current position and where he'd last seen Maurice. Maurice had either fled back to the ladder or he was dead.

"I have no mouth," said Rod in apology and farewell.

His mind immediately went to Omar and the others at the consular mission. He took his phone out. There was no signal. He tried to call Morag nonetheless, but the phone could not connect to the network.

So, he was trapped and had no means of contacting the outside world. No help would be forthcoming.

He looked at the shelves of treasures around him. A dolly made from twisted black wheat stalks. A jewellery box inset with pearls. A glass dish with scalloped edges decorated with eye motifs which never seemed to be quite still. A ceramic skull. A melted crucifix. A rusted spearhead.

"…And a cuddly toy," said Rod, and chuckled at his own weak joke. "Another cultural reference you wouldn't get, Nina."

On a higher shelf he saw a red jewel resting in a bronze dish. It was an unevenly-carved jewel, almost in the shape of a crouching cat. He laughed, a full and honest laugh this time. Rhythms of the bloody universe.

He had seen the jewel for the first time years before, in an underground chamber (but not like this), in a moment when death seemed close at hand (but not like this). He could feel the tug of it already.

It was the *Azhur-Banipal shad Nekku*. "The stone of the King in Crimson," he said in recognition and acknowledgement.

He had seen it that one time, beneath the Syrian Desert, and managed to resist its demonic lure. Even now it was whispering without words, promising him his heart's desire, if he simply picked it up. But he knew the offer came with a terrible price. In the desert tunnels, he had felt arms wrapped in ragged cloths reaching out for him. The image had invaded his dreams in the years since. To touch the jewel was to give oneself to the King in Crimson. Rod didn't know who that was. The who's who of the Venislarn world was not his area of expertise.

"Yeah, not today, mate," he said and looked elsewhere.

On a middle shelf on the other side of the room was a pendant necklace. He would have assumed the material was gold, except it was marked with a mottled tarnish. The pink sphere of the pendant stone was mounted on baroque filigrees of metal.

"The *Gellik* orb," he said and picked it up.

This was a perversely annoying turn of events. He had come here to find the orb, so it could be used to summon the potentially world-saving Vivian Grey back to the mortal realm. And here he was, orb in hand, with no way of returning it.

He pocketed it and moved to the leading edge of the cave-in. Huge clay clods of earth made up the majority of the material. Rod dug his fingers in and heaved. Although fistfuls came away in his hands, there was no way he could move those massive chunks. He shook the muck from his hands and forced himself to consider his situation clearly.

"Got the orb. That's a positive. Not currently dead *and* not injured. That's another. Trapped and alone. No back up. Air will run out in—" He sniffed as though that could somehow magically give him some idea. "—a few hours' time."

He looked at the lights on the wall and sought out a switch. There was none. That was a disappointment. If the whole chain of wall lamps could be controlled from this end, he might have been able to use the on-off switch to send a Morse code message to Maurice, if Maurice was somehow still alive. If there had even been the smallest air vent, he could have tried to signal out, even pass the necklace orb up to someone on the outside. He looked through the shoe boxes stacked underneath the shelves on both sides, hoping to find that mysterious something that might help him, but found only more occult knick-knacks and weird objects. He discovered little of note (although he found out Omar possessed two mummified severed hands – both right hands, not even a matching pair).

"I'm trapped. In a tunnel. And I'm going to die," he said finally, then wondered how many times in his life he'd had cause to say that.

His gaze returned to the blood-red stone of the King in Crimson. He sighed. "Do you actually grant wishes?" he said wearily.

The act of addressing it made him shiver. He felt a presence directly behind him. He could not see the King in Crimson's shadow looming over him. He could not smell the rot of his ancient flesh. He could not hear the rustle of his bandaged limbs or the rasp of his tomb-dry breath. But Rod could sense the King, fully realised, inches away from him.

He resisted the urge to turn round. This was not merely because he was afraid (and he was afraid of seeing the foul god-king in the flesh) but because he suspected he would see nothing at all, yet feel a fresh presence behind him. Always behind.

"You grant wishes," he said, making it a statement this time. "If I take the jewel, you will grant my wishes. You will take this orb thing and give it to someone at the consular mission so they can use it. You will do that before you drag me to hell, or whatever."

There was no reply, and he'd expected none. Rod had set out his stall and that was as much of an agreement he hoped to get. He reached forward and, hesitating only to lick his suddenly dry lips and flex his suddenly sweaty fingers, he took the stone of the King in Crimson from its bronze dish.

It was cold to the touch.

A hand came down on his shoulder and long thin fingers gripped him like a vice.

Rod stilled his quivering breath. "How do," he said.

Something brushed his back, touched the hair on the back of his head. The cowl of a robe brushed his ear. Rod felt breath on his cheek, the smell of dry rot and old meat.

"Your soul is mine," whispered the King in a voice like the wind.

"Right you are," said Rod.

A second hand gripped his other shoulder. "I had a school P.E. teacher who did that," said Rod.

"P.E.?"

"Come behind us and put his hands on our shoulders, like. Stand real close. I'm not saying the man was a pervert. Mr Crockleton. I'm sure he thought he was just being all friendly and… Point is, I didn't like it then and I don't like it now." Rod attempted to shrug him off but the King held tight.

"You're mine. The deal is done."

"Aye, but the wishes."

"One wish."

"What? No way, mate. A deal like this, I should get as many wishes as I like and then—"

"One wish, patron!" hissed the King.

"Don't take the bleedin' mick. At least three. Three wishes is traditional."

"Three then…" said the King. Rod wished he'd driven a harder bargain.

He took the orb from his pocket and held it up high so that the creature behind him could see it clearly. "First wish then. See this? This orb?" he said, just in case the damned King thought he was referring to his hand. "I need it to get to Morag at the consular mission office. I need her to get it now and safely so that she can use it. That's Morag Murray. The Birmingham consular mission office." He wanted to give a postcode but couldn't remember it.

The King was silent.

"Got that?" Rod tried to look aside, get some acknowledgement from the King and when his eyes looked back, his hand was empty. Necklace and orb pendant had vanished. "Right. Good."

Rod felt a renewed fear. The orb was gone. Hopefully delivered to where it could do the most good. Now all Rod had left to worry about was himself.

"Now, getting me out of here," he said. He turned to the collapsed tunnel beyond the doorway. "I want to be able to shift that lot." He tried to face the King in Crimson but the risen horror turned with him. Rod glimpsed the skeletal fingers on his shoulder. They were black and cracked, like rotten banana skins. "Can you make me stronger?"

"How strong?" the demon rasped.

"You know, super strong."

"How strong?"

"How strong?" Rod held up his hands in exasperation. "Super strong. Strong enough to knock out a bleedin' god with a single punch," he said peevishly. "*That* strong!"

The King in Crimson was silent.

"Is it done? Have you done it?"

The King in Crimson was literally breathing down his neck. *"It is done."*

"Good. Fine." Rod hurried to the landslide and dug his hands into the nearest chunks. He pulled at them ferociously, expecting new energy to flow through him. He clawed and scrabbled and nearly ripped off one of his nails in his haste.

"I said super strong, yeah," he said, sensing that nothing had changed.

"Strong enough to knock out a bleeding god with a single punch."

"Aye, and that should mean..." Rod stopped and straightened. The hands never left his shoulders. He spoke slowly to savour his rising temper and to stave off the answer that he knew, just knew was coming. "Did you make me strong enough only in terms of punching gods? Like only so I could punch a god?"

"You asked..."

Rod whirled and almost shook the King in Crimson from him. "You right tricksy bugger! I knew you were going to do summat like this. Mess with the wording. You better have sent that orb to Morag like I asked. I was careful how I phrased that, but this!" He pushed angrily at the hands but they held his jacket. He tugged and pulled and then just slipped out of his jacket completely. He turned, pistol already drawn and aimed.

Ninety percent of his anger dried up at the full sight of the King in Crimson. He was a hunched figure, but was still a full head taller than Rod. His limbs were emaciated, coarse and black, mummified even within the sleeves of a threadbare red coat. But his chest and face, where it was visible, were alive and wet. Open sores and gaping wounds fed his skin with a constant layer of weeping, glistening pus. The tumorous holes in his face shifted constantly like tiny murmuring mouths. His mouth and nose were invisible, covered by a stained rectangular mask. The line of the mask over his nose framed his sunken eyes, which were hateful and very human. The fabric glistened and moved with the King's breath. With the mask and the King's ragged, uniform-like coat, Rod couldn't tell see where fabric ended and flesh began. He couldn't tell if the black-red colour of the clothes was dye or drying blood.

Staggered by the dreadful sight, Rod might have lost all of his anger to terror, but for the fact the King in Crimson still held onto Rod's work jacket by the shoulders, holding it up in confusion. Like a cloakroom attendant who had lost their customer. Rod grasped onto that ten percent of his anger.

"You knew what I wanted," he said.

"You dare challenge me?" Black pus flew in flecks from face wounds.

"Until I get my three flamin' wishes, you'll do what I say, sunshine."

He knew he was pushing it. He was riding a wave of anger- and fear-fuelled adrenaline, and suspected it would all go very badly for him when it was over. What did it matter? It was going to go very badly for everyone when this day was done.

"All I wanted was to get out of this bloody hole and away from here. Can you not do that?"

"That I can do, patron," said the King in Crimson.

And, in an instant, they were gone.

02:15AM

Morag straightened out the spine of her policy document and sipped her fresh cup of tea. The flow of people in and out of the meeting room had settled. With many pulled away by more urgent missions and other distractions, there were now only five of them in the room: Morag, Lois, the army major Sanders, and the two councilmen.

"Okay, if we can all turn to page seven," she said. "We can proceed with the plans for mass euthanasia."

"Killing people," said Major Sanders.

"Yep," said Morag. She wiped a tear from her eye. It wasn't a tear for the billions of people who were suffering or about to suffer. That would have made sense, even if it might have looked unprofessional at this juncture. Tears had sprung unbidden to her eyes because her mug, found from gods knew where, had a cheery cartoon cat and dog on it. As post-natal hormones washed about her body, she couldn't look at the bloody mug without a catch in her throat.

"Stupid, stupid mug," she muttered, then cleared her throat. "Right, yes, murdering the local population?"

"Killing," said Major Sanders. "Not murdering."

"Right. Right."

"I have given the order for the Fifth Fusiliers to begin shooting civilians on sight."

"I want it put on record that I am not happy with this," said Councillor Rahman. "I'm not signing off on this one. I want to know where these orders are coming from."

The major sighed. "Well, given that my commanding officer has run away to his holiday cottage in Wales and isn't answering his phone. Given that the Prime Minister disappeared mid-broadcast and has possibly been eaten. Given that it appears the US Commander-in-Chief has ignored internationally agreed protocols and is trying to fight off the alien menace single-handedly. Given all of that, I'd say it's pretty bloody clear that the chain of command has collapsed. I've given out the order to start shooting civilians to all troops in this city."

"My objection's been noted?" said the councillor.

Morag and Lois looked at each other. "Are you taking minutes?" Morag asked.

"No," said Lois. "Didn't seem to be any point."

Morag looked at Councillor Rahman. "You can make a note of it yourself if it makes you any happier." She turned to the major. "We've got a volunteer force administering suicide pills door to door throughout the city. And we've also got soldiers shooting people on sight. Won't there be some form of ... overlap?"

"Undoubtedly," said Major Sanders. "Unfortunately, there's no co-ordination between the branches of government in charge. We should expect some suicide pill volunteers to be killed by army personnel, possibly before they have distributed their supplies."

"I suppose there's little we can do about that now," said Morag. She caught a glimpse of the cat and dog mug. Their big soulful eyes brought new tears to her eyes. "Damn it."

As she turned the mug around there was a tiny electrical pop, and something appeared in the air directly in front of her face. It dropped heavily to the table. The council CEO swore in surprise.

It was a chunky piece of jewellery. Yellow metal worked around a rose-coloured glass ball.

"The *Gellik* orb," Morag said, as surprised as any by its sudden appearance.

"What is it? Is it dangerous?" said Councillor Rahman.

"It's a way to get Vivian back," said Morag. She would have pushed herself from her seat and sprinted for the lift, but her lower torso was still a big old bag of wrongness and she could only do a tender high-speed hobble. "Talk amongst yourselves," she called back to the attendees as she left.

She took the lift to the floor above.

Security Bob was in the lobby area of the Vault.

"Omar?" she said.

"Inside. With that girl of yours," he said as he unlocked the doors to let her through.

Omar was exactly where she'd left him, in his wheelchair by one of the many workspaces he'd created for himself around the Vault. He was leaning gingerly over an open book.

"Working out how to save the world?" she said.

"Huh?" said the professor, shaken from a reverie. He sat back and treated her to a weak smile. "Nothing so practical or noble, my dear. I was looking over one of our little travel albums." He put a hand on the scrapbook page. Photographs, ticket stubs and notes had been painstakingly taped onto its pages.

The photograph on the open page was of Omar and Maurice on a grassy clifftop. Maurice was nearly swamped by a cream cable-knit sweater. Omar's arms were expressively wide as he talked about something that both of them could see but the photographer could not.

"Shetland. Fourteen years ago," said Omar. "We stayed at a charming hotel with a very poor breakfast menu. We went to see the puffins. We visited an old Norse settlement. And one evening we summoned the *Voor-D'yoi Lak* from its cave and barely escaped with our lives." He sighed nostalgically. "A fine time was had by all."

Only then did he see the *Gellik* orb in her hand. He clutched at it. "They're back?"

"I've not seen Rod or Maurice. This just appeared. Literally appeared."

A dark look passed momentarily over his face.

"My daughter somewhere?" she asked, casting about.

"Around and about with that amoral rag doll," he said.

"Prudence!" she called.

"Yes, mother!" came a distant reply.

"You being good?"

"Yes, mother!"

Omar turned the gem around in his hand. "If I had known this had previously opened a passage between earth and *Hath-No*, we might have been able to effect her rescue earlier."

"So you can do it?" Morag said, trying not to sound so pathetically eager.

"Dimensional tunnelling devices are child's play," he said. "Ten a penny, frankly."

02:17AM

Prudence ran her hands across the cement surface of *Crippen Ai*. Her mum's call had distracted her, pulled her out of the worlds beyond which the trapped and tortured creature had shown her.

Now, she felt the surface again, seeking a reconnection.

Steve the Destroyer interrupted her with a "Look! Look! I have found it!"

His land-squid had climbed up a shelving unit and now Steve was shoving a carved wooden cube along the shelf. It was not a large thing but it was a significant challenge to him.

"Just on a shelf with all this junk!" he grunted as he pushed. "Clearly its proper display case is not yet ready." He turned to put his back against it. "Such things take time."

"I'm busy," said Prudence, tilting her head towards *Crippen Ai*.

"Pah! Who are you to say when you are busy, morsel? Steve's business is the only important business. Come help me. Come stare in wonder."

Prudence ignored him and turned her attention back to…

……

......

......

...With startling ease, Prudence slipped back into the mental realm of *Crippen Ai*. She felt a momentarily alarming jolt as she found herself transported into a space that was this space. Prudence, a spiritual observer only, stood in the consular mission Vault. In front of her, a girl with an explosion of ginger hair and a loose dress made from a T-shirt leaned against the entombed form of *Crippen Ai*.

"That's me," she said. She had never seen herself before.

Prudence moved forward to take a better look at herself. She looked at the concentrating face, the screwed-up eyes. She seemed to be putting in a lot of effort to do nothing at all. Prudence the observer saw Prudence the observed blush at the thought of being watched.

"Come help me, indolent child!" commanded Steve. He had given up pushing the cube and was now attempting to twist its sliding surfaces.

At the end of the shelves, the burned form of *Crippen Ai* twisted and shuddered in the shadows, a tormented figure at the edge of this vision.

"Why are you showing me this?" said Prudence. Immediately she was looking along the aisle to where her mother and the professor were. Did she choose to look that way, or had *Crippen Ai* directed her? She couldn't tell. Prudence drifted towards the professor. He had his hands on a pink jewel her mother had brought him and speaking softly in Venislarn. Prudence was confident if she concentrated a little, she would know what the words meant. The jewel began to glow as though a strong light was shining through it.

This, Prudence knew, was what *Crippen Ai* wanted to show her. The pink light was one end of a thread which linked this place and another.

"Show me," she said and *Crippen Ai* hauled her away along the length of the thread. The transition was too fast to understand, the journey passing through something other than mere geography.

They came to a halt so suddenly that Prudence fell to her knees and rolled across the gritty floor of this new place. It was a gloomy cavern, filled with a subtle stench of rot. Old rot, new rot and everything in between. It was like flicking through the pages of a book at speed and each page was an essay in decay. Sounds of horns and drums and shouts echoed in from the world beyond this cavern.

There were shelves here too. The total experiences of her life so far indicated that everywhere was filled with shelves. And, yes, books also. Like some of the books in the Vault, nearly all of the books here were alive. They were restless, like roosting birds jostling for space.

The floor of the cavern was taken up by a machine. It merged with the floor in a crust of grease and filth. Higher up, its articulated arms were pale grey and shining silver. The arms curved up and over like cresting waves to touch down on the pieces of paper arranged on the counter surface before it. Prudence noted the see-through tubes running up the arms from the machine's base, carrying a ceaseless supply of dark red ink to the fingertips.

Despite the noisy activity coming from elsewhere, the *skrit skrit skrit* sound of pens on paper seemed to fill the place. The machine itself moved silently and Prudence (who had never seen a spider) was very much put in mind of a spider weaving its web.

She stepped closer and, as she did, noted the form of *Crippen Ai* watching from the darkness of the high ceiling. Prudence stepped onto the lower levels of the table (which was no table at all but an extension of the machine's body) and climbed up to look at the paper. The pens, several of them working on each sheet at a time, produced a fast-emerging block of prose.

. . .

T*he* kaatbari, *Prudence Murray, peered closer. Although she could not read, filtered through the senses and mind of the Venislarn pariah* Crippen Ai, *the words made sense to her and she saw her own current actions being narrated to her as they occurred.*

Prudence drew back a little in shock but curiosity held her there. She looked at Yoth-Kreylah ap Shallas, *fascinated by the machine's working and saw, amid the arms and pistons and inner gears, the face of* ap Shallas. Ap Shallas's *eyes looked up to seek out the kaatbari.*

T*he* old woman in the centre of the machine sat back and the whole apparatus of her machine body moved with her. She stared directly at Prudence, although Prudence was not present in any true sense.

The woman stared. She frowned. It was not a happy or friendly face. It was human and all the more unhappy and unfriendly for that fact. Dirt etched the many lines on the woman's face and outlined her irritation and displeasure. "Boo," she said.

Prudence shrank back. The woman continued to stare.

"*Barry!*" she called.

There was a succession of dull clonks and clangs and a short *thoggan* creature ran into the room.

"*Yeth, mithtreth,*" he said, clattering to a halt. He spoke Venislarn, but passed through the intermediary of *Crippen Ai's* mind, Prudence understood it clearly.

"Barry, can you see someone—" The *Yoth-Kreylah ap Shallas* stopped. "What are you wearing, Barry?"

The *thoggan* was wearing what might charitably be described as a suit of armour. But one would have to be very charitable indeed, as it appeared to only consist of a number of pots and bowls bound to his head, chest and limbs with rags and lengths of filthy sinew.

He smiled. Prudence automatically tried to count his teeth.

"*Thith is my armour. I am drethed for war.*"

"*You look ridiculous.*"

"Hath-No *dethendth upon the earth at thith very moment, mithtreth, and when the time comth, I will fight at your thide, my anthethtral weapon thworn to you.*"

Ap Shallas scowled. "*I have told you that I will not be fighting. I am close to finishing the book. Furthermore...*" A twisting mechanical arm prodded the shoddy little axe he carried. "*That is not an ancestral weapon. I saw you making it earlier.*"

"It could be," said Barry, "*if I gave it to my offthpring.*"

Ap Shallas ignore his idiocy and pointed at Prudence. "*Tell me, can you see someone standing there?*"

The *thoggan* made a good show of looking in Prudence's direction. "*No, mithreth,*" he said eventually.

"*Me neither,*" she said.

"*Riiight.*"

The many arms came in to scribe once more. Prudence watched and read and thought.

THE KAATBARI WATCHED as ap Shallas *noted down the conversation she had just had with the* thoggan, *Barry. Prudence thought that* ap Shallas *was, if not exactly cruel, at least a rude and dismissive master to the* thoggan. *She felt this even more so upon reading that Barry had been in servitude to* ap Shallas *for a length of time that was beyond all human comprehension.*

"OH, WHAT DO YOU KNOW?" said the *ap Shallas* out loud, and glared at the spot where Prudence stood.

Prudence blinked. "Can you see me?"

"Not at all," said the *ap Shallas* as she continued to write.

"*...but I know that you are here. I am recording everything that is happening in this instant and I can read my own writing which tells me exactly what you're saying and doing.*"

"So, you know that I'm saying because you've read it?"

"Correct."

"As you're writing it?"

The ap Shallas *nodded sharply.*

"It makes perfect sense if you're able to make certain leaps of logic," said the *ap Shallas*.

Barry gave *ap Shallas* a gentle pat on the side. "Who are you talking to, mithreth?"

"*The* kaatbari. *Prudence Murray. Morag's daughter.*"

Barry nodded slowly. "*There'th no one there.*"

"*I know!*"

Barry gave this due thought. "*Maybe you'd like a cup of tea, mithreth.*"

"What?"

"*Or a bit of a retht. You have been overdoing it of late.*"

"*I have worked ceaselessly for an eternity,*" she said.

"*That'th what I'm talking about.*"

She made a disgusted huff and attempted to return to her writing.

Prudence Murray observed her quietly for a while. She studied the movements of the pen arms, the glistening ink as it flowed across the page and then dried. The Yoth-Kreylah ap Shallas *worked to a task that, to Prudence's mind would be one without end. To try to write down everything that ever happened was impossible.*

"You'd have to write down everything that happened," said Prudence, "and then you'd have to write down what happened when you wrote the book. And then you'd have to write about writing that bit. And then you'd have to write—"

A*p* S*hallas* slammed a writing hand down on the desk. "Stop it," she said.

"Stop what?" said Prudence.

Ap Shallas glanced at the writing she was still producing to read what Prudence had said. "Stop trying to complicate things."

"I'm not complicating things."

"You are and you know it, young girl. And you're wrong anyway."

"Wrong how?"

Ap Shallas continued to write.

Y*oth*-K*reylah* *ap* S*hallas* *could have explained to the impudent girl—*

—"H*ey*!" said Prudence—

*—*how the Bloody *Big Book made use of recursive and self-referential systems to encapsulate the sum totality of all things without unnecessary repetition. Just as the twenty-six letters of the Latin alphabet can be used repeatedly to describe all things, so certain pieces of text could be used time and again to reference those many events that were utterly identical.*

. . .

"That sounds like nonsense," said Prudence.

"That shows how little you understand," said *Ap Shallas* as she wrote. "The recording of an infinite universe might require an infinite book but that doesn't mean—"

"Flibble," said Prudence.

"Pardon?" said ap Shallas.

"Flappy poppy wapple babble," said Prudence and looked at the page where the words were being written.

"Quiddy biddy ungle faff-a-taff-a wap," *said the* kaatbari *and laughed as the words came out on the page.*

"Oh, I see," *said* ap Shallas. "Very juvenile."

"Bum," said Prudence.

"Yes—"

"Bum bum."

"Stop it, now," *said* ap Shallas, *mildly surprised to feel a very human anger she had not known in aeons.* "I have better things to—"

"Bum bum bum bum bum bum. Squitty squitty poo poo."

With great effort, ap Shallas—

The writing machine woman pushed her papers aside and addressed the spot where she took Prudence to be.

"This is all you have left to offer the world, is it?" She snapped in a violent tone that jolted Prudence. "Clowning about as the world falls into darkness? And don't think I can't tell you're up there, *Crippen Ai*!" she yelled at the rafters. She looked back to Prudence's approximate location. "He probably decided to inflict you on me because I stopped him stealing the throne of *Hath-No*. He's a sore and spiteful loser."

Prudence looked up. *Crippen Ai* continued his agonised tremors in the dark but there was now a note of embarrassment in his twitches.

"Your sole purpose was to herald the end of the world," *ap Shallas* said to Prudence, "and you have done that. Back in your own time, the August Handmaidens of *Prein* have come to take ownership of you, but only as a trophy, a plaything. And if they knew what you were, half the humans would gladly hand you over. You are a spent thing of only fading ornamental value. If I were to wax poetic, I would say you are an exploded firework, the discarded wrapping paper. You are an empty Christmas stocking. And for that—" She paused and swallowed with difficulty as though true emotional sentiments caused her physical pain. "—For that I'm genuinely sorry. There's a whole wide world out there, a beautiful world and you're not going to get to enjoy any of it."

"*Mithtreth*," said Barry, trying to get her attention.

"*Not now*," she said. "*I'm talking to this young girl here.*"

"What girl?"

"Now, your mother was – or is – a foolish woman. Far too headstrong, with a monstrously unbecoming chip on her shoulder but she was – or is – a woman of passions. She was full of grit and determination…"

Prudence's attention wavered as she saw what Barry had been trying to point out. A pink sparkle of light had appeared in the air directly behind *ap Shallas*. From it wisps of light, like strands of hair, cascaded out towards *ap Shallas*. Prudence walked towards it and passed her hands through the growing curtain of colour. The *Gellik* orb…

"But mithtreth!"

"*Do not interrupt me mid-sentence*," said *ap Shallas* and then, perhaps spotting the pink reflection, turned. The machine swivelled on feet or wheels – Prudence could not see. It pivoted with much effort, long arms swinging out. When *ap Shallas* saw what was happening, she gave a shout. *"No! It is not time!"*

Prudence realised it was a shout of annoyance, not fear.

"This is most inconvenient! Come back later!" she commanded the expanding portal.

The glowing light pulled her in, pulled the woman from the machine. She emerged, shedding braces and straps, clamps and girdles, clothed only in filth and rags. Prudence thought of the angry whelks, the vulnerable creature in its hard shell, and felt something that wasn't quite pity for this woman, shouting in pathetic protest as she was extracted.

The *thoggan* dithered in panic, running backwards and forwards in his clanking pot armour. *Ap Shallas* didn't seem to even notice him. She frantically grabbed for the papers and the one huge book that were sliding off her desk-lap, and Prudence realised the woman only had one arm. The other ended just above the elbow in a knobbly and ugly stump.

"Don't!" she yelled, tumbling slowly into the light.

Prudence felt a peculiar dissonance as she heard *ap Shallas*'s yell with both *these* ears and her *actual* ears, in another plane of existence. She pulled back to hear more clearly...

......
......
......

...Prudence stepped back from the cement surface. There was grey dust on her hand. Away in another corner of the vault, pink light glowed and a woman yelled in unrestrained fury.

"What is that?" said Steve, still working on the wooden puzzle cube.

Prudence brushed the dust from her hands. "It is the *ap Shallas*. Mrs Vivian Grey. They've brought her back from *Hath-No*."

"Is that so?" he said, walking to the shelf end to seek her out.

"Do you think I'm an empty Christmas stocking?"

Steve gave a whole-body shrug. "What's a Christmas?"

"I don't know."

"Does it wear big stockings?"

"No, I don't think it's like that."

"You would make a big stocking, apprentice," Steve assured her. "Although only a thin leg would fit. We would need to break your jaw and scoop your insides out—"

"No, not like that," she said, impatient for the right kind of reassurance. "Am I useless? Has my purpose already been served?"

Steve gave her a deeply thoughtful inspection. "To what use would you like to be put?"

Prudence didn't know how to answer that one. "No one wants me here. Mrs Grey said there's a beautiful world out there and I'm not going to get to enjoy any of it," she said.

"Everyone else is having all the fun," agreed Steve. "I would like to burn things."

Prudence wasn't sure if burning things was how one went about enjoying the world, but it had an instinctive appeal.

"We should go see it while it's still there," said Prudence, then thought about the imprisoning circle that the professor had cast around the place. She took the heavy walkie-talkie from her pocket and pressed the button. It squawked. There would be no point asking her mother. She released the button.

"We should leave," she said and, seized with by an impulse, took the wooden puzzle cube from the shelf.

"Be careful, mortal," intoned Steve in as ominous a voice as the squeaky doll could manage. "The great artefacts of *Prein* can transport you to realms of infinite pleasure or relentless pain."

"I thought we could just go outside and look at, I don't know, the stars. And flowers."

"There are no flowers in the realms of infinite pleasure," sneered Steve.

"What about for people who really like flowers?" she said, and twisted the sides. The symbols, written in an alphabet that did not want to make life easy for beginner readers, glowed and shifted. Three turns, four turns; move that inner segment round. There was the screech of planes of existence tearing themselves apart and a tunnel of blue lightning opened before them. The land squid warbled in alarm and tried to hide between two hardback books.

"Your mother is going to think this is my fault!" Steve shouted against the interdimensional winds that had sprung up. "She will punish me!"

"Then you'd best come with me," said Prudence.

Steve considered the logic of this and, spear pencil held tight, jumped onto her outstretched hand. "Stars and flowers and burning things," he instructed. "And then we will come straight back."

Prudence held him tight. "Let's see what there is to see while it is still there," she said and stepped into the crackling vortex.

02:30AM

Nina explored the back of the police van while Ricky drove. She was checking to see how they might accommodate a donkey. She wasn't a hundred percent on the dimensions of a donkey, but was doing her best to imagine it.

"This van is pretty cool. There's an actual cell in here," she said. Reinforced steel sectioned off a tiny bench seat from the rest of the interior.

"It's one of the newer ones," said Ricky. "It's got unbreakable plastic in the windscreen too."

"Sweet ride," said Pupfish, who reclined in a passenger seat up front.

They were on the Aston Expressway, heading north out of the city centre. From its elevated position, there were views across a good part of the city. The horizon was filled with burning buildings and huge shapes silhouetted against the glowing skyline. Over to the left there was some sort of smoky flaming vortex above Villa Park. It rose like a cartoon beanstalk, swirling so tightly it looked solid enough to climb up. The swirling pulsed in time with distant screaming sounds. A pungent smell, somewhere between 'overzealous barbecue' and 'undiscovered dead mouse behind the radiator', seeped into the van.

"Can we do something about that stink?" said Nina.

Pupfish stabbed buttons to try and turn off the van's air conditioning, but only managed to engage the sirens. Ricky swatted his hand aside, turning off both sirens and aircon.

"We'll get a donkey through here, won't we?" said Nina. She held up her hands to gauge the size of the gap between the cell and the caged storage racks. They stood on either side of the rear door, and were optimised for humans. "Is a donkey about this big?" She turned round and held up outstretched hands to Pupfish.

He shrugged. "How many donkeys do you – *ggh!* – think we get on the Waters, dog? Uh, think we might have trouble up ahead." He pointed.

Nina crouched behind the front seats to peer through the window and tried to make sense of what she could see. Sure, it was the middle of the night, and the city was burning, shifting and being consumed, but something was seriously off about the view.

"What's normally there?" she asked, waving a hand at the middle distance.

Ricky Lee gave her an incredulous glance. "Spaghetti Junction? The M6 motorway? Those things, you mean?"

"Right. Yeah. So not like a great big Drayton Manor rollercoaster?"

"No, they tend to keep them at Drayton Manor."

Nina knew that, but it was the only thing her brain could liken this to. Colossal loops corkscrewed away from them, high into the hideous sky.

Spaghetti Junction was a motorway interchange arranged over five elevated levels and composed almost entirely of slip roads – connecting and redistributing traffic headed along motorways west, east and south. Sutton Park was in the suburbs to the north, and they had to pass through Spaghetti Junction to get there. Now someone had stuck a giant invisible fork into the bowl of spaghetti and hoisted it, twisting, into the sky. The road they were on ran straight into the chaos.

"That looks bad," said Nina.

"What the fuck happened?" said Ricky.

"Gods don't want us leaving town, po-po," offered Pupfish.

"We could find another route," said Nina.

"Cars are still going along it," said Ricky.

Nina could see them too. Like the other city streets, the impossible loops of the distended Spaghetti Junction were dotted with abandoned and crashed wrecks of vehicles, but some were definitely moving up there. They were even driving right round on the upside-down bits, looping the loop.

"Do you think we need to go really, really fast to do that?" she said.

"Those ones don't look as if they're going all that fast," Ricky replied. "In fact, does that one look as if it's trying to turn around to you?"

As they drew nearer, they could see one car, which looked like her dad's BMW, turning around in the road. It performed the manoeuvre while completely upside-down.

"We should see it in a minute," said Ricky. "It's coming up."

"We doing this? We going in?" said Pupfish.

"We loop the loop to get to Erdington, then carry on," said Ricky.

"Thought I was the reckless one," said Nina.

Ricky sighed. "I don't see that we have much choice. We could try and get off the main road, but we still need to cross over that thing, Whatever it is."

It dominated the skyline, and they watched in fascination as more cars scaled its sides.

"This reminds me of a bridge in Normandy I went over on a coach trip once," said Ricky.

"*Ggh!* You mean Kings Norton, cop-man?" said Pupfish. "Canal over that way's got—"

"Normandy in France," said Ricky. "This massive bridge, a proper engineering miracle, but it's really scary when you drive up to it. Looks as if you're gonna just drive off the top into thin air or something."

"Sounds like someone made it that way on purpose," said Nina. "You can bet it's right next to a Venislarn dumping ground, or something."

"We ain't gonna drive off into thin air or nuffin, are we?" said Pupfish.

"What goes up must come down, I'm guessing," said Nina. "So let's just all hold our bottle and pretend this is normal."

"Is that your guide to life?" Ricky asked with a smile.

"Pretty much." She gave him a peck on the cheek, nearly poking him in the eye with the corner of her hat.

Ricky gently increased the acceleration as they approached the upward slope of the road.

"Shouldn't we have seen that BMW by now?" asked Nina. The road ahead contained nothing but a taxi that was travelling along in the same direction as them, about a quarter of a mile ahead.

Ricky shrugged. "Maybe it came off at one of the other exits?"

Nina craned her neck to look up at the road stretching above them. As they crawled up the slope, it became more difficult to picture exactly where they were, relative to the ground. There were loops and twists of dual-carriageway in every direction, with just the turbulent night beyond. Nina wanted to say something, because there were definitely no other exits from this dreadful loop, but she clamped her lips shut. Ricky had enough on his plate.

"*Ggh!*— Where's up?" said Pupfish.

Nina knew exactly what he meant. It felt as if they had been driving up this crazy slope for long enough that they ought to be on the way down. "Can you tell, Ricky?" she asked.

"Not really," he said. "It's still like driving up a really steep hill, in terms of what the engine thinks it's doing. We're in a low gear and I'm accelerating hard."

"So what would happen if you weren't?" Nina asked.

"I'm not prepared to put that to the test. Nobody wants to be rolling backwards, completely out of control."

"No." Nina was not convinced their current situation could accurately be described as under control, but she would leave Ricky with the mechanics of driving. "Pupfish, let's try and find a reference point. Anything at all you can identify?"

They both stared at the surroundings as Ricky kept them moving forwards and upwards.

"I think that thing over there is Villa Park," she said, pointing at a whirling, flaming blur in the dark. "We passed it earlier."

Pupfish gave a nod. "So which end of that thing is pointing at the sky?" he asked.

Nina wasn't sure. "Well, we have a choice of two, I guess. Keep looking."

Pupfish had an advantage when it came to scanning a wide view, given the placement of his eyes, but he surprised Nina when he pointed straight ahead at the windscreen. "Canal is right there," he declared.

"What? I can't see anything. How do you know?"

"*Samakha* superpower, we always know where the waters are at."

"You chat *muda*, Pupfish," she grinned. "You ain't got no superpowers."

"I have."

"Making mysterious fishy smells is not a superpower."

"You's racist, Nina. You know that?"

"It's banter."

"That's how they keep us down, man."

Ricky swerved without warning. A flash of headlights, a roar of an engine. Nina rolled in the back and landed uncomfortably against the storage racks.

"The BMW," said Ricky. "Took its time getting back to here."

Nina grunted as she sat up. She looked out the back window at the receding red lights of the speeding car. Something huge and flat and fingered flapped over the safety barrier at the side of the road, swatted the BMW flat and dragged it off the side. It all happened in a couple of seconds.

"Um," said Nina and then swallowed. "Did anyone else see the massive hand thing?"

"What?" said Ricky.

"*Jingu bis adn-bhul made!*" swore Pupfish, his eyes wide (wider than normal) as he stared ahead.

Several hundred metres down the road, another giant hand – grey, slick and translucent in the light of nearby fires – reached down and plucked the taxi from the road, lifting it away.

"Oh, fuck," whispered Ricky.

"We're on a sushi conveyor belt," said Nina.

"Don't say 'sushi', man," said Pupfish. "*Ggh!* That's one of them trigger words."

"This was a bad idea," said Ricky. "We've got to get off this thing."

"We need to work out where the ground is first!" Nina pointed out.

"Water's that way," said Pupfish, pointing.

"No time for your bullshit!"

"It's there, dog! Don't be *adn-bhul* doubting me!"

"There is a canal right underneath Spaghetti Junction," said Ricky.

Nina revised her opinion of *Samakha* superpowers

immediately. "Okay. You keep pointing at the canal, Pupfish. Then we'll know when we're done on this loop."

Pupfish kept his arm rigid and tracked the canal. Nina tried to picture what that meant in terms of their trajectory. If the canal was straight ahead, they were completely upside down, surely? She expected Ricky to report they were coasting down the other side, as Pupfish's finger moved gradually downwards, but the engine noises, and Ricky's grim expression remained the same.

Soon enough, Pupfish's finger pointed right back at the position it had started. Nina had been watching the screaming column above Villa Park, and it confirmed the same story. "We've been right round the loop," she said.

Ricky shook his head. "And yet, it's like we're always climbing. What do we do?"

"We could – *ggh!* – jump out of the van when we're over the canal," said Pupfish.

Nina looked at the indistinct smear that Pupfish had identified as the canal. "Does that sound achievable? To anyone?"

"Also, I feel compelled to point out that gravity is not behaving like it normally does," said Ricky. "So jumping for it doesn't necessarily mean you would fall in the right direction."

Nina cast around the cab of the van. "What would Rod do? This is one of those times when he would whip out a gadget to test gravity."

"Pretty sure anything you have in your pocket will test gravity," said Ricky, his eyes fixed on the road and signs of hungry hands.

"Huh," said Nina. "Oh, right." She leaned over and felt around in her jacket pocket. She located a coin and held it in her outstretched palm. It was a silver shilling from her travels in the past. It was marked with a shield pattern on one side and an engraving of one of the King Georges on the other. She didn't know which George it was, but she did recall this coin could pay for a cheap night's entertainment at the King Street Theatre.

She turned her palm downwards. The coin stayed in place. She took it between her fingers and let go. It stayed where it was, appearing to hover in mid-air. "Ah."

"Maybe that means we can fly?" Pupfish said.

"This is just a bubble of Venislarn weirdness," said Nina. "There's no sense in any of it." The thought of a bubble gave her another idea. She cracked open the window and held the coin outside. She let go, and it dropped away. "OK. So gravity's fine outside, apparently."

"Great," said Ricky. "Maybe getting out of the van is a good idea *when* we're sure it's at the bottom."

"We gonna do this?" Nina said to Pupfish. He nodded. "Right. We go round again and do a countdown to when we think we're properly at the bottom – so that gravity is under our feet, yeah?"

They all nodded. Pupfish traced the canal with his finger again. They joined him in the countdown, voices getting louder as the van approached what they hoped was the bottom.

"Ready?" said Ricky, unclipping his seatbelt. He dropped the speed.

Nina flung open the van's rear doors. Some items of police equipment dropped out, skittering and sliding unnaturally along the road.

"Three, *bhul tamade*!" shouted Pupfish. "Two, *bhul tamade*!" He grabbed the door handle as he yelled, "One, *bhul tamade*!"

Nina leapt.

She hit the ground squarely. She was ready for the momentum to tip her over, but it caught her by surprise, rolling her in a different direction.

Pupfish shouted in alarm. Nina turned and tried to stand, looking for him.

Nina felt the plunge of vertigo. Her legs buckled beneath her. Why couldn't she walk? Even her feet were slipping out from under her. Pupfish seemed to be having similar difficulty. She leaned her upper body towards the concrete balustrade at the side of the road. She saw the van, stalled, starting to slide backwards, drawn by whatever bizarre gravitational pull held it. She pressed herself against the crash barrier to stay out of its way, and as it fell back past her she caught sight of Ricky Lee halfway out of the door, his face rigid with fright. Was this what he had feared when he took his foot off the accelerator? She twisted to watch. He called out, but the words were lost as the van dropped away at an acceleration that seemed impossible. It swerved over to the side and slammed hard against a steel post. Nina couldn't see whether Ricky had managed to get out of the van, but at that moment she lost her footing and started to slide along the road. Pupfish scrabbled to grab her as she slid past him. His hand hooked under her armpit and they collided hard together against the balustrade.

Nina had Pupfish's armpit in her face. She twisted to look back – or was it down?

The van peeled itself away from the side of the road where it had crashed, careering and bouncing away. As it spun, the crushed remains of Ricky Lee toppled soggily from the driver's door. There was a faint slapping sound as his too-thin corpse hit the tarmac and slid out of sight.

Nina couldn't breathe.

"I can't – *ggh!* – hold you for long!" It was a stupid thing for Pupfish say. What did it matter? Ricky Lee was dead.

"No," she told herself. "He's not dead."

"I need to get you to the side, Nina," Pupfish grunted.

"He was the sensible one," she said.

"Grab that metal post!"

"He had to go last. He had to make sure we were out."

Pupfish grunted and swung her hard against the crash barrier, forcing her to take hold of the vertical struts that were now, in this tilted world, rungs on a ladder. She grabbed the crash barrier with both hands.

"We need to get off this," said Pupfish. "Over the side."

Nina grasped the low wall of the balustrade with one hand and tried to bend over it. She brought her other hand over, and clung on. Pupfish followed. The two of them peered over the edge.

"Canal's right there," said Pupfish, pointing straight down.

The road they stood on had some lighting, making it hard to pick out anything in the gloom below. Nina could see something that might have been a fire, or it might equally have been a reflection of fire in the water.

"Do you think that the gravity gets more … normal if we go over the edge?" Pupfish asked.

"I don't know." What she meant to say was she didn't care. "We should just do it anyway."

Nina wriggled forward until her hips were on top of the balustrade and pivoted for a moment, unsure which way she was going to fall. Pupfish overbalanced before she did, maybe because he had a greater upper body weight, maybe because he was already arcing into a dive. He disappeared into the darkness below.

Metal and concrete screamed. In the corner of her eye Nina saw something intercept the tumbling van. There was a spit of flame and sparks.

She pushed herself over the barrier. She thrashed and yelled as she fell. The tumbling empty darkness seemed to last an age and still she didn't care. She hit the water at an angle and sank fast. The cold ejected the last of the air from her lungs in a sudden blast.

She was grabbed by the arms and pulled briskly out of the water. Pupfish plonked her on the bank of the canal.

"You alive?" he said. "*Ggh!* I don't know CPR."

Nina laid on her back and looked up at the hideous glare of the crazy looping road.

"You lost your hat," added Pupfish.

She got to her feet, surprised she could even stand. She was dripping wet and even colder now she was out in the air.

"I didn't love him," she said, looking at the death trap highway. "I didn't love him, but I really liked him." She glared at Pupfish. "More than I like you," she added, which was unfair and cruel, but she was too torn up inside to resist.

Pupfish just nodded.

"Let's get out of here," she said.

02:35AM

Even though the pink light of the *Gellik* orb had faded, the gasping and screaming from the bundle of human parts on the floor had not. Morag stared, frozen in incomprehension. Limbs were held close, contracted. A face lined with black filth, teeth gritted, eyes wheeling madly. The body, bones jutting, joints twisted, was covered in a collage of rags: flaking, dirty, indeterminate layers, like sections of tree bark, peeled away in places to reveal skins of ages past.

"Mrs Grey?" said Omar, aghast. It was only at that moment Morag realised this creature – this castaway, this cavewoman, this wild thing – was Vivian Grey. She struggled to accept it, struggled to see how this tensely-bunched and twisted thing was human, but she kickstarted herself into action and dropped to Vivian's side to help.

Vivian's hands – no, her one hand – clawed at her throat as she gasped. She barked a single syllable over and over, although Morag could not make it out.

Professor Omar had picked up the telephone and was urgently requesting medical assistance in the Vault.

"It's okay, Vivian," said Morag. "Help is coming."

Vivian wheezed and shuddered and Morag realised the word Vivian was gasping and shouting was "*Chor!*" The Venislarn word for air.

"Can't you breathe?" said Morag.

She hoped the woman wasn't choking. If she tried the Heimlich manoeuvre on this frail creature, she might just snap her in two.

Vivian nodded distinctly, taking deep, if hurried breaths. Morag could see her making a conscious effort to slow her breathing in order to speak.

"*Mech ar—*" deep breath "*—dey-ah chor—*" deep breath "*—Frein paz u-hrei?*"

"What day? Er, Friday," said Morag.

Vivian launched herself at Morag and wrapped her in a tight and foetid embrace. "*U-hrei! Gre'nh siv u-hrei!*"

"Yes," said Morag, not sure what to make of all this. "There are days and weeks and hours and minutes. We have time."

Vivian pulled away sharply. Tears had washed little tracks of near-cleanliness down her filthy face.

"*Shet,*" she said and searched about herself. Under the sprawl of her legs and disintegrating rags, Vivian scrabbled for the thick, church-Bible sized book which had materialised with her.

The Vault doors opened and two women hurried in: Lois the receptionist and Angie, one of the office nurses. Angie carried a green plastic first aid kit and Morag felt the urge to laugh. What relief from the symptoms of a visit to hell could be found in there? She doubted such things had been covered in any medical training.

"What's happened?" said Lois.

"*Jae rhho chor!*" Vivian gasped.

"How does the air hurt?" asked Angie the nurse.

"Mrs Grey has just returned from a long sojourn in hell," said Omar, helpfully.

Angie took this at face value and was already opening the medic kit. Vivian's eyes widened at the sight of a small hypodermic.

"It's just some droperidol," said Angie. "Just to help calm you."

Vivian tried to scoot away, gripping her book tight.

"Mrs Grey!" said Omar sharply.

Vivian looked up and collapsed to the floor, instantly unconscious. The professor was already screwing up the piece of paper he had shown Vivian. Angie the nurse paused with the syringe of sedative.

"She'll be out long enough for you to fetch a stretcher," Omar suggested.

Angie nodded. She raised her eyebrows at Omar, pasty-faced and more than a little slumped in his chair. "Don't look so chipper yourself, mate."

"I think I can soldier through to the bitter end," he replied.

Angie headed out and took Lois with her.

Morag sat on the floor. With the tenderness and aches of childbirth still upon her, she felt no hurry to get back up again. Now that Vivian was still, Morag had time to look at her properly. She asked Omar to pass her the jacket he had tossed over a nearby chair.

"That's my second-best corduroy," he said, reluctantly handing it over. "A little Egyptian tailor. Marvellous man. Probably dead now."

Morag bundled it up and placed it under Vivian's head as a pillow. She straightened Vivian's head – it felt so light – and tried to disentangle some of the hair stuck to the side of her head. Much of it was matted down with blood. There were wounds on each side of her head, gouges from the crown to just above the ears, pink and barely healed.

Thoughts of injury drew Morag's attention down to Vivian's amputated arm. There was no forearm and no elbow. Her upper arm ended in a mess of knotted flesh, like some badly tied-off sausage.

"Christ, what happened to her?" Morag whispered.

"I'd say she looks remarkably well," said Omar. "All things considered."

02:42AM

The tunnel of lightning dumped Prudence and Steve onto a hard floor. Prudence banged her knee and rolled. Steve the Destroyer landed with a soft *"Oof!"* next to her. The floor was hard and white, like that of the Library Vault, but not cold, and slightly tacky to the touch. That was not the only difference. There was also the screaming.

A man yelled in horror and fled from them, abandoning his metal trolley of bottled drinks and packet food. As the residual blue lightning sparked off overhead strip lights, Prudence heard other screams. The quality of the echoes told her this was a large space.

She looked at the long aisle of shelves (stocked with plastic bottles of drinks on one side, glass bottles and metal tins on the other) and shook her head. "Is this whole world nothing but shelves?"

Steve thumped his stuffing back into shape and picked up his spear pencil. "This is a supermarket, youngling."

Prudence looked round. "It's okay, I s'pose. What's it for?"

"It's a shop, fool."

Prudence understood that much. "There's a lot of drink."

"Humans drink spirits to obliterate the terror of their own continued existence."

Prudence gave the abandoned trolley an experimental push. It was heavy. "He wanted a lot to drink."

"A lot of terrors to obliterate," said Steve. He jabbed upward at the swinging blue and white sign above the aisle. "The floating placards tell us what wonders can be found in each corridor."

Prudence had not really wanted to visit the outside world in order to go shopping, but now that she was here...

"I like pink wafers," she said.

"Then we must find an aisle advertising wafers, pink or otherwise."

"This way."

A high and distant siren had started up. The screaming still continued, although it seemed to have moved off to a distant corner.

They entered an aisle containing boxes in various bright colours. There had been an accident: dozens of boxes had been tipped onto the floor and trampled, spreading nuggets of crunchy cereal grains everywhere. Down the far end of the aisle, Prudence saw a window and the night beyond.

"It is an odd time to be shopping," she commented.

Steve grunted. "Humans are like *sandajj* tree-crawlers. When startled they gather up all their nuts and run for a place to hide."

Prudence picked up a box of cereal and inspected the image on the front. "Does the monkey boy make the cereals? Or are the cereals to be fed to the monkey boy?"

"I do not care about monkey boys," said Steve.

"Maybe I'll like them," she said and tore open the packet. The little brown grains were hollow, crunchy and sweet.

There were sudden fresh shouts elsewhere in the supermarket: less panicked, more commanding.

"Maybe I shouldn't have done that," said Prudence.

"Give me the cube!" commanded Steve. "We need to leave this place."

She looked at him. "I don't have it."

"Of course you have it!" he snapped. "You were holding it."

Prudence looked at her hands stupidly, as though they might suddenly contain a portal-opening cube instead of a handful of puffed rice grains and a yellow box with a monkey boy on it.

"I didn't mean to drop it," she said.

"You dropped it! When?"

"While we were travelling, I think."

"In the inter-*yadella* vortex? Idiot child!"

"Don't shout at me!" she snapped, wounded by his words. "I'm not an idiot."

Three men came running into the aisle. They had heavy clomping boots, brown-green uniforms, helmets and big guns.

"I'm sorry. I'll put them back," she said, placing the yellow cereal box back on the shelf.

"Come on outside, lass. Let's find your parents," one said, before the soldier next to him shouted "Hostile!" and took aim.

For a split second Prudence thought he was aiming his weapon at her – which seemed a bit of an over-reaction for cereal theft – then she realised he was looking past her. Steve dived towards a gap in the display of cereals as the soldiers opened fire. Prudence expected the gunfire to be loud but she wasn't prepared for just how loud it was. Cereal packets burst in tatters of card and showers of cereal.

Prudence had cowered automatically and now a hand grabbed her under the armpit. "Let's get you out of here. It's okay. It's gone now."

She was hauled out of the aisle, lifted past a row of conveyor belts and through the sliding doors. There was further sporadic gunfire elsewhere in the shop.

"Steve!" yelled Prudence, but there was no reply.

Outside, in a paved area in front of a car park, the soldiers had gathered dozens of people from the supermarket. The sky above crackled with a sheet of light that washed over everything. There were noises on the warm breeze, unhappy sounds from far away.

"Does this little girl belong to anyone?" called out the soldier who held her.

There were mutters and whimpers from the people lined up outside the shop, but no other reply.

"You stand there," said the soldier and thrust Prudence into a gap between two women. "You! Stay where you are!" he barked at a man further along.

"I weren't doing nothing wrong!" the man replied.

"Step back! Step back!" A rifle was raised.

One of the women gripped Prudence's shoulder. It wasn't a reassuring grip. Prudence could feel the woman's fear vibrating through her.

"Ladies and gentlemen, I need you all to turn around and face the wall," commanded another voice. This one didn't bark. It spoke with loud self-assurance, with the assumption it was going to be obeyed. "Face the wall. This is for your own good."

"What's going on?" someone called out.

"All will be explained," said the commanding one. "Face the wall. That's right. You too."

Prudence was one of the last to turn. The soldiers didn't seem so focused on her, only on the adults. The commanding soldier pressed his hand to a device at his chest. He said something rapidly and the only words Prudence could make out were "Tesco's Shirley" and Prudence wasn't sure if "Tescos Shirley" was the soldier's name. He signed off, nodded grimly and raised his rifle to aim at the gathered shoppers. The other soldiers did likewise.

The commander, Tescos Shirley, caught her looking.

"I'm sorry," he said. "This is really for your own good. The things that are coming…"

There was a crash by the entrance to the shop. A soldier staggered out, tumbling a pile of shopping baskets before him. "There! It's there!" he shouted, pointing at a darting shadow.

Shoppers turned. Some saw the guns. Some began to raise their voices in frightened protest. Half the soldiers had turned to see what the darting thing was.

In the momentary confusion, Prudence ran. She ran towards the darker area of the car park off to the right. There were further shouts, then the soldiers opened fire. As well the bang of gunfire, there was the duller, more frightening sound of bullets striking the walls.

Prudence ducked, or maybe fell, picturing bullets slamming into the wall above her. She pushed herself on into the dark and around the corner of the building. There was a small triangle of car park, then a tall hedge and fence. She ran blindly into the hedge, hoping for a way through, finding one where hedge and fence met. A rough post scraped against her arm. It was a hot, dragging sensation, and she knew it would hurt a lot later.

Gunfire followed her. She pushed right through and surfaced, gasping, by the side of a house on a quiet street. There was an alley between the houses opposite, and a narrow gate framed in the light from beyond.

Something, a soldier perhaps, thrashed and grunted in the gap between the hedge and the fence.

"Come—It's for your own good— *Nnh*."

Prudence ran for the gate. Stones on the tarmac road stung her bare feet. She hit the gate and bounced off, her head reeling. She found the latch, lifted it and ran through. There was a large open space beyond, a few trees here and there, and rows of irregular stone markers jutting out of the ground. Gravestones. A cemetery.

With thoughts of soldiers who might still be chasing after her,

Prudence ran along the perimeter and found a spreading bush in which to hide. She hunkered down among the prickly branches and took out the walkie-talkie. She pressed the button.

"Mum. Mum, it's me. I'm in a graveyard and they're chasing me."

She released the button. The walkie-talkie made a light hissing sound but nothing else happened. She pressed the button again.

"Mum. Mum, it's me. Can I speak to my mum please?"

Nothing but a quiet static hiss.

She wondered if she was doing it wrong. There were a couple of twiddly knobs on the top, and a dial with numbers. But her mum had shown her how to use it: press the button and talk.

"I need to talk to my mum. I need help."

02:45AM

Yoth-Kreylah ap Shallas awoke. The light fixed to the concrete ceiling above was bright, a clean white light unlike any in *Hath-No*. She scrunched her eyes up and put her arm in front of her face.

"Hey, bab," said a woman's voice nearby. "It's okay. I'm here."

Ap Shallas lay on a soft, yielding surface: a bed. Air, cooler and thinner than the soupy atmosphere of *Hath-No*, washed across her face. And *Yoth-Kreylah ap Shallas* was breathing it; not just breathing it but drawing sustenance from it.

"*Ye-hurgech bal…* oxygen *ghon dikraa*," she murmured.

"You're breathing just fine," said the woman.

Ap Shallas shook her head. She felt the softness of the pillow beneath her. "*Peneth xar chor av-a boa hauh.*"

"Everyone breathes, bab," replied the woman.

Ap Shallas opened her eyes fully, blinked against the light and sat up.

"Easy now," said the woman.

The woman wore a spotty blouse and carefully styled black hair with little kiss curls. The frivolity of her clothes and the preciseness of her hair appeared at odds with the weary and anxious hypervigilance on the woman's face, but *ap Shallas* was not used to reading human expressions and did not put much stock in her own analysis.

"It's me," said the woman. "Lois. Remember?"

Ap Shallas did remember. The woman's name was Lois Wheeler. She worked as the receptionist at the Birmingham consular mission to the Venislarn. *Ap Shallas* remembered these as clear facts, statements without emotional content. It was a distant memory, possibly something *ap Shallas* had read or written a long time ago.

Ap Shallas swung her legs off the bed. They were thin limbs with little brown feet. The long bones of her feet were clearly visible through the skin, radiating spokes from leg to toes. *Ap Shallas* flexed her toes. She had not seen them in aeons. It came as something of a surprise to find she had them at all.

"*Kaeron.*"

"Pardon?" said Lois.

Ap Shallas struggled for the word. "Toes."

"Er, yes," said Lois. "All there, Mrs Grey."

Ap Shallas pushed herself from the bed, tottered only for a moment, and stood. She and Lois were in a small windowless chamber. There was the bed, a counter with a ceramic basin set into it, and a mirror above. There were two doors. One was closed and the other led to a square chamber with a larger ceramic basin plumbed into the floor. The name and function of that basin eluded *ap Shallas* in a way that caused her disproportionate annoyance.

"Toilet!" she blurted at last.

"You need the loo?" said Lois, arms out to assist her.

Ap Shallas made a dismissive puffing sound. *Ap Shallas* had no need for toilets. She had not eaten or drunk in an eternity. There was nothing inside her to expel.

She moved across to the counter and, with her hand on the surface to support her, looked in the mirror. A strange creature gazed back. There was almost nothing of its shape or outer appearance that she recognised, although there was a glimmer of life and familiarity in the sunken eyes.

Ap Shallas put a hand to her face and followed the contours of lines and wrinkles.

"Reward for long service," she said, recalling something someone had said a long time ago.

"You all right, Vivian?" said Lois.

Yoth-Kreylah ap Shallas looked at her and then back to the woman in the mirror. "Mrs Vivian Grey?"

"That's right. You do remember who you are, don't you?"

The question hurt her profoundly. *Ap Shallas* remembered Mrs Vivian Grey. Mrs Vivian Grey was a woman, an Earth human. Vivian had lived for little over half a century, maybe half of that time in service to the consular mission. And then Vivian had fallen into *Leng* space, to hell. From the plains of hell to the fortress of *Hath-No* had been but a fleeting episode, a transition, and then Vivian had become the scribe of *Hath-No*, briefly under the service of *Bakhan Sand* and then alone, the author of the Bloody Big Book, an unknowable infinite age as *Yoth-Kreylah ap Shallas*.

To identify her as Vivian Grey was a nonsense. Vivian Grey was a speck of time and matter at the start of her existence, a characterless sperm, an egg. *Ap Shallas* knew Vivian Grey, but she could hardly *be* Vivian Grey.

"*Skex au thuein*?" she asked.

"Your book?" Lois nodded. "Professor Omar has it."

"*Daen're so!*" she snapped. "*Yeh'a shyuata!*"

"Sure, bab, sure," said Lois. "I'll get it. And what was the other thing?"

Ap Shallas stared at her fingertips. Useless soft round fingertips, not the tools she had wielded for an eternity.

"Pens!" she enunciated in the alien language of English. "I haven't *finished* the book yet!"

Nina and Pupfish walked towards the residential streets that climbed the hill away from Spaghetti Junction. Nina had stripped off her soaked Georgian coat and left it at the roadside.

Buildings all around them were smouldering and crushed, as if a giant flaming monster had trodden a path through this neighbourhood, but the streets were quiet. It was a warm night but Nina stood by the burning ruin of a building to drive some of the damp from her dress.

Pupfish took off his baseball jacket and held it out to dry.

"I thought you didn't mind being wet," said Nina.

"This is an authentic Ralph Lauren copy," he said. "Allana bought it for me."

Nina jerked her chin. She didn't want to talk about boyfriends and girlfriends. "Do you know how far away Sutton Park is?"

"Never been there," he said with a shrug. "*Ggh!* Never been outside the motorway."

"Really?"

She looked at her phone for directions. The phone was working, had survived the crash and the swim, but it was picking up no phone or data signal at all.

There was a petrol station on the other side of the road. Nina walked over to it, sidestepping the spots of flaming wreckage here and there. A young man with a hipster man-bun on his head stood at the night counter.

"How do I get to Sutton Park from here?" she asked him.

"We operate a no-smoking policy for our retail premises," he murmured emotionlessly. "I told them that the safety of our customers is the most important thing to us."

Nina glanced over her shoulder at the smoking plastic ruins of the forecourt. "You did a great job. Now, I need to get to Sutton Park. How do I do that?"

"Do you want to buy a map book?" he asked.

"A map? In a book? Are you from history?"

"You may as well take the map book," he said in that dead tone. He pushed it underneath the glass screen.

"Thank you." Nina took the book. "Can I have some chocolate Minstrels as well, please? Actually, what I really wanted to know is whether there's any way of getting to Sutton Park that's quicker than walking."

"Don't know that I would be making unnecessary journeys. Conditions are a bit dangerous."

"Believe me when I say that this is a necessary journey."

"You could take a car, I see quite a few that seem to have lost their drivers." He pointed outside to the forecourt, which was a wasteland of crushed cars. Some of those towards the edge might have been driveable.

"What if I don't know how to drive?" said Nina.

"Take one that is an automatic, maybe?"

"Automatic is not the same as self-driving, is it?" Nina had been caught out by these weasel words before.

"You can probably manage stop, go and steering if you've ever been on the dodgems."

"Huh. Maybe."

"Or someone has left their moped," he said, pointing.

Nina saw the abandoned moped. "The minstrels then, my good man."

He turned to pull a bag of chocolates off the rack behind him. As he did, she saw that his hipster man-bun was not a bun at all. A hairy creature had plugged itself into the back of his open skull.

Wire-thin needle limbs pumped up and down into his brain cavity, steering him.

"Here," he said. "Was I helpful? Did I do well?"

"Oh, fabulous," said Nina. She moved away swiftly, only then seeing dozens of other hairy balls with needle legs walking in a leisurely manner across the forecourt towards her.

"Pupfish!" she called in a deliberately controlled voice. "To the moped, please!"

"What?" said the *samakha* on the pavement.

"Moped! Now!"

She speed-walked to the moped. Nina was no expert, but this looked like one of those old lady mopeds that was only one step up from a mobility scooter. She could sense Pupfish was as clueless as she was when it came to cars.

"I'm driving," she said, straddling the seat.

She found the unhurried threat of hairy brain spiders was an excellent tutor, and in no time had it turned on and was accelerating away. With the weight of Pupfish on the back climbing the hill, the moped barely made walking pace. Once they had reached the peak, it sped up a little.

It turned out to be a sound choice when they reached a crater in the road. It had obliterated both carriageways and a row of houses. They paused at the edge to take a look.

"I can't see the bottom," said Pupfish.

Nina wondered if it was made by something massive falling from above, or something massive emerging from below. They skirted the hole using the remaining strip of pavement and drove on towards Sutton.

02:54AM

Crouched in the bush, Prudence looked out across the cemetery. She could see the tombstones in clear silhouette, even though the night was not black as she had expected. A shimmering light covered everything. It shifted and pooled in the sky above. The way it rippled made Prudence feel like she was underwater, that she was being held under something. Its colour refused to resolve itself in her mind. If she had to pinpoint it, she would say its nearest approximation was pink. But it was certainly not pink, nor any shade of it. Wisps of light gathered where the light was thickest and brightest, touching down on the ground like lazy unhurried lightning. Where it met the earth, the grass twitched and wriggled at its touch.

A leaf stroked Prudence's cheek. She shuddered at the accidental contact, standing and moving away from the bush. As the light moved in the sky, the bush seemed to move with it, but it was just a trick of light and shadow.

A voice cried from across the cemetery. "Help! I need help!"

It was a child's voice. Automatically, Prudence went towards it.

"Help! They're chasing me!"

She moved swiftly. The grass was warm and scratchy on her feet. The voice sounded close, clearly audible against the background sounds of a crackling sky, occasional gunfire and the fainter shouts of violence and fear, but she could not see the child. The voice appeared to be coming from beyond a large sagging tree with dangling limbs.

"I need help! They're chasing me!"

Prudence looked about but could see no pursuers. Ahead, streamers of lazy lightning touched down in the tops of the tree. The limp dangling limbs of the tree swayed softly in the wind.

"Help!"

The voice was very close but Prudence couldn't see the girl. It sounded like a girl. She cupped her hands to her mouth. "Where are you?"

"Where are *you*?" the girl called back.

Possibly she was hiding in the cover of the tree. Prudence ran forward. The thin dangling limbs of the tree hung low and she reached a hand up to brush them aside.

"Get back, brainless morsel!" yelled Steve.

Prudence looked round. The tiny cloth man was skipping and jumping across the ground towards her.

"Steve! I—"

A tree limb, thinner than string, wrapped itself around Prudence's wrist. She gasped and pulled away. It tightened automatically.

"Ah! It's got me!" she shouted, instinctively.

"It's got me!" cried the girl's voice in response.

More tree limbs, lifted by a wind Prudence could not feel, drifted towards her. She felt a sharp fear, but also a profound sense of stupidity – that she could be snared by a brainless tree. She pulled, but the tendril round her wrist held firm. Other branches tugged at the hem of her T-shirt dress.

She yelped at a touch on her heel and the back of her leg. It was Steve, scrambling up her. He rose up over her shoulder, tottered unsteadily down the length of her arm and, with precision, jabbed the tip of his pencil-spear into the narrow strip of tree flesh digging into her wrist.

"Your mother will not be pleased if I only bring home your corpse!" he spat. The tree abruptly let go of Prudence, as if he had found a nerve.

She fell on her bottom. As the other tendrils whipped out to get her, she scooted back, crabbing out of reach. She coughed and panted, staring alternately between the flailing tree and the raw red mark on her wrist. She hissed as sensation and pain came back to her.

"I thought you were dead," she said.

Steve crowed with laughter. "Kill Steve the Destroyer? Pah!" He did a little jig and a smooth moonwalk in the leaf mulch. "I am *Qulsteyvan* the Destroyer, ex-outrider of the entourage of *Prein*, former emissary of the shattered realms and once loyal servant to the blind gods of *Suler'au Sukram*! Takes a lot to kill the likes of me!" He slapped his flower-patterned lower half. "And I think these might be my lucky legs. Bulletproof!"

"That's nice," said Prudence.

"There's nothing to fear, it's just a tree," came a man's voice from the tree.

"Hang on, I'm gonna take a selfie," said a woman's voice.

Shapes moved in the upper portions of the tree. Round, wet, dripping shapes, held in place by the branches. A human foot dangled floppily.

"I need help!" yelled a girl's voice that was not quite Prudence's.

"Stupid tree," said Prudence and winced. The red line around her wrist glistened. Not blood, but a glistening of broken skin.

"You are hurt?" said Steve and bounded up onto her arm again. He inspected her wrist. "Mmmm. Is it going to fall off?"

"What?"

"Give it a shake and see if it falls off."

Prudence did no such thing. The injury burned. She blew on it and that made it sting sharply. A moan of self-pity and pain escaped her lips, and there were tears in her eyes. She didn't want to cry, she really didn't want to cry, but the tears in her eyes made it almost irresistible. As though tears demanded crying, that one could not exist without the other.

"I want my mummy," she said and the last syllable was lost in a silly sob that exploded from her lips and dribbled spit on her T-shirt dress. She absently picked up Steve and used him to mop the spit mark.

"I am not a dishcloth, youngling!" he screeched.

"Sorry," she mumbled.

"You must be quiet!"

"I'm sorry."

"Look!" He pointed with his chubby little fist.

Far across the cemetery, there were figures silhouetted in the not-pink light. Prudence could see their guns, the bulk of their helmets and packs.

"Are they soldiers?" she said.

"Human warriors. Nothing compared to the hordes of *Suler'au Sukram*."

"But they were killing people," she said, perplexed. "Ordinary people."

"I dare you to touch it. It won't harm anyone," said a man's voice from the tree.

"Fuck! Derek, it's got me!" screamed another voice.

"Shut up, you'll give us away," Prudence told the tree. "And that's a bad word."

"Shut up," said the tree. "I am not a dishcloth, Derek!"

"The soldiers were going to kill me," she said to Steve. "They shot all those people. They said 'It's for your own good.'"

"The Soulgate is closing, gobbet," said Steve. "And death is a way out, until the arrival of *Yoth-Bilau*."

"I don't want to die, yet."

"It might be better than hell."

"I dunno," she said. "Depends what hell's got to offer."

The soldiers were getting nearer. Prudence stood. "It's time to go." She circled round the tree's reach and made towards the far end of the cemetery.

She crept low to the ground. The soldiers moved purposefully, perhaps drawn by the voices from the tree. Ahead, in the shifting not-pink, there was a tall gate with stone pillars.

"Stupid tree. It won't hurt anyone," said the tree.

A soldier was beneath the tree, reaching up to it. Drooping branches reached slowly for him.

Prudence paused.

"Do not lally-gag, morsel," said Steve.

"But he can't..." said Prudence and shouted, "Don't touch it! It's dangerous!"

The soldiers heard that. The one beneath the tree lowered his hand. There was the flash and bang of gunfire. The turf to Prudence's left ruptured as bullets struck the soft ground.

"Fool! Get down!" snapped Steve.

The tree lashed out to grab the nearest soldier. He was ensnared, hand, neck and thigh and pulled upwards. "There's nothing to fear. It's for your own good," said the tree voices.

The soldiers' attention was diverted by the predatory tree. Prudence ran for it.

"Next time, you do as I say!" grumbled Steve.

"I was only trying to help."

"Fah! Look what trouble that brings!"

There were further gunshots, and there were screams. Multiple screams.

"Here!" ordered Steve and beckoned her into the shadow of a

tall tombstone topped with a statue of a winged angel. He scaled the back of the tombstone and peered out around the angel's robes. "The tree has got at least three of the human warriors. That is good."

Prudence, squatting in the dark, nodded, not sure what she was nodding to.

Beyond the veil of the distorting light, a white dot of light winked at her in the sky above.

"Is that a star?" she said.

Steve looked up. "No, that's a helicopter."

A dark form dived into view and the white light was noisily swallowed by a yellow explosion. The flaming chunks of helicopter rained down beyond the cemetery perimeter. The dark form swooped in a wide circle, its wings tipped with lines of green luminescence.

"And that?" asked Prudence.

Steve studied it thoughtfully. "*Eyahl-cryd* flyer, I believe," he said. "Let's go."

She pushed herself up and sprinted after Steve. For a tiny dolly, he moved at a pace she struggled to match. She ducked automatically at the sound of shooting, although it possibly wasn't aimed her way.

"I didn't think the outside world would be this violent!" she called to Steve.

"I know!" he replied joyfully.

Perhaps Prudence was too focused on escape and not the area around her, for a few seconds from the cemetery gate a man ran out from the side. He collided with her, tripping her through the gate and onto the pavement of the road beyond.

"Here ... here..." he panted.

Prudence tried to get to her feet, but the soldier grabbed her by the waist and lifted her up into a painful hug.

"Marko," called a voice further behind, running to catch up. "Where are the others?"

Prudence kicked and squealed. Steve had doubled back, leapt high and stabbed his pencil-spear down into the soldier's boot. Above the grunts and breaths and the background noise of hell's descent upon earth, Prudence heard the click as the pencil tip broke.

"Curse you, impenetrable boot!"

Prudence managed to bring an elbow up and connected with the soldier's eye. He cried out and dropped her. She landed squarely on her feet and jumped away. As she looked back, the soldier was swinging his gun down from his shoulder. There was a long red wound across his face, a bloody whip mark – probably from a tree branch – which cut through one eye and across his mouth. Prudence realised her elbow was wet with the man's blood.

He brought the rifle round, there was a stutter of gunfire. He fell backwards. Prudence turned. In the not-pink light, she saw four figures. None were much taller than her. All were carrying bulky rifles. The one who had just shot the soldier had spikey pigtails in her hair.

A soldier came through the gates, a pistol drawn but held low. It was Tescos Shirley, the commanding officer. He looked at the soldier on the floor, at Prudence, and at the four gun-toting children.

"Children shouldn't have to live to see this," he said faintly, and the girl shot him – three bullets, two in the shoulder and one in the throat. He fell, gurgled briefly, and was still.

Prudence stared at the four children. There were two girls and two boys. They all wore striped ties and blazer jackets with a badge on the lapel. Three of them held guns aimed at Prudence. The other boy had a phone in his hand.

"Deficient weapon," muttered Steve, examining the broken tip of his pencil.

The phone flashed and clicked.

"Get that out of my face, worthless one!" said Steve. "Pass me a sharpening implement."

"What is that thing?" said the short boy with the phone.

"Take another one after I've shot it, Elon," said the girl with the long blonde hair.

Prudence saw when they talked there was something obviously wrong with their faces. Was it the way their lips moved? Was it the shape of their jawlines? Or was it the arrangement of their eyes which were either too close or too far apart or … something?

"What are you?" she said.

The girl with the dark pigtails tapped the badge at her lapel. "Thatcher Academy."

"Is that a school?" Prudence hazarded.

Pigtails snorted as though Prudence was only pretending not to know. "You?" she said. "How old are you? Eight? Nine?"

"I don't know," said Prudence. "What time is it?"

"Your school?" demanded pigtails.

Prudence shook her head.

"She's human collateral, Yang," said the taller boy.

"She lasted longer than form 8Y," said the blonde girl.

"They were weak. So's she. The time of testing is at hand."

The one with pigtails, Yang, shook her head slightly. "Is she worth the cost of a bullet? It would be more fun to let her live. For a time."

"Mammonites," said Steve.

"What are they?" said Prudence.

"She's ignorant," said the tall boy.

"Thick," said the shorter one, Elon. "Kill her and I'll take a picture."

Yang waved the gun at Prudence. "What are predicted in your SATs?"

"What?" said Prudence.

"I got top grades in English, Maths and Science. You?"

Prudence wasn't sure what answer would appease this girl. "I ... I just want to find my mum."

This caused laughter among the children.

"Poor little girl wants her mummy," said Elon.

"Pathetic," said the blonde girl. "And where is your mummy?"

"At the Library," said Prudence. She did not care for being mocked and, despite the guns, felt anger rise within her. "I'm Prudence Murray."

"She's the *kaatbari*, pup," said Steve.

"Bullpoop," said the blonde girl.

"You're lying," said the taller boy.

"He's calling you out," said Yang. "You going to refute Prester's accusation or shall we punish you now for dishonesty?"

"I don't know what that means," said Prudence. "But, um, I am the *kaatbari*."

"And she's got laser eyes!" said Steve dramatically.

"I haven't really," said Prudence.

"Show us," said the blonde girl.

"I don't really know how." She did her best stare.

"Nothing," said Yang.

"I thought I saw a bit of a twinkle," said Elon.

Yang gave him a piercing look. Her slightly *off* face could produce an unnervingly piercing glare.

"Don't talk nonsense, Elon Mogg-Mammonson," she said. "You're the weakest member of this group. I've been keeping score. Don't make me eject you from the team."

Her hands curled around the grips on her rifle. Elon licked his lips nervously with a tongue that was not the right shape (if only just).

"Maybe there's a reward for her," he said and tapped his phone.

"You got signal on that yet?" said Yang.

"No."

"Then who would we go to for the reward?"

"*Yo-Morgantus*?"

The taller boy, Prester, cuffed him round the ear. "You would go to our divine mother's rival and—"

What Elon might do was interrupted by the blonde girl raising her rifle and firing a short burst past Prudence. A man – a soldier or not, Prudence couldn't tell – fell at the roadside.

"You keeping the scores?" she said.

Yang nodded. "One more for Ayesha."

"Girls beating the boys."

"I'm not pooling my score with yours," said Yang coldly.

Prudence did not understand these children. They were older than her – okay, everyone was older than her – but they were more mature and their ways were a mystery to her. "My mum will give you a reward if you return me to her."

"I'm not going to the city centre," said Yang. "This is our turf."

"We do not know where the divine mother will rise," said Prester.

"We could take her to a phone box," said Elon.

"Like a 'Doctor Who' phone box?" said blonde Ayesha witheringly.

"There still are some," said Elon. "I think there's one near the Co-op. It's not blue though. It's just a phone box."

"What's she going to pay us?" said Yang.

Prudence felt in her pockets. She had the walkie-talkie in one and the tin containing Mr Angry Shell in the other. She took out the tin and considered it.

"I could give you what's in here."

"What is it?" said Elon, already reaching for it.

"It's special," said Prudence, holding it out of reach. "It bites people if they're not careful."

This got their interest.

"For safe passage to a phone box?" said Yang.

"We don't need them," said Steve. He tapped Ayesha's leg. "That knife at your belt. Lend it to me so I might sharpen my weapon."

"What's in it for me?" said Ayesha.

"I promise not to stab you with it, runt."

This seemed an agreeable deal. Ayesha passed Steve a short flick-knife that nearly crushed him to the ground.

"Safe passage to a phone box in exchange for the box and its contents," said Yang firmly, having come to some decision. She held out her hand, palm flat.

One of the others had to tell Prudence she had to shake it to seal the deal.

02:59AM

Morag re-entered the conference room. "Apologies," she said, returning to her seat. "What have I missed?"

"On the plus side, I've heard a rumour that the nuclear missiles are to be launched imminently," said Major Sanders.

"Plus side, yes," she said. "We're all looking forward to a quick fiery death. And there's bad news? A negative side?"

Sanders nodded tersely. "My men have encountered some of the Venislarn and have suffered losses."

"Their job was to target civilians."

"The Venislarn god they encountered in Aston is apparently unaware of this."

"Ah, well, yes."

"The men were issued with protective wards which should have prevented this."

"What wards?"

Major Sanders searched under his papers and pulled out a clip-on badge of the sort used as company IDs everywhere. He passed it to Morag. Inside the plastic sleeve was a rectangle of pink card printed with Venislarn writing.

"*Shan-shan prui otpeh. Shi feyden pi qhurri'or,*" she read.

"Is that an effective Venislarn repellent?" asked Sanders.

"It basically says, 'Don't mind me. Pretend I'm not here.'"

"It's not magical?" The major sounded like the child Santa had forgot.

"Not in the least. You might want to tell your men they'll have to watch their backs."

The deputy council leader and his CEO were both staring at his mobile phone.

"Councillor Rahman? Are you with us?"

"This..." he whispered dumbfounded, pointing at his phone.

"Is it people panic buying at Tesco's again?" Morag said. "What they think extra packs of toilet roll will achieve at this point—"

"No, I..."

He fiddled with his phone and was able to cast the image to the conference room screen. Insets on the big screen shuffled around. Morag's eyes went to a rolling news broadcast.

"Another preacher blaming the apocalypse on the gays?" she said.

"No, that!" said Rahman, pointing wildly. "What the hell is that?"

On another portion of the screen, a news reporter on a stormy seafront was trying to hold his waterproof hood in place while delivering a currently silent but definitely impassioned report on what was occurring out at sea. The news channel ticker-tape identified the location as St Elijo, California. Beyond the horizon of foamy green waves, a shape had risen from the sea. It was steep, like a volcanic island, but clearly a constructed thing. Ruined temples crowded its slopes. Broken arches of twisted geometry crowned its walls. Even at a distance, it was evident no human hands had built the place – the insane lines and obscene angles were an anathema to the human mind.

"It's *Cary'yeh*," said Morag. "The sunken city of *Zildrohar-Cqulu*. Not sunken anymore, I guess. I've met him," she added conversationally. "I was covered in chocolate at the time."

Great worm creatures churned their way across the sea and up the beach. Prickles and slime covered the bloated bodies of the *yon-bun* dwellers. Their blind heads twitched and their mouth parts flexed.

The news reporter was screaming now. He held the seafront railing with both hands, attempting to head-butt himself to death against the top rail.

A pair of fighter jets flew out across the stormy sky. Missiles soared. Explosions peppered the terraces of the dreadful city.

"Our American colleagues deciding to meet the apocalypse head on," said Sanders.

On the screen, a dark limb lashed upwards from the waves and swatted a plane out of the sky. The other banked away, looping up and round into low clouds. A moment later there was a flash of yellow fire in the clouds and wreckage spilled down towards the sea.

The video feed cut out a second later.

"What a rich and colourful apocalypse we are living through," said Morag, for want of anything better to say.

03:36AM

So the four children were Mammonites. Prudence pieced the details together from the children's conversation, with extra titbits thrown in by Steve, plus the knowledge that simply fell into place as Prudence's consciousness grew. Prudence had been born less than four hours ago and understood that her life, apart from the matter of being the *kaatbari*, was a quite extraordinary one. As she had grown taller (a fact only measurable by the fit of her clothes) so her thoughts had branched out. There was nothing magical in this; she was stretching like a person waking up and, as she did, her mind brushed against facts that were so obvious she did not need to pay them attention.

Facts like that thing there in the road ahead was a zebra crossing. That there was a post box. The weapons the children carried were assault rifles. The clothes they wore were their school uniform. And the children themselves were Mammonites.

The Mammonites were Venislarn, the offspring of *Yoth Mammon* the corruptor, the defiler of souls, the dredger in the lake of desires. *Yoth Mammon* was off in some other Venislarn realm at the moment, and had left her children in a corner of Birmingham that they could call their own. The Mammonites had thrown themselves into the human way of life with great gusto. The greed, avarice and competitive consumerism of modern society appealed to them deeply. They had taken great pains to adopt a human-like form and, in coming closer than any other Venislarn, had missed by a mile. Mammonites sat in the deepest part of the uncanny valley, nearly human and disturbingly unhuman.

Mammonites might have struck most humans as greedy and selfish, but they rejected such assertions. They possessed two key clear truths which humans were rarely willing to accept. Firstly, everything had a quantifiable value, from food to air to life itself. Secondly, that truth was rarely pleasant but that didn't stop it being true. For example, both humans and Mammonites allowed the poor, old and weak in their societies to die. Humans might wring their hands, give bland platitudes, and maybe even talk about the boundaries of medical science and the limits on hospital funding. Mammonites would simply pop round to granny's house with an axe and some plastic sheeting to protect the furniture.

Upon the onset of the apocalypse, as indescribable horrors poured out of rifts in the sky and pits in the ground, many Mammonites decided it was time to tally up the final ledgers and settle all debts. For many of the school children of Thatcher Academy, this meant equipping themselves from the school armoury and engaging in a battle royale with their classmates, a very final school exam for which there would be no resits.

Yang, Elon, Prester and Ayesha were all in year seven and had acquitted themselves well against their schoolmates. As they cut a swathe through the population from the Mammonite village of Dickens Heath and into Shirley, their targets had switched from Mammonite to human. The debt-settling had become interracial.

To hear Elon Mogg-Mammonson talk about it, the major

crimp in their success was their inability to brag about it on social media.

"No 5G. No 4G. No basic phone signal at all," he complained as they walked down a suburban avenue.

The houses here were quiet. The Mammonites took pot shots at any lit windows, any twitching curtains. No humans dared venture into the street.

Elon waved his phone about above his head. "The cloud's out there, but we can't access it. I thought the end of the world would be better than this."

"This is definitely the time foretold," said Prester. "'Mankind has become as the *em-sho'ven* gods, wild and free and knowing no laws or morals, rejoicing in murder and torture'." He said it like he was quoting something.

"No mention of dodgy phone reception," muttered Elon.

"Maybe the strange light is stopping your phone working," said Prudence.

The inability of the light around them to conform to any known colour was not only irritating, it was starting to give Prudence a headache. It washed about overhead, pooling thickly in places, stretching out in brighter shades in others.

"It's the unholy colours of *Ammi-Usub*," said Steve as he marched in the gutter. "We fought them in the realms of *Suler'au Sukram*."

"Did you win?" said Yang.

Steve growled. It was a little growl, but audible nonetheless. "Have you ever tried fighting a colour, sprogling?" he said bitterly. "You ever tried taking a blade to a pigment?"

"So you lost," said Yang with a superior grunt of amusement.

"Let's see you do better. Go on. Pick a colour. One of the weak ones."

"I don't need to prove myself to you."

"Green! I challenge you to fight the colour green."

Yang laughed.

"See?" said Steve. "We could have beaten green with one arm tied behind our backs. Possibly even yellow. But *Ammi-Usub* … the realms were shattered and our gods blinded."

"Is it dangerous, then?" said Prudence.

"It changes things," said Steve. "The tree that attacked you. That insect."

He waggled his spear at a not-necessarily-pink insect on a nearby gatepost. It was a fat creature, bigger than Prudence's hand. It had large, possibly-not-purple eyes and membranous wings with nearly-silver veins running through them.

Ayesha took aim and fired a single shot. The insect was blasted away but for a pair of wings drifting in the air.

"Your possessed dolly is a coward," she said to Prudence.

Three more insects landed on the gatepost. Prudence walked in the road to give them a wide berth. "So this has all been foretold?"

Prester didn't look at her as he answered, his attention and rifle aim was on the houses opposite. "'Our great mother will rise this day. Then the liberated *em-sho'ven* Venislarn will teach us new ways to kill and conquer and all of this world will burn in a sacrificial fire of exultation.'"

"Er, that sounds nice," Prudence said, politely.

"Will everything burn?" said Elon.

"Everything," Prester nodded.

"I mean *everything*?"

"It is foretold."

"Right. Just I was waiting for the new *Sniper Elite* game to come out on PlayStation."

"There will be none of that in the new world," said Prester.

They walked on in silence for a few seconds.

"I ordered some Vans from Amazon yesterday," said Ayesha.

"Gone," said Prester. "All will be fire."

"But they were Prime Next Day Delivery."

"It matters not," he said.

"*Bhul* that," she said. "Prime Next Day is, like, a promise. You can't stop that."

"This is the final day! Our mother rises. The Soulgate closes. The promises of humanity mean nothing."

"You didn't see these Vans though…"

Yang whirled. The nose of her assault rifle swept over the midriffs of her school friends.

"I will shoot the next one who bitches or whines," she hissed. "*Bhul* your Vans. *Bhul* your stupid PlayStation games. Yes, our mother will rise. *San-shu chu'meyah*. But right now, we have everything that we should desire. We have vanquished our enemies—"

"*Adn-bhul* hate form 9F," said Elon.

"—and we have trampled the weak under our feet. This city is ours by right and we have the weapons to take it. As the whole world descends into the hell of our ancestors, we take what we wish and fear no one. We are bathed in glory. This is all we could want. Nothing else matters."

Her hands were shaking with passion when she'd finished speaking. Ayesha fretfully watched Yang's finger on the trigger.

"We should want nothing else," said Yang with quiet conviction and turned to carry on.

The rest followed obediently.

"I wouldn't mind some KFC though," said Elon. "To go with the glory, I mean."

There was a heavy pause.

"Yes, obviously," said Yang. "We all like KFC. KFC *and* glory would be nice."

They walked on.

"With like one of them Krushem milkshakes," said Ayesha.

Another pause.

"Which one?" said Yang.

"Oreo Krushem, of course."

Yang nodded slowly. "I prefer the salted caramel."

"Or that, or that," said Ayesha quickly.

"What's a Krushem?" said Prudence.

The Mammonites laughed.

"Never had a Krushem from KFC?" said Elon.

"I don't know," said Prudence, feeling defensive. "Maybe if you told me what one was then I could tell you if I'd had one."

"She's never had a Krushem," said Ayesha, shaking her head. "Don't reckon you've ever owned a pair of Vans either. Why haven't you got any shoes?"

Prudence looked at her dusty feet and then the bright clean trainers Ayesha wore. "I don't think I need shoes," she said.

"The *kaatbari* doesn't need shoes," said Steve.

"There will be no shoes in the world to come," said Prester.

"Oh, really?" said Ayesha sarcastically. "There's a prediction about that too?"

Prester seemed momentarily unsure. "'And in the sight of *Yoth-Bilau* and her dead children the *skolori* races will swarm, unseen and unformed, their passage marked by colossal footprints with talons spaced in a circle.'"

"Didn't say nothing about shoes," said Ayesha.

"If the *skolori* have circular feet, they won't wear shoes."

"Tenuous."

"Our divine mother – *san-shu chu'meyah* – doesn't have feet," argued Prester.

"She could if she wanted," Ayesha countered.

"I wonder," said Elon slowly, "if our divine mother coming back will be as much fun as our parents told us it would be." He was already flinching as he said it.

Prester aimed his rifle at Elon's head. "You don't want *Yoth Mammon* to rise from the pit of *Leng*? Is that what you're saying?"

Elon stuttered and shook his head, eventually managing to say, "You need me to find the phone box."

Yang huffed. "We do."

"But he's a blasphemer," said Prester.

"And you talk too much," said Yang. "And he's right."

Prudence could see Prester tempted to turn his rifle on Yang, but fear of the small girl held him back. Whatever social ties bound this little group, they were very loose.

"Oh, I am sure the arrival of our divine mother will be wonderful," said Yang tartly. "But our parents do go on about it. They've lived their lives. They've hatched, grown, experienced the joy of eviscerating an enemy, made some savage acquisitions and they get to, I don't know, twenty-five and there's nothing to look forward to except children and death. That's why they bang on about the end of the world."

"You blaspheme," said Prester.

"I would like to make my mind up for myself, Prester Hurst-Mammonson. I don't have to want what my parents wanted."

"My mum just wanted me to stay at the Library and hide, stay safe," said Prudence, only thinking about it as she said it.

"We came out to see flowers and burn things," said Steve.

"We haven't really seen any flowers yet."

"Or burned anything," said Steve with heartfelt disappointment.

Ayesha pulled aside her blazer. There was a fabric band slung from shoulder to hip underneath. She unclipped one of the silver cannisters on the belt, pulled out a pin and lobbed it into the garden of the nearest house. Seconds later a searing white flare of light engulfed the small lawn, a bush, and the wooden porch of the house.

Prudence stepped back from the heat and tried to rub the flashes of colour that spun across her eyes.

"Phosphorus grenade," said Ayesha. "For when you absolutely have to set things on fire."

There were shouts from within the house. A door opened. The Mammonite school children opened fire.

Afterwards, when the shooting had stopped, the bush had been reduced to a black skeleton, and the porch was burning with a lazy yellow flame Steve ran around the edges of the scorched lawn.

"That was most entertaining," he declared. "Give me one."

Ayesha put her hand to her bandolier of grenades. "They're bigger than you."

"I am stronger than I look, puny mortal."

He clearly saw her look to Prudence for confirmation.

"Don't look at her!" he shrieked, offended. "She's my apprentice. I'm the one in charge!"

"Is he?" said Ayesha.

"He's the one who will get into trouble if I don't get home safely," said Prudence. "I think he's scared of my mum."

Steve crossed his arms furiously. "Steve the Destroyer is scared of no one."

Ayesha drummed her fingers on the grenade. "I will give you one when we are at the phone box, if the *kaatbari* will speak a word in our favour."

"Speak a word?" said Prudence.

"I'd like Vans. After the world has ended. I want there to be Vans and KFC."

"And PlayStation," said Elon. "Oh, and bring back the phone data signal. And wi-fi."

"I don't know what I want yet," said Yang, "but you can also speak on my behalf."

"Who to?" said Prudence, perplexed.

"You are the *kaatbari*, aren't you?" said Prester. "You're the herald of the Soulgate. You must have influence."

Prudence blew out her lips. "Don't know about that."

"Some god must have invoked you."

"Would I have noticed?"

"Some god must have spaffed his beans into your mum," said Elon.

Yang looked at him in disgust.

"What?" he said. "That's how it works. We watched that video in Personal Development."

"You are a foul creature and I will shoot you before this night is through," said Yang.

"The phone box," Elon reminded her.

Yang grumbled, then jerked for him to lead on.

Ayesha walked beside Prudence. "*Yo-Morgantus*," she said. "He's the one you need to have words with. Then he can speak on your behalf to the ones above him."

"I'll try," said Prudence, but the words sounded empty. The world was an unfolding mystery and she couldn't speak with much certainty about any of it.

03:10AM

"Then left here," said Pupfish, reading the map in one hand and holding onto Nina's waist with the other.

"Here?" shouted Nina above the noise of the puttering engine and the wind.

"Here."

The side road took them past the turning for the train station and through dark residential streets to a high pillared entrance to Sutton Park. Nina wove the moped through the pedestrian entrance. She reflected sadly on the fact that if she'd been driving a car she would have been compelled to crash through it instead.

"Right, we're here," she said to Pupfish.

"Where? I don't see no donkeys."

It was dark once they were off the streets. There were not so many things on fire in Sutton Park, which took some getting used to.

"It's a big park isn't it?" said Nina.

Pupfish looked at his map. "Is all this green stuff the park?"

"Yeah."

"It's like crazy big. *Ggh!* Where's the donkeys at?"

Nina twisted and shone her phone torch on the map. "The Donkey Sanctuary," she said, pointing.

The gleam of her torch picked out something pink and slick on the floor. Nina scanned across the ground: the pink slick led to the ravaged corpse of a small deer. Her mind flipped automatically to what little she had glimpsed of Ricky's crushed corpse. She grunted and forced her mind away from it.

"*Bhul.* Someone killed Bambi," said Pupfish. "Like some NC17 Bambi *muda.*"

"Something is loose in this park," said Nina, automatically shining her torch around.

"Donkeys do this *muda*?" said Pupfish.

"No."

"You sure?"

Nina met his gaze. Expressions were hard to read on *samakha* faces, but she guessed Pupfish looked more than a little spooked. It might be the sight of the half-eaten little deer or, more likely, it was the culture shock of the urban youth being thrust into so much open green space. "Donkeys didn't do this," she said.

"Squirrels?"

She shook her head. "It's this way."

They rode slowly along a track, through thick woodland that only deepened the darkness, to a gate and a compound of little sheds. The noises from inside suggested they were filled with donkeys, and that the donkeys had cottoned on to the fact that things were not normal.

"Man, that noise!" Pupfish said, with a grimace.

It sounded like a death metal bagpipe orchestra. There was honking and screaming and all of the tonal variations in between.

"They'll probably quieten down when we go and see them," said Nina with a confidence she did not feel. They crossed the yard and tried some doors.

"You need to break this open, Pupfish," said Nina.

"How'm I gonna do that? You want me to shoot the lock off?"

She'd forgotten he had a stolen pistol stuffed down his codpiece. "No. Let's save the bullets for actual dangers. Must be something we can use." She went back to the moped and swung its headlight around. "A spade!"

Pupfish used it to pry the locks off the sheds. Nina followed along, making sure the donkeys all emerged into the yard.

Nina's more recent experiences with horses back in Georgian times meant these donkeys seemed like small, scruffy imitations. There had been a donkey tied up in the yard of The Old Crown at one point, but it was a sad and dusty creature that belonged to the laundry woman. These donkeys looked positively brimming with health in comparison, although they were clearly agitated and restless.

"*Azbhul*!" yelled Pupfish as the donkeys began to fill the yard and come close to him. "These bastards ain't dangerous, are they? They smell funny."

"They're donkeys," said Nina. "Just donkeys. You have seen donkeys before, haven't you?"

"Nah, never," he said. "'Cept on *Shrek*, you know. You?"

"Yeah. Seaside donkeys as a kid. Weston-Super-Mare. Thought they were bigger than this, to be honest."

She dashed back to close the entrance gate properly when she realised that these donkeys were seriously agitated and there was a risk they might all take off into the darkness. She turned to address them all. Two dozen grey-brown creatures nuzzled and half-reared at each other in a mixture of curiosity and fear. Somewhere amongst them was Mr Giles Grey, a transformed human.

"Hi!" she said loudly to the crowd. "I'm Nina Seth. I work for the consular mission to the Venislarn. This is my friend, Pupfish. We're looking for Mr Grey. That's his donkey name and his real name. Mr Grey! We know you're in here somewhere. Make yourself known!"

She had half-expected a donkey to step nobly from the throng, perhaps even address her with a deep Shakespearean gravitas and say something like, "Greetings, Nina. I … am Mr Grey," with dramatic pauses and everything.

Nothing happened at all.

"We need your help," she said. "We know you're a donkey and everything, but the Soulgate is going to close around the world and Professor Omar says you might know a ritual or a spell to stop it."

There was no notable response from the animals.

Nina huffed. "Pupfish, can you see names anywhere?"

Nina and Pupfish pushed through the crowd of donkeys looking for clues. There was a torch mounted just inside one of the shed, and Nina quickly learned donkeys did not enjoy having a light shone in their faces.

"I thought they would have badges or something. Wait, are you trying to tell me something?" A tall brown donkey had shoved her twice now. She peered into its face, searching for a spark of acknowledgment, but it looked like all of the others. "Are you Mr Grey? Stamp your left foot for yes and your right foot for no."

"They ain't gonna know which is left and right," Pupfish said.

"We have to assume Mr Grey is an educated donkey. Look! Did it move its foot?"

"*Ggh!* It's just walking over there."

Pupfish was right. Another donkey was now leaning into her personal space.

"We can try something else. If Mr Grey is anything like I imagine him to be, he'll like refined things." She brought up the digital assistant on her phone. "Play some classical music!"

You don't have any classical music. Would you like to go to the store?

Nina grunted in frustration. It wasn't as if she knew any tunes that she could whistle. "Play some rock music!"

OK, playing rock music.

If she couldn't draw Mr Grey out with something he liked, maybe she could goad him into a reaction with something louder.

She held up her phone and stalked amongst the donkeys. "Which one looks the most annoyed, Pupfish?" she asked.

He shook his head. "Man, I don't know."

"I know it's hard, but concentrate," urged Nina.

"It's not that. I don't think your phone knows what rock music is. Surely that's Taylor Swift?"

"Yes it is. We don't need to get into a debate. I've got no connectivity."

"That's your Taylor Swift music?"

"Maybe."

"*Ggh!* Like you think Taylor Swift is rock?" he said and laughed. "*Bhul tamade* dweeb."

"We don't need to discuss whether it's rock or not. We just need to assume that Mr Grey probably won't be a fan."

Pupfish peered into the face of one donkey, then another. He worked his way through them as systematically as he could, given the fact they were milling about in a way that seemed like determined chaos.

"They all look the same," he declared. "They all got an expression that says 'I'm going to laugh about you behind your back, soon as you're not looking.' *Adn-bhul* Taylor Swift, dog."

Nina looked from Pupfish to the nearby donkeys saw what he meant. Each donkey had a unique set of colours and markings, but the same set of basic features. She tried to read the expressions on their faces, but they all looked a bit like Rod when he had a new gadget. It was a look that could best be described as distracted and a little bit over-excited. She failed to pick up on the idea they were all desperate to share a joke, though.

Nina thumbed her phone to turn off Taylor Swift. The donkeys were not responding visibly to the music. "What else can we try? We need a test that a human would be able to pass in a donkey's body."

"Maybe he's gone native," said Pupfish.

Nina had been nursing the same suspicion. If Mr Grey had forgotten his human side, he would not respond. "Gone deep, you mean," she said firmly. "If Mr Grey is buried inside one of these then we will get him out. We have to."

Nina took a step back and started a slow, deliberate clap. "Let's try this. One two, one two."

She nodded at Pupfish and he joined in, clapping along with her. Nina stomped her feet in time with the clapping. "One two, one two."

The two of them kept the rhythmic stomping going for a good couple of minutes, making eye contact with as many donkeys as they could, but none of them showed the slightest inclination to join in, or even pay attention.

"Right, there's only one thing we can do here," she said to Pupfish.

"Yeah," he nodded. He stopped clapping and stomping. "What's that?"

"We need to take them all. We need to get them back to the vault and Omar can figure out which one is which."

Pupfish turned from side to side in a silent but agitated mime that tried to convey their isolated location, their lack of transport options, and just how many donkeys there were. "We ain't gonna fit them on the back of the moped," he said.

"I know," she said, irritated at herself.

"So donkeys," Pupfish said. "They like horse babies, or what?"

"Course they're not horse babies, they're, um—" She paused, not really sure whether a donkey and a horse were related at all.

"Okay, cut-n-shut ponies. Whatever. *Ggh!* We can ride them, yeah?"

"Yeah, you can ride them. Well I can ride them. You might be a bit big."

Pupfish gave a donkey an experimental pat on the head. "Will they follow us?"

"No," said Nina. "We're going to need to rope them together, then lure them with food." She headed into the sheds and found some bridles hanging up. "We need to put these on them."

"You know how to do that?" asked Pupfish, taking the odd, strappy bundle and holding it in various ways against a donkey to see how it might fit.

"I do," said Nina, showing him. "I had a boy to do this for me when I had to ride a horse. Dick his name was."

"The horse?"

"The boy. Proper bloody perv he was. Obsessed with my tits."

"Ha! That's funny cos you don't have none."

"*But* at least he taught me some horse stuff."

It took them a good while to get bridles onto all of the donkeys and then find a shiny blue twine to fasten them all together. Pupfish tossed her a flick knife to cut the trailing end of the rope.

Nina had been observing the donkeys, and she had singled out the one that she thought was the most inquisitive. She hoped if she put him at the front he would encourage the others to follow. "You are now the lead donkey," she told him, as she led it round and tied it to the gate. "I will call you Donk. I hope you and I can get along Donk, because we have a hell of a journey in front of us."

"Did you find some food to lure them?" asked Pupfish, as they completed work on the donkey train.

"No, there's none in the sheds. They must keep it somewhere else," said Nina. "Let's try with some grass or something. Maybe if we get them moving they will just keep going."

Pupfish opened the gate as Nina took hold of Donk's halter.

"Come on, hup!" Nina led Donk through the gate. It was straightforward to begin with as Donk seemed keen to get out and look around.

Pupfish stood by the gate as the other donkeys filed past. He gave some of them an affectionate slap on the rear as they passed. Nina thought perhaps he'd seen it in a film. Whether it was a cowboy film or one of the questionable pornos that the fishboys liked to peddle, she did not care to contemplate.

Nina had a plan for transport which she had not yet shared with Pupfish, on the grounds that it was so absurd he might just stalk off into the night. Walking all the way back into central Birmingham, probably ten miles in all, was the slow and difficult option, but there was an outlandish alternative she might be able to pull off.

She and Pupfish had counted as they'd put the bridles on, and there were twenty-eight donkeys in total. Nina led them through the spooky darkness of Sutton Park. The night sky glowed with the reflections of fires and the sickening luminescence of flying horrors, but here there were pockets of utter blackness on every side.

A chilling howl erupted from the darkness, and Donk froze. Nina could see the rolling eyes of several terrified donkeys who were trying to decide which way to bolt.

"*Muda*," said Pupfish, pointing. "*Dendooshi*."

Nina saw a large beast slink forward from the shadows. There were more behind it. She lifted the beam of the torch. They were *dendooshi* all right. She'd seen them in the consular mission Menagerie in Dudley recently, loping beasts with gnashing fangs and spittle-drenched fur. She knew Pupfish and his very unfortunate girlfriend Alanna had encountered them during a brief excursion into hell. Pupfish's description of them as big-ass wolves was fairly spot on.

"Any handy tips for defeating them?" she whispered urgently.

"Naw, man! Mostly you just gotta keep well out of their way," said Pupfish.

That was no longer an option, as the pack advanced in a semi-circle. Donkeys must have seemed like a tasty, slow-moving snack to the *dendooshi*. Nina could not afford to lose a single donkeys, as she still didn't know which one was Mr Grey.

"Back off!" she yelled at them in her fiercest voice, just in case they might be easily spooked by a woman who was much smaller than they were. Then she remembered the pheromone spray Rod had given her. It was still in her dress pocket. It was supposed to repel wolves, so maybe there was a chance it would work on *dendooshi*. She reached for her pocket, but Donk chose that moment to bolt in panic, dragging her along.

"Donk! Stop! This is going to get you killed, you're playing right into their hands!"

Nina discovered she was not as strong as a donkey and it continued to haul her along in its determination to run away.

"Donk, I really don't want to get rough with you, but you're leaving me no choice." Nina scrambled forward and smacked him hard on the nose. This was something that she'd seen Dick do when a horse nipped his hand. Donk stopped and looked up at her.

"What? I'm trying to save our lives, you idiot."

Now she could reach her pocket, she pulled out the spray can. The nearest *dendooshi* were so close she could see the glistening drool hanging from their mouths. She popped the top and aimed it. Then she paused. What was a pheromone spray supposed to do, exactly? It sounded like something for stopping wolves pooing in the garden, now that she stopped to think about it. She tried to read the text on the can without compromising her aim, but it was too dark. She waited a few more seconds and then lunged forward with a blood curdling scream and sprayed the nearest *dendooshi* in its eyes. It hissed and shrank back, pawing at its face. It stumbled into one of the other *dendooshi* and turned blindly to attack it. Nina seized the opportunity to blast another that was within reach, then she dragged Donk forward, skirting round the pack.

She was about to yell to Pupfish when there came the pop-bang of gunfire. The *samakha* had decided now was the time to get violent. She didn't know how much damage a bullet would do to a six-foot wall of wolf, but Pupfish had taken it from one of Kathy's Forward Management goons; maybe it was loaded with blue Venislarn-killers.

"Pupfish! Guard the rear of the donkey train!" she yelled.

They made their way out of the park and onto the roads of suburban Sutton Coldfield. The *dendooshi* were still following, more warily now. Pupfish had the good sense to ration his shots. Many Birmingham folk were familiar with the sound of random gunshots in the night, but she doubted that kind of experience extended to genteel Sutton Coldfield. No one came out of their houses. No one came to investigate. Hiding or dead, she couldn't tell.

CARCOSA

Rod opened his eyes, saw white stars in a black sky and immediately knew he was far from home. He half-entertained the notion his brain saw those constellations and knew they were not any constellation visible from Earth. But, no, the truth was much simpler. The sky above was black, and the sky of home was never truly black. This was the sky as seen from the Moon; from space: black and speckled with cold unlovely stars. Rod felt painfully lonely just looking at it.

Something prickled his back and arms through his shirt. Rod sat up. Brittle, colourless grass rustled and disintegrated beneath him. Crumbling headstones, headless statues and half-complete or half-demolished masonry littered the field around him.

"Graveyard," he told himself.

Speaking made him think of who he might be listening, and he looked around. There was no one in sight. The King in Crimson was not with him. He patted himself and checked the ground.

"Bugger's got my jacket," he muttered.

There was no wind, but for a moment something carried

voices to him: the *cher-ta-cher-ta-cher* of conversation. Brushing fragments of dead grass from the seat of his trousers, Rod looked round for the source. Some distance away, obscured by various headstones, there was movement. Beyond was a high wall, a street and city buildings. The buildings were old, some with medieval arches, others with the forthright square stonework of Victorian institutions. None seemed to be intact or complete. Rod had seen bombed cities up close in Iraq and this looked similar, although not quite the same.

He tramped across the thick, dry grass towards the sounds of talking. Something shifted nearby, low to the ground. It possessed a near-human skull coated in a thick, translucent gloop that bulged away to create a long, boneless, slug-like body. It probably had an unpronounceable Venislarn name – Nina or Morag would know it – but Rod was content to think of it as a giant slimy skull-slug. It slid between gravestones towards him. Its skull mouth was wide open, ready to bite down on him, even though it was still several feet away. It inched closer, its back arching like a cresting wave, pouncing upon him in nature documentary slow motion.

"Back off, mate," said Rod and moved away from it with ease.

There were other skull-slugs in the graveyard, all equally slow and unhurried. In the dark of the night they weren't easy to spot until they moved against the grey gravestones or the ash-white grass.

The sounds of conversation came from a family of four sitting in an open space between rows of graves. A tatty patterned blanket lay on the ground, and the four of them sat on it around a wicker picnic basket. The mother and young daughter were buttoned up in long dresses with heavy frilled petticoats, the son in a rough-weave jacket and short trousers. The father wore a suit and high-collared shirt. All four wore linen masks across their mouths and noses, held in place with elasticated strips around their ears.

The girl held her empty hand to her mouth. Her jaw moved up and down behind the mask.

"May I have another sandwich, mother?" asked the boy.

"Do not speak with your mouth full," the woman replied with prim formality. She leaned forward to open the wooden lid of picnic basket, reached in, and placed nothing at all on the boy's plate. The boy set upon the imaginary sandwich with gusto.

It was make-believe, child's play, yet there was no playfulness or warmth in their eyes or voices.

The father raised a cane and pointed into the distance. "The ships would come in across the lake and moor up there. Of course, you can't see them now."

The mother nodded but did not turn to look.

"Mummy," said the daughter. "The thing."

She pointed towards Rod but, he realised, not at him. A skull-slug was by Rod's feet, pooling its viscous goo beneath the bone face, giving it height and mass.

"Yes," said the mother. "Now shush."

She turned her attention from the creature. She didn't even see Rod. She picked up a light china cup and saucer. Rod couldn't see if there was imaginary tea in the cup to go with the imaginary sandwiches.

"Aren't you going to move?" said Rod. "Don't you think you should ... run, or something?"

The father's moustache twitched as though irritated, but otherwise no one seemed to be aware of him.

The skull-slug's skull was now at a level with Rod's waist, and so close it could lash out and attack him, if it moved at anything faster than, well, a slug's pace. Rod stepped away from it. A hand took hold of his shoulder.

He shuddered in surprise and tried to turn to look round, but the King in Crimson held him tight. A diseased and bandaged foot lashed out and connected with the skull-slug's jaw. It snapped shut with the click of teeth.

"*This one's mine,*" said the King in Crimson.

The family of four continued to eat their invisible lunch and paid no heed to the arrival of the King in Crimson.

"Can't they see us?" said Rod. "Are they ghosts?" The daughter looked at Rod out of the corner of her eye while she ate. Rod thought for a moment. "Are we the ghosts?"

"*No such luck for you, patron,*" said the King, clicking his tongue and drawing Rod back and away. "*Now...*"

He spun Rod round. Rod was faced with the King in Crimson looming large, seeming to grow taller on tapering legs, like some weird camera effect. His breath was a long inward gasp, a deep breath before the plunge.

"What do you think you're doing?" said Rod.

The King flicked at the edge of his bandage mask and it slipped off one side, revealing his mouth. The teeth, in his bloody and lipless mouth, were cracked and translucent with age, a mouth of nicotine fingernails. "*You have your wishes, patron.*"

Rod was shaking his head. "No, no. You don't get to cheat me like that."

The looming King in Crimson paused in his supernatural looming. "*Cheat? Cheat?*" He spat the words as though spitting out an unpleasant taste.

"You promised me three wishes," said Rod.

"*Three indeed, valued customer.*" The King held up ancient bony digits. "*The gem to your friend. Unnatural strength. And you wished to be away from that tomb in which you were trapped. Three!*"

"What strength?" said Rod. "You cheated me and you know it. I could not move those stones."

"*The strength to knock—*"

"To knock out a god with a single punch, aye. I see no gods and I've not punched anyone. That wish has not been delivered."

"The wish was for the strength."

"Unproven," said Rod with a forced tone of conviction. He had never been a gifted persuader. His general inclination was to let truth and common decency speak on his behalf and hope people would be similarly decent and fall into line. Actually, trying to wheedle his way out of a bargain with a Venislarn demi-god or whatever did not play to his strengths.

"As far as I'm concerned, Sunny Jim, until I've actually punched a god in the face, that wish is unfulfilled. Still out for delivery. Sorry, you were out when you called, we will try to deliver it another time."

"The three wishes have been granted," said the King in Crimson, but his dramatic looming had ceased and he was shrinking, subsiding.

"But they've not been collected," said Rod. "My soul is not yours, not yet."

He saw that the King's hands were empty.

"Where's my jacket? You had it before. I've got valuables in there, in the pockets and sewn into the lining."

Seeing that the conversation had moved on, that the claiming of Rod's eternal soul was no longer under discussion, the King pointed in a surly manner to a gravestone some distance away. Rod's jacket was draped over it. A scrawny masked figure was making her way across the graveyard towards it. Rod could read her intentions clearly.

"Oi! Oi! That's mine!" he called and jogged over.

Threats were not necessary. The opportunistic thief reached out a hand, reconsidered her options and fled, tattered skirts flapping around her pale ankles.

It belatedly occurred to Rod to warn her about the skull-slug things but, by that time, she had vanished among the graves. He lifted his jacket up, dusted it, inspected it and slipped it on.

The King in Crimson was at his elbow, mask back in place, present without any sense of having moved.

Rod looked at the broken architecture of the city. "Where am I?"

"*Carcosa,*" said the King in Crimson.

"Carcosa," Rod repeated. It seemed a familiar name, but he could no more place it than he could Atlantis or Brigadoon. "We're no longer on Earth? My Earth?"

"*You wished to be somewhere else.*"

Rod gritted his teeth and took a deep breath. "There's a word to describe what you are," he told the King in Crimson. "It's more than contrary, more than a jobsworth. You're an arse, mate. Worse than flamin' riddles, and that's saying summat."

He didn't have a plan, but he wanted to show his general contempt for the King in Crimson, so he walked away in the direction of the nearest street. He had to side-step a few skull-slug creatures on the way, but he didn't look back.

The cobbled streets were quiet but not empty. City residents drifted along in twos and threes. Clothes were mostly ragged and frayed and even the clothes of the better dressed had the air of museum pieces, carefully preserved and mended. Everyone wore masks across their mouths and noses; many filthy, some spotted with blood. No one spoke.

There was a strange rhythm to the way the people walked. They did not tiptoe as such, but moved with careful and slow footsteps as though fearful of making a noise. They were people pretending to be ghosts.

There were a number of market stalls in front of the ruins of what might have been a church. The sallow-faced stallholders averted their gaze as Rod approached. The nearest stall held a number of open boxes, all empty, save for labels and prices written on torn squares of brown paper. Next to Rod, a man in top hat and mask walked his fingertips from box to box, seemingly unable to decide between one empty box labelled 'nectarines' and one labelled 'figs'. The man nodded his appreciation to the stallholder who silently doffed his cap in response. Not a word was spoken.

Rod stepped away. The King in Crimson was close. Rod was about to ask what the hell was going on here when he heard, clearly in the near silent city, the sound of music: the swirling sounds of an organ.

He hurried in the direction of the sound: some signs of life in a dead metropolis. People pretended not to look as he went by with unseemly haste and noise. Mothers physically turned their children away from him.

The music was coming from the archway entrance of a tall and possibly once grand building. Decorative columns topped with statues ran along the front of the building. Portions of the columns had fallen away, revealing them to be nothing but a plaster façade over a dull stone front. Several of the statues had lost their heads. The rest had had their faces removed.

A woman, in a dress so ripped and ragged that the bones of her corset poked through, stood beside a stout music box with a small array of organ pipes and a curved brass handle. As she cranked the handle, a melancholy tune wheezed from the box and she sang without enthusiasm or skill.

"A<small>LONG THE SHORE</small> *the cloud waves break.*
    "The twin suns sink behind the lake.
    "The shadows lengthen...
    "In Carcosa."

T<small>HE YOUNG WOMAN</small> saw Rod watching and met his gaze. In a city of creeping introverted souls, the gaze of this tired-looking lass was like a physical jolt. She did not stop her singing, but her eyes smiled and she nodded to him encouragingly, waving him towards the entrance.

Rod was wary of smiling and encouraging women beckoning him into strange buildings. He had heard enough apocryphal tales from armed forces colleagues. They all started with blokes being beckoned into foreign drinking dens by strange beautiful women and ended with the bloke waking up in a bathtub minus a kidney. But Rod had nowhere better to go, he was armed, and the people of this place were so uniformly pale and gaunt he couldn't imagine any of them being much of a threat to him.

"Evenin'," he said and stepped past her through the entrance.

The lobby was carpeted and lit by long rows of gas lamps. The carpet was so threadbare that the pattern had gone completely from parts of it and the coarse under weave dominated. Maybe a third of the gas lamps were working.

A slight lad in the remnants of a uniform, on which gold brocade was nothing but unravelling rope strands, scuttled forward. "Come, come," he whispered. "You're just in time."

"Oh, is that right?" said Rod.

He followed the youth. The lad capered on the spot to try to get Rod to speed up. Rod followed him through a series of heavy dusty drapes and into a theatre auditorium. Hundreds of empty seats were gathered in tiers before a curtained stage. The air tasted of dust.

"I think we have a seat for you," said the usher.

"Aye. I imagine so," said Rod.

He followed the usher down to a middle row and a middle seat.

"I can't really stay," he said politely, feeling himself adopting the language to suit the dream logic of this place. "I must get back. The end of world is happening."

"Please, sir. Don't spoil the story for the other patrons."

03:17AM

There was a knock at the door and then, "You've locked yourself in, Vivian," said Lois.

Yoth-Kreylah ap Shallas squatted in the corner with her back against the sink unit, the Bloody Big Book open across her knees while she tried to continue her writing with the deficient biro Lois had initially brought her.

"*Besh-e cudj yeh'a*?" said *ap Shallas* and then remembered to speak in English. "Have you brought more pens? *Good* pens."

"What I could find, bab."

Lois's tone did not fill her with confidence. Nonetheless, *ap Shallas* shuffled over and flicked the door catch. Lois all but fell in. She had a bunch of pens and pencils clutched in her hand.

"Oh, you've been busy, haven't you?" she said in a deliberately cheery tone. "You all right down there?"

"The world as we know it has hours left," said *ap Shallas*. "We are not all right anywhere."

"Yes, I just meant—"

"I know what you meant," said *ap Shallas*. She frowned and

interrogated her own memories. "I did know what you meant. I recall knowing what you meant."

Ap Shallas gripped the edges of the Bloody Big Book as though it was the handrail of a ship in the middle of thrashing seas. Dropped here, back in the mortal world once more, *ap Shallas* could feel her life in hell slipping away from her. An eternity of memories, an active omniscience granted by the eyes of *Hath-No*— As *Yoth-Kreylah ap Shallas* she had seen everything and transcribed everything – nearly everything! – into the book. But now, trapped once more on the mortal plane and in the pathetically finite body of Vivian Grey, she could not hold onto that mental power. Her brain wasn't large enough. Her *vision* wasn't wide enough.

"I need to finish it!" she said. "A line here. A reference there." She held out her hands for the pens.

Lois showed her what she had found.

It was evident that during the construction and equipping of this Doomsday HQ, scant budget had been set aside for quality stationery. There were several of the cheap transparent biros that *ap Shallas* was already struggling with. She hoped they were cheap; if anyone had paid good money for nasty pens that snapped under the slightest pressure and which produced gunky ink, emerging in sporadic and miserly spurts, then they had been horribly duped. She ignored the few similar pens Lois held. She picked up a four-colour retractable biro.

"The blue and the black have run out but the red and the green are still good," said Lois.

Ap Shallas made a doubtful noise and selected the most promising pen on offer. It was a rollerball and produced a smooth track of black ink on the edge of the current page in the book (which she turned with millennia of practice into a minor decorative border).

"And what is this?" she said, flicking the plastic animal head on the end of the pen. It wobbled on its spring mounting, cartoon eyes bulging.

"It's a unicorn," said Lois.

"I can see it's a unicorn," said *ap Shallas*. "I meant ... why?"

"Unicorns are fun," said Lois. "Now, what's so important that you need all these pens, eh? Wouldn't you like maybe to get a shower, some nice fresh clothes and maybe a bite to eat? Nina's mom's brought in some delicious samosas."

"I need to write," said *ap Shallas*. "I need to describe it all, recount it all, before the world is ended." A horrible, nervous and wretched energy flowed through her.

"But why?" said Lois.

Ap Shallas flicked back to a partially completed section. Dipping to a precise location in an infinite book should have been impossible but *ap Shallas* clung to vestiges of her power as its creator. It obeyed her touch and command for now.

Lois turned round and looked down awkwardly to see what was being written.

"You understand what needs to be done?" Vivian Grey asked Steve the Destroyer (for the fourth time) as they walked to the throne room of the regent Sha-Datsei.

"Get the pathetic humans back to Earth, find any remains of Crippen-Ai, notify the authorities," said the pabash-kaj doll.

"And the authorities are...?"

"The consular mission. The ginger one, Morag Murray, if I can."

"Failing that?"

"Scientists. Doctors. Anyone who is not a brainless fool."

Vivian made a sceptical noise, a vocalisation of her lack of trust in the doll's abilities. "This mission might be harder than it appears."

"You could come with us. You're not half as annoying as some of these creatures," said Steve.

"No. I am staying here. I have to write the Book of Sand. It's self-evident."

Steve shook his head. "You have to write it because you know you're going to write it?"

"And I must therefore be writing it for some greater purpose. Perhaps it is the key to this whole thing."

"Thing?"

Vivian Grey looked at her hand. It was a delaying action, time to gather some unconnected thoughts. "The end of the world," she said. "Judgement Day."

"I SEE," said Lois once she'd read it all. "Then you'd better crack on with it. With any luck we'll be dead before long. Now, can I bring you a cuppa?"

That gave *ap Shallas* cause to pause. Food and drink as sources of nutrition had vanished from her routine aeons ago, but the ritual of drinking tea – the act of heating the water, soaking the leaves, savouring the taste – these had stayed with her a lot longer.

"I know how you like it," said Lois.

Vivian remembered cups of tea that Lois Wheeler had brought her. They rarely matched her expectations.

"No," she said. "Bring me pens. More pens. Not—" She flicked the plastic novelty head on her pen. "—*Unicorn* pens."

IN THE CONFERENCE ROOM, a map of the northern hemisphere, green lines on a black background, dominated the wall of screens. Nothing at all was occurring on the map but it held everyone's attention.

Sanders had explained the appearance of dots on the screen would indicate nuclear missile launches.

Mrs Seth bustled quietly around the table, collecting plates and replacing untouched hot drinks with new ones. She maintained a low-grade cheerful muttering to herself but kept her head down so as not to disturb the fretful watchers. Morag didn't know if she comprehended what was happening on the screen, and what it meant for the world at large. If she did, she was truly taking it in her stride.

Chad from marketing strode into the room, a cluster of presentation boards under one arm and a heavy folder of notes in the other.

"Prepare to be astounded," he declared loudly. "Prepare to be amazed."

"Be quiet and sit down," hissed Morag.

"But I've got the mood boards for our communication campaign. I've decided a triadic colour scheme is called for. Bold? Yes. Occasionally over-powering? Perhaps. But I think we're beyond the looking glass here, folks, so why don't we—"

"Just shut up," Morag snapped.

"There!" said Sanders, pointing at a spot on the screen. "Scotland."

"Oh, God," quailed Councillor Rahman softly.

The board was starting to light up. Orange glows appeared along the North Mediterranean coast, central Asia and up into Russia.

"That's pretty," said Chad. "What is it?"

"Nuclear missile launches," said the major.

Chad blinked. "What? No, nonononono. That can't be!"

"This was what we always planned for," said Morag, even though the words themselves sickened the pit of her stomach (although she did not properly understand where the pit of her stomach was located in the deflated ruin of her lower abdomen). "This is our best-case scenario." She thought about that. "Our least-worst-case scenario."

Chad floundered in distress. "But – but my presentation. My

vision. I had a five-part programme for keeping the public on board and informed. There would have been live broadcasts by our esteemed leaders." He gestured open-palmed at the deputy council leader. "A Q&A with trusted journalists. We get some buzz going. Some sure-fire twitter trending for the older market segments."

Morag and simply pointed at the screen.

"How long have we got?" said Chad.

The major took a deep, weary breath. "Our own nuclear arsenal will reach local targets within five to ten minutes, but we don't have the stockpiles we used to have. We will rely on partner countries to finish the job."

"We've asked the Americans to nuke us?"

"Among others. In which case we could have anywhere between thirty and forty minutes until thermonuclear annihilation."

Chad twisted his lip. "I mean it was going to be a whole hour presentation, but I suppose we could ditch the icebreakers, and the word association thought shower. I could bring it down to a half hour."

"You want to do a marketing pitch with the last half hour we have left to live?" asked Morag.

"That would be great!" said Chad, pleased by the suggestion and thoroughly missing her tone. "I can set up in five minutes. Anyone need any comfort breaks?" he asked the room. "It's going to be an emotional and intense ride."

Chad took his presentation cards to the front of the room and rested them against a flipchart in front of the screen currently detailing creeping flight paths of thousands of nuclear warheads.

"Not the best backdrop," Chad noted. "Could we perhaps change it to…?" He looked around his audience but didn't find any willing volunteers to change the image. "Okay. We work with what we've got. Now I'm going to hand these out. Just for fun. Just for fun. But it's to get you thinking."

"'If I was a yoghurt, what kind of yoghurt would I be?'" read the council CEO.

"Just for fun," said Chad. "But it will prove relevant later on. Just you wait and see." He glanced at the board of flying missiles. "Yeah, I think we'll get to that bit. Just."

Morag put her pen down and with an aching grunt, got to her feet. "I'm going to leave now."

"But the presentation…" said Chad.

"Yeah. I'm going to spend these final precious minutes with my daughter."

She walked out – walked, not waddled, she told herself – and made for the lift. As she waited for it to arrive, her thoughts went momentarily to Nina and Rod and where they might be spending their final moments. She didn't know if Nina had even reached Sutton Coldfield, let alone found the donkey she was looking for. She wanted to picture Rod driving back to base from the university, but it felt like he'd been gone a long time. She couldn't help thinking something had delayed him; perhaps permanently.

She rode up to the Vault level. Security Bob was in the lobby area. He let her through to the Vault without a word. Belatedly it occurred to her that he might not know about the missiles. Why would he? She considered saying something pleasant and reconciliatory to him, but it would sound awkward, and wouldn't make their final moments any better for either of them.

The Vault was quiet but for the hum of the aircon and the low-level scratches, clicks and ululations of those artefacts which refused to stay still. She found Professor Sheikh Omar walking with obvious discomfort down an aisle of confiscated books. His head swung from side to side as he looked about.

"Professor?"

He turned slowly. Pain etched the tall man's face, ageing him, maybe making him look a little closer to his true age. "Now, I don't want you to panic, dear," he said.

"What?" said Morag.

"I'm sure she's around here *somewhere*."

She felt it like a punch. How could it impact her so much? Daughter or not, she'd only known her a short time, and yet his words took hold of her innards and twisted hard.

"Prudence!" she yelled.

03:31AM

Nina and Donk kept up the momentum, dragging the donkey train with them. From the park it was a short walk through terraced streets up to the car park of the train station. The station building had that old Victorian school look. There was a light on inside.

"Nina," Pupfish called from the back of the line. "Sure the trains aren't running, man."

Nina ignored him and walked out onto the platform. Her best scenario was that a train was waiting at the platform with the engine running. No such luck, but there were two figures down the end of the platform: an older woman in a wheelchair and another beefy-armed woman in a railway uniform. The beefy woman had armed herself with a gigantic wrench. Nina saw that it glistened stickily under the lights as the woman wielded it as a warning. It had clearly already been in a fight.

Nina approached with her hands held up, so she did not alarm the woman. Unfortunately, the donkey procession undermined her efforts. The woman looked at Nina, the donkeys, then Pupfish as he entered.

"Go away!" she shouted. "No trains here!"

Nina held up her ID, not that the woman could see it. "We need to get a train."

"Not another step," said the beefy woman. "I will fucking brain you, darlin'."

Nina tossed her the ID. She had hoped it would fly like a frisbee into the woman's hand but instead it wobbled and fell like a falling leaf.

"What's that?" said the woman.

"It tells you who I am. I'm Nina Seth."

The woman shrugged. "Hello Nina. There are still no trains."

"I work for an organisation. We are some of the only people who are briefed on the current situation and equipped to deal with it."

"Deal with it?" scoffed the woman.

There was a growl from the ticket hall. Donkeys bunched together nervously. They weren't stupid. Pupfish raised his pistol and fired in the direction of the *dendooshi*. There was a yelp and a long silence.

"Ooh, that was loud," said the old woman in the wheelchair. It was said in a mildly amused and jolly tone. Wherever the woman's brain was it, it wasn't orbiting Planet Normal.

"I need your help," Nina told the railway employee. "I had a police escort when I set out on this job, but he— " Nina didn't want to talk about Ricky Lee to this stranger who didn't care. "I don't have one anymore. Now I need a train to get this group to central Birmingham. If you can't make a train happen, then I urge you to put me in touch with someone who can."

"Donkeys," said the woman. Her face crunched with confusion and she opened her mouth to ask a question but abandoned that. "Karl's looking for a train."

"Karl?"

"He's a driver. We tried to use the computer to see where the trains are on the network, but the system's not working. So he went old school."

"What does that mean?" Nina asked.

The woman pointed up the track. "Walking up the track to find a train then bringing it back here. We're taking his mom into Birmingham with us. We need to get her somewhere safe. There are men with guns…" She pursed her lips. She clearly had her own horror stories.

"It's not easy to know what 'safe' even means at the moment," said Nina. "He went that way?"

The woman nodded.

Nina jumped down from platform to track. "Pupfish will guard you while I find him."

"I'll unlock the ramp while we're waiting, shall I?" said the woman.

"Ramp?"

"You'll need the ramp to get the donkeys on."

Nina ran down the track and only tripped a few times on the sleepers. She soon caught up with Karl.

"Woah! Woah!" he shouted in alarm, waving a heavy-duty torch about.

"It's okay," she told him, a little out of breath. "Human. Normal human. Here to help."

"No hi-vis? No hard hat? This is a place of work, not the Wild West, mate." He was apparently more alarmed by her lack of health and safety considerations than the possibility of her being a monstrous thing from beyond.

"I forgot to bring them," she said.

He was younger than Nina had expected. She gave him a deeply abbreviated version of her situation, reassured him that his mom was still fine, and might have entirely neglected to mention the donkeys in her haste to get him up to speed.

They walked up the side of the track, while shining his

powerful torch in front of them, so that any trains would see them coming.

"Train!" she shouted, pointing to a stationary carriage ahead.

Karl nodded with satisfaction, as if he'd known that there would be one here. It wasn't very far away from the station, so maybe it was a train car park, or a train park, or whatever. It had three sections which was quite possibly enough for their donkey crew.

Karl climbed into the cabin.

"You can make this work?" Nina said.

He ignored the question. "We can't go full speed into the city. We will need to proceed at a speed where we can apply the brakes if we need to. We have no idea what we might find on the line."

"Uh-huh. Makes sense."

Nina ran back up to the platform (taking Karl's hard hat and torch because he insisted) to help get the ramp in place and the donkeys loaded.

"Only two bullets left," said Pupfish. "The donkeys ain't happy neither."

Karl and his train slowly pulled into the station. The beefy woman pulled the ramp into place and wheeled Karl's mother on board. Pupfish tried to haul Donk up and onto the train. The donkey wasn't all that keen on the idea, and strained on his halter, hooves skidding on the platform.

"Come on Donk!" Nina called. "We need to get you moving."

She ran to a platform vending machine and shovelled in some coins. There was the hint of sound and movement from the ticket hall. The *dendooshi* were wary but hadn't left.

"What are you doing, Nina?" called Pupfish.

"Crisps!" she replied. "What flavour do you reckon?"

"Did I mention the bullets and the *teglau* wolf monsters?"

That wasn't a helpful response, so she got cheese and onion because she imagined donkeys might like onions. She ran back, opening the bag and then went to Donk, getting the scent of the open bag under his nose. "Come on! We'll get you some proper donkey food as soon as we can, but I bet you'd like a crisp, wouldn't you?"

Donk did seem interested, and he followed Nina up the ramp and onto the train. Nina was well aware they needed to move right down the carriage if they were to accommodate all of the donkeys, so she kept going along the aisle, while Donk squeezed his tubby frame between the seats in pursuit of the snack. She opened the door to First Class and continued into the next carriage.

"How many are left?" she called to Pupfish.

"Ten."

She shuffled back to the end of First Class and emptied the crisps onto a seat so that Donk had something to keep him absorbed. She squeezed back down the crowded aisle, checking that the donkeys were all installed comfortably. There was a gunshot.

"One bullet!" yelled Pupfish. "Let's go."

The doors shut. Nina could see three *dendooshi* devouring the corpse of one of their own in the ticket hall. Another, one of the largest, came prowling onto the platform.

"Can you look after all of our passengers while I ride up front with Karl?" Nina asked Pupfish.

"Sure. Can I get some of your crisps?"

"I gave them all to the donkey," she said.

The train pulled away slowly to the sound of huffs, nickers and whines of nervous donkeys. The *dendooshi* kept pace with the train to the end of the platform, then stood there and watched them go.

03:33AM

The unholy colours of *Ammi-Usub* seemed to be gathering more thickly the further Prudence, Steve and the Mammonites travelled. Prudence wondered if the unknowable colour was following them, or if they were by chance following it. Plant life swayed to its rippling powers. Colour danced around the street lamps. The tops of wooden telegraph poles warped and sprouted new growth, anaemic shoots reaching for the alien light around them.

A puddle of water that had gathered around a blocked drain was oily. When Prester kicked through it, it oozed and rippled in a way that water shouldn't. Even the air seemed changed. It would have been easy and simplistic to say the air stank, of fire and fumes and filth, but that would be wrong. Such expressions were only a human approximation of the indescribable change that had come over the atmosphere.

"Are we in danger?" Prudence had asked. "Is the light changing us too?"

"It will have me to deal with if it tries," said Yang.

"Still think you can fight a colour?" said Steve.

Shortly afterwards they were attacked by The Things That Used To Be Dogs. Prudence thought they looked cute, with their scruffy fur and floppy eyes and bright glowing eyes. Then they ran at the children and one of the big ones grabbed Elon Mogg-Mammonson by the shin and tried to drag him into the bushes. The Mammonites shot The Things That Used To Be Dogs. Even when several of the dogs had been killed, and it was clear that children were off the menu, they kept coming, until every one of them had been slaughtered.

"I thought they looked cute," said Prudence.

Elon hissed as he inspected his ripped and bloodied trousers.

"Are you hurt?" said Yang.

He nodded, his teeth gritted.

"Can you walk?" she said.

"I think."

Yang Mammon-Mammonson ejected the ammo clip from her rifle, checked it and reinserted it. "You think?"

Elon looked at the rifle. "Yeah. I can walk. Sure."

"Good."

They carried on and passed through a housing estate. Mutated creeper plants curled into lettering along the side of boxy housing.

"*Hello,*" Prudence read before realising what she'd just done. "I can read!" she said.

Prester grunted dismissively. "I have a reading age of sixteen."

"I heard you cheated on that test," said Ayesha.

"Are you accusing me?" he said bluntly. "I am recording this conversation for monitoring purposes."

"I am only recounting what I heard," she replied smoothly.

"Who from? I could sue them."

"They're dead now," said Ayesha. "We shot them."

"*Muda,*" said Prester. "Can't sue the dead."

"Cheating – cheating successfully – is an accomplishment in itself," said Yang.

Prudence waved at the plant-writing on the house. "Hello, house," she said.

"Do not talk to the literate vegetation, gobbet," said Steve. "Nothing good will come of it."

It was not the only plant trying to communicate. Along the road, wildly growing ivy contorted itself into strange ideograms and near-triangles that hurt Prudence's eyes to look at. In the garden of another house, a bush had produced an array of giant white flowers. The five petals mimicked the outline of human arms, legs and heads. The largest flower was only slightly smaller than Prudence herself. A petal bent towards them as they passed. Through the front window, she could see the interior of the house was filled with dense plant matter. The tip of a shoe poked out of a cluster of leaves, but she could not see if there was a foot within it.

Yang slowed as they neared a grass covered roundabout. Twenty or so humans were gathered in a circle on the roundabout, hands linked and faces raised to the *thing* above them.

"What is that?" asked Prudence.

"An *ulah weyskin*?" said Prester.

"It could be a *sholog'ai frei*," said Steve.

"It looks like a stupid blobby jellyfish," said Ayesha.

Whatever it was, Ayesha had perhaps summed it up best. Ten feet above the circle of people – chanting, dancing, worshipping people – a shape had congealed out of the light. It wobbled and distended like an unstable soap bubble. Tracers of light crackled over its surface, ephemeral tentacles questing blindly. Where they touched the human devotees, they burned skin and left black scars. The humans moaned in religious ecstasy.

"They've picked that as their god?" said Yang disdainfully.

"I guess," said Prester.

"With all the gods of beyond coming to earth, they picked that one?"

"Humans are stupid," said Steve.

"That's why democracy is such a bad idea," said Ayesha.

"Look," said Elon.

"We are looking," said Yang.

"No, look. The Co-op."

Prudence followed his pointing finger and saw a shop on the far side of the roundabout.

"And the phone?" said Prudence.

"The booth thing on the corner," he said.

The group made their way slowly round. Ayesha and Prester kept their assault rifles trained on the blob-worshippers. A woman screamed as the jelly-god burned her face and chest. It was hard to tell if it was a sound of joy or agony.

"I could take out half of them from here," said Ayesha.

"To put them out of their misery?" said Prester suspiciously.

"Target practice," she said.

The shop was open or, at least, the lights inside were on. They crossed the last road and Prudence approached the phone box. It was hardly a box at all, just a battered metal stand with a scratched plastic cover. She looked at the graffiti covered phone unit and the number buttons. "What now?"

"I'm going in," said Ayesha and jerked her toward the shop. "Prester, are there sweets in the 'glorious world to come'?"

"Our divine mother – *San-shu chu'meyah* – is hardly concerned with sweets and snacks."

"Thought so," she said. "Gonna go stock up on Haribo."

Yang adjusted the shoulder strap of her rifle and didn't quite point her gun at Prudence.

"We brought you here. Now you pay us."

"Oh." Prudence had almost forgotten. She took the tin from her pocket. "Here."

Yang took it and appraised it from various angles. "Special? Bites people?"

"Uh-huh."

Yang struggled with the lid for a second and then prised it off. The angry whelk inside clattered and snapped and grabbed onto Yang's thumb with its sharp shell. Yang grunted but did not flinch. She watched it as it tried to chew the flesh from her.

"This is sufficient," she said, prising the creature off and back into the tin. She stowed it away in her blazer, sucked her thumb and then stepped back to take aim at Prudence. Prester followed her example. A cold feeling passed over Prudence.

"Safe passage you got," said Yang. "And now our deal is concluded."

"You going to shoot us?" said Prudence.

"Traitors," growled Steve, readying his spear.

"Don't blame me if you're poor negotiators," said Yang.

"That's really unfair," said Prudence.

"We are nothing but fair and honest." Yang smiled. The smile contorted her unnatural face. "We pride ourselves on that."

"Well, it's certainly not nice," said Prudence, who was sure there was a point to be made and that the Mammonites would put their guns away if she could only make that point clearly enough.

"'Nice' is a coward's word," said Yang. "Meaningless."

"We can take these weaklings," Steve said to Prudence.

"They have guns."

"You can dodge bullets, can't you?"

Prudence bit her lip. "No. I really don't think so."

The shop's automatic door slid open and Elon and Ayesha came out. Ayesha's arms were full of packets of brightly coloured sweets. Elon chewed on a wriggly snake sweet as long as his arm.

"What's going on?" he mumbled.

"Hey, I thought we had a deal," said Ayesha.

"What deal?" said Yang.

"The *kaatbari* was going to put in a good word for us. With *Yo-Morgantus* or someone."

"No one needs to put in a good word for us," said Prester. "When our mother rises—"

"She'll be bringing a family bucket of Kentucky Fried Chicken with her, will she?" said Ayesha.

Prester turned to her, anger on his fractionally lopsided face. In a single action, Ayesha dropped her stash of sweets, aimed her assault rifle from the hip and fired. Prester stumbled back.

"You just—" he began to say and she shot him again: a concentrated burst that spattered his chest and knocked him back into the road where he fell down.

"And gravy," said Ayesha. "KFC always tastes better with the gravy."

There was a long moment of stillness. Ayesha stared at the body. Yang watched Ayesha. Prudence stood, stunned. Even Steve held his position. The only sounds were the blob worshippers on the roundabout and Elon slowly chewing a red jelly snake.

"He cheated on his reading test," said Ayesha eventually.

Yang tilted her head on one side, conceding this.

"Couldn't read an *adn-bhul* situation though," said Ayesha.

"Good one," said Elon.

Yang's attention turned back to Prudence. Difficult though it was to judge the expression on her uncanny face, there seemed to be a calmer contemplative air about her.

"You going to speak to *Yo-Morgantus*?" she said.

"Maybe," said Prudence.

Yang jerked her head. "I know there's not going to be any KFC or sweets—"

"Or phone data," said Elon.

"Right. But you could put in a good word for us."

Prudence shrugged. "I guess."

"Don't make any promises to these creatures," said Steve.

"I can ask my mum," she said.

Yang lowered her rifle and took a little red plastic wallet from her blazer. She slipped a rectangular card from it.

"They gave us those when they came to do an assembly," she said and passed it to Prudence. "The consular mission think they're like ChildLine, or something."

The card simply read DAY OR NIGHT, ANY TIME followed by a long number.

Yang passed her a coin. "For your call."

Prudence nodded, not fully understanding.

Ayesha unclipped one of the phosphorus grenades from her belt.

"Give it to me!" commanded Steve in his most booming voice (which was not booming at all).

"It's twice your size," said Prudence.

"Only physically," said Steve.

Prudence took it from Ayesha on his behalf.

Yang gestured to the others. Ayesha and Elon picked up the dropped sweetie bags, Yang took ammo clips from Prester's corpse and checked his pockets for anything of value. Then they made off down the road. They didn't look back.

Prudence went to the phone box, lifted the handle and put it to her ear. "Hello?"

"You have to put in the number," said Steve.

Prudence read the instructions on the box, inserted the coin, tapped in the numbers and waited as it rang. The woman who answered was not her mum.

"I want to speak to my mum," said Prudence. When the woman didn't seem to understand, she added, "I'm Prudence Murray."

The woman told her to *"Hang on"* in a suddenly alarmed voice, as though Prudence was in imminent danger of doing something else.

Steve was up on her shoulder now, trying to listen in.

"I'm hanging on," she informed him.

There was a scrape on the line and then her mum's voice. *"Prudence?"*

"Hi mum."

"Prudence? Prudence, is that you?"

"Yes, mum. It's me."

Her mum made a very strange noise on the phone, a sort of wheezing sigh, as though she had forgotten to breathe for the past two hours and was only now remembering. *"Oh, God. Where are you? Are you okay?"*

Prudence nodded. "I'm fine. I was nearly shot, but then there was an argument about KFC – but I've never had KFC – and so we were fine in the end. I gave Mr Angry Shell away. I hope that's okay."

"What? Where are you?"

"I'm at a phone box next to a Co-op."

"Which Co-op? Where?"

Prudence looked around. "Near a green bit where some people are worshipping a blobby jellyfish thing."

"It's a *sholog'ai frei*," said Steve.

"Steve thinks it's a *sholog'ai frei*," said Prudence.

"Steve? Steve is with you?"

"Yes, mum."

There were mutters on the line and then her mum said, possibly to someone else, *"I'm going to kill him when I get my hands on him."*

"See how she blames me!" said Steve with righteous annoyance. "Steve does not take well to persecution!"

"I need to work out where you are. Hang on. We've got the number up. Acocks Green."

"Yes?" said Prudence who had no idea.

"That's five miles away at least. How the fuck did you get that far out?"

"Mum, you used a bad word."

"I'm about to use a lot more."

"You're angry with me," said Prudence and felt something crumple miserably inside her.

"I'm not angry with you." Her mum's tone was abruptly and deliberately light and did not fool Prudence one jot.

Tears trickled down Prudence's cheeks. "We just wanted to go out and see things while they were still there and…" She had to stop to sniffle and rub her eyes. "Flowers," she managed to say.

"And burn things," said Steve.

"Flowers and burn things," Prudence spluttered as she cried. "But then the soldiers tried to shoot us and we had to run and then we made some friends—"

"No friends of mine," said Steve.

"Okay, okay," said her mum. *"Okay, it's going to be fine."*

"I didn't mean to—" Prudence didn't know how that sentence ended, so stopped.

"We're coming to get you right now." There were conversations elsewhere and then raised voices. *"Someone. Someone is coming to get you. I'm coming to get you. You need to get out of sight and stay hidden."*

Prudence sniffed snot noisily and nodded.

"You hear me, Prudence Murray?"

"I can hear you, mum," she said.

"Get out of sight, now."

"I tried the walkie-talkie but it didn't work."

There was another noise from her mum and Prudence couldn't tell if it was laughter or crying. *"Go. Hide. I love you."*

Prudence nodded and hung up the phone.

CARCOSA

The whole bloody theatre was empty. Up in the boxes it was impossible to tell where the ruined drapes ended and the sheets of dusty cobwebs began.

"You said there were other patrons." said Rod, but the usher had withdrawn, and now the gas lights around the theatre walls were dimming as the stage curtain lifted. It creaked alarmingly, threatening to fall apart and crash to the stage at any moment.

The backdrop was a faded and mildewed painting of a city not entirely unlike the one outside. Tall spires, buildings of glass, wide squares marked by fountains and statues. The backdrop was torn, great hanging flaps of fabric revealing the darkness behind, but this only added to the effect of a decadent city, clinging to faded glory as its veneer of civilisation rotted.

Actors took to the stage. Their costumes were old and shabby, like everything else, but Rod could see they had made some effort to highlight the significance of their costumes and characters. The severe wig and dark outfit of one woman marked her out instantly as some witch or evil stepmother figure. The narrow suit, large spectacles and surely prosthetic nose of one man presented him as a dusty scholar. The long, pointed beard and overly tailored jacket of another spoke of a more sinister form of academia; magic even.

And then the actors spoke and Rod held back a groan. Memories of Miss Pringle's English Lit GCSE lessons at Wickersley Comprehensive, and enforced school trips to plays at Rotherham Civic Theatre sprang uncalled to mind. It wasn't that Rod specifically hated Shakespeare or Shakespearean language. He was a Yorkshireman: he at least had an advantage over most people in that 'thee's, 'thou's and 'thy's came easily to him. He was sure that old Billy Shakespeare had some cracking stories. But it felt to Rod that he had only ever been exposed to one type of Shakespearean performance: the kind in which the actors strode meaninglessly and self-importantly about the stage and, in lieu of acting, just shouted the lines at the audience in the hope they could convey meaning by sheer volume.

To Rod's ear (and he was sure he wasn't alone) the shouted delivery of a string of "verily"s, "i' faith"s and "anon"s prevented him from gleaning any natural meaning. By the time he'd deciphered one line, the actors had moved on five more and he was lost.

The witch, the scholar and the magician strode about declaiming this and that, speaking of some sort of great terror. Rod didn't have a clue what was going on until a Venislarn god took to the stage.

"Ah, right," he said, much happier. You knew where you stood with a Venislarn.

There wasn't actually a god on stage. That would have been alarming and quite impractical. The amorphous and tentacled thing appeared as a cardboard shadow puppet, projected against the backdrop from somewhere up above. It approached from stage right and proceeded to menace the human actors. There was then a great deal more declaiming and shouty prose.

Rod frowned and hunched forward in his seat, trying to make sense of it. The characters were arguing. The magician was all for one course of action and the witch was clearly opposed. There was a brief volley of convoluted abuse. If this had been an English Lit lesson, Miss Pringle would have stopped here to explain the wonderfully clever and surprisingly filthy jokes which had been encoded in the text, but Rod just accepted the magician and the witch weren't right happy with one another and were having it out on stage.

From nowhere, the magician had hold of a baby, dangling from his hand by one leg. Of course, it was not an actual baby – just a cloth and stuffing thing – but he wiggled it with such ferocity that its dangling limbs danced with unnerving realism. The magician held a knife high to stab the infant. There was the flash and sharp bang of stage pyrotechnics, and the magician had magically acquired a horse's head, in true *Midsummer Night's Dream* fashion. The magician fled and the other actors left the stage. It was the end of the scene. Rod automatically started clapping, then hearing how hollow it sounded in the empty space, stopped almost immediately. The sound of one man clapping in a theatre sounded downright disrespectful, sarcastic even.

Fresh characters entered the stage: two young women in white dresses and a silent, swaggering warrior with an empty sword scabbard and shiny helmet that had lost all but two feathers from its plumed crest. More impassioned but impenetrable speeches followed. All Rod could work out was that the taller, red-headed woman was generally angry and driven about something or other, and the shorter dark woman was happy to throw in the odd quip and toss an occasional saucy wink at the front rows of the audience. The front rows were still empty, but maybe it was hard to cast a saucy wink further into the auditorium. Rod wasn't a theatre type. He didn't know.

"Peanuts, sir?" The usher was back, with a tray held by a strap around his neck.

"I don't have any money," said Rod, trying to maintain focus on the play.

"It is not a problem, patron," he said. "They are complimentary." The lad picked up the edge of a brown paper bag from his tray and did a squeaky voice. "'Oh, Mr Rod, you are the nicest man we ever did meet.' See? Complimentary." The usher had the grace to not laugh at his own joke.

"Sure, peanuts," said Rods.

The lad rustled through his tray. "I'm sorry, sir, we're out of nuts. Can I offer you some candies instead?"

"Aye, whatever."

On stage the young trio, occasionally accompanied by the witch from the prologue, encountered other walk-on characters and various Venislarn projected into the stage area through numerous effects. Rod, despite his struggles with the dense language, found himself getting drawn into the narrative. The theatre company might have seen better days, and the actors lacked much in the way of skill or nuance but, by ruddy heck, they threw themselves into it with enthusiasm and hard work.

The usher leaned closer. "I'm afraid to report that we have no candies either. Perhaps sir would care to order in advance next time."

Rod waved the irritating man away. The usher sat down two seats along and watched the play along with Rod.

There was a fight with sinister fish men with wobbly papier-mâché heads. There were horrible spider women on stilts. And there was a peculiarly delicate but brief romance between the tall lass and a willowy chap, maybe some sort of fire sprite, who flitted around the stage in a toga-loin cloth thing and not much else.

Despite the impenetrable script and the negligible production values there was something undeniably familiar about the play.

Rod wondered if its themes were somehow universal and that it presented tropes and clichés that sparked half-recollections in his mind. The truth came to him in a horrid rush during a later scene in which the lewdly winking dark girl and the mostly dumb warrior protector had met the scholar from the prologue in his arcane lair. The scholar had refused to assist the two in their unclear quest unless the warrior engaged the scholar in a challenge of wits. This caused the warrior some consternation.

"Thy stratagem is that I commit a bawdy ode to memory and pray that I might playeth some of its component words?" he said to the short woman.

"'Tis so," she replied sweetly.

The scholar and the warrior took it in turns to lay down large tablets on a table, each with a letter inscribed on it.

"Wait a minute..." muttered Rod, entranced.

"What word art thou composing?" demanded the scholar.

"A grave word indeed," said the warrior. "I know all the words of man. Maid, ready thyself to consult thy dictionary."

The short woman was shaking her head. "No bestiary canst hold a word such as that. 'Tis the final word of unmaking!"

Rod looked from the warrior to the woman to the scholar, from each to each to each. The warrior picked up a tile with overexaggerated motions. Backstage, there was the rumble of thunder. Brief explosions puffed on stage.

Rod stood up, pointed at the musclebound warrior and said loudly, "Is that supposed to be me?"

The cast on stage glanced his way momentarily. The scholar froze in his dramatic pose. The warrior coughed.

"Er, 'tis the final word of unmaking!" said the woman, repeating her previous line.

"Mayhap it is. Mayhap 'tis not," said the warrior. "Mayhap I do not have the making of it. How many letters doth it have?"

"Eleven," said the woman.

"That's me, playing Venislarn Scrabble," said Rod.

The usher reached across and pulled him down into his seat. "Dear patron, I must ask you to stay seated for the full performance."

Rod turned to him. "That's me – *meant* to be me – and Nina on the day when we went to see Professor Omar. We needed his help to stop *Zildovar Fruity Loops* destroying the city."

"*The King in Crimson* is a work of fiction," insisted the usher. "Any similarity to persons living or dead is purely coincidental."

"And that looks nothing like me," continued Rod, waving angrily at the stage. "What's with the silly helmet?"

"As a playwright, I reject all accusations of plagiarism. A homage or two, here and there perhaps…"

Rod continued to watch. The action had leapt forward. The white-clad Nina character (who had never worn anything as modest and innocent in Rod's recollection) was trading sharp insults with a wild-eyed priestess while the red-haired woman, obviously meant to be Morag, battled with a shadow monster projected onto the stage.

"The play is not perfect," said the usher, who Rod now abruptly realised was the King in Crimson and had been all along. "Truth be told, it is more than a little … derivative."

"It's a bloody rip-off is what it is," said Rod. "Of my life."

"Oh, it goes back way further than that. My own sources of, um, inspiration are quite apparent, but I like to think I've covered that up with some light jokes and self-referential asides."

The battles on stage concluded with the death of priestess Ingrid Spence and the placating of the shadow monster with a rousing song. The debris of the titanic struggle was swept off stage and a twisted and scarred figure hobbled on, cast in the green-filtered limelight of a pantomime villain. A jigsaw of lines had been drawn on the actor's face in red make-up. The youth affected a hunched back and swung a long arm about as he launched into a loud soliloquy.

"Jeffney Ray?" said Rod, recalling the human door-to-door salesman who had traded souls for cash with the Mammonites and did not care how much chaos or pain it caused. Rod shook his head. "This is like having my annual appraisal in play form. I'm not right sure I'm enjoying it."

"Speak kindly," said the King. "It is the only play we have left."

Rod half-recalled something from a conversation with either Nina or Vivian, memories of an item stored in the Vault. *The King in Crimson*, a play.

"Is this the play that drives folks mad?" he said.

"It was not my intention when I penned it," said the King. "I can't be held responsible for how audiences respond to my art."

"You, the King in Crimson, wrote a play called *The King in Crimson*? That's a bit ... isn't it?"

"I told you it was more than a little self-referential. Ah! Here's my first appearance. Even if it is merely a dream."

A white curtain and a wrought iron bed were sufficient to represent a hospital ward on stage. The warrior Rod sat in bed, delivering a hand-wringing and emotional speech to the imperious and buxom actress portraying Kathy Kaur. As he did, a portion of the stage darkened and a fancy-dress mummy in wine-soaked rags prowled around behind Rod, performing a bit of what looked like interpretive dance.

"Not exactly true to life, is it?" muttered Rod as the scene concluded.

"Everyone's a critic," said the King next to him. "Best not peer too closely. Nothing survives close scrutiny. Take our fiery heroine."

In a fresh scene, the red-haired woman strode on and challenged the disfigured Jeffney character.

"Here we have a woman employed as a diplomat," said the

King. "A go-between the mortal world and the *em-shadt* Venislarn. Yet her primary trait is that of anger. She is like a dog tied to a stake. It defies logic."

"Don't be telling Morag that," said Rod and wondered where she was now, what she was doing. He pictured her in the Vault with her impossible child. He did not know how long they could stay safe down there. He wasn't even certain how much time had passed here in Carcosa. A creeping fear came over him.

"Where are we?" he asked the King. "Are we in another dimension? Is this a different planet?"

"What do you think?"

Rod thought of the ruined city and the silent lifeless people. "Is this Earth's future? Is it hell?"

"All will become apparent by the end." The King extended a bony finger towards the stage. "Or not."

A full choir in dark robes and lopsided theatre masks chanted a portentous choral while Nina and Rod contended with imaginatively realised horrors on stage. The severe witch figure – Vivian, Rod realised with a jolt – stepped through a cardboard portal into the red-lit realms of hell. She carried an oversized book with her. Sheets of parchment fell from its pages, and Rod saw the sheets were threaded along a length of string so that she carried a trail of handwritten papers wherever she went.

As the play continued, the witch Vivian adopted the role of narrator. Every word she wrote in her hellish prison was enacted on stage.

"It's a play about the book about the real things that happened," said Rod, unimpressed.

"Self-referential," said the King. "The play is the book is the reality. And I don't care if you don't like it."

BIRCHINGHAM - 03:45AM

At the sound of the announcement, [Ap Shallas wrote] Mrs Vivian Grey realised she would have to tear herself away from her work in order to intervene as the Book of Sand dictated.

"This is most inconvenient," she declared.

She put down her pen (she had not yet found a pen with a better flow and ease of use than the frivolous unicorn-head one) and stood up.

Lois Wheeler had put some clothes on the chair in the room for her. Vivian Grey looked at them, then looked at herself in the mirror above the sink. Hell's grime mired her face, and her hair hung in lank strands, framing it. Elsewhere amongst its infinite pages, the Book of Sand held tables and charts which, for those who could read it, enumerated every one of those hairs. The Bloody Big Book encompassed the finite and the infinite, the microscopic to the macroscopic. At this moment, in the macroscopic world, Vivian was aware that her appearance was out of keeping with the rest of the human world and entirely unsuited for the workplace.

She stripped off her clothes and washed. She sponged herself down with warm water quickly and efficiently, watching the rivulets trickle *across her loose, emaciated skin. She held her head under the tap and rinsed her hair and paid little attention to the amount of hair coming away in her hands and accumulating around the plughole. She dried herself off with two small towels and dressed in the clothes Lois had provided.*

There was a formal jacket, a skirt, a blouse, underwear and shoes. Vivian struggled with the buttons of the blouse for a few moments. She had had little practice with buttons in Hath-No and buttons did not favour the one-handed woman. It only occurred to her as she zipped up the skirt that these were her own clothes, a suit she had kept in storage in the office for those (surprisingly frequent) times when encounters with the slimy and bilious Venislarn necessitated a quick outfit change during the work day.

In the medical kit on the bedside cabinet, she found a safety pin with which to pin back the empty sleeve of her jacket. She used a fabric dressing, snipped short, to tie back her hair. She picked up the Bloody Big Book, consulted the last few paragraphs she had written and decided, inconvenient or not, now was the time. She slipped on the shoes, sensible formal shoes with a decent rubber grip, and stepped out.

She knew from what she had written that no one would challenge her in the corridor. The people of the consular mission had just been informed that they would soon be killed and released from the prospect of eternal hell by a contingent of nuclear missiles. Their minds were preoccupied with personal matters and Vivian reached the lifts without hindrance or distraction.

A VOICE SPOKE over the public address system in the consular mission bunker.

"Okay, folks," said the man's voice. "*Just got confirmation that the missiles are in the air. Central Birmingham is one of the targets. The blast will easily penetrate down to this level. Um, instantaneously.*" He gave a sharp breath, half-gasp, half-laugh. "So, I guess that's it. Take care. Take care? Jeez..."

On hearing the announcement, *Ap Shallas* looked at the pages she had just written in the basement room and saw her immediate future written out for her.

"This is most inconvenient," she said to no one.

The book said she would go upstairs to the ground level, and so she would.

While the lift carried her up (now dressed in the clothes Lois had given her) she thought that donning her earthly work clothes again was a resumption of her earthly duties. She would have to ask Lois to provide her with a new ID badge. Perhaps it was time to readopt a name she had not used for an eternity.

Vivian Grey stepped out of the lift.

The sounds of the world beyond penetrated the glass and steel edifice of the building. The roars of beasts and flames were a constant background hum to the final day of Planet Earth, punctuated here and there by the fainter sounds of explosions and the unique (and frequently mind-melting) calls of certain Venislarn deities.

The single human in the lobby sat on a chair by the open street door of the library. Outside, held back by Dee's Ward of Perfect Intersection, were the August Handmaidens of *Prein*. Vivian approached with firm strides, giving herself a stature and an imperious energy that her frail body truly did not feel.

"Vaughn Sitterson," she called as she approached. "I would ask you what you're doing, but I already know full well."

Vaughn swivelled in his comfy office seat. His wrists were pinned to his chair arms with cable ties. His shirt collar and jacket were askew, twisted round so that the knot of his tie was only inches from his shoulder. He stared at her with a wild-eyed look that indicated he had perhaps been through something of a physical and emotional journey to get here. "Don't try to stop me," he said.

"I'm not going to stop you," she replied. "I am only here because it is written I am here."

"You have no idea how difficult it has been to move around on this thing."

"Refreshing insights into access problems for wheelchair users," she nodded. "If you had time, you could use it to rewrite our equal opportunities policy."

The corner of his eye twitched.

The Handmaiden by the door tilted her carapace and her etched shell shifted from one angry baby face to another.

"We have a deal?" she said smoothly to Vaughn.

Vaughn turned to answer but Vivian spoke ahead of him. "I have a better deal for you," she said.

"You are Mrs Vivian Grey," said the Handmaiden. "We were told you were dead."

"You are *Shara'naak Kye*. This man is going to tell you where the *kaatbari* can be found. Overheard the call the young girl made to the switchboard, did we, Vaughn?"

"I just want it to be over," he said. There was a terrible bitterness to his voice. It turned into a sob by the end of the sentence.

Vivian put her elbow to his headrest and propelled him hard out of the door. *Shara'naak Kye* had to step aside to avoid him colliding with her legs. He rolled across the brick paving of Centenary Square until the chair came to a juddering halt and tipped over in front of the semi-circle of Handmaidens. Vaughn gave a high-pitched wail of surprise and pain.

"Please, do kill him," said Vivian.

"He was going to provide us with key information," said *Shara'naak Kye*.

"Why do you want Prudence Murray?"

"We are owed vengeance against Morag Murray," said the Handmaiden smoothly. "She murdered our sisters."

Vivian shook her head and exhaled through her nose. "Such petty motivation. And on today of all days. Still, I will tell you where she is."

"We had a deal!" Vaughn cried. "She's in Acocks Green!"

"But he doesn't know precisely where," said Vivian. "And you will need to be quick. We have perhaps less than twenty minutes before the nuclear missile strike on the city."

Shara'naak Kye bent closer, presenting her shell face right up to Vivian's. "What nuclear missiles?"

Vivian kept her position and her composure. "Our deal. You and I. You inform *Yo-Morgantus – san-shu chuman –* about the inbound missiles and I, in return, will disclose that Prudence Murray is on Gospel Lane in Acocks Green."

Shara'naak Kye swayed in hesitation. Perhaps she was contemplating asking how Vivian could know such a thing. Perhaps she was going to make some parting remark about rejecting Vivian's offer (even though she wouldn't).

"And just kill him." Vivian pointed at Vaughn.

"Thank you!" said Vaughn, tied into his chair on the ground. "Thank you! Yes! Yes! Ye—!"

His gratitude was cut off by a claw foot driving into his skull.

Shara'naak Kye ran off, and her sisters followed. Vivian noted with unsurprised satisfaction that they headed west towards *Yo-Morgantus*'s court in the Cube and not south towards Acocks Green.

She turned away to return to her writing. There were glass display cabinets near the centre of the lobby showcasing Birmingham souvenirs, and a few Library-specific souvenirs which could be purchased by visitors. In one cabinet were a number of copper-barrelled ballpoint pens in presentation cases.

Vivian contemplated the unicorn-head pen held between her hand and the book.

"This will be much better," she said and slid the display case open.

She laid the Bloody Big Book out on a side counter and tested the pens one at a time. One of the lobby lifts opened and Morag Murray emerged, followed by Professor Sheikh Omar. Morag was hurrying and Omar was hurrying after her, but since one had given birth not many hours ago and the other was in a wheelchair and nurturing a possibly mortal chest injury, neither moved with as much haste as they imagined.

"Think what you're doing, dear," Omar called. "You simply cannot go out there."

"I know," said Morag. "It's hell. You said. And then you chortled."

"An absent-minded turn of phrase juxtaposed with the literal hellscape out there. It was inadvertent humour. And I did not chortle."

"You did."

"Tittered perhaps. Chuckle maybe. But never chortle. A man has standards."

Morag whirled on Omar. Neither of them had yet seen Vivian at the reception counter and she watched their furious spat with aloof interest.

"Are you going to help me find my daughter or not?" snapped Morag.

"Find her?" said the professor. "If she or we encounter the military out there, they will kill us. If she or we encounter the Venislarn, they will kill us. Or worse. The roads are blocked. Half the city is engulfed in fire. That's an *Esk'ehlad* death hymn you can hear out there. *Yo-Kaxeos* is rising from his tomb. *Yoth-Thorani* has summoned all the trees of the city to her army and is trampling anyone who even looks like they might once have so much as held a pair of pruning shears. *Qahake-Pysh* is making haste here from Carcosa, and even the gods don't know what will happen if she bumps into her ex-husband. That's going to be an earth-shattering lover's tiff and I don't mean in a 'Christmas Eve at the Queen Vic' kind of way."

"You don't watch *EastEnders*!" said Morag.

"No, but Maurice is fond of serial dramas and one can't help picking up a thing or two. We have all of that to contend with and – oh! – we will be engulfed in a blessed thermonuclear explosion before we even get halfway to your daughter!"

"But I have to try! Who knows what's happening to her right now?"

"She is going to be captured by the August Handmaidens of *Prein*," said Vivian.

Morag and Omar stopped and turned. Vivian had settled on a pen she liked.

Morag took a stunned step. "How long have you…?" She gave Vivian a full look up and down as though she had not seen her in ages. "You look … better. Have you recovered?"

It was an odd question. Vivian met Morag's gaze levelly.

"Recovered, Miss Murray? I'm not sure if, after all that has happened, there was much of me left to be recovered. I can say that, at best, I am functioning as a fair facsimile of Mrs Vivian Grey." She looked at the post-natal Morag and the wounded Omar. "Under the circumstances, 'functioning' seems as much as any of us can hope for."

Morag stared at her for a long moment before saying, "How do you know Prudence is going to be captured?"

"Because I have written it so and I have seen it written," said Vivian. "Also, I told them where to find her."

"What?"

"Vaughn was going to do that anyway."

"But why?"

"Why capture her or why tell them?" asked Vivian. "It doesn't matter. Despite their threats, they will have to take her to *Yo-Morgantus* before being allowed to kill her. If you have any hope of finding her, it will be there, at the Cube."

"But the bombs!" said Omar.

Vivian ignored him. "I do have to ask you one thing, Miss Murray. I don't yet understand, not satisfactorily."

"What is it?"

"Your daughter. The world is descending into a hell, a true hell. All wise people are seeking death right now. Why do you have this need to find Prudence?"

Morag recoiled, affronted. "Because she's my daughter. My little girl."

"Well, exactly. You've only recently given birth to her. You barely know her."

Morag gave a disbelieving cough of laughter.

"Oh, God, you really are Vivian Grey. A perfect facsimile. I forgot how mad you are."

Vivian was surprised. "Honest and practical, Miss Murray. Never mad."

03:49AM

Nina stood in the train's cab with Karl the driver.

"Keep looking as far forward along the track as you can manage, we can't afford to miss any obstacles," said Karl. "You've got to keep your eyes peeled in this game."

Nina peered forward. The track was lit up by the train's light, but there was a purplish glow across the horizon that drew the eye away. It was either the approaching dawn or the burning city.

"So they're important, these donkeys?" Karl asked eventually.

"Yes, they are. Well, one of them is, and I don't know which one. That's why I brought them all."

"Makes sense."

Nina was impressed by Karl's ability to assimilate highly improbable information. Either he was in shock, or he would score a high abyssal rating. She pointed. "What's that on the track up ahead?"

Karl slowed the train while they tried to make sense of the obstruction up ahead. "Is it a person?" he asked.

It was a man, lying prone and staring at them.. He scrambled to his feet and moved away from the track, but then stuck out his thumb like a hitchhiker.

"Am I stopping?" asked Karl.

"Absolutely not," said Nina.

Karl nodded grimly and accelerated as they passed the man.

They came across other pedestrians, using the train tracks to navigate the city. They passed buildings on fire, some of them so close to the track that their faces felt scorched. They heard the sound of breaking glass from further back in the train.

"That'll be the heat," said Karl.

The unspoken question hanging between them was whether it was a window which exposed some, or all of their passengers to the appalling heat. They pressed on in silence.

The station signs were the only reliable markers of where they were. As they passed through Gravelly Hill station, Nina strained to see whether the railway line would be affected by the madness that had taken Ricky Lee's life.

"It was a bit screwed up round here earlier," she said, quietly.

She could see no sign of the loop-the-loop road from this angle, which was absurd. It was hundreds of feet high; they should have seen it miles back.

"You'll see when we go past Spaghetti Junction," she said, nodding to the concrete structures towering over them. They crawled underneath. There was a sudden, appalling pressure in the cab. They both cried out in pain. Then it was gone.

The donkeys further back in the train brayed loudly in alarm.

"Calm down, you bitches," Pupfish could be heard shouted.

"What the Jesus and Mary Chain was that?" Karl said, shaking his head.

"I think it's some sort of barrier," said Nina. "We made it through." She gave him a weak smile.

"That's Aston station," he said as they rumbled over a bridge. "Just Duddeston to go before we reach the city centre."

"Doing a great job, Karl," she said, shifting the oversized hard hat back onto her head.

"Not doing so bad a job yourself, mate."

She left the cab and went back to check on the passengers. The donkeys shifted restlessly. Nina liked to think they were excited by the experience of being on a train, but figured they were really just spooked as fuck.

The railway woman sat with Karl's mum, employing her powerful arms to keep a donkey at bay. It clearly felt it would be most comfortable standing with its rear end pressed up against Karl's mum.

"This is quite undignified," Karl's mum told Nina.

"I run the best train service in the city."

"Certainly ain't no Virgin Trains," said the railway woman.

Nina carried on, squeezing past uncooperative and occasionally bitey donkeys until she reached the rear carriage and Pupfish. Some of the windows had been blasted in by the heat. Pupfish stood with the rearmost donkeys. He had his arm round the neck of a skittish one to keep it under control. Nina saw the seats at the very back were scorched and smoking.

"You guys okay back here?"

Pupfish stared at her. He blinked broad golden eyes. "*Ggh!* This ain't like Shrek at all!" he complained.

Nina shook her head. "You're a film star. Consider this a helpful experience. Research for a role."

"For what film, huh? *Ggh! Donkey Train of Death?*"

"I'd watch it."

There was a small lurch as the train slowed.

"We nearly there?" said Pupfish, peering through cracked and smeared windows.

"Don't think so," said Nina. She hurried back through the crowded carriage, squeezing past and elbowing donkeys that got in her way.

"What's up?" she said as she re-entered the driver's cab. Then she saw it. Up ahead, just about picked out by the train lights, a large form blocked the track. "Is that a tree?"

"Fallen from where?"

The giant object was fat, round and tapered at each end. Its surface was brown and cracked like bark, but there was a glistening smoothness to it too.

"Looks like King Kong took a dump on the track, 'scuse my French," said Karl. "Beyond this it's viaduct – elevated railway – all the way into New Street, but if we can't shift that…"

Nina picked up Karl's torch from the console. "Open the door for me and I'll go check."

"You sure?" he said, a tremor of concern in his voice.

"No," she said and shrugged. "But, hey, YOLO."

He grunted, unconvinced, and opened the cab door for her.

03:54AM

P rudence tried to stay out of sight. She went into the Co-op with Steve.

There were two dead people on the floor in one aisle. There were biscuits and crisps in another aisle, and a cabinet full of drinks. She ate a chocolate Penguin, a packet of Hula Hoops and drank from a bottle of Dr Pepper. The Dr Pepper fizzed and made her nose hurt, so she didn't finish it.

She sat outside on the pavement between a rubbish bin and a parked car and waited. She could see Prester's twisted body in the road. There was no traffic, no vehicles to swerve around or drive over it. The circle of humans on the grass (who hadn't even looked round at the sound of gunfire earlier) continued their meaningless, painful worship. Several had collapsed with blackened limb or faces, scorched by their new god. They seemed perfectly happy with that.

Steve pestered her for the grenade, but she was firm and said no. He attempted to threaten her with his pencil spear, so she picked him up and told him firmly this was not okay and he would get the grenade when the time was appropriate. Steve threatened her with untold tortures before running off in a sulk.

A short while later the shop set on fire. Steve claimed he had nothing to do with it, but he was quite sooty and smelled of smoke, and Prudence didn't believe him. She was forced by the heat to move further along the pavement. She sat next to a lamppost and watched the fire. The rolling swirls of flame brushing the windows and pouring from the doorway were very pretty and impressive. As the heat warmed her face, she decided the fire was the prettiest thing she'd seen in her entire life.

Watching the fire, it took her a few seconds longer to realise there was movement on the street corner. Prudence stood, sure it was going to be her mum, that she had waited long enough.

It was not her mum.

Three August Handmaidens of *Prein* approached. Prudence had seen them through the vision mediated by *Crippen-Ai*. She recalled her mum's encounters with one while Prudence was still in the womb. In the flesh, seen with her own eyes, she was struck by their size, and the noise their scraping plate armour made as it shifted and turned.

Prudence saw two of the Handmaidens carried prisoners in their crab claw forearms. Yang Mammon-Mammonson was held by her shoulder. She occasionally tried to swat or grab at her captor with her other arm, but her muscles seemed not to work and she could only twitch ineffectually. Ayesha was gripped tightly around her waist and hung limply, arms and legs swinging in unison.

There was a tickle at Prudence's back as Steve wriggled up and squeezed into the waistband of her baggy trouser-shorts. "Shh!" he hissed. "I'm not here!"

She had no time to question him. The lead Handmaiden was upon her, many-jointed legs folding to bring her faceless shell down to Prudence's level. Prudence didn't even think to run.

"So, this is her," said the Handmaiden. Her voice was smooth, almost emotionless, and came from nowhere in particular.

Prudence, despite her alarm, found herself wondering if the Handmaidens of *Prein*, having no real voices of their own, had stolen their voices from human beings, just as they had stolen the images of tortured children which dotted their shells.

"There," croaked Yang weakly. "We showed you. Now let us go."

The Handmaiden holding her squeezed. Yang let out a sound that was more strangled cough than scream.

"We had a deal," she whispered.

The lead Handmaiden ignored Yang. "You're Prudence Murray," she said.

"I'm the *kaatbari*," Prudence acknowledged.

"We know your mother."

"My mum is coming to get me."

The three Handmaidens shifted, piton feet stamping loudly on the pavement. Was that excitement? Was it fear?

"I am *Shara'naak Kye*," said the Handmaiden before her. "I am one of nine sisters. There were once twelve of us."

"I know who you are," said Prudence. "You don't like my mum, do you?"

"We have been sent to collect you."

"You've come to take ownership of me, as a trophy, a plaything."

Shara'naak Kye tilted, a questioning stance.

"That's what *Yoth-Kreylah ap Shallas* told me. That's what's written in the Bloody Big Book."

"And are you afraid of us?" said the Handmaiden.

"Do you want me to be?" asked Prudence.

The baby face nearest Prudence rolled away to be replaced by another, this one of gasping and breathless horror. "You're not important. We want vengeance and our rightful place in the order to come. You are just a token."

"A trophy," said Prudence.

A claw came round. Prudence automatically tried to push it away. It made no difference. The two concave halves slipped around her and closed in. The stubby teeth of the claw gripped her stomach, squeezing to the point of pain, but no further. Prudence put her hands on the claw edge. The shell was cold, no sense of life within. Yet there was a sense of restrained power, the notion she could be crushed in an instant.

Shara'naak Kye lifted her off the ground and set off. The other two followed. Yang mewled in pain, half unconscious. The August Handmaidens of *Prein* moved at a startling pace. Their legs clicked and flowed over road and verges and even vehicles, always keeping their huge bodies balanced and aloft, pale boats on a sea of legs.

04:01AM

Nina picked her way along the tracks towards the strange obstruction. The railway was at a point where it ran a considerable height above the surrounding buildings, and it gave a decent view of the city. To the left, the city was flame and ruin. The motorway was a dancing and twisted ribbon of concrete and tarmac. The spinning vortex of fire over Villa Park stadium had shifted and expanded.

To the right of the track several titanic god-things had already gathered close to the city centre. Picked out by the sort-of-but-not-quite purple light in the sky above, she saw an obese mountain of a creature tossing buildings into the air. Several miles away, tornados clustered together like talons driven into the earth. Even further off, an elongated humanoid giant stood, surrounded by its children, all of them so tall their upper portions were lost in the clouds.

Nearer to, down a steep grassy embankment, Nina saw a large compound, surrounded by high metal railings and filled with cargo containers. She realised it was the Dumping Ground: the consular mission's large scale facility for storing Venislarn substances and by-products. That might explain the strange thing on the track. If a truck-sized turd had come from anywhere, the Dumping Ground was a fair candidate.

"But how did it get out here?" she said to herself.

As she played her torch over its rough, glistening surface it rippled. A row of four eyes opened in its side and rolled around as they sought her out. The thing bellowed from a flabby lipless mouth, trying to stand on feet that were somewhere under the fat wobbling bulk of its body.

"What da *bhul* is that, man?" Pupfish had appeared behind her. His pistol was drawn but aimed down.

"Herd-beast of *Nystar*, I think," said Nina. "Never seen one before. They're kept as sacrificial offerings to the gods of *Leng*. No idea what it's doing out here."

"*Ggh!* That's one ugly mofo, fasho."

The herd-beast bellowed again. It sounded like a lorry in a tunnel, revving its engine and blasting its horn.

"Do not upset the massive cow thing," said Nina. She looked down the embankment to the road beside the Dumping Ground.

"We're in Nechells, very near the city. We could get off here and walk the rest of the way."

"Donkeys can jump, can they?" Pupfish asked.

Nina considered how high up the doors were when there was no platform. She peered back up the line. "We get Karl to reverse the train so a door lines up with the bridge back there. If we use that yellow ramp, I reckon we can get the donkeys onto the brickwork, and they'll find a way down the side."

"I prefer to stay on the train. *Ggh!* It feels safer."

She waved a torch at the herd-beast. "We can't move that. It'll derail the train if it wants to."

"Nina man, I don't like walkin', I'm a film star now," he said, but dutifully went back to the train to begin unloading.

. . .

WHOLE STREETS AFLAME. Corpses arranged as art installations or summoning circles. Humans, animals, plant life and buildings fused together in new and startling forms. All these flew past and were gone as soon as Prudence glimpsed them.

Prudence, grunting as she propped herself up to alleviate the pain of *Shara'naak*'s grip, pushed aside her windblown hair and looked around, trying to spot stars beyond the rooftops and the trees. The sky was deep purple and grey. There were clouds, but no stars.

The August Handmaidens of *Prein* slowed on a wide avenue, lined by houses on one side and broad green space on the other. As they came to a halt, Prudence realised the breeze around her was not just from the speed of their travel. Sharp, blustery winds whipped around them. The faceless Handmaidens seemed to be looking ahead. In the dark sky there were flying fragments of tile and brickwork, and a distant groaning of buildings being torn apart.

"*Yam Schro dat Kaxeos, feschaq bet mye'kha,*" said one of the Handmaidens.

"What's happening?" said Prudence.

"*Chand'a. Ven-se rghn Kaxeos,*" said another.

The Handmaidens moved from the road, through a grand gateway which looked as if it belonged in front of a stately home, but led onto a park area in the shadow of several tower blocks.

Shara'naak Kye dumped Prudence beside a curving, slightly-fish-shaped concrete sculpture. "Stay here."

"What's happening?" asked Prudence.

The Handmaiden half turned away, then reconsidered. "The Balti Triangle blocks our route. The Winds of *Kaxeos* are trying to excavate their buried master. We wait."

Yang and Ayesha were deposited beside Prudence. Yang was dropped carelessly onto the sculpture. Her face slapped bloodily off the surface and she slid, moaning, to the ground. Ayesha collapsed as she was dropped and lay still.

The August Handmaidens stood in a loose formation around them. As much as Prudence could judge anything, she thought they were watching the sky and the destructive forces of the nearby winds.

Prudence crawled over to Ayesha to check on her. The mammonite girl's eyes were closed, her hand limp and clammy. Prudence didn't think she was breathing. She went to Yang who lay equally still. She put a hand to Yang's cheek and whispered over her shoulder to Steve. "How do you tell if someone's still alive?"

"Bite it and see if it screams," Steve whispered back.

"Touch me and I'll kill you," murmured Yang.

"Okay," said Prudence.

There was a large bleeding bruise on Yang's face, covering one eye and her cheek. Her blazer had been ripped open by a Handmaiden claw. Her school badge flopped down and hung by a single thread. Prudence wished there was something she could do, a dressing she could press to the wound, a pillow she could make, but he had nothing to offer.

"You're going to be okay," she said and stroked Yang's hair.

"I object to the insinuation that I'm not," said Yang.

"Ayesha—" Prudence glanced at the other girl.

"Is she dead?"

"I think so."

Yang slowly pushed herself up into a seated position, wincing at a new pain. She prodded Ayesha's body with her foot. Ayesha rocked but did not stir. "Good."

"Good?"

"She would have been a threat to me one day."

The fringes of tornadoes ripped the tops off trees. Violent

winds whipped cladding and broke windows in the topmost floors of the tower blocks.

"And why are you hiding?" Prudence whispered to Steve.

"Steve the Destroyer never hides," he answered. "I'm utilising appropriate camouflage."

"These are the *Prein*. I thought they were your people."

"Were!" he hissed. "We are not ... in accord at this time."

"Did you do something to upset them?"

Steve scrambled around in the space beneath Prudence's T-shirt. "It's not something I did. A *Skandex* paladin, a brother, took objection to my current form. The *Prein* do not accept weakness, and definitely not squidgy, fluffy, cuddly forms like this."

"They're bullies," said Prudence.

"They are not! They just punish those who they judge to be lesser than them."

"I think that's the same thing."

Yang shrugged, wincing at the pain it caused. "Bullies are just visionaries with poor PR."

There was a screeching wrench and a large dark form came bouncing end over end across the grass towards them. The August Handmaidens of *Prein* adopted defensive stances. Prudence wondered what wild, crazily spinning Venislarn this might be, carried on the powerful winds. A Handmaiden slashed at it, but it bounced up and right over them, wobbling towards the road.

"Trampoline," said Yang.

Prudence shuffled back against the protective shelter of the sculpture. It had initially appeared fish-like but now, Prudence could not say what it was meant to represent. It was twice as long as she was tall, and twice as high as her when she crouched next to it. The bulbous 'head' end of it was a hollow cylinder of concrete, and the eye opening stretched out backwards along the thing's scoop-shaped 'tail'.

"I do not like waiting," said one of the Handmaidens of *Prein*. "We should kill the humans and move on."

"We have orders," replied *Shara'naak Kye*. "We're not to kill the *kaatbari*."

"Why? What does *Morgantus* want it for? To be his sport, not ours?"

The third one turned and pointed at the night sky. Three sharp points of light were approaching from afar, moving at speed.

"There are plots," said the Handmaiden. "Plots within plots."

PUPFISH LED a train of donkeys in a zig-zag down the grassy embankment next to the bridge. The donkeys were surefooted and unhurried. Several paused to nibble the grass en route. Pupfish didn't seem to mind. He held onto Donk's bridle for support as much as anything and focussed on not slipping.

While he dealt with the donkeys, Nina stood beside the cab of the train and discussed the situation with Karl.

"You saying we shouldn't get off here?" he said.

Nina slowly shook her head. "I don't know what's for the best," she said honestly. "The beast of *Nystar* might move and you could carry on. But the city centre..." She gazed into the night. "It looks as fucked up as everywhere else."

What could they do? An honest answer might be to seek a swift death. Trying ramming the herd-beast at seventy miles an hour, or setting the train in motion and lying on the tracks. Nina wasn't in the mood to give out that kind of advice. "Back up the track as far as you can. Find somewhere to hide."

"For how long?"

"Until it's all over," she said.

"And how long will that be, eh?"

Nina had no answer for that. Then she spotted the three lights in the night sky. They weren't large, but they were clear, and there was something about the speed and the directness in which they were approaching that fixed her attention on them.

"Not long at all," she whispered.

Nina didn't feel fear at the sight of the nuclear missiles, but she was torn by a sudden and powerful yearning to be with her parents, or with Ricky. With anyone.

She grabbed Karl's hand.

There was light without sound. Sunlight, an all-encompassing sun, exploded across the city.

CARCOSA

"Oh, no," said Rod, seeing what was coming up. In a smoky alchemist's laboratory, the haughty but shapely Kathy character was being held against her will by some nebulous spirit. The warrior, Rod, had entered from the wings to rescue her. Rod did not listen to the speechifying dialogue. He knew what was coming and he had zero desire to see it recreated on stage.

"I'm going," he said, standing.

The King in Crimson gripped his wrist. "No. You do not leave yet. You must wait for your cue."

"Cue?"

"Sit."

Rod sat but kept his gaze away from the stage.

"What I did—" he began. "When I had sex with Kathy, that was purely professional. And I don't take kindly on people snooping on my ... bedroom antics and turning them into an all-singing, all-dancing stage production."

The King in Crimson flinched. "No, I have never been satisfied with this character."

"Who? Me?"

The ravaged King threw a contemptuous hand at the stage. "This man. Who is he? What is he?"

"Well, it's me, isn't it?" said Rod.

"The man is a trained killer, resourceful and experienced—"

"Aye?"

"—and yet socially he is lacking confidence. As bumbling and as innocent as a schoolboy. He is a contradiction, and an unsatisfying one at that."

"I'm not bumbling," said Rod. "And I'm definitely not innocent."

The King waved his comment away. "You're just trying to make me feel better. This one is no better."

Rod risked a peek at the stage. The alchemy workshop was gone, along with the embarrassing lovers, and now the Nina character was prancing about the stage with a threadbare hobby horse between her legs.

"I'm losing track," admitted Rod. "Is this Nina in the past?"

"This character," said the King. "She is part *ingénue*, part *fille fatale*."

"I'm not particularly *au fait* with French," said Rod.

"She constantly announces her sexual experiences, but is otherwise ignorant. Yet here – in this adventure – her competence and intelligence know no bounds."

Nina in Georgian England, identified by a rakish cavalier's hat, bamboozled various stuffed shirt characters with a blank verse commentary that Rod could not follow at all.

"You are aware that she, Nina, is a real person?" he said.

The King in Crimson shrugged. "The play invites us to view all of these characters as simultaneously real and fictional."

The play progressed. Rod was no longer sure how much time he had spent in the theatre. Scenes galloped from one to the next with baffling speed. The ingenuity of the scene changes and physical effects, however cheap they might have been, however much the ropes and the beams creaked with each rising or falling backdrop, kept his attention.

The red-haired actress now flitted between two roles, mother and daughter.

"Our budget is not inexhaustible," the King in Crimson commented.

The Nina character sang and danced through a chorus of horse-headed mimes. Rod recalled the magician character in the very first scene. A papier-mâché fish man tumbled like a fool in amongst the animals.

"It borders on the incomprehensible, doesn't it?" said the King.

"This didn't happen, surely?" said Rod.

"Happening now, eternally happening," said the King in Crimson.

The dance routine came to a sudden and abrupt ending. There were drum rolls from the orchestra pit, thunder crashes from above and magnesium-bright lights flared.

Rod stood, as though height could give him clearer understanding. "Is that—?"

Nina, the fishboy and the horses fell as the ever-brightening light consumed them and the curtain fell.

"Was that a nuclear explosion?" said Rod. "Is that ... is that what happened?"

The King in Crimson patted his arm. "It's good to end on a cliff-hanger," he said, and when Rod looked at him, added, "Do not worry. It is only the end of the first act."

PART II

04:16AM

Abruptly, the sky over the park where the Handmaidens had stopped turned a searing white. Prudence lowered her gaze to protect her eyes. Night had vanished. The light made stark shadows. Prudence saw her hand as a black silhouette against bright green grass.

"Is this day?" said Prudence.

"No," whispered Yang. "It's— I think it's a nuclear explosion but ... they've stopped it somehow."

The initial brilliance dimmed fractionally.

"Humans," said Yang contemptuously. "Attempting to destroy everything, just because they were losing."

Prudence noticed that where Yang had fallen against the sculpture, blood was smeared across its rough surface. As she watched, the blood seeped, quite purposefully, into the cracks and pores. Prudence put her hand on it and felt a tingling run across her flesh: thousands of microscopic incisions. She pulled away. "It's a Bridgeman sculpture."

"What's that?" said Yang.

"It drinks blood and..." She looked at the way the fish-like form was fixed to the ground by a concrete foot. She leaned close to it. "Can you move?"

In the dark, she felt along the sculpture for signs of movement, and felt a rippling tension pass through the concrete form.

"What is it?" said Yang.

Prudence pursed her lips and thought. Despite not particularly liking where her thoughts took her, she said to Yang, "Bring Ayesha over here."

"Why?"

Prudence crawled over and tried hauling Ayesha along the ground by her shoulder. She had no success until Yang joined in. Together they dragged her the short distance to the sculpture. Prudence took Ayesha's hand and, with a silent apology to the dead girl, placed it on the sculpture's skin. It held automatically.

Yang shook her head, frowning.

"Feeding it," said Prudence.

"A human ploy to kill us has failed," said one of the Handmaidens. "We should question the *kaatbari* and find out what she knows. Something that is useful to our cause."

"*Yo Morgantus* will see us rewarded," said *Shara'naak Kye*. "We will have vengeance."

"We should avenge our lost sisters now," said the dissatisfied Handmaiden. "Kill them and then join the fray."

"We have instructions. And a promise that our honour will be restored," said *Shara'naak Kye*.

The Handmaidens were watching the fiery glare overhead and the violent storm beyond it. They were paying no attention to their prisoners. Ayesha's body throbbed as the Bridgeman fish sculpture drank from her. In the new light, the dead blonde girl was pale, colourless. Prudence didn't know if this was because her blood was being drained, or if it was something that happened to all dead people.

"Get on," Prudence said to Yang.

Yang frowned again, then blinked, struggling to keep her injured eye open.

"Get on," insisted Prudence.

"You won't escape them," whispered Steve.

"Whose side are you on?"

"I am merely stating facts, child."

"Let someone else come collect this prize so we may be about our slaughter," said a Handmaiden. Prudence looked up to see if the creature had turned to face them. Apparently not.

"And let them get all the praise and glory from *Yo Morgantus* for doing so?" said another.

"No," said *Shara'naak Kye*. "We obey *Yo Morgantus* until the Fortress of *Hath-No* brings the armies of the blind gods and we can—"

Something powerful struck the tower block opposite. A whole corner, a wedge of glass and stone, sheared away and exploded on the road below.

Prudence pushed Yang into the broad eyehole of the sculpture and climbed onto the scoop tail behind her.

"What do you expect this to do?" Yang hissed. "It's not a motorbike!"

"What's a motorbike?" said Prudence. She leaned in close, felt the sculpted creature's uncountable tiny bites tickle her skin. "Get us out of here. Please," she whispered.

The creature shivered but did not move. How long had it been standing here? How long had it been dormant, forgetting that it was anything other than a statue?

"Please," she repeated.

A Handmaiden turned. "What are you doing?" she asked. "Are you trying to hide?"

Shara'naak Kye turned. "Are they playing?"

Prudence and put her forehead on the fish's curved top. "Please!"

"I believe—" said the first Handmaiden. Her words were lost as the Bridgeman fish shot forward, whipping the Handmaiden's legs out from under her. There was a violent crack and crunch of concrete against shell, and a spray of something cold and wet that Prudence viciously hoped was Handmaiden blood. Yang screamed – not in fear or elation or surprise – just screamed.

04:18AM

It had taken Nina longer than was perhaps necessary to work out they weren't going to be vaporised by a nuclear fireball. There was a new smell in the air, the charred dust smell of an electric heater that had been unused for a while.

Karl had taken the train, empty now but for his two female passengers and the mess the donkeys had left behind, and reversed up the track. There was nowhere for them to go. Sutton Coldfield, beyond the motorway and the barrier, was gone. Maybe they would find a tunnel, maybe find somewhere to hide.

The thin, wrong light illuminated the area around them. It did not look good. Nina had helped Pupfish get the line of donkeys hurriedly down the slope and out of sight. The donkeys didn't share her sense of urgency. Either they were too stupid to be frightened of magically thwarted nuclear explosions and Venislarn shit, or they were just badass quadrupeds.

Down on the narrow lane, with the steep railway verge on one side and the high railings of the consular mission's Dumping Ground on the other, Nina and the rear of the donkey line caught up with Pupfish.

"We're *bhul-detar*, ain't we?" he said.

"Why'd you say that?"

"*Ggh!* The look on your face."

Nina didn't realise she'd been frowning. She stopped. "Nah. I was just wondering if badass, you know, the word 'badass', had anything to do with these animals being bad asses. They act kinda badass."

Pupfish was shaking his head dismissively. "Donkeys ain't asses."

"Aren't they?"

"Asses are horse, bro."

"Are they?"

"Aren't they?"

She realised they had slipped into conversational territory where neither of them had an answer. She'd have googled it, but there was no phone signal and no internet. No internet. The world had already gone to hell. And, if Rod and Vivian hadn't been lying, this was how the world used to be *all the time*. It was no wonder that underage drinking used to be so popular.

"Anyway, yes," she said.

"Yes what?" said Pupfish.

"We're *bhul-detar*. The situation's fubar, as Rod would say." She pointed up at the railway track. "That herd-beast of *Nystar* up there wasn't just blocking the way randomly." Her pointing finger swung round to the Dumping Ground. "When the nukes blew, I saw movement in there. Priests of *Nystar*."

Frowning with fish eyes on the side of his head and no eyebrows wasn't easy, but Pupfish managed a curious head tilt like an intelligent dog who had just heard the phone ring. "Priests of *Nystar*. *Ggh!* We met those evil *pabbe-grru shaska* in that nightclub."

"And they dragged you and your girl into *Leng*-space. Right."

"I owe them bitches some payback."

"Maybe another time. We've got twenty-eight donkeys to get back to the consular mission. Obviously, we should give this place a wide berth, except—" She pointed ahead. A mash of articulated lorries – three or four, it was hard to tell – blocked the end of the road, sealing the space between the elevated railway and the consular mission's storage compound. "—we're going through the Dumping Ground."

Whatever crazy force had destroyed those lorries had also ripped through a section of the fencing, and a wall of containers shielding the place from prying eyes.

Nina and Pupfish walked together with the lead donkey, Donk. The train of twenty-eight beasts of burden produced a constant soundtrack of grunts, snorts, and the very occasional bray of alarm. Nina would have preferred them to be quieter, but these seemed to be untrained donkeys and didn't know any command words at all. The ever-present howls and shrieks of a city being torn apart masked the noise a little.

At least Donk was a biddable leader. His long, hairy ears flicked and twitched as they moved down the road to the gap in the high steel fence. Nina shifted her grip on his bridle, sniffed her fingers, and wiped them on her long Georgian coat. "I stink of donkey."

"I can't tell," said Pupfish.

"Cos fish don't have noses."

"*Ggh!* That's racist, girl. I mean everything stinks of donkey. And fire."

She nodded. "When this is over, I am going to lie in the deepest, hottest bath for a week. And then it's Nando's, Pizza Hut and Maccy D's every night."

"In the bath?"

"In the bath. And then clothes shopping."

"Because you'll have put on fifty pounds."

Nina ran a hand down her side. "Lean, mean, calorie burning machine, this. What will you do?"

Pupfish's gill-gasp was a scoff of disbelief. "You think this will ever be over?"

"You've got to believe it," she said, and found herself immediately, unexpectedly and unhelpfully thinking of Ricky Lee: images of his crushed body sliding away down a twisting road. She didn't wipe the sudden tears from her eyes, partly because she didn't want to acknowledge them, partly because she didn't want to get donkey stink in her eyes.

"Nando's sounds good," said Pupfish. "Allana and me. Nando's. Extra hot on the Peri-ometer. *Ggh!* Bottomless soft drinks."

Nina nodded approvingly. "God, I'm hungry."

Pupfish dug into his baseball jacket pocket and held out something to Nina. "Chupa chups? My emergency stash. They might've got wet in the canal."

She unwrapped the head of the sticky lolly sweet with her teeth. The head had part-melted against the wrapper, but she tore it away and jammed the lolly in her mouth. Pupfish unwrapped one for himself.

"Started buying them for Fluke and me – *ggh!* – when he tried to give up smoking," he said.

"You never smoked."

"Solidarity with a brother," he said. "Even if he is banging my mom."

"Yeah. That *muda* ain't right."

They slowed at the ripped entrance to the Dumping Ground. Nina tied Donk to a railing and beckoned Pupfish through to scope the way ahead.

The Dumping Ground (or the Venislarn Material Reclamation Centre to give it its correct name) occupied a large plot of land in an unlovely industrial corner of Birmingham, a mile out of the city centre. Placed conveniently near a railway junction, it openly operated as a cargo containment facility. The only thing the consular mission had to hide was the contents of those containers. Nina climbed crab-wise over the smashed fence and the loops of razor wire which had been torn free, and moved through the alley between two stacks of containers. As she came to the opening into the main yard, she crouched.

"*Ggh!* That's some crazy stackin', man," said Pupfish.

Nina rolled the lolly in her mouth and sucked thoughtfully.

The centre of the Dumping Ground contained an open area of dirt and weathered concrete, dotted with a small number of containers. There was probably some operational reason for this spacing. Nina imagined it was possibly because the contents of some containers didn't react well to being next to others. The Venislarn, even their dribblings, secretions and other waste materials, could be tetchy about personal space. There were lights on in the office cabin, and a big yellow straddling crane was trundling about with a container slung beneath it. There was a human at the controls. It would have to be a human; the Priests of *Nystar* were too massive to fit in the cab and they'd only mash the controls with their tentacles or sharp hoofs. Nina gave the human only a moment's thought. Collaborator, slave or mind-controlled zombie, people were just doing what they could to survive now.

The crane was moving the container over to a circle of others which had been put into place recently. Nina could tell they had been recently moved because, on an ordinary day, no one would stack containers like that. A number of them had been placed on end, in a circle, and others were placed horizontally, on top of and between upright pairs, to create square archways.

"Reminds me of that thing," said Pupfish.

"Jenga?"

"I was gonna – *ggh!* – say Stonehenge."

Priests of *Nystar* stomped around in their weird ceremonial circle. In the stretched dusky light, their skin shimmered red and green, the colour of rotten meat. Their hoofs (or were they toenails? Nina could never be sure) dug at the earth as they spun and sang. It was definitely singing, even though it was about as tuneful as modern jazz. The masses of tentacles springing from the place where sane creatures would keep their heads swayed in time with the chanting.

"Are they doing some – *ggh!* – sort of ritual or something?" said Pupfish.

Nina listened to the words. "*Ouka ha'ya phik-no...* 'It is time. It is time. Is it the time? Yes, it is the time.' I think it's more of a pre-match warm up."

"And the main event...?"

"Won't be good. There's the main entrance over there. We've got to sneak round—"

"With twenty-eight donkeys."

"—with twenty-eight donkeys, and out that gate. If they're busy with their ritual, it might be doable."

"I can sneak." Pupfish gave a small throaty chuckle. "This reminds me of a film I did."

"You've only done one Hollywood film."

"I mean from my old days."

Nina gave him a frank look. Pupfish's earlier movie output had been of the decidedly top shelf DVD variety, catering to a very niche audience of those people who wanted to see fish-on-woman action. "I don't see how this could remind you of any sort of porn film."

"It was a remake of this really old film, *Die Hard*."

"A porn version?"

"Yeah."

"*Dick Hard*?"

"It was called *This Guy's Hard*."

"My title was better."

"And my character, Dong McLayin'—"

"Jeez."

"—had to sneak through this building swarming with sexy lesbian terrorists who were – *ggh!* – gagging for a bit of *samakha* dick."

Nina wanted to ask why lesbians would be gagging for dick, but there was only so much time before the world truly ended, and they were getting way off topic.

"Do you have a particular plan in mind?" she asked. "And can I check, cos this is important, does it involve you getting your fishy tackle out?"

04:20AM

Prudence clung on as the Bridgeman fish skimmed the grass of the parkland at a speed faster than any person could run. She clung to the fish's head and peered over the side. She could not tell if it was propelling itself on its one foot or really flying. The fish hopped over the low rail separating grassy park from the road. Prudence whooped at the momentary weightlessness. Yang, clinging desperately, fell back against Prudence's legs.

"This is madness!" yelled Steve, who had clambered up through Prudence's T-shirt neck onto her shoulder.

"It's amazing!" Prudence yelled back against the wind.

The fish swerved and swam along the road at the park's edge.

"I should steer the rock creature! I should be in charge!"

"No one's steering!" shouted Prudence, filled with a strange and misplaced joy.

Two Handmaidens scuttled at furious speed out of the park on a course that would intercept theirs. Yang shouted and pointed.

"I see them!" said Prudence. She leaned against the Bridgeman fish with no understanding of how to steer this creature, apart from asking. "Watch out," she told it urgently. "Get away from them."

A Handmaiden clambered over a parked car and into the road to block their path. The Bridgeman fish swerved. Prudence pressed herself against it to hold on. The fish's base collided with the Handmaiden, squashing her against the side of the car before bouncing off and away. Yang gave a high squeal as her leg slipped outside of the fish's eye. She grabbed Prudence's legs and hauled herself back in.

"You're going to kill us!" Yang yelled.

"We've got to get away!" she shouted in reply. "Are they following us, Steve?"

Steve shifted and wriggled. "You have too much hair, unruly child! I cannot see!" He pawed and tugged at her hair as he tried to push it aside.

The Bridgeman fish shot out of a narrow drive, across a large traffic island and down the grassy central reservation of a dual-lane road that ran beside a petrol station with a brightly lit forecourt.

Steve slapped Prudence's cheek. "Go faster! Go faster! She is almost upon us!"

Prudence looked round. "Where?"

The Bridgeman fish tilted back abruptly as something – a claw tip no doubt – grabbed the end of the scooped tail and forced it down. The fish wobbled and tilted.

"No! No!" shouted Yang. Her voice was whipped away as she tumbled out onto the ground.

Pushed down further, the fishtail dug into the ground and ploughed a noisy juddering furrow in the turf. It swung side to side, each turn over-compensating for the last, until the Bridgeman fish passed beyond a point of equilibrium and tipped over. Prudence flew out. She managed to land on one foot before spilling forward and rolling.

A distance ahead the fish's nose dug into the earth. It bounced up, spinning end over end, before landing again with a dull and final thump.

Prudence groaned and coughed. There was a broad deep ache in her thigh. She rolled over and realised it was the grenade in her pocket sticking into her. She pulled it out of her twisted shorts and tried to get her breath back.

"Steve?" she called, realising he was no longer with her.

She looked round and saw the Handmaiden of *Prein* just before they collided. The Handmaiden rolled and nearly trampled Prudence before grabbing her by the arm and hoisting her up.

"You are a tiresome pinprick like your mother," said the Handmaiden. The voice was precise and calm and far too human, but there was an evident rage in her restless stance. "We should have killed you when we first saw you."

There was no sign of *Shara'naak Kye* or the other Handmaiden.

"You can't kill me because I'm the *kaatbari*," said Prudence.

"Really?" said the Handmaiden, squeezing with the powerful claw. "What can you do to stop me?"

Prudence battered at the shell with the grenade she was holding. She whacked the screwed-up, bawling baby face before her. The grenade made pathetic *tink tink* noises against the thick bone-white shell. The Handmaiden rocked and turned. Prudence's next strike rammed the grenade between carapace and the shoulder plate of a leg. As she pulled away, Prudence lost her grip on it.

"The pin! Pull the little pin!" screeched Steve, somewhere on the ground below her.

"What?" said Prudence, then saw the dangling ring of metal jutting from the little cannister.

As Prudence reached, the Handmaiden belatedly moved her out of reach. Prudence came away with the little ring and attached pin in her fingers.

"No!" said the Handmaiden and immediately dropped Prudence, using both claws in an attempt to reach the grenade jammed in her shell. The Handmaiden struggled and twisted, plates shifting, as she tried to reach the awkward spot. As one movement opened up a gap, a shiny metal lever pinged away from the grenade. The Handmaiden froze for a second, then her struggles became more frantic. She spun and turned and danced, feet stomping, chasing a point on herself she couldn't quite reach—

The grenade exploded in fizzing white light. The Handmaiden continued to gyrate in a frenzy. There was a high-pitched squeal. At first Prudence, blinded by light and wheeling images, thought it was the Handmaiden screaming. It wasn't. It was the hiss of steam as the Handmaiden cooked and her blood boiled.

When she had presence of mind, Prudence scrambled to her hands and knees and fled. She saw Steve the Destroyer running towards her and scooped him up.

"We are victorious!" he crowed.

Yang was on the ground, lying in the groove ploughed into the ground by the crashing fish.

"You okay?" said Prudence.

"I could sue," Yang mumbled.

"I really don't know what that means."

Yang held out her hand. Prudence grabbed it and pulled the mammonite girl to her feet.

"She's not dead," said Steve.

For an instant, Prudence thought he was talking about Yang, but he was tugging Prudence's hair so she looked round. The Handmaiden was hauling herself towards them, the legs of one side clawing the earth, pulling her along and dragging brittle, black and smoking limbs behind her. Even crippled, she moved at a lick.

"Not dead," agreed Prudence, ready to flee.

Gunfire flashed in the night, a constellation of flaring lights. The Handmaiden slumped sideways as her shell cracked and shattered. A few more wounded steps and she keeled over completely.

Men and women approached, stepping into the light cast from the petrol station forecourt. They wore grey and white combat fatigues and carried assault rifles not unlike the ones the mammonites had used.

"The soldiers again," Prudence said. "We have to go."

As they began to move off, a voice shouted. "We're not going to hurt you!"

Prudence wasn't prepared to take such things on trust. As they began to run, she immediately came up against two more of them, approaching from the other direction. A tall man slung his gun behind his back and held out his hands, open-palmed.

"It's okay," he said. "We're here to help." He must have seen the doubt on her face. He grinned. "We're not regular army troops. We're the good guys."

There was a stutter of gunfire as the soldiers shot the Handmaiden again. Prudence jumped at the sound.

The tall man made a gentle shushing sound. "I'm Captain Malcolm McKenna with Forward Company." He looked at Yang and the bleeding bruise that covered one half of her face. "You okay, kiddo? You don't look so good. You come with us. We'll look at that. Get you some food."

"The other soldiers…" said Prudence.

Captain Malcolm shook his head. "We're not with them. We're not like them." He tapped his assault rifle. "We've got the ammo to kill these Venislarn monsters. You're safe with us. What are your names?"

"Prudence," said Prudence.

"Yang," said Yang warily.

"Sir!" shouted a man ahead. "Got some sort of animated concrete thing here! I think it's wounded."

"Deal with it!" Captain Malcolm called back. There was a bout of sustained gunfire. "See?" he said. "We're the good guys."

Forward Company had a van parked on the far side of the abandoned petrol station. Prudence and Yang were instructed to hop in and sit on the benches nearest the driver's seat. A soldier climbed in after them and took down a medical pack from among the racks holding weapons, ammo and armour.

"Let's take a look at you, then," he said and began to clean the cuts on Yang's face.

Prudence suspected, even feared, that Yang's injured face was the only thing preventing them denouncing her as a Venislarn monster and shooting her at once. The cuts and the bruise drew the eye away from the fractionally, but disturbingly uneven quality of her features. Her bad symmetry was no symmetry at all with a great purple welt running down it.

He carefully removed her blazer to check her shoulder. Her shirt was ripped but nothing more.

He taped a dressing to her forehead. "The rest of it you'll just have to be careful with," he said. "Okay? Anything else I can get you?"

Yang pointed to the rack opposite. "The SA80 rifle and two thirty round magazines."

The medic laughed. He looked back at the gun and laughed again.

"She means we're fine, thank you," said Prudence.

The amused but confused soldier shook his head. "We'll get you somewhere safe soon enough. Got a fortified base in the city centre. That's a nice dolly," he said, nodding at Steve clutched in Prudence's hand.

"Play along," said Prudence when the medic had left the van.

"I'm not afraid of him," said Steve.

"And I do not lie," said Yang. "Did he mean I could have the rifle or not? He was unclear."

"They think we're a couple of ordinary girls," said Prudence.

"I am an extraordinary girl," said Yang.

"I could be even more extraordinary if I wanted, gobbet," said Steve.

Prudence sighed heavily. "You're both going to get us killed."

"Let them come," said Yang. She put her blazer aside and inspected a belt on the wall from which a long knife hung in a sheath.

"Or maybe," said Prudence slowly, like she was talking to idiots, "we let them think we're perfectly ordinary girls and get a ride to the city centre. My mum is there."

Yang's fingertips lingered on the knife grip. "I suppose. But I will not lie."

"Then we need to think carefully what we will and won't tell them."

Yang sat down cautiously.

"Am I also to be a perfectly ordinary girl?" said Steve the Destroyer.

"I don't know what you are," said Prudence.

04:29AM

Golden light played over the invisible dome that covered the city. It was like someone had taken the sun and rolled it out to the thickness of pizza dough and draped it over them. The city inside was bathed in a horrible fake daylight. The world beyond was burning. The light didn't seem to be fading at all, as though the nuclear explosions which should have killed them all were merely on pause. It wasn't frozen, though. The light energy swirled and bubbled on the cusp of consuming them all.

"My mum was watching Coronation Street on the day she died," Morag said.

Vivian stood at a counter in the Library lobby a short distance away, flicking backwards and forwards through the Bloody Big Book, annotating and making additions. She was working with a machine-like intensity and didn't look up.

"I am *Yoth-Kreylah ap Shallas*, the living black and white. I am functionally omniscient, or at least was, and know all things. But even I found that utterance meaningless and baffling."

"I was just thinking," said Morag. "When we didn't die just now, I was relieved. I was glad we didn't die."

"Even though—"

"Even though death is definitely the preferred option right now. Yes, yes, of course." Morag shifted her stance. She felt occasional dull tugging sensations in her lower body. She hoped it was her body moving back towards its normal shape after childbirth.

"That's your illogical animal brain," said Vivian. "Only thinking in the short term. Death would have been the preferable option for you."

"I don't think it's illogical," said Morag. "I was thinking of my mum. On the day she died she was in terrible pain. Morphine wasn't even touching it. She knew she was dying. She told me. And yet she decided to watch Coronation Street."

"Certain types seek escape through mindless television soap dramas."

Vivian Grey might try to hide her callous nature behind the excuse she was an honest pragmatist, but there was an audibly vicious glee in the way she said 'types'.

"It wasn't that."

"You're questioning my omniscience?"

"No," said Morag. "I'm telling you you're wrong."

Professor Sheikh Omar, who had been sitting, pale and silent in his wheelchair, gave a snort of laughter.

"There was this storyline," said Morag. "This psycho, Richard something, was brutalising Gail and her family."

"Richard Hillman," said Omar.

"Right. I didn't know you were a Corrie fan."

"One can't help but pick up some titbits if it's on in the room. Maurice finds the northern accents charming, apparently."

"Anyway," said Morag, "you could tell this storyline had some way to go. This guy, Hillman, drove them all into a canal in the end, not that you need me to tell you that, what with your omniscience and that."

Vivian grunted but said nothing.

"But even though she must have known she wasn't going to see the end of that storyline, my mum watched it on the day she died. We have this insatiable desire to see how things turn out. We want to know what happens next."

Vivian apparently had no insights to offer on this and continued her writing. Morag knew the woman had only recently escaped from Hell, but it wouldn't hurt her to join in a bloody conversation. To see that Morag was only talking so much because she was worried. About Prudence, about what the hell she was going to say to *Yo-Morgantus* when she confronted him, about the infinite tortures that still awaited them all.

"You think the world outside this ... this shield is destroyed now?" she said.

"Some of it," said Vivian, still not looking up. "Much of it. Other places will have been preserved."

"This is *Morgantus*'s doing, right?"

"Yes."

"Because you told the August Handmaidens of *Prein* about the missiles?"

Vivian nodded, turned over a billion pages and jotted something in the margins.

"She's got a plan," said Omar. Normally, he might have injected this statement with a sly tone and a darkly playful look, but the professor didn't have the energy. Whatever magical shellfish were working at his chest, his injury was slowly but certainly getting the better of him.

"I simply need to finish the book," Vivian said.

That seemed to be her answer to everything. Morag sighed, but kept the sigh silent; she didn't want Mrs Grey to know she was getting to her. She stepped closer to the door and looked out.

"Are you sure this taxi is coming? I could have walked to the Cube by now."

"Across streets filled with slaughter and fire?" said Vivian. "I think not. The taxi is coming. I am omniscient, you know."

"Really? You've never mentioned that before." It was cheap sarcasm, but the woman was indeed getting to her. From hauling Vivian out of Hell, to jokingly wondering if she could send the damned woman back, had been less than two hours. It took a special kind of person to generate that level of irritation.

"Ontological necessity," said Vivian.

"I beg your pardon?" said Morag. "Did you just swear at me?"

Vivian raised her gaze from her book and looked at Morag. "Your former lover, Cameron Barnes, introduced me to the concept while we were discussing the mysterious appearance of OOParts in the city. He stated that the objects might exist because they had been comprehensively described in the Bloody Big Book, and the describing of them made them real. The cosmologist, Max Tegmark expressed the view that all structures which mathematically exist also exist as physical structures. The complexity of the concept is indistinguishable from the reality."

"Sounds like flimflam to me," said Omar.

Vivian shot him a pointed look.

"Oh, I'm all in favour of flimflammery," he said.

Vivian briefly returned her attention to Morag. "I must write the book because the world exists."

"Not sure that makes sense," said Morag.

Vivian's stillness conveyed the notion that Morag's opinion was as unwanted as it was obvious.

The lifts dinged. For the first time, Morag wondered if the Library had its own backup power systems so the consular mission could keep going after the rest of the world had been plunged into darkness.

Chad from marketing stumbled out. "Ah!" he exclaimed and

tottered over. His jacket was gone and his shirt sleeves rolled up. This usually implied Chad had slipped into total marketing mode; that his mind, hammering away at the coalface of corporate bullshit, had reached some sort of epiphany. "Shouldn't the world have ended by now?" he asked.

"It did," said Vivian. "Over four hours ago. And we have maybe an hour or two before the arrival of *Yoth-Bilau* and the closing of the Soulgate around our world."

"I meant..." He sighed. "Shouldn't we all be blown up? I was delivering my pitch vis-à-vis the apocalypse. I've got some great ideas about remarketing to the disaffected and providing calls to action via micro-influencers. It was an idea blizzard and totally buzz-generating. You should have been there."

"We really shouldn't," said Morag.

"The nuclear missiles didn't kill us," said Vivian. "*Yo-Morgantus* or someone he could call upon put up a protective shield over the city."

The wavering emotions of surprise and elation and fear flickering across Chad's stupid face mirrored how Morag had felt at that moment of non-annihilation.

"We're going to live?" he said.

"And then we're going to hell, young man," said Omar.

"*Yo-Morgantus* doesn't want us all dying before we can become his tortured playthings," said Morag.

Vivian made a mark in her book. "It is impossible for you to comprehend what hell will be like."

"Well, you've been there," said Morag. "Tell us."

Vivian shook her head. "I fell into *Leng*-space and travelled from there to *Hath-No*. We might call those places hell because that's where the gods and demons live. That's hell as mere geography. We are about to experience hell as a state of being."

"Huh?" said Chad.

"We are confined by the limits of our language. 'Hell' is an

English word, one we're making convey far more meaning than it is capable of. Say what one will about the Venislarn, their language has a gift for expression that ours cannot compete with. *Shar'as yon ke-eh-delah.*"

"Amen to that," said Omar.

"I think I attended enough Sunday School to know a little something of hell," said Chad. "Mrs O'Brien painted a powerful mental picture. Now there was a woman who should have had a career in sales."

"Again, language is letting you down," said Vivian. "We use the word 'hell' and you think of it in terms of English translations of the Bible. Hell, Hades, Gehenna, Tartarus. All these words come with cultural baggage—"

"If you're going to turn this into a lecture, I'm going," said Morag.

"You will find this relevant," Vivian said. "My point is, I say 'hell' and Chad here thinks of flames and little imps with pitchforks."

"Mrs O'Brien had this thing for 'beds of fire', actually," he said.

"I say 'Hades' and you think of some vague notion of an ancient Greek underworld, filled with ironic tortures concocted by fantasists with too much imagination and too much time on their hands. The hell of the Venislarn is neither of these things."

"Hell is hell," said Morag.

"The Christian hell, Islamic hell, ancient mythical hells – the thing they all have in common is that they are purposeful. You are being tormented for a reason. And, odd though it seems, that is a comfort in itself. We know full well that we cannot understand the Venislarn. *Yo-Morgantus* and *Yo Daganau-Pysh* and the other temporal rulers of this world are not even true Venislarn gods. They are foot soldiers. They are the first colonists. Things with unknowable names are descending on us right now. They don't care about us. They can't even see us. We are flesh and bone, and whatever mental or spiritual energy we apparently possess. They will not see us, but they will grind us under their metaphorical feet for eternity without even knowing we exist." Her thin chest heaved. "There is no negotiation."

Morag gave Vivian the decency of pretending to consider this for a second or two. "Bollocks," she said.

"Profanity is quite uncalled for."

"It's entirely called for when you're talking bollocks, Vivian. You're saying we should do nothing, because there's nothing that can be done. Out there, our colleagues are trying to do what they can. The world outside the shield *Morgantus* has thrown up might be burned to a crisp. We've not heard from Nina. Or Rod and Maurice. But they're out there."

"Doing what?" Vivian snorted. "It's all in vain."

"Nina went to Sutton Park. If she can manage to bring Mr Grey back here—"

"Ah," said Omar loudly.

Morag frowned at him. There was a pained and uncomfortable look on his face, and it didn't look like it was merely because of his injury.

"What?" said Morag. Then she saw the corresponding look on Vivian's face. Vivian was a woman who generally functioned on a range of minor emotions: disapproval, smug contentment, mild irritation. She made a little emotion go a long way. Right now, she looked absolutely aghast, and cued up behind the pained horror on her face, seething anger was already bubbling through.

"Omar," she whispered. "You told them?"

"Barely anything," he said. "Nina Seth had very much worked it out for herself."

"Nina Seth?" Vivian spat the words. "The girl can barely recall what day it is. You dared to bring my late husband into this."

"Clearly not late," muttered Morag.

"Be quiet, you jabbering Scot!" Vivian snapped. "You mess

with things you do not understand! You think my husband's dangerous and theoretical rituals will do anything more than bring calamity upon us?"

"What? Worse than what's already happening?"

Vivian Grey slammed the Bloody Big Book shut. The slamming of an infinite number of pages produced a dull thump which echoed around the lobby.

"Some things should be left as they are!" Furiously, Vivian gathered the clumsy book under her one arm. "If someone happens to be a donkey, perhaps you should consider they are a donkey for a very good reason!" She exited from behind the counter and strode to the lifts with a "You're all children meddling with things you don't understand!"

Morag watched her get into the lift and the doors closing behind her. "So, she knows her husband's a donkey and doesn't want anything to be done about it?"

"That's the long and the short of it," said Omar. "Vivian's relationship is a complicated affair. But what do I know? I've never understood them."

"Relationships?"

"Donkeys," said Omar.

04:32AM

It took a long ten seconds to convince Donk it was safe to cross over the uneven clanking ruins of the Dumping Grounds fence. Once he was through, the rest followed. He had an inquisitive and watchful manner, definitely a philosopher among donkeys.

"I think this one really might be Mr Grey," said Nina. "You're Mr Grey, aren't you? You can tell me."

Donk snorted and jerked his head.

"That was a nod!" said Nina. "Definitely a nod. You see that?"

"No," said Pupfish. He had ejected the magazine from his pistol to inspect it once more.

"Still only one bullet?"

He sighed noisily and slid the magazine back in. "I don't like going into a hostile situation unarmed."

Nina still had Pupfish's flick knife in her coat pocket, but one knife and a single bullet were hardly sufficient.

They reached the end of the gap in the container wall and looked round the corner at the priests of *Nystar*. The priests' ritual circle of upended cargo containers filled a space fifty metres across. While the main foot-stamping, tentacle-waving action was going on in the centre of that circle, the nearest priest of *Nystar* was only a hop, skip and a jump away from them. The straddle crane finished depositing another container and wheeled around to get another.

"If this was *This Guy's Hard*—" said Pupfish.

"Why don't you just say *Die Hard*?"

"I've not seen the original, man. We don't get to see many films on the Waters. Cable companies don't dare come near – *ggh!* – and I ain't exactly got the kinda face they like to see at the multiplex. If this was *Guy's Hard* then we should use the air vents to sneak around – *ggh!* – steal the detonators and try to alert the cops."

"Okay," said Nina. "One, there are no air vents."

"I'm just sayin'."

"*Two*, we *are* the cops in this situation. I've got a little ID badge and everything. And, three, that is *exactly* the plot from *Die Hard*. I don't know how your dodgy porn version was any different from the original."

Pupfish turned away in disappointed embarrassment. "I'm just, like – *ggh!* – speaking metaphorically and maybe—"

She slapped him on the arm with the back of her hand as an idea struck her. "Course, what we could do is search through some of these containers for stuff to use as weapons. This is the Dumping Ground. Half the stuff here can melt your face or steal your soul."

"That's what I'm *sayin'*, dog. I was in this one scene and I'm doing it with the head terrorist, this girl, Salty Boobstone—"

"The head terrorist was called Salty Boobstone?"

"Nah. The character had some funny German name. The girl, the actress, she was called Salty."

Nina didn't want to be drawn in but couldn't help herself. "No.

No, you've got that wrong. No woman is called Salty, let alone Salty Boobstone. Sally, maybe?"

"Nah. It was her stage name."

"Her porn name?"

"Whatevs."

"No. No woman would willingly have that name." She shook her head in irritation. "I'm going to go find something we can use as a weapon or distraction, then you and I are going to have a proper talk about porn names." She moved off through the shadows of the cargo container wall, but couldn't help muttering a bitter, "Salty Boobstone, indeed!" as she went.

Nina sucked hard on her lolly as she looked at the containers. The consular mission did little to distinguish its cargo containers from those in general circulation. Clandestine movement of goods and materials on the UK rail network would be a hell of a lot less clandestine if all the boxes had big *WARNING! – May contain horrors from beyond our universe!* stickers on the side. Dumping Ground containers were just marked with a three-digit identifier, plus, if you were lucky, a plate with some sort of description.

She passed by a container marked Needles (Lamisal), Casings (Whurrikin) and Shells (Yetsid). On the ground in front of the next container was a human body in a yellow biohazard suit – a Dumping Ground employee. Nina didn't need to check if he was dead; even though she had no medical training, she reckoned a person would struggle to survive without a head or spine. It was clear having *Please do not kill me* on your suit in Venislarn did not guarantee one's safety. Even if it was in a nice jolly font and everything.

The container was marked with the number 655 in big painted numerals, and on the smaller plate, The Tree of Chippenham (Weird). The door was slightly ajar; she slid inside. Maybe the guy had been trying to hide, or maybe, like her, he'd been looking for weapons. Nina knew the branches of the weird tree (apart from weeping blood and driving people mad) made excellent wands. Nina had once been on the receiving end of a wand of *quirz'ir* binding, a gut-punching and sickening experience which nearly knocked the life out of her.

The paltry amount of outside light which trickled inside the container only helped her see for the first few feet, but it was enough to discern the shape of the tree. It had been rammed into the container roots first. The branches, folded in by the sides of the metal box, all pointed towards the door, and Nina was faced with the pokey ends of a hundred gnarly branches, like the rear end of an enormous porcupine.

The tree is *an enormous porcupine.*

The words came into Nina's head not as a voice, but as an insistent thought, measured and authoritative, like a posh stage actor. She was bright enough to recognise it wasn't one of her thoughts.

The branches rippled as though the tree was indeed a porcupine shifting in its sleep.

"Enough of that nonsense," she told it. "I've just come for one branch."

You already took a branch, came the thought. *You took a branch and you don't remember.*

She looked at her hands and could almost imagine having been here before, playing through the exact situation.

You've been here a hundred times.

Nina crossed her arms. "No, I haven't. Stop being silly." She reached out for a thin nobbly branch, one that seemed to have the air of a cool Hogwarts wand about it.

That's not a wand. That's a child's finger.

"Stop it. You're just being annoying now."

You will break the child's finger and cause untold pain.

"Why would a child be in this container?"

You're not really here. You're at home with your children.

"I don't have children."

But you do. You just don't remember.

"Oh, really? Then what are their names?"

Er – Timothy and Lola.

"Shows what you know. My kids will be called Jaxon, Taylor and Tiktok. Seriously, tree? Is this how you're supposed to drive people mad? Just by telling them things that aren't true?"

Maybe this isn't the tree talking. Maybe I'm the voice in your head.

She sniggered. "A voice in my head? Sound like that? I mean, you're not even female."

Maybe you're not female.

"It's pathetic. Stop. You're just crap." She twisted the branch. A foot-long section snapped off drily. "It's embarrassing really. I bet the other trees talk about you behind your back."

They ... they don't.

"All the trees in Chippenham threw a party when you got taken away."

They didn't. I was – I am king among trees!

"Tell yourself that often? Now, shut up. I need to remember an enchantment."

A wand of *quirz'ir* binding was a forceful weapon. Even so, Nina was confident she had the magical know-how to focus and encase the tree's energy. Nina didn't regard herself as any kind of wizard, and she certainly wasn't any kind of academic occultist like Sheikh Omar or Mrs Grey, but she felt she had a certain *knack*. It was like when she was a teenager, trying to copy Maddy Ziegler's dance routines off YouTube – sure, she didn't have all the moves, but the bits she couldn't get right she could sort of finesse so they didn't look totally wrong.

She held the wand loosely across both palms.

You don't know what you're doing.

"Shut it," she hissed. "You had your chance." She closed her eyes as she began her chant. "*Eh hoch in ur'allad bye-zhu…*" It was a good chant. It felt right. "*Bhullos fro a jai'r Katouraz…*"

It felt right, and the biggest part of it feeling right was the chant didn't cause her mind to fragment in a billion screaming shards, or turn her internal organs into her external organs. As she finished, she opened her eyes. The wand was encased in a fading blue nimbus of magic light.

"Score," she said, then realised the whole tree was glowing faintly. "Hey, I only meant to charm this bit of it."

I told you. You don't know what you're doing.

She was about to throw some quality shade at the tree when there was a hollow clang and a tremor ran through the container. Nina glanced up.

"*Muda*. The crane."

It's your imagination – woah!

The tree's mellifluous thought-voice took on a momentary warble of panic as the container shifted and began to rise. Nina bolted for the door, jumped down the three feet (and rising) drop to the ground, and scrambled for cover behind the nearest container as the weird tree was hoisted up by the straddle crane. The crane reversed away with it, the container door flapping.

Nina gripped her new wand and made her way back to Pupfish. The *samakha* actor-turned-donkey-handler raised his pistol as she appeared from the shadows.

"It's me," she said.

He shifted uneasily. "You were gone a while."

"I was arguing with a tree."

He looked at her wand. "Where did you go? Diagon Alley?"

"Says the man who reckons he doesn't get to see regular films."

"I seen *Harry Poked-Her and the Half-Fucked Pricks*."

"Seen it or was in it? Stop. I don't want you ruining my childhood anymore." She held the wand. "This should knock any priests who get in our way sideways."

"Then let's move. *Ggh!* I don't like hanging around."

Donk threw up his head and produced a throaty rasp as though in agreement.

"That's definitely Mr Grey," said Nina. "Probably definitely."

Pupfish and Nina led the donkeys into the maze of cargo containers.

CARCOSA

Just as the interval was ending and the second act of the play about to begin, a tar-like creature oozed up beneath the rows of seats in front of Rod and attempted to eat him. The King in Crimson stamped on it and drove it away.

"Normally, I would permit it, but I'm enjoying your company. What do you think of it, so far?"

On stage, action resumed with Nina, the fishman (Pupfish presumably) and a final horseman (or possibly donkey), fighting and acting their way through an army of tentacled creatures. The creatures were represented by other members of the troop in oversized smocks, waving their long arms about like whips. They shouted indignant gibberish.

"It's nonsense, isn't it?" said Rod.

In amongst the charades and confusion on stage, two more characters had appeared on stage. As Nina and Pupfish moved away, warrior Rod and the mummified King in Crimson sat on chairs, backs to the audience. The other actors slowed into tableau as the on-stage King and Rod launched into fresh speeches. The warrior stood and faced the audience. He shielded his brow with one hand and stared at Rod several rows back.

"Are these counterfeits our own selves, a mirror of this moment?" said the warrior. "'Tis a chasm of shadows, vastness beyond comprehension, yet do I see my own visage?"

The mummified King also stood, and gave the auditorium a cursory glance. "I see naught but shadows."

"Hang on. Is this now?" said Rod. "Is this a representation of now?" He got to his feet. "Are they being us, in this instant, right now?"

Rod shuddered, feeling the inevitability of a nightmare controlling his actions. He turned to look back up the rows of seats behind them. The tiers rose steeply, falling away with an abruptly stretched perspective. The theatre was suddenly too large. The space from the stage to the seats and behind was a rising curve, an exponential line on a graph, a landscape with no horizon.

"Do you see our audience?" said the King in Crimson, amused.

Rod stared as though through a sequence of tarnished mirrors, looking for movement in the gloom above. He saw movement, but could not tell if it was a trick of the light, or the mind, or if there were other figures up there. Other Kings and other Rods, the Rods turning back and gawping upward themselves.

"Thou didst do this to me!" cried the warrior on the stage.

"It is as it is writ," replied the King with him. "The word is penned, the player doth move across the stage. The storyteller's tale is his covenant."

Rod gripped a chair back as his stomach and mind lurched. He was overcome with a strong sense of vertigo, mixed with a vile déjà vu. He had been here before. He could see every instance, stretching away from him like a bottomless pit.

"I feel sick," he said.

"The truth unsettling you?" said the King.

"You did this to me."

The King smiled. "I wrote it so, if that's what you mean."

Rod swung about giddily, drunk.

"There's nothing you can do about it," said the King, smugly. "The word is written. The stage is set. Perhaps this is the major criticism of the piece. From the outset, the tragic destruction of your world – as of mine – is set in stone. It is the one promise the story makes. Your world must go to hell, all human endeavour must fail. In such a story, what is the point of a *hero*—" he spat the word "—such as you?"

Drunk, enraged by his surroundings and the King's mocking words, Rod bunched his fists. The King grinned, chin jutting. Rod felt the tension in himself and the desire to lash out. If all the world was damned then there could at least be some satisfaction in smashing this undead loon's face in.

He hesitated. Enough strength to knock out a god and then his soul would belong to the King in Crimson...

He laughed at himself. He had come so close to sealing the deal.

"What's the point?" he said to the King, shaking his fists out, forcing himself to calm. "I'll tell you. Even now, there's always summat a feller can do, even when there's nowt he can do."

"What will hath a man when his course is fated?" continued the on-stage warrior. "Nay! Even in the face of gods and hell, even in the mouth of madness itself, a man must act, sire."

"What he said," smiled Rod.

The King in Crimson seemed unconcerned. "Then that's your cue."

On stage, the warrior adopted a melodramatic pose and rushed into the wings. Rod pushed past the King and hurried for the exit. He didn't know if he was going to throw up or scream, but whichever it was, he would rather do it in the street.

BIRMINGHAM - 04:45AM

The donkey train halted at a junction of containers. The priests of *Nystar*'s on-going chant was ramping up but, as far as Nina could judge, it was some way off from its final crescendo.

Pupfish looked along the avenues. "What do you reckon?"

Nina twitched her nose as she thought. "I reckon you heard her name wrong. No one is called Salty Boobstone."

He glared at her. Up close in the glowing pre-dawn of Hell-on-Earth, his fish eyes were huge. No one glared like a *samakha*. "*That* is what you're thinking about? *Ggh!*"

"I'm not dying with you thinking some stupid *muda*."

"It was her stage name."

"Porn name. And everyone knows porn names don't work like that."

"Oh? *Ggh!* You know something about the adult entertainment business?"

"Everyone knows your porn name is your first pet and the street you grew up on."

"That's not a thing!"

"That's absolutely a thing!"

"Honey Mayfield. That's mine. A proper porn name."

"I never really had a pet."

"No porn name for you, then."

Nina moved forward. With almost no guidance, Donk followed close behind. They snaked through the yard, always trying to keep at least one row of containers between them and the priests.

"I had a pet *ghadik* crawler for a while," said Pupfish thoughtfully. "Kept it in an old takeaway box with holes punched in the top."

"What was it called?" she said.

"*Damz'ian. Ggh!* So, my porn name should be *Damz'ian Daganau-Vei*?"

Nina gave it some thought and tried to be charitable. "Hardly rolls off the tongue, does it?"

There was a scream behind them, anguished and inhuman. As Nina turned it was joined by more. She realised it was the donkeys.

"*Bhul!*"

The rear end of the train was out of sight around a corner. Like idiots, they had left it unguarded. Now the donkeys at the front were starting to panic.

"Lead them on!" she told Pupfish. "I'll go!"

She pushed her way past swaying and agitated donkeys. Many yanked forward, others backwards, pulling each other about on the line of rope binding them together. The rope went taut and the whole line was dragged to the right. Stumbling beasts slammed into container walls. Nina was momentarily pinned into place by the tight, straining rope.

She crouched and slid under the rope. She jumped between two donkeys just as they were yanked backwards. Whatever had the rear of the train was reeling them in.

She ran to the corner and came onto a scene of savage violence. Priests of Nystar had stumbled upon the rear of the line and, maybe seeking an alternative post-ritual banquet to *Nystar* herd-beast, had leapt upon the rear donkeys. Head tentacles were wrapped around the animals. Slit-belly mouths slobbered and drooled over donkey flanks. The animals just in front of those that had been seized were jerking and yanking in a terrified frenzy to pull away.

And the noise...

Nina closed her mind to the noise. The flick knife was in her hand. The rope nearest to her was pulled so taut that the strands pinged apart like snapped guitar strings as she ran the blade against it. The freed donkeys shot forward, some nearly thrown to the ground. Then, like a runaway rollercoaster they whiplashed round the corner, the hindmost donkey almost flying, screaming as it went.

The priests of *Nystar*, angered by the interruption and the theft of most of their walking buffet, raised their voices in angry song and advanced on Nina. To the average human, the priests would be an utterly terrifying vision but, on a practical level, they really didn't look like a credible threat. Their basic body shape was turnip, the fattest and most ungainly entrants in a giant vegetable parade. They had no eyes – or no apparent sensory organs of any sort – and no hands or claws or whatever. Yes, they had many legs, but they weren't arranged in any meaningful way. Their legs weren't a spider-like circle, or a neat arrangement like a team of horses. They were more like a bunch of abandoned bar stools.

Despite these physical failings, and Nina's rock-solid fearlessness, the sight of several priests of *Nystar* trundling angrily towards her, head-tentacles flailing, compelled her to back away hurriedly. As she reached a corner, she pointed and twisted the wand. There were no magic words of activation – only a moment of mental application. A priest fell back, and a car-sized dent appeared in the container next to it. The wand's blowback nearly snapped Nina's wrist.

"*Nyal-hu amh! Saheek bro amh!*" the priests sang which, roughly translated, meant, 'Why'd you have to come here and spoil everything?'

"*Bhul-zhu, vangru dolot!*" she yelled back, threw another wand bolt at them, and fled.

Nina thought she'd taken the same route as the fleeing donkeys, quickly realising this wasn't the case. She turned into a dead end, doubled back before the priests could trap her and, from that point, took turnings at random. The priestly chanting was a helpful if ominous reminder of how close they were.

Nina slid between two containers that were, she hoped, too close together for the priests to follow and pushed herself into the open. She ran several steps before she realised where she was. Around her, upended containers and cross pieces formed the giant ritual circle of the priests of *Nystar*. More than a dozen of the interdimensional priests stood at key points in the circle. Their tentacles were raised high in quivering religious fervour, and Nina was unhelpfully put in mind of those inflatable wavy-arm dudes outside car showrooms and carpet shops. Spiritually speaking, things were hotting up. If these had been regular human nutjobs, a white-clad minister would already be telling the blind they could see and wheelchair users they could walk. Nina guessed nothing as inoffensively stupid was going on here. At the centre of the circle, she thought she could glimpse a twist in the air, a kink in the fabric of reality. She didn't want to see what was going to come through that.

Priests in the circle were turning to regard her. Behind her, shuffling, grunting and singing indicated the ones behind were trying to get round to flank her.

She raised her hands in greeting. "*San-shu chuman'n, het Nystar. Nehah unurl e'naan.*"

From their body language (if walking monster spheres could be said to have body language), Nina guessed they weren't happy to have someone drop in on their special moment.

"Okay," she said. "I'll come back another time..."

There was an anguished holler and a bang. A bunch of donkeys, set loose from one another, ran across the circle in wild panic. One bounced into a priest of *Nystar*, knocking them both in separate directions. Another ran straight into the space-time wrinkle in the circle centre. There was a noise Nina hoped never to hear again, and a graphic demonstration of what happened when a donkey-sized object leapt into a less-than-donkey-sized hole. The priests roared in outrage and charged at her.

"Ah, fuck it," she spat and ran to the side, blasting with her wand as she went.

The wand was powerful, but the recoil was shocking. A single use sent a shudder through Nina's arm, and she had to use both hands for fear of breaking bones. Nonetheless, when it struck one of the fat priests square, it delivered a body-bruising blow. If there had been a fraction of the number of priests, or an entire squad of wand-waving Ninas, it might have been a fair fight. But there were too many, and she could only manage a limited number of blasts as she sprinted for a way out.

The cargo container Stonehenge seemed to groan in protest, making metal-stressed moans each time she fired at the priests. The sounds were coming from overhead. She looked up at the nearest doorframe arrangement of three containers. The one across the top had the number 655 daubed on its side.

"The tree..."

"*Nyal-hu amh!*" sang an angry priest, closing in. Nina fired. The blast sent it rolling away like a misshapen bowling ball. Above her, the three-part configuration rocked and creaked. She had enchanted the wand but had caught the entire tree in the enchantment.

A wildly stupid but irresistible idea seized her. She retreated under the archway, facing the advancing priests, the tree's container directly overhead.

"I was prepared to live and let live!" she called to them. She put her hand to the side container. It was rough with rust and flaked paint. The priests marched at her. "But you had to go and eat my donkeys!"

Nina waited for them to come closer still. She glanced up at the overhead container. Activating the wand was only a matter of willpower, so she turned her will to the container above her and gave a mental shove. The weird tree of Chippenham in the crosspiece container fired as a single giant wand. Nina heard the doors explode off the container. The sound was immediately eclipsed by the groan of a two-tonne cargo container trying to blast off like a rocket.

The horizontal force propelled it sideways, dragging the upright containers with it. The square archway teetered and began to collapse. Nina ran to get out from underneath. Priests, stubborn or oblivious or both, chased after her, even into the collapsing archway. The falling arch collided with the next container in the circle and slowly but inevitably tipped that one too. Nina retreated further as the containers came down on the priests.

Metal shrieked as more containers fell, but Nina didn't stop to watch. She ran for her life, hoping the priests were sufficiently distracted by the carnage in their ritual circle. She could see the railway embankment beyond one wall of containers and made a simple decision to go in the opposite direction. She stumbled upon the main Dumping Ground exit without plan or expectation, and ran out into the road. There were no priests tailing her, but she heard the continuous screech of buckling containers as they fell.

Pupfish stood in the middle of the road. He had three donkeys with him.

"Three?" said Nina, dismayed.

"Man, what happened – *ggh!* – in there?" he asked. Clouds of dust billowed over the Dumping Ground, thrown up by the cargo catastrophe.

"What happened to the rest of my donkeys?" she demanded, her voice going shrill with anger.

"They got loose, innit," he said. He pointed down the road. In the pale light, Nina could see half a dozen donkeys running away. They moved at a speedy trot, not looking like they were ever going to slow.

"Damn it all, Pupfish," she huffed. She looked at the donkeys they had. "At least we've still got Donk. That's clearly Mr Grey."

She looked at Donk. He looked back at her with a directness and intelligence that surely no donkey could possess. From twenty-eight donkeys down to three.

"Donk, Dink and—" She waved her hand over the third donkey.

"Duncan," said Pupfish.

"Yeah. Sure. Donk, Dink and Duncan."

Nina took one last look back at the Dumping Ground and then stowed her wand by slotting it through one of the buttonholes of her coat. She turned to the road ahead and the uncertain journey back to the city centre and the Library.

04:51AM

Morag paced the Library lobby. This wasn't entirely due to impatience and nervous energy. Whatever damage Prudence had wrought on her way out into the world, it made any single standing position uncomfortable.

"Vivian says Mr Grey's ritual won't work," she said.

"She said it was dangerous and theoretical," said Omar.

"So, it will work?"

He attempted a shrug, but it was an effort.

"She said we couldn't negotiate with the Venislarn too," she said.

"That is correct. You marching off to the Cube and demanding satisfaction from *Yo-Morgantus* will not end well."

"But she said we can't negotiate with them because we can't even understand their motives. That they're unknowable."

"That is also true."

Morag wasn't content to let that stand. Ideas were circling in her head. She was certain if she'd had an easier day, then she'd be able to grasp hold of them more easily. "We do understand some of their motives," she said carefully.

"Oh?"

"*Yo-Morgantus* has a thing for gingers."

"That's hardly a searing insight."

"He enjoys human degradation and naked ginger people—"

"And early Electric Light Orchestra," added Chad.

"He does!" said Morag. "And as for *Kaxeos*. He literally owns a curry house and runs a fleet of taxis."

"That's not motivation," said Omar.

"It's his engagement with our world. Just as *Daganau-Pysh* owns a section of canal."

"Even though he resides in the metaphysical deeps below."

"But his children – both the true *samakha* and the half breeds we deal with – have made their home there. Same with *Yoth Mammon*. She might be a mile-wide flying mouth, but her children have embraced earth culture. They even play at being stockbrokers and other twattish things. The local Venislarn have gone native."

"That does happen," said Chad. "I spent that six months working for an agency in Los Angeles and I came back with an American accent and a coke habit."

"Morag, you're missing the point," said Omar. "All those things may be true. But they're just snippets. There's layers of misunderstanding hidden away there. And half the things you mention are about their children who are, culturally if not genetically, fifty-percent human anyway. And, without sounding like Mrs Grey's broken record, we have not seen the true gods yet. The deep ones, elder ones, outer ones – whatever you want to call them, because we don't have the words for them – are going to turn up and we'll either not notice or the first thing we'll know is our brains leaking out through our ears and our *shufas-gherr* spiralling into a million drops of *yeradi'o*."

"No," she replied firmly. "*You're* missing the point. It doesn't matter if we can't understand the true Venislarn. Like flies trying to understand humans. But the fly understands the ways of the spider. And the spider understands the … I dunno, frog. Do frogs eat spiders? I don't know what eats frogs."

"Cats?" suggested Chad. "Sheep?"

"Point is, there's a chain. We do know that *Yo-Morgantus* likes gingers and, thanks to the nuclear missiles, gingers are suddenly in short supply."

"Are we going to sell redheads to the Venislarn?" said Chad.

"We're going to sell the Venislarn whatever they need," said Morag. "And in exchange we'll save what souls we can for as long as we can."

"Save souls already in hell?" said Omar. He was amused rather than dismissive; Morag took that as a positive sign.

"We get them to … ringfence certain humans. Protect them."

"Put us in a zoo?"

Morag shrugged. "Sure. Whatever. Cos hell is here, and we are going to be here for a long time and, no matter what happens, win or lose, we'll wish we did something – anything! – to ease that suffering. There's a post-hell existence awaiting us, and we might as well prepare."

"Well, I'm in," said Chad.

Morag looked at him. "I wasn't necessarily inviting you."

"Excuse me, Morag, but you've just described a doorstep advertising campaign, a conference roadshow. You are heading out into the great unknown on a sales mission. You need a team at your side. Not just *a* team but the 'A Team'." He spread his arms wide. "And I'm here to align your vision paradigm with the real-word sales matrix."

Morag didn't feel particularly enthused. She looked at Omar.

"Me?" he said. "I was planning on getting a cup of tea and dying slowly. You're not going to get me to walk, and certainly not into the lairs of gods."

There was a flash of light outside. Morag saw a silver Mercedes pull onto the paved area immediately outside the library. There was a uCab sticker on the driver's door. All the uCab taxis in the city were controlled by the god *Kaxeos*, their drivers his slaves.

"That's cool," said Chad. "You said you weren't walking anywhere and – *sha-pow!* – a taxi appears."

"It's smug," said Omar. "If you were an all-knowing fire god, timing is not a challenge."

"Taxi for three," said Morag.

"Destination 'deal with the gods'," said Chad.

"Part of that car is on fire," said Omar.

"Mmmm," Morag nodded. "The driver doesn't seem to mind."

Omar gave a long and exhausted sigh. It was the sigh of a man giving in to the inevitable.

On the short taxi journey, Morag saw how much of the city centre had been destroyed. It wasn't just fire, or explosive acts of demolition. Strange and unstable things had oozed from between the gaps in this world.

The god *Kaxeos*, who until tonight had been buried beneath the Balti triangle, was a being of infinite wisdom playing his own inscrutable game with the other Venislarn gods. A taxi sent by him was a nudge best not ignored. And, at that moment, it was possibly one of the safest ways to get around the city. Nonetheless it was unnerving to have only a single window between oneself and the unfolding madness.

The driver was a bearded man, although half of his beard had been burned away in some recent trauma, and the left side of his face was a shiny and tender pink. He said nothing. He didn't ask for a destination and did not offer a comment. They got in and he simply drove away. Morag was prepared to trust *Kaxeos*'s judgement (as much out of general tiredness as actual faith). She soon saw where they were being taken.

Mammon-Mammonson Investments was a tall white building that had once been the Birmingham stock exchange before technology had rendered regional stock exchanges redundant. The building seemed to have been untouched by the ravages of Armageddon. This might have been pure luck. Morag suspected otherwise.

It was a three-metre hop from taxi to the lobby of Mammon-Mammonson Investments. Being out in the open had never felt so exposed. Omar, who had left his wheelchair at the Library, offered his hand to support her as she offered a hand to support him. Chad, the only one of them who was not injured (either by the passage of a bullet or a baby through the body) was hyped up by the prospect of making deals with the Venislarn, and his arms were too animated to offer support to anyone.

They passed through the marbled vestibule and into the main lobby.

Several dozen men, or things which more of less looked like men, stood in the lobby, ringing a large uneven stack of boxes. As the door swung closed behind Morag, they turned as one to look at the intruders. They had sharp suits, with sharper knives in their hands. One of them grinned, exposing sharp teeth.

04:56AM

Forward Company's van moved slowly through the city streets. Abandoned, crashed or burned-out vehicles forced the van to zig-zag along wider roads, and avoid narrower roads altogether. Captain Malcolm explained to Prudence and Yang that they were being forced to take a large detour back to the city centre through Moseley and Edgbaston to avoid what he called "the big wind monsters ripping up Sparkbrook and Sparkhill".

Once Yang and Prudence had established their story that they both lived on the far side of Shirley, but neither had living family in the area, Captain Malcolm declared the girls would come with them back to their base. The nine other soldiers crammed into the van didn't seem to care one way or the other. There was an unfocused faraway gaze in the eyes of more than one of them. The sour smell of sweat was strong in Prudence's nostrils.

One of the men twitched in fear when a dragon-winged creature glided over the van. It hooted a challenge, before swinging round towards some woodland.

"This ammo works on all Venislarn," Captain Malcolm told Prudence. He ejected a round from his pistol and showed it to them. It had a blue metallic shine to it. "It's made from this gooey slime from one of the monsters. It's poison to them all."

Yang quietly pressed herself against the wall of the van to create distance between her and the bullet. Malcolm didn't notice. He was looking out of the window in the direction the dragon creature had flown.

"We could kill any of them," he said, "but we've got a list of high priority targets. Those nasty spider crab things you met. There's eight more of them somewhere in the city. And we've got plans to deal with *Yo-Morgantus*. He's one of the big nasty ones. And *Yoth-Bilau*, when it shows itself. Isn't that right, guys?" He looked to his men and women for confirmation. Half of them seemed not to hear.

"Can't fault you for your optimism, sir," said a woman whose long hair was plastered to her face with sweat.

Malcolm grunted. "It's been a long night already," he said to Prudence. "Things will look better when we're back at base. You'll meet my son. He's five years old. How old are you?"

Prudence's brain blanked. "How old do you think I am?" she asked.

Malcolm shook his head. "Eleven?"

"Good guess," said Prudence.

On one long high street, all the shops to one side had fallen away, as though sideways had become downwards. It looked as if the pavement was a cliff edge. The van stayed well away from that side of the road.

"Local spacetime is coming apart in places, but that's okay," said Malcolm. Prudence didn't know who he was trying to reassure with that comment. He pointed out an area over to the left. Giants, only visible as needle-thin legs, moved in a circle in a field of light.

"I think that's where Edgbaston cricket ground used to be," he said. "Can't imagine what damage it's doing to the pitch. We'll want to see test matches played again when this is over, eh?"

"What's cricket?" said Prudence.

Malcolm made a horrified sound. "And we'll have to do something about kids' education, too."

"Whatever, sir," said the sweaty woman.

Vivian entered the conference room in the command sub-basement. Three men sat at a table which was far too big for just them. One wore a light purple tracksuit, another a business suit, the third the uniform of a British army major. If Vivian reached for the fading knowledge of *Ap Shallas* still within her, she would have been able to conjure their names. She had neither the time nor the desire.

"Are you using this room?" she said curtly.

The tracksuit wearer looked at her, open mouthed. He had probably had a confusing and long night, but that wasn't reason enough to be gawping like a slack-mouthed frog.

"We were expecting to be dead," said the major. He gestured at the big wall of monitor screens behind them. It was black and lifeless.

Vivian spared it a glance. "*Yo-Morgantus*, possibly in conjunction with the unholy colours of *Ammi-Usub* has erected a shield over the city. The nuclear explosion did not penetrate it. That was some minutes ago. Aren't you meant to be doing something useful?"

"That dramatic fellow from marketing was doing a presentation," said the tracksuit wearer.

"We had to imagine what kind of yoghurt we were," said the suit.

"I was a Muller fruit corner," said tracksuit.

"Squeezy froob," said the suit.

"I believe I need to rejoin my men," said the major, standing.

"I will be using this room," said Vivian and slid the Bloody Big Book onto the table. "I have a book to finish."

As she sat down, the door opened and a round woman reversed in with a tea trolley. "Pretend I'm not here," she told everyone in a loud voice, and proceeded to collect mugs, cups and plates.

"We should give you some room to—" As tracksuit stood, he waved his hand to encompass whatever it was he thought Vivian was doing.

"Is there anything we can do to assist?" asked his suited companion.

"Pens," said Vivian. She waggled the expensive-looking copper-barrelled pen. "I picked this up from the Library gift shop not half an hour ago and I can already sense it's running out."

The men gathered what few pens they had on the table.

"And that would be a council-run gift shop, then," said the tea lady with dark emphasis. She glared at tracksuit and sucked her teeth angrily.

Tracksuit visibly quailed. "I can assure you, Mrs Seth, that Birmingham City Council is not responsible, directly or indirectly, for the items sold in library and museum gift shops."

The woman wasn't interested, and muttered foully as she continued tidying.

Once the men were gone, the crockery collected and Vivian had a dubious pile of cheap pens by her open book, she was ready to continue writing.

"I'll come back with a nice hot pot of tea for you," said Mrs Seth.

"I prefer to make my own tea," said Vivian. "I don't wish to be disappointed."

Mrs Seth produced an open-mouthed laugh of disdain. "Oh, let's see, shall we?" She wheeled her trolley out noisily with a muttered, "Where does she think tea bloody comes from, eh?"

Knowing the gift shop pen was on its last dribbles of ink, Vivian found her page in the Bloody Big Book and wrote.

CARCOSA

Rebounding off a foyer wall, tearing away a long patch of flaking wallpaper as he did, Rod stumbled out of the theatre and into the streets of Carcosa. He wanted to throw up, he wanted to scream. He didn't have the energy for either.

This world, far from Earth, was a nightmare of decay and silence.

"I need to get back," he muttered to himself, realising he had been muttering it over and over.

Realisation gave him strength of purpose. He grabbed a man in the street. "I need to get out of here. How do I leave?"

Between the man's mask and the brim of his stovepipe hat, eyes widened in both fear and disgust.

"Please!" Rod called to the surrounding crowd, which was doing its best to ignore him. "I need to get back home. Birmingham. Birmingham? Anyone heard of it?"

There was no flicker of recognition or sympathy from any of them. Rod ran on. He paused at the end of the street, breathless from nausea, and leaned on the corner building. Motes of dried and worn stonework crumbled at his touch.

A family of four – the family from the graveyard – emerged through the fallen gate archway opposite. The father walked ahead. The mother held the daughter's hand to stop her falling behind. A skull-slug covered the girl's back, its ooze around her shoulders, its skull face perched next to her own, grinning. The girl wept silently.

"What's done is done," said the mother softly, more annoyed than worried.

Rod stared. "What is wrong with you people?" he shouted.

The parents clearly heard him, but kept their eyes ahead. The son glanced momentarily at Rod, then took a bite from a pretend apple and carried on.

"What the flamin' heck…?" Rod whispered.

"Plague grips the city," said the King in Crimson, next to Rod once more.

Rod was too tired to give a start of surprise but shot the bastard a furious look. "Do you have to creep up on me all the time?"

"I never leave your side," said the King.

Rod shook his head. "This plague, then."

"A shortness of breath, sharp pain, sudden dizziness and then bleeding at the pores."

"And then death," Rod nodded.

"No one is allowed to die in Carcosa anymore." He fingered his mask. "They wear the masks as penance and try not to draw attention to themselves."

"And they do nothing to fix things, to save themselves?"

"If the horrors are coming – if the horrors are *here* – and there is nothing they can do about it, best to pretend nothing's wrong and carry on as normal."

"Idiots," said Rod.

"People," said the King.

"Well, I'm getting out of here," said Rod, pushing himself away from the wall.

"That's the spirit!" said the King. "Across Lake Hali, away from the Hyades cluster and all the way back to home!"

If he was mocking Rod, Rod chose to ignore him. "If you got me here then you can take me back," he said as he marched back towards the busiest streets.

"Three wishes requested. Three wishes given."

"You're a cheating scoundrel, I'll tell you that for nowt."

"Slanderous in the extreme."

"Sue me." Rod walked the city, looking for any signs of how he might leave. The father in the graveyard had mentioned boats or ships or somesuch, so maybe there was a way out from this place. But the King in Crimson had said they were in the Hyades cluster and the word 'cluster' suggested stars and distant galaxies to Rod's mind. Whether he needed a spaceship or a wizard to get him home, Rod would seek one out.

He stepped from one side of a partially flooded alleyway to the other. "What happens at the end of the play?" he asked the King.

"The end?" the King said.

"If I'm in it then what do I do next? How do I get out of this?"

The King in Crimson coughed, a laugh perhaps. "The play is unfinished. Perhaps if I had finished it things would be different."

Rod grunted at the unhelpful and empty comment.

They passed through a street of densely packed, empty shops and into a long, wide square. The remains of high buildings marked the sides. The arcades of shops at ground level were whole and complete, but the upper levels were nothing but empty windows and jagged brickwork. The square was crowded, far more crowded than any other portion of the city. Men, women and children stood silently.

Nearby, a child played idly with a whirling toy. He stood next to a woman who ignored him.

Rod halted when he saw the toy properly. At first he had taken it to be some sort of windmill. He recognised the three arms and the rings set into them, the almost frictionless spinning of the body.

"That's a fidget spinner."

The boy didn't look up.

He took hold of the boy's wrist and lifted it. "This a bloody fidget spinner. Don't tell me they make fidget spinners in—" Rod plucked the toy from the boy's fingers; he mewled pathetically for a moment. Rod turned it over and inspected it closely. The words MADE IN CHINA were embossed on the plastic body.

He shook it in the woman's face. "Where did he get this? Did you find it? Did you buy it?"

The woman shifted aside so that his hand and the fidget spinner were no longer in her eyeline. Rod turned to a man who might have been with them.

"Oi, mate. Did you buy this?"

The man didn't respond so Rod – who had had enough of these bloody people – gave him a shove. The man's eyebrows shot up in disbelief.

"This!" growled Rod. "Where did you get it?"

Stunned, the man pointed off to an alley leading off from the square. "The canal," he mumbled. "The traders."

"Thank you!" snapped Rod, who was an intrinsically polite man.

He looked to the boy, thinking to give the fidget spinner back to him but the boy's blank-eyed attention had moved on: now fixated on the bright stars above the empty windows.

Rod ran to the alleyway the man had pointed out. He paused, standing on the protruding lip of a building foundation stone, and shouted across the square.

"You lot need to wake up! Do something! Repair your bloody houses, sort out the mess in the streets!" He saw skull-slugs here and there, leisurely grazing on the unresisting herd. "And flamin' heck, do something about the vermin, will you? Your world needs fixing! It's not rocket science, you know! If I have to come back here and sort you out myself, I will!"

Of the hundreds of people in the square, maybe a handful momentarily turned their faces in his direction. But it seemed a colossal effort; within seconds he was forgotten. Silence fell. There was no wind, no warmth, no movement beyond the strictly functional.

"Christ on a bike," he muttered, and left.

The alley from the square sloped down before descending in uneven steps. The buildings leaned in close. Rot had eaten away the wooden timbers of some of the simpler buildings and, here and there, upper levels had literally collapsed against one another across the road, like drunkards leaning on each other.

Poorer people, their rags filthy and shapeless, moved wordlessly, backs hunched. Baskets and crates were carried underarm or across their shoulders. There was little actual produce that Rod could see. Scraps and rubbish were in abundance, but there was no fruit, vegetables or baked goods. Perhaps they moved through habit, repeating the actions of a working day but with none of the end results to show for it.

He tried to engage them, tried to meet their gaze. "Do you know where I might buy something like this?" he asked more than once. The people offered him nothing.

He followed the intermittent steps until the alley simply stopped at a plain wall where forked cracks made a crazy pattern on the damp plasterwork. He turned and looked back up the alley and did not recognise it.

"What are you doing, dear patron?" asked the King in Crimson.

"I'm finding a way out," he said tersely. "If fidget spinners can get here from China, then there'll be a way that Rod Campbell can get back."

"To China?"

"Don't be a smart arse." Rod climbed back up the slope and took the first right. More stairs, more crowded buildings, more people carrying meaningless cargo on pointless errands. This passageway ended at an open sewer, a narrow and deep channel that didn't seem to be flowing anywhere. Despite the foul-looking grey and brown detritus floating its surface, it didn't smell much at all, as though it had given up its stench.

Rod backtracked and took a different turning, this time through an archway that appeared older than the building around it. Further steps up and down and, because it made him feel more productive, a turn here and then there, taken at random.

A V-shaped chunk knocked out of a step struck him as annoyingly familiar. As he looked up, a rotund woman in a black cloak passed by. He was sure he had seen her before.

"Going in circles?" suggested the King.

"Trapped in a maze," countered Rod. "I've been here before."

"Limited budget for sets," said the King. Rod ignored his meta nonsense.

"As long as it's not like that one where the stairs go up and down and the whole universe is folded in on itself, up is down and left is right. You know the one?"

"The picture by Escher," said the King.

"I don't know who directed it. I mean that film where David Bowie is the Wizard King or whatever," said Rod. "Spiky hair. A disturbing codpiece that ten-year-old Rod Campbell did not need to see. And screwy geography." He was angry with this city and its inhabitants. He didn't want to get into an argument with its streets as well.

Rod removed the paracord bracelet from his wrist. Like many

of his wearable tools, the bracelet had started out as a catalogue-bought item, before he had added to it. On top of the ten feet of handy paracord, he had woven a monofilament garrotte wire and a long spool of heavy fishing line. All told, he had nearly two hundred metres of line at his disposal.

On the next street corner, seven feet up a wall, there was a rusty bracket on which a shop sign might once have hung. Rod made a loop of tied fishing line, hooked it over the bracket, and began to feed it out from his unravelling bracelet as he moved down the street.

"This labyrinth isn't going to fool me," he told the King.

Progress was slow and awkward. Rod had to hold the bracelet directly above his head so it wouldn't accidentally strangle passers-by. But he made progress. He asked people about 'traders' and even showed them the fidget spinner, but the city folk were unresponsive, and he went on his way, hand high, cursing them all under his breath.

He didn't cross his own path once. He might have thought that an awning looked like one he had seen earlier, the pair of girls he saw walking solemnly hand in hand might have been uncannily like the two he had seen minutes before, but he did not see his string again. There were dead ends and he backtracked more than once, only coming to a full stop when he reached the end of his cord. Fishing wire had given way to monofilament to a final ten feet of paracord rope.

Rod looked about, hoping for a final revelatory sight of something that might be his end goal but, no, nothing. He sighed, composed himself, and began to make his way back, gathering the cord around his hand as he retraced his steps.

"I suspect someone is playing silly buggers," he said out loud.

"Silly buggers," said the King in Crimson.

"And I suspect that someone is you," Rod added.

He was heading up a road when he felt a new rhythmic tension in the cord. He craned his head to look over the people and picked out a figure who seemed to be moving directly towards him. When the crowd parted sufficiently, Rod saw a scarred and filthy man winding in the cord from the other end.

The scarred man tugged at the cord, frowned as he found resistance, and tugged again.

"This is mine, mate," said Rod. "I tied it to the wall for a reason."

The man tried tugging it one more time, then looked up at Rod. "I can do you a ... deal." He spoke slowly, as though he rarely did so and struggled to remember the mechanics of it.

"I was looking for something," said Rod.

The man dipped into the grimy waistband of his ruined trousers and pulled out something that looked like a wand. Only when he pressed the button on the side and it buzzed into life did Rod realise it was a filth-caked electric toothbrush.

"For cleaning," said the man. "Zzzzzzzz." He mimed polishing something with the whirring brush head. "Good for shoes." He nodded, glanced at his own feet, appearing to be surprised there were no shoes on his own dirty feet and choked back a sob.

Recognition hit Rod. "Jeffney Ray!"

The scarred man – his face an utter ruin since Rod had last seen him – blinked tears from his eyes. "Good for shoes," he said.

Rod took the electric toothbrush from him and found the manufacturer's logo. It was another Earth product.

"You got this from somewhere," Rod said. "You came here somehow."

The man, Jeffney, looked at him uncomprehending.

"Don't you remember?" said Rod.

Jeffney nodded and licked his torn lips. *"Skeidl hraim yeg courxean. Oyo-map-ehu merishimsha meren'froi,"* he whispered.

"Do not kill me, honoured friend," the King translated. "I was only admiring your beauty."

Jeffney nodded, weeping, and still holding onto Rod via the length of cord, scampered barefoot down the street.

BIRMINGHAM - 05:09AM

Hans Mammon-Mammonson, the current managing director of Mammon-Mammonson Investments sat at the top of a long table that seemed to have only one purpose; to make the people at the other end feel as small and as insignificant as possible. Morag put her hands on the table, half expecting to feel it sloping from the big man in his big chair down to what currently felt like the kiddy end of the table.

"*Ven'bruch* geometry," Professor Omar whispered as though reading her thoughts. "Don't look at the gold inlay too closely."

Blinds were drawn against the apocalypse outside, the only illumination coming from concealed lights in the marble cornices. Hans Mammon-Mammonson stared at the three humans. Just to the side of him on the table was one of the smaller plastic crates that had been on the pile downstairs. He had brought it along when he invited them to speak with him in the board room. He cleaned out his fingernails using the large curved and spiked knife he held. He didn't take his eyes off the three humans as he moved from fingernail to fingernail.

The Mammonites were the closest approximation to actual

humanity the Venislarn had ever achieved. The August Handmaidens of *Prein* had embossed their shells with human faces. The *samakha*, the *Ken'bet* marionettes and the *Voor-D'yoi Lak* had adopted a vaguely humanoid two-arms-two-legs form, but not much more. Only the Mammonites had taken a shape that was almost passably human.

The fact they were almost human made them all the more disturbing to look at. Hans Mammon-Mammonson's eyes were slightly too far apart, or perhaps just a fraction too narrow, or maybe it was something to do with the symmetry of his nose. Whatever it was, the uncanny effect of his appearance was just downright creepy. Omar had once shared a personal theory with Morag that humanity's ancestors had evolved the 'uncanny valley' fear for a purpose. Way back in human history, early man had a good reason to be afraid of things that looked almost human.

Morag didn't want to think about such things.

"The consular mission to the Venislarn," said Mammon-Mammonson. He grinned, impressed, but the grin revealed something achingly wrong with his jawline. "I would have thought your job on this earth was done. The only reason we didn't kill you on sight is I'm curious as to how your employer maintains such loyalty. Stock options? A share of the profits?"

"The consular mission is a public sector body," said Morag. "There are no stocks, no profits."

Mammon-Mammonson flinched as he frowned. "No profits?"

Morag knew such a concept would confuse, even disgust the Mammonite. "We do it because it needs doing."

"Gratis? No commission?"

She made a vague agreeing motion, then looked around the room. All the computer screens and TVs were dead. "And how is business? How are profits?"

Mammon-Mammonson bristled. "Our mother rises presently. The priests of *Nystar* are welcoming her to this world as we speak." He glanced at the chunky watch on his wrist. It was probably obscenely expensive, but Morag wouldn't know. She didn't know any normal human beings who still wore watches.

"Is she running a bit late?" said Morag.

"Our unholy mother's schedule is none of your business."

"It's hell out there," she agreed. "Probably got held up."

Mammon-Mammonson stopped cleaning his nails and laid the knife down on the table, blade angled towards Morag. "Did you come here simply to goad me into killing you?"

"No, sir," said Chad with sudden energy. "We've come to make a deal."

"What do you want?"

Chad waved such notions away. "It's not what *we* want. We're here to see what we can do for *you*."

"For us?"

"As my esteemed colleague Morag puts it, there's a post-hell existence coming our way. This isn't the end. This is just the next stage."

Mammon-Mammonson held Chad with a contemptuous gaze. Most people gave Chad contemptuous gazes once they'd got to know him.

"Go on," he said, eventually.

"We've looked out the window. We know what's going on. And your mother, *Yoth Mammon*, sure she's on her way, but are you really happy? Really?" He dipped into his jacket and pulled out a wallet and flipped it open. He removed a bank card. "Visa. Up in smoke." He pulled another. "HSBC. Melted into slag. Lloyds. Got my Costa reward card here. Don't think they're serving any more chai lattes. Tesco Clubcard. All those points ... gone." He dug out a pair of bank notes. "What are these worth now, eh?"

Mammon-Mammonson grunted and pulled up the clips on the plastic box he'd brought into the room. From it he took bundle after bundle of wrapped bank notes. Morag looked at the piles and could not guess if each was worth a thousand pounds, or ten thousand. Were the boxes piled up in the lobby downstairs full of such cash?

"The value attributed to something is what its value is agreed to be," said Mammon-Mammonson. "It is a contract of agreement."

"Business is business, right?" said Chad. "You've always understood that. You've been waiting for this day forever but, maybe, it hasn't gone the way you planned."

Mammon-Mammonson nodded grimly. Chad, a man whose bullshit just tended to flow over people, ignored or shrugged off, actually seemed to be getting through to him.

"Even when the last blade of grass has been burned away, the last living thing driven to extinction, and the last drop of water poisoned with our mother's bile, it would still be nice to be rich," said the Mammonite.

Chad grinned. "Hans, we are here to save the day. We are engaging in a multi-lateral, cross-deity set of negotiations with a focus on aligning best practice with the current reality framework. There is a new world order. This—" he brushed his own cash off the table "—is part of the old world. It's VHS. It's vinyl – and not in a good way. It's horse drawn carriages. If there's to be order—"

"We like order," said Mammon-Mammonson.

"Of course you do. And this new order is to be built on commodities of value."

"Such as?"

Chad pretended to look about himself. "Not many humans around these days, are there?"

Mammon-Mammonson guffawed sharply. "You think currencies of the new world should be built on the – what should we say? – the 'human standard'?"

"Untouched living humans," said Morag.

The mammonite laughed again. "You've come here to tell me

we shouldn't harm human beings because they will be more valuable that way?"

"We're saying we want you to actively protect the surviving humans."

Mammon-Mammonson was genuinely amused. Morag couldn't gauge whether that boded well or ill.

"And that's a marvellous notion," he said. "But it's not the basis of a negotiation. You have no authority to offer anything. All you've done is give me an idea and three healthy human specimens to start our collection."

Sheikh Omar grunted with laughter. "Shows what you know, you *curran khe'ad*. I am far from healthy. There's every danger I might shuffle off the old proverbial before I leave this room. And Chad ... healthy in body but he's a ha'penny short of a sixpence." He placed a hand on Morag's arm. She could feel him trembling. "Morag here, however is the *a-made kaatbari*."

Mammon-Mammonson's eyes widened in gentle surprise.

"Her daughter aside, she's possibly the most significant human being on the planet. A holy mother, if you will."

The mammonite didn't question this assertion. They had moulded themselves physically and mentally to the world of finance and trading. Could they smell lies?

"She is going to *Yo-Morgantus,* so you might wish to think about what sway she holds in his court."

Mammon-Mammonson put his hand on the pile of cash he'd made. Even now, Morag could see him drawing solace from the memory of wealth it represented. "We want the *lo-frax* field," he said.

Chad looked questioningly at the others. Omar coughed.

"You want to own the spiritual field which surrounds our world?" he said. "You want to own the net, not all the human souls within it?"

Mammon-Mammonson gave a genial shrug, a sign of his

reasonableness. "If human *fraxasa* are to be the currency of this new world, if you want us and our unholy mother to protect you, then we also want to control the borders. Import, export. Tariffs and taxes."

"Excuse us a moment," said Morag. She wheeled her chair back and turned Omar to face her. She crouched low to whisper. "Can we do that?"

"Do what?" said Omar. "The Mammonites want the *lo-frax* field. You know what that means?"

"What does that mean?" whispered Chad, who had scooted round to join them in their huddle.

"It's like—" Omar gestured with his long fingers, reaching for a concept. "It's like wanting to own the horizon. Or midnight. It's not ours to sell."

"Does anyone own it?" said Morag.

"Does anyone own the horizon?"

Chad had spun back to the table. "Hans, baby. That's definitely doable," he said with a firm confidence that he did not deserve to wield.

Morag was instantly beside him. "We will certainly look into it."

Mammon-Mammonson rocked with mirth. Something shifted in his cheekbones as he smiled. Slowly, he reached for the knife on the table and spun it. It twirled frictionlessly, a silver blur. Mammon-Mammonson watched it, perhaps hoping to divine some meaning from its movement.

05:15AM

The Forward Company van took a wide road. Prudence began to see buildings taller than she'd seen elsewhere in the city. "Are we near the centre?" she said.

"We're here," said Captain Malcolm.

The van swung around an elevated roundabout. At the centre of the roundabout stood an intricate concrete tower, too small to be a building, but large nonetheless. It was not a Venislarn thing, but it reminded Prudence of the Bridgeman fish sculpture nonetheless. She remembered these people had killed that with their special bullets, and wondered if perhaps they were no more her friends than the soldiers who had first tried to kill her.

The van mounted a pavement and passed through an archway into a shop front. Under dim lighting, the van was met by other soldiers in the Forward Company uniform. Prudence and Yang followed the soldiers out. Yang tripped as she picked up her blazer and stumbled against the rack of weapons.

"Careful," Prudence whispered. "And don't threaten to sue them."

In Prudence's hand, Steve continued play the part of a grubby ragdoll, one that tightly clutched a pencil to its body.

"Downstairs," said Malcolm and pointed. A double width flight of stairs descended into the ground. Prudence held the wooden handrail as they went down.

"This used to be a cinema," said Malcolm. "The Smallbrook Queensway Odeon."

"Your military base is a cinema?" said Yang, unimpressed.

"An abandoned cinema," said Malcolm. "The main auditorium is forty feet underground. Doubles up as a handy bomb shelter."

They passed another band of soldiers coming up.

"You've heard of Odeon, the cinema chain, right?" said Malcolm. "Started by a local man. Oscar Deutsch Entertains Our Nation."

Gritty dust crunched under Prudence's bare feet. The stairs turned onto another flight, then into an area crammed with desks, equipment and computers. The flow of humans in and out was matched by the volume of voices. Instructions, requests and questions were called out.

"Maybe this was what war used to be like," said Malcolm. He spoke briefly to a woman at a desk, told her here were two more for registration, then led the girls into the next room.

This, Prudence surmised, was the main auditorium. From the entrance, large concrete steps ran across the length of the space, down to a stage area some distance below. Knots of people and gear dotted the amphitheatre steps: working groups, small encampments. As well as the dim lighting from above, torches and lamps provided illumination for the different spaces. It had a dank and fusty smell, as if the air in here didn't get out much.

"See that?" said Malcolm, pointing to the stage area. "The tall cage of blue john?"

On one of several tables near a group of people in deep

discussion was a cylinder, maybe three feet tall, composed of shards of purple-blue stone encased in a wire mesh.

"Put an explosive core in that, and we've got a bomb powerful enough to kill gods." He laughed and directed them down the steps to a small clutch of people by a wall.

Three women sat together. A small boy slept on the stair, wrapped up in a quilt patterned with colourful steam trains.

"Mary," said Malcolm and one of the women looked up. There were tired red rings under her eyes. She looked at Prudence and Yang without emotion.

"More refugees?" she said.

"Prudence and Yang," said Malcolm. "I've got to go speak to the leadership. We found Handmaidens of *Prein* in Acocks Green. Killed one."

Mary nodded. Another woman shifted and pulled out blankets from the pile she sat on. She gave each of the girls one.

"How much?" said Yang.

The woman ignored her and opened a round tin. Inside were golden biscuits, several of them broken, which she offered to the girls. Prudence took one and Yang followed her example.

"Find somewhere to sit," said Mary. "Don't wake the boy."

Prudence moved up a step and carefully, watchfully, sat a distance away from the women. She unfolded the blanket and pulled it over her shoulders. She wasn't cold, but it felt good to have the soft pressure around her.

"And now what?" whispered Yang, sitting close but at a measured distance.

Prudence had no idea. In her hand, Steve the Destroyer tapped at her wrist. She glanced down.

"Kathy Kaur," he said.

"What?"

He furtively pointed down to the stage area. Prudence looked across at the various people.

"Dr Kathy Kaur," said Steve, as though clarification was needed.

Prudence had never met Kathy Kaur, not directly. The woman had been present at her birth, but there'd hardly been time for formal introductions.

"You think she'll recognise me?" said Prudence.

"You've grown a bit since then," said Steve.

Morag felt as though she was holding her breath all the way from the boardroom to the lift to the taxi still waiting on Great Charles Street. She did not speak. She did not make any movement beyond the strictly necessary. Only when she was in the back seat of the taxi next to Omar did she release the metaphorical breath and look at the professor.

"Yes," he said simply.

Chad twisted in the front passenger seat to face them as the taxi pulled away. "I think that went well."

"Well?" Morag laughed despite herself. "We walked in there with nothing, promised the CEO the Moon on a stick, and walked out again with our lives. That was nothing short of a fucking miracle, mate."

Omar nodded readily. "It is the beginnings of negotiations. They are prepared to accept human survival as a prerequisite for future business."

It was what they wanted. It was hardly a cheery thought. Human existence continuing at the whim of the psychotic children of a monster god. And Morag could easily picture the day when some Mammonite investor decided the way to increase the value of an individual human soul would be to destroy as many of the others as possible.

The taxi had swung round onto the A38 dual carriageway and was gently weaving between the wrecked vehicles, collapsed buildings, and general carnage that dotted the way ahead. Morag did not see another human being anywhere.

"Where to now?" she said.

"We talk," said the driver. "*Liq glun-a-siscu.*"

Kaxeos's zombie taxi drivers never spoke. Their minds were not their own. If this one was speaking then it was *Yo Kaxeos* speaking through him.

"*San-shu chuman'n Yo Kaxeos,*" said Omar. "I wondered when you might speak to us."

"*Prah ley espli'ch. Murrei do'papli a-shren,*" said the taxi driver and Omar chuckled drily.

"What's that?" said Chad. "My Venislarn isn't as good as..."

"Basically," said Morag, "he wanted to see if we would get out of the Mammonite building alive. He would talk to us if we did."

"That was a … that was a test?"

"I'm surprised we passed, dear chap," said Omar. For a man who had been nursing a mortal wound all night, the prospect of sudden death had brought out his whimsical side. "So, Lord *Kaxeos*. One takes it you have a stake in what follows? Demands even?"

The taxi driver began a long litany in Venislarn.

"I might need to write this down," said Omar.

Chad immediately had a phone in his hand. "Chad in notetaking mode."

The taxi driver's waxy pink burned jaw moved as he spoke his god's words. Omar rapidly translated and Chad swiped his phone screen to jot them down. Morag watched the dying world drift by their window.

When the list of demands was done, Chad sighed mightily.

"You okay?" said Morag.

"I just realised," he said, cradling his phone, "I had eight thousand Instagram followers. All gone now. Like tears in rain."

"Uh-huh. So, what's the gist of *Kaxeos*'s requirements?"

"In short, freedom," said Omar. "What else does a chained god want?"

"*Dhye pehaesh qan khurid!*" said the taxi driver, somewhat petulantly.

"Paraphrasing, of course, my lord," said Omar. "Perhaps Lord *Kaxeos* does not crave the same systemic order as the Mammonites, but he hopes to retain a rational post-apocalyptic world in which to enjoy the same powers as he has now."

"He wants to keep running taxis and selling curry."

"Not specifically – figuratively. And humans are definitely valued as mobile processors."

"Wow. Brains on legs. I can't tell if that's a compliment or not."

"And although his children, the Winds of *Kaxeos*, are by their nature destructive, Lord *Kaxeos* does admire our facility for construction."

Morag nodded. The taxi took a roundabout and drove past a burning fire station towards Eastside and the canals. "So, skilled workers are welcome in the new world."

"Oh, definitely."

"*Pao-shibbu mape rashad Thorani*," said the taxi driver.

"And he wants our help defeating *Yoth Thorani*?" said Morag.

"Tree goddess and a fire god might be natural enemies," said Omar.

"*Me'ah adn-bhul pabbe-grru shaska!*" growled the driver.

Morag blinked. "Did I hear that right? 'Nut-fucker'?"

Omar lowered his voice. "I think there's some bad blood there."

CARCOSA

Jeffney led Rod around a few short turns until they came down to a body of water. Canal, river or lake, Rod couldn't tell. The water rippled, but there was no flow to it. A dozen yards from the bank, thick mist sat on the water, piled high like ground level storm clouds, fading from white to silver to the black of night. The path at the water's edge was narrow: a stubby lip between city wall and the water. Rod followed the broken little man along the path. Jeffney moved without care for other people, dodging between them where he could, bouncing off them when he couldn't.

The path widened and Rod saw boats moored along the side. A good number of them were abandoned things, rotting, sinking or sunk. Long rowboats were tied up beside steam-driven paddle boats and untidy sail ships. Bigger boats were positioned further out, along precarious and twisted jetties. There were the shapes of tall vessels, intermittently visible in the mist. Most leaned at angles that did not suggest seaworthiness.

There was movement around a few of the boats on the quayside. Cargo crates were being unloaded and stacked, unstacked and reloaded. Carts moved. Ropes were coiled. Sailors strolled. The impression of industry was unmistakeable but, as with the workers of the city, Rod failed to see any end result. It was simply habit.

Jeffney tugged him further on.

They passed a man clutching a single toilet roll to his chest. He looked blissfully pleased with his possession.

"Was that toilet paper?" said Rod. Jeffney ignored him.

Moments later they came across a masked man squatting on stone steps beside a waterside gateway. He had a plastic rectangular box with dials on it resting on his drawn up knees.

"That's an Etch-A-Sketch," said Rod.

The man drew his knees up further, wrapping his arms protectively around the old toy.

"I used to have one of them as a kid," said Rod.

"It is mine now," hissed the man behind his mask.

Rod shook his head and allowed Jeffney to pull him on.

As they neared a long sail-less barge, Rod saw other locals clutching various consumer goods and items of tat. More toilet rolls, individual biro pens, soap, toothpaste. One woman cradled a vegetable spiralizer. A man explored a plastic egg filled with silly putty. Several couples carried contraptions of metal tubing and plastic joints: exercise equipment or DIY aids straight off teleshopping channels.

Rod saw a fat man conducting trade at the far end of the long vessel. Although Rod did not recognise him personally, a connection clicked in his mind. "The Black Barge."

Jeffney nodded in pathetic and eager agreement.

The Black Barge was not actually black, but Rod guessed people preferred alliteration over accuracy. The narrowboat was grey and windowless. The hull and cabin were formed around a long ribcage, surrounded by some hard, uneven material. To Rod's eye, it looked like a mummified whale corpse, dried and emaciated. Now he understood how Jeffney Ray had come here. The young man had got himself into debt with a number of Venislarn, back in Brum. When he'd disappeared some months ago, it was assumed he had died or run off. Instead, Rod could see someone had called in his debts, and Jeffney – poor stupid bugger – was paying for them.

The bargemaster was a lardy, barrel-chested man. He wore a long sleeveless leather coat and not much else. As he bartered and bargained with the Carcosan folk on the jetty, he mopped his sweating brow with a dark rag. Rod had not met him before, but he'd heard Nina mention him. Rod grasped for a name. Something Scandinavian or Eastern European. Bjorn or Ivan or—

"Sven!" he called.

The bargemaster looked his way and nodded, one businessman to another, before turning back to his customers. Intense haggling took place, resulting in the exchange of an occult-looking Carcosan book for two disposable cigarette lighters.

Sven held a squeezy tube out to Rod. "For you," he said. "Latest thing. Keep teeth white and minty fresh."

"I don't need toothpaste," said Rod.

"No. You have good teeth. For discerning customer though…" He opened an age-worn chest on the deck and removed an orange and yellow boxy toy. He flicked it on and pressed a button. There was an electronic trill.

"*Spell 'cat'*," said a robotic American voice.

"I never had one of those," said Rod.

"It is very good," said Sven. "Home computer. All the rage with cool kids."

"It's a Speak & Spell," said Rod. "Think it's older than me."

"Still good," said Sven. "You got enchantments to sell? I take all magic items, any condition. Not taking children though. Slump in market." He saw Rod's lack of interest in the Speak & Spell. "I have other items. All mod con. You want NutriBullet? You want cotton buds? Very delicate. The best."

Rod showed him his consular mission ID. Sven squinted to read it.

"This isn't Birmingham," he said. "Also, only joking about children."

"You are buying them?"

Sven forced a laugh. "I don't trade in children. Not here. Not Birmingham."

"You going back to Birmingham soon?"

Sven tilted his head. "Final visit. Fire sale. Everything must go, huh?"

The mists ebbed and shifted on the water.

"Have you got room for a passenger?"

"Paying passenger?"

Rod dug out his wallet. He looked for banknotes and produced a ten and a five. Sven blew out noisily in contempt.

"You do contactless?" said Rod.

"Pound worthless soon enough," said Sven.

Rod put his money away. He pointed at the wire and cord Jeffney held. "Paracord, monofilament, fishing line."

Sven inspected it. Jeffney flinched in reflex as the bargemaster moved.

"Is good," agreed Sven. He tested the tension of the wire between his thumbs. "This will get you halfway there."

"What's halfway?" said Rod.

Sven laughed heartily. "Nothing at all."

"Great, and the other half?"

Rod went through his pockets and his belongings. His tobacco tin, containing wax-headed matches, sewing kit, superglue and water-purifying tablets, drew some interest but not enough. He showed Sven his phone.

"I don't get good coverage," said the bargemaster. Rod had zero bars, which wasn't a surprise.

Rod stripped off his jacket, hoping the guy could be tempted with clothing. Sven immediately eyed Rod's pistol in its shoulder holster.

"Glock 21," said Sven. "Fires point four-five auto round. Thirteen round magazine. Very reliable."

Rod was loath to part with his pistol. He wouldn't want to admit to feeling lost or naked without it, but back on Earth there was something approximating a war going on. He needed a weapon.

"I live on barge, what use do I have for handgun?" said Sven. He waved Rod's jacket away too.

As Rod shrugged his jacket back on, the pack of tissues Maurice had given him fell onto the jetty.

"What that?" said Sven.

Rod picked them up. "Napkins," he said, unenthusiastically.

"Mint in box?" said Sven and, when Rod frowned, asked, "Have they been opened?"

"No. Still sealed."

Sven nodded slowly, his chins undulating. "Collector's item?"

"Er, sure."

Sven held out his hand and Rod handed them over. The bargemaster held them reverently for a moment before giving them a tender squeeze, as though testing fruit for ripeness. "This will do. Passage to Birmingham. We leave soon."

"Ta muchly."

Sven returned his attention to the customers he had been neglecting on the jetty.

"This is redundant effort," said the King in Crimson, putting an unwanted hand on Rod's shoulder. "You go back and for what? Your world is drowning in torrents of blood and fire."

"You don't have to stay with me," said Rod. "You don't have to talk. I'm going home to do what I can. You can do whatever pleases you." He stepped aboard the Black Barge, past Sven, jerking a thumb over his shoulder. "I'm not paying for him, by the way."

"Who?" said the bargemaster.

Rod looked back at the King in Crimson and then at Sven. Sven shrugged.

BIRMINGHAM - 05:34AM

Daganau Vei, or The Waters, was a *samakha* shanty town in crisis. Considering its position, leaning over the Warwick and Birmingham Canal, it was surprising how much of it was currently on fire. Morag was sure the warped and soggy plywood was so sodden it should have been practically fireproof. But one side of the canal was completely ablaze, plumes of steamy smoke pouring from crappy apartment windows, and dark alleys which led into warrens of impossible geography.

Much of the population was gathered on the other bank, including many of the true *samakha* (who rarely came above surface or out into the open). Morag, Omar and Chad were spotted the instant they appeared at the brick-built steps leading to the canal side. *Samakha* hissed. A number of the human fish-wives, who had sold themselves to the *samakha*, advanced towards them.

"'Bout bloody time you turned up," one said.

"We've been calling your number for hours," said another.

"What'd you call all this then?" said a third, waving her arms at the crazy pre-dawn sky.

"It's the end of the world," said Morag.

"I know it's the bloody end of the world," said the woman. "I wanna know what you're doing about it!"

Behind Morag, Omar grunted in pain, struggling on the stairs.

Morag cast about the crowd for the familiar pair of fish faces she'd recognised earlier. "Fluke! Death Roe! Give the professor a hand, please."

They were big lads. Fluke, tall and athletic in a tight black t-shirt worn to show off his biceps, was still a head shorter than the haddock-faced fish-mountain Death Roe.

"Fasho, miss," said Fluke and hurried to assist.

The consular mission might be naturally distrusted and despised by most of the *samakha,* but the lads of the Waters Crew gang had had their bacon saved by mission staff often enough to owe them a level of respect.

Down on the crowded towpath, a band of true *samakha* squatted on crooked limbs beneath an ornate canopy carried on poles by four attendants. The true *samakha* had the glistening grey skin of bloated sea fish, and rigidly wide mouths that could offer no readable expressions. Servants bathed them constantly with little saucepans filled in a chain from the canal side. The canopy and constant watering suggested they had a persistent fear of being dried in the sun, but sunrise was a good hour or more away and they were in more danger of being barbecued by the conflagration on the other side of the canal.

The human/*samakha* chain fetching water from the canal drew Morag's attention to the water itself: for the locals, a potentially greater cause of concern. The canal was half empty. Dark stains marked the previous high-water mark on the canal side. Whether the canal had been breached and was draining, or whether the water was simply being boiled away by the fires of judgement day, she couldn't tell.

A failing canal and a town on fire was both opportunity and

threat for Morag. It meant the *samakha* had wants and needs that could form the basis of a trading deal. It also meant they were scared and angry and, therefore, dangerous.

"*Skeidl hraim yeg courxean*," she said in greeting as she approached the canopy and the half dozen fish elders within. "*Shan-shan prui beddigo fesk.*"

An elder spoke in a throaty bubbling Venislarn. A half-breed fishman immediately began to translate into English, as though the *samakha* did not respect Morag enough to believe she could understand. Morag was silently grateful; the guttural fish elder had one hell of a thick accent, and she didn't want to appear impolite by asking him to repeat himself.

The translator wore a soot-stained kitchen apron and cradled a large green crab in his arms, stroking it soothingly as he spoke. "The time of victory is at hand. Humans are not welcome. *Ggh!*"

"String 'em up!" shouted someone.

"Make them do real-life hangman!" shouted another.

"All humans will be sacrificed to the great-father *Daganau-Pysh*!" agreed Hragra.

"What you chatting about, Hragra?" called one of the human women. "You hate us people all of a sudden?"

"I'm just translating, ain't I?"

"Fuckin' racist is what it is!"

Down in the canal a monstrous frilled tentacle rose from the shallow water, dripping with mud, curled into a supple S-shape and then sank again.

"Looks like your god is running out of water," Morag noted.

"*Shas va adanei gheyn-ri'n, meh yo*," Omar concurred.

The elder burbled.

"*Daganau-Pysh* is lord of all the waters," said the translator.

"*Zildrohar Cqulu* might disagree with that," said Morag.

"Or *Yoth-Qahake-Pysh*," said Omar. "She is on her way here now."

"*Zildrohar Cqulu*'s sunken city has already risen."

There was an angry splash from the water. The canal seemed more mud than water now. Although *Daganau-Pysh* had undoubtedly conjured greater depths beneath the canal than its original builders had ever imagined, there was no getting away from the fact that the god was now paddling about in a few feet of silty water.

"Are we *trying* to antagonise him?" Chad whispered.

"Just getting his attention," Morag replied.

An elder waved a clawed hand. His fingers were long and webbed, and the hand made a fan-like slicing sound as it cut the air. "*Skzza' ineneo. Aen-su du guhes' pysh!*"

Strong hands seized the three interlopers – Fluke and Death Roe went from supporting Omar to restraining him. All three were driven towards the edge of the canal.

"Okay, we've got their attention now," said Morag. "Hey! Easy! I've just given birth."

"*Yo Daganau-Pysh*," called out Omar. "*Me'a pen dhorri*. We have come on the behalf of others – *Kaxeos, Mammon* – with proposals for the world that is to come. Gods who have spent silent aeons in their own realms are now coming here to take what you have worked to build for yourself."

As if to punctuate this, helpfully or not, a large bamboo gantry high up on the far side fell away, cracking and burning. It crashed into the canal, flying apart in smoking chunks on impact. Samakha responded with wails and angry shouts.

"*Em-shadt car-eh ben durrigan!*" said Omar, struggling in the grip of the young *samakha*. "You have made this world your home! You! You colonised it! Are you going to let nameless things come here and take over? Gods who have not the slightest inkling of how this world works. No concept of ... time, of gravity, of ... of..."

"How you can make chocolate chip cookies without melting the chips!" shouted Fluke.

"How to pop a crisp packet when the crisps are gone," nodded Death Roe.

"How to steer a coracle with your knees, to impress the honeys!"

"Yes! That!" agreed Omar.

His impassioned plea had set the elders burbling to one another. There was room for discussion. Fluke patted Omar's chest, eliciting a pained moan from him.

"Eh? Why you got – *ggh!* – seashells down your shirt, man?"

"They're whelks," Omar grunted. "Angry whelks."

"He's got whelks down his front," said Death Roe. "Some kinda whelk smuggler."

"Whelk mule!" declared Fluke.

Mutters of suspicion rippled through the crowd.

"*Ggh!* Something fishy going on," murmured Hragra the translator.

Morag resisted the urge to shout of course something fishy was going on.

"Ladies! Gentlemen! Please! Let's not get distracted!" It was Chad, adopting his smoothest salesman voice. "We've come not just to offer something to your—" he waved a hand at the murky shallows "—you know, but to every one of you."

He raised his hands high. The fishmen holding him loosened their grip.

"Canalside living! It's the best, isn't it? City centre dwellings with nature and the calming waters outside your window. But you can do so much better than this. This place is – and do forgive me – a right bloody shambles."

There was a mixture of angry disagreement and surly acknowledgement from the *samakha*. Chad's phone was in his hand, displaying a picture to those nearest to him. "Sherborne Wharf. Gas Street Basin. New apartment complexes."

"Mrs Grey promised me a new apartment months ago!" a woman yelled from the crowd.

"And hundreds of them have just come on the market," said Chad. Morag guessed that was sort of true if the human occupants of the city were, for the most part, dead and gone.

An elder made a dismissive gesture, but he was clearly in the minority.

Samakha and human slaves crowded to look at Chad's phone. There was no internet, so he must have had that picture stored already. Did he have a stock of random images? Was it where he lived? Was it an aspiration of his? Whichever, as he chatted to individuals, Chad weaved them a homeowners dream of living on a stylish wharf with a café-bar on every corner and nothing but cool fresh water around them.

"You'll need a workforce to repair the canal here," Morag added loudly. "Humans to work alongside *samakha*. We have a deal with *Yoth Mammon*—"

"A deal of sorts," corrected Omar.

"We have an *understanding* that an enclave of humans will be protected in the world to come," said Morag.

The elder with the massive webbed hands objected in violent Venislarn. "*Map-ehu! Map-ehu! Ouril set-ehu!*"

"Well, you can be pure *samakha* all by yourself, if you like—" Morag began, but the elder wasn't listening. He raised his voice in garbled and angry speech.

"The time of purification is at hand," translated the crab-handling Hragra. "No more the mixing of – *ggh!* – blood with the dog species."

"Who's 'e calling a dog, eh?" shouted a woman.

"The unclean *samakha* will be driven into the waters to become food for our lord and god. None shall—" Hragra was cut off by sudden violence beneath the canopy. An elder with a massive dorsal fin had leapt up and shoved the one who'd been speaking hard, out from under the canopy and off the side of the towpath.

Shouts went up. Morag couldn't see what was happening. She looked to Chad, but he was deep in discussion about stamp duty for first time buyers with a young fish couple. She looked to Omar.

The professor had a thoughtful look on his face. "It would appear that *Reyah-Sku* – the shover there – felt that *Muyori'n Fee* – the shovee – was far from being a pure blood *samakha*."

The big-handed *Muyori'n Fee* surfaced in the canal, gargling invectives and beckoning.

"And now *Muyori'n Fee* is inviting *Reyah-Sku* to come in the water and settle the matter, *mano a mano*."

"Or fish-o a fish-o," said Morag.

"Oh, that's a common misconception," said the professor. "'Mano' does not mean 'man' but refers to—"

He was interrupted by further shoving and shouting beneath the elders' canopy. Elders had risen from their frog-like squats, pushed aside their attendants, flung away watering pots and set to full-blown skirmishing.

Omar watched with interest. "So, *Rilk Hasp*, who is *Muyori'n Fee*'s brother, is keen to point out that *Reyah-Sku* has no claim to racial purity since his grandmother was a ... a Rhode Island whore, I think he's saying. Ah, but now *Sho'loffa* is interjecting and sharing the 'well-known' belief that the *Krel-asan* clan, including *Rilk Hasp* and *Muyori'n Fee*, are all half-bloods and have so much Scandinavian blood in them they might as well ... ah, *vest ghading plas'iah penti-o*. It doesn't translate well and is quite racist, to *samakha* and Scandinavians alike. And now *Vand'ab-oby* is weighing in with some moral philosophy about purity being spiritual in nature and— Oh well, that's him in the drink."

Shoving, stabbing and slicing had resulted in various *samakha* elders being pitched into the canal. And now, *Daganau-Pysh*, Lord of the Deep Places, was lazily picking them up one by one in his slick coils and dragging them down to be consumed. Perhaps he agreed those who had been ditched were less than worthy. Perhaps he really didn't care. Perhaps he was pissed off that his home was draining away to nothing and was simply comfort eating.

In a few short minutes the canopy had been reduced to shreds, and the number of self-important, racially pure elders had been reduced to a sorry trio who stayed out of the fight.

The waters of the canal slurped and sucked. There was one last cry from an entangled fishman, then silence – but for the crackle and roar of the fire on the opposite bank.

One of the elders spoke, barely a whisper.

Hragra the translator held out his hand (the one not holding a crab). "Those apartments. Could we have a look?"

05:35AM

In the end, Prudence ate Yang's biscuit too. Yang didn't trust the biscuit because it didn't come in a wrapper.

"I'm sure it's fresh," said Prudence.

"Yes, but what is it?" said Yang.

"It's a biscuit."

"What brand?"

Prudence looked at Yang's biscuit, since she'd already eaten her own. She shrugged. "No brand. It's just a biscuit."

"How can it be *just* a biscuit? You can't have a product without a brand. The brand is the message. If I eat it, am a fun-loving party girl? Am I a much-cherished grandma? Am I a dedicated office-worker taking a break from my labours?"

Prudence tried to be helpful. "It tastes buttery."

Yang huffed, unimpressed, so Prudence ate Yang's biscuit.

There was movement on the stage.

"Something's happening," said Yang

"We should leave," said Prudence.

"We are not safe here," Yang agreed.

Soldiers were meeting on the stage, chatting in a manner

which Prudence could tell was formal, even without hearing what they were saying. Malcolm, the soldier who had brought them here, had a map spread out on a table. With Kathy Kaur at his side, he was discussing matters with those around him.

"I'm going to have a look before we go," said Prudence.

"Why?" said Yang.

"They've got a map. It can tell us where we are. My mum is at the Library of Birmingham."

"They'll shoot you as a spy if they see you," said Yang. "I would."

"So, would I," whispered Steve in agreement.

Prudence was certain that Yang was far too cynical, and Steve's wisdom wasn't to be trusted. She stood, tucked Steve in the blanket beside Yang and moved to the edge of their concrete step to get to the stairway.

"Where you going, love?" asked one of the women, the one who had given them the blankets.

"I need to stretch my legs," said Prudence. It was a phrase she had never used before, but she automatically felt it was the right kind of thing to say.

"Do not get in anyone's way."

"I won't."

It was easy to move through the abandoned cinema's auditorium without being noticed. The place was crowded and, although people were gathered in groups, there was very little organisation. Here, a bunch of people slept under green blankets, some of them on low metal beds. There, a family sat around a glowing screen, watching some animated film. A person in uniform sorted through a bunch of heavy rucksacks all stacked together. A soldier brushed past Prudence to get something from one of them before returning to the stage. At a table, another soldier handed out ammunition magazines to a short queue.

Prudence tiptoed past all of these. She didn't actually tiptoe.

Tiptoeing would have looked suspicious. Prudence decided the best way to move was sort of like a breeze, wafting through, causing no fuss, acting like she was not worth noticing.

Kathy had joined in with Malcolm's briefing. "I will carry the pack and move forward with alpha team. It will be connected to a fail-deadly dead man's switch which will be activated once we enter the Cube. I will also be carrying a *Yandi voors* amulet and enacting certain charms to keep any Venislarn at bay."

"And that will keep you safe?" asked a soldier.

"No, Jackson," said Malcolm. "*You* will keep her safe as you approach from the forming-up point and into the building."

There was mild joking and some side chatter. Prudence used the distraction to step up onto the stage area. The space was crowded, but she kept herself behind the back of the gathered men and women, and worked her way round. The closer she got to the table and the map, the more obvious her movements would be. She began to edge towards a gap between two men next to the table.

"Captain McKenna!" called a voice across the auditorium.

Captain Malcolm and many soldiers looked over. It would have been an ideal opportunity for Prudence to slip in and look at the map, but she glanced over too, just for an instant. Three soldiers were standing with Yang between them.

"What is it?" Malcolm asked.

One of the men approached. When he was halfway, Yang shoved one of the other soldiers and tried to run off. The soldier grabbed her by the arm, nearly toppled by her momentum. They spun around together, stumbled and fell, the soldier pinning the mammonite girl to the floor. There was a screeching from Yang and shouts of pain and effort from the soldier. Many people were now on their feet, the volume in the room rising. As soldiers moved to intercept, to see past one another, Prudence lost sight of Yang.

She could have looked at the map. She could have pushed through to get to Yang. Fear and uncertainty gripped her, and she did neither. She stood, immobile, until the soldiers cleared a space. Yang was being marched forward, held firmly between two soldiers. One had a bleeding nose and long scratches on his cheeks. Somewhere else, a thin voice moaned, "Broke my arm. The tiny bitch broke my arm."

"What's going on?" demanded Kathy Kaur.

Yang's mouth was pursed in lip-whitening tightness. Her eyes bulged with silent fury.

"Peters saw her badge," said one of the soldiers.

"Badge?" said Kathy.

The soldier carefully let go with one hand and lifted the torn badge on her blazer.

"Thatcher Academy," said Kathy.

"The mammonites?" said Malcolm.

Kathy reached out and pulled Yang's fringe away from her face. Yang flinched. Kathy picked up a dark blue stone which was holding down one corner of the map. In a simple innocent-looking movement she pressed it against Yang's cheek. There was a sizzle, a hint of burning vapours, and Yang screamed as though stabbed.

"No!" shouted Prudence and eyes were suddenly on her. Hands grabbed her too. Captain Malcolm stared in shock at Prudence, then Yang.

"We found them in Acocks Green," said Malcolm.

Yang was panting and groaning in restrained agony. There was a blistered pink circle on her upper cheek, wet and raw.

"And you brought them here?" hissed Kathy.

"But look..." he said, gesturing at Prudence's face. Kathy Kaur put the blue stone ball to Prudence's face. Prudence gasped and began to shriek – but the stone was cool against her skin.

"Mammonite and human children. Together?" said Kathy.

Prudence was filled with heart-thumping energy and emotion. "I'm Prudence Murray and I'm the *kaatbari* and you have to let us go or I will ... I will burn you all with my laser eyes!"

The wide-eyed stares of the adults grew wider, but no one made a move to let them go.

"Impossible," Kathy whispered. "I was there. I saw you." She glanced at a device on the table and then touched Prudence's curly ginger hair with her fingertips. "Not even six hours old ... Morag's baby girl."

"My mummy will be very angry if she finds out you've taken us," said Prudence, with as much menace as she could muster.

This didn't have the desire effect at all. Kathy smiled, a little lip twist at first and then a big grin. "This is excellent beyond words." She looked at the cylindrical cage full of Venislarn-killing rocks, then at Prudence. "Carrot and stick. Now we've got two bargaining chips for when we go see *Morgantus*."

"No, you have to let us go—!" said Prudence, but it sounded rubbish even to her own ears as she said it.

Kathy pointed at Prudence, then Yang. "Restrain her and get ready for departure right now. Dispose of the mammonite, outside."

Yang struggled as the soldiers holding her pulled her away. There was a last silent glance at Prudence, an unreadable stare, neither pleading nor condemning.

"No!" Prudence yelled. "You can't! You can't! Bring her back! You can't!" She fought against the hands holding her. "I'll tell my mum!" she cried.

Kathy crouched and looked at Prudence, Yang already forgotten. Kathy Kaur was a big woman. She had broad shoulders and a tall face. Her eyes were large, made larger by the makeup that accentuated her eyes and eyebrows.

She tried to give Prudence a kindly look, but didn't make it look convincing. She put her hand against Prudence's shoulder. "We're going to go see your dad. We'll tell him together."

There was noise at the back of the auditorium, the thump of doors and a muffled shout. Prudence tried to see, but the soldiers were in the way. She looked back at Kathy's face. The fake kindly look was still there.

05:39AM

The two soldiers pinning Yang between them pushed through a pair of double doors and into an above-ground courtyard. Brick walls from three different buildings hemmed the area in. A downpipe emptied into a leaf-clogged drain in one corner. The rest of the ground was littered with rusting drink cans, old food wrappers and unidentifiable crud.

Yang Mammon-Mammonson, heir to the Mammon-Mammonson fortune, grand-daughter of the goddess *Yoth Mammon* the corruptor, the defiler of souls, the dredger in the lake of desires, would not have pictured this death for herself. She had perhaps never been able to encompass the concept of her own death. She was Yang and only saw herself with a destiny of limitless avarice and wealth. To die in this grimy courtyard at the hands of humans was unthinkable.

And yet Yang found herself approving of this execution spot. This would be an ideal place to bring someone to kill. The cul-de-sac with high, unscalable walls was ideal. The squalor of the space added to the degradation that Yang would want to inflict on a victim. It was brutal and unpleasant. She approved. She just wished she wasn't on the receiving end.

"Is it going to be you or me?" said one soldier.

The other shrugged. "Both. It's not human."

One loosened his grip and the other gave Yang a forceful shove she was simply too small to resist. She was propelled into the corner of the courtyard. She could hear the minute clicks and knocks of rifles being raised to fire.

Yang braced herself against the wall and turned. She was too far from them to attack before they fired.

Steve the Destroyer ran out of the doorway with a miniscule war cry and stabbed one of the soldiers in the ankle with his pencil. The weapon barely put a crease in the soldier's trousers.

"What the hell?" said the unhurt stab victim.

The other soldier looked down. "What is it?"

It was distraction enough. Yang leapt forward. The men saw her coming but were not quick enough to react. Yang dodged to the side of one, grabbed the barrel of his service rifle, and pushed it aside as the man automatically fired. She felt the heat of the discharge and ignored it. She twisted the surprised man so that he partly shielded her from the other.

Yang let go with one hand and found the knife on the man's belt. "Got your grenade," she said.

As he turned one way, she turned the other, pulling the knife free, before sticking it in his back, underneath his armour and into his kidney. He grunted in shock.

The other soldier was shouting now. Yang thought he ought to have started firing. Having concerns about shooting his fellow soldier was a weakness. Yang slipped forward under the falling man's armpit and took control of his rifle. She fired at the stupid, shouty soldier. One round went into his throat, but the second missed. Then the falling man managed to rip the rifle he was still loosely holding from Yang's grip.

Yang stepped neatly forward, taking the rifle from the one she'd shot as he staggered, hands going to his bloody neck. He seemed to have completely forgotten he had a rifle, the strap slipping from his arm. One bullet finished off the knife-wounded soldier. The one shot in the neck tried to stagger back through the doorway. Yang shot him in the back of the head. He fell, blocking the door from swinging shut.

Yang knelt and aimed down the short length of corridor, waiting for any reinforcements to arrive. As she watched and waited, she controlled her breathing to maintain her aim. She mentally reviewed the sequence of events as it might sound from elsewhere in the building: shouts, then four shots spanning no more than three seconds. The soldiers had been told to kill her. Was there any reason why those particular sounds should draw suspicion?

Steve regarded the mashed end of his pencil, then kicked the corpse of the nearest soldier. "And that's what happens when you mess with Steve the Destroyer, petty mortals!"

"I killed them," said Yang.

Steve adopted a masterful pose, leaning on his blunted spear. "Did you though? Did you really?"

Yang looked at him. "Yes. Yes, I did."

"The prawn thinks it's in charge, but that's just what chess master Steve wants it to think."

Concluding that no one was coming, Yang relaxed and began to search the bodies for ammo and weapons. "Why did you follow me?" she asked.

"So you can help me rescue Prudence," Steve said. "We should never have come here."

"That's what I said."

"That Prudence Murray is a wilful one for such a little gobbet," he said. "Her mother is even worse."

"Is that so?" Yang pulled the knife from the dead soldier's back.

"Pass that here," said Steve.

Yang threw it so that it clattered to the ground inches from Steve. Blood spattered over his shapeless cloth feet. He turned his pencil around in his hands and, standing on the blade to hold it in place, began to sharpen it.

CARCOSA

Rod watched the slaves as the Black Barge prepared to disembark. In the last hour, he had seen the antiques, art and knowledge of Carcosa traded for a Poundland selection of household goods and mail order tat. Jeffney Ray, a gaunt-eyed blonde girl, and a shuffling zombie dressed in the remnants of a Harry Potter T-shirt stowed the goods below and cleared the deck.

The barge set off silently with no engine noise, or any visible means of propulsion. It pulled away from the jetty and stone quayside, moving straight out across the water. To keep out of the way, Rod placed himself on the roof of the cabin and watched Carcosa fade away. Under cold starlight, the city's stone buildings shone white like chalk, like teeth. The city's silence was even more painfully obvious at a distance. As the mist parted before the barge, Carcosa was reduced to a bleached image, a reproduction, a jagged white sculpture on the shores of a dark lake in a lifeless world.

When they had left the city far behind, and even the mists had curled away to the horizon, food was brought to Rod. A packet of three out of date shortbread biscuits, a plastic pot of peach slices in syrup, and a can of beer with a name in Russian script were presented to him on a paper plate by the blonde slave. He thanked her, ate the biscuits and drank half the beer.

In his jacket pocket, he found the crushed remains of the macaroon Maurice had given him to eat in the car. It was nothing but crumbly cakey dust now. He scooped it out and gathered it together, so he had a small pile of crumbs in his hand.

He looked at the pile for a time and thought of Maurice, then of Omar and Morag and Nina, and the other people he had left far behind. After that, he tipped the crumbs over the side onto the water. He didn't mean it to look or feel like he was scattering ashes, but it felt like that anyway.

"Why do you bother?" said the King in Crimson, who was now seated next to him.

"Why do I bother what?" said Rod.

"Bother with any of it. It's all over for you now."

"Me personally? Or the world generally?"

"Both," said the King.

Rod stared across the lake, although there was nothing to see. Black lake, black sky.

"Don't you know? Didn't you write me as a character in your play?" offered Rod. The half drunk beer was making him flippant.

"You're only delaying the inevitable," said the King.

Rod snorted softly. "That's the whole point, surely?"

"Is it?"

"It could be our organisation slogan. 'The consular mission: only delaying the inevitable.'"

"You achieve nothing."

"We gain time."

"For what?"

Rod sipped his beer and waved his arm in the direction they were heading.

"I'm going back to Birmingham. I'm going to find my friends. I will help hold off the Venislarn as long as possible, maybe punch a god in the face while I'm at it, and do what I can for as long as I can."

"Achieving nothing, saving no one."

Rod ignored the miserable creature. He finished his beer and briefly considered throwing the can into the water. He didn't, not sure what monsters from the depths he might anger, and unwilling to pollute the waters of another world.

He swung around to look at Sven who was manning the tiller. "You've been everywhere, haven't you, Sven?"

The bargemaster shrugged.

"Are any of the worlds you visit actually nice?"

"Apart from yours?" said Sven.

"Given that ours is about to be destroyed, aye, other worlds."

Sven gave it some thought. "Yeah, for sure. Some. Port of *Celephaïs* is very nice."

"And safe?" asked Rod.

"Sure."

Rod hesitated before he spoke again. He needed to get his thoughts in order and not disappoint himself by mentally leaping ahead. "And your hold. How many people could it carry if you were taking passengers?"

"I do not usually take passengers."

"But if you did, Sven. If you did."

Sven wiped his forehead with his rag and, because he was still thinking, gave his armpit a rub too. "Hundred. Maybe more."

Rod gave the King in Crimson a look. "We could save a hundred people."

"What difference does that make in a world of billions?" the King sneered.

"It'd make a difference to the hundred," he said.

BIRMINGHAM - 05:40AM

The taxi journey from the canalside in Digbeth to the Cube was a short one. Though the end of the world had blocked some roads, obliterated others, and even co-opted a few into becoming things that defied description, the lack of traffic and freedom to ignore one-way signs meant the uCab driver could zip straight across the city centre, past the ruins of the Bullring shopping centre and the Peace Gardens (now reduced to ash and fallen stone) and round to the Cube.

"I probably ought to do this alone," Morag said, the thought coming to her somewhat belatedly.

"You think that, out of all the gods, *Morgantus* is the one you can manage single-handed?" said Omar.

"I think he will destroy you on sight," said Morag. "Me, he has a soft spot for."

Omar's expression was grim. "Like a prized beef cow, ripe for slaughter."

"I'm a ginge. We're special."

Omar shook his head and opened the car door. "I've got nowhere better to be. I've never been to Morgantus's court."

"Never?"

"Never. I hear the view from the top floor is quite stunning."

Morag looked at him levelly. Going inside armed with just their own demands and those of other local gods was probably a death sentence, and Omar knew it. But, as he rightly said, he had nowhere better to be.

"If it's all the same with you," said Chad from the front seat, "I might just stay here. Guard the car."

Morag patted him on the shoulder. "A wise decision. Thanks."

She hoped she'd put the right level of gratitude in her voice, and didn't make it sound like she was glad he wasn't coming with them. His surprising spiel with the *samakha* had possibly saved their lives (and committed them to finding more than a hundred luxury canalside apartments for the fishfolk), but she didn't want to go walking into the most dangerous den in the city with Chad's mouth ready to go off at any moment.

She got out and waited for Omar to shuffle round to meet her. "I don't know which of us is the most decrepit invalid at this point," she said.

Omar looped his arm through hers. His hand rested on her wrist. It was oddly pleasant to have the comfort of simple human contact.

"One of us is healing," he told her.

The Cube was, as its name suggested, a cuboid building, over twenty storeys of businesses and apartments, overlooking the Peace Gardens on one side and a large junction of the Birmingham Canal on the other. The canal side of the building linked to bridges and elevated walkways which could take a Cube resident to any number of bars, restaurants, boutiques and galleries, along the waterfront or inside the Mailbox shopping centre. Morag imagined most of those swanky eateries would now be gutted by fire or demolished. Coming from the street side of the

Cube, she wouldn't get to see unless she walked all the way through the building.

Before they entered the lobby area, Morag looked up the side of the building. The shield of light and energy over the city cast a peculiar glow on the glass and plastic cladding, but otherwise it appeared the same as always. As the seat of power in this city, on this Day of Judgement, Morag would have expected more. She didn't know what. Maybe some sort of crackling energy column bursting from the roof. Maybe *Presz'lings, Uriye Inai'e* or *Croyi-Takk*, clinging to the outer structure, screeching and hooting in victory at the ravaged world. There was neither.

"We might die in here," she said.

"Death – actual death, the cessation of being – would be a victory at this point," said Omar.

"Cheery bastard, aren't you?"

They went inside. Beside the bank of lifts there was the concierge desk. The concierge was a servant of *Yo-Morgantus*, a corpulent chap of few words, with crazy pattern baldness that looked like he had been frenziedly attacked by electric clippers. He was not at his station today. Somehow the man had been fused and cemented into the wall behind his desk, skin and hair blended into the fabric of the building so that only his face, belly and one forearm protruded beyond the surface. His eyes followed them as they walked to the lift. Morag gave him a nod of greeting. Neither spoke.

The lift doors closed and carried them up. Omar's arm twitched against Morag's.

"Do you remember when we first met?" he said.

She thought for a second. "The Caledonian Sleeper. Edinburgh to Birmingham. We sat in the buffet car and drank whisky."

"Glenfarclas," said Omar, savouring the word.

"You knew me. I had no idea who you were or what I was getting myself into."

He murmured, a hint of laughter. "I knew *who* you were. I didn't really know you." He shifted a little closer, not quite leaning on her. "I do have to say, Miss Murray, you are quite possibly one of my favourite human beings."

"What the fuck?" she laughed.

"A refreshingly unrepentant human being. If there was true power in anger, *Yo-Morgantus* would have a lot to fear from you."

"Instead we've got—" she puffed out her cheeks. "—some Venislarn denizens who want new homes, functioning taxi services and some semblance of an economy. Plus a half-hearted promise to co-operate with each other and protect at least some of the remaining humans."

"Very half-hearted."

"Will it be enough?" she asked. "I mean, you seem to have known what was happening from day one. Me. My pregnancy. Prophecies and predictions and some ritual that only Mr Grey knows."

"His invention. His life's work."

"You know it all. You've studied all the sources."

"No more than Vivian has. Since the world is ending, I will admit to you, privately, that of the two of us, she is the far more knowledgeable."

"But you know how this is going to play out?" she said.

"Would you respect me more if I said yes?"

She gestured upward at the floor they were now fast approaching. "This. A deal with *Morgantus*. Do we stand a chance?"

He smiled as he squeezed her hand again. "Not a hope in hell, my dear."

She was too tired to be shocked. "Then why? What's the point?"

"Misdirection."

"What?"

"If *Morgantus* is watching us, then his eyes are not where they should be."

"You mean Mr Grey's ritual?"

"No. Not that, either."

Before she could ask him what he meant the lift dinged and the doors opened.

05:44AM

Prudence heard a series of bangs as she was marched back up the steps of the cinema auditorium. She had pleaded with Kathy Kaur and Captain Malcolm to not kill Yang. She had demanded, asked, pleaded, and finally wept silently. Malcolm kept his distance from her, as though embarrassed, speaking with some of the thirty or so men and women who accompanied them. Kathy occasionally glanced towards Prudence, each time nodding as though, yes, this was normal.

In the covered driveway area through which Prudence had entered the cinema, they paused. A unit of soldiers, guns at the ready, crossed the deserted road and moved swiftly but cautiously alongside the dual carriageway. Kathy and Prudence moved with the second group. The chatter among the men had dampened. Prudence sensed a tension, a fear, among them.

Stunned – depressed more than stunned at what had happened – Prudence barely had the energy to wish a building would fall on them all. She stumbled, swept along with the battalion of murderers down the carriageway, and into the area before a square red-fronted building.

"Five minutes to form up inside the Mailbox," Malcolm said to Kathy. "Another five for the marksmen of bravo team to get into position on the roof. We've had intel from spotters on Commercial Street that a man and a woman have just entered the Cube, descriptions matching Sheikh Omar and Morag Murray."

Prudence perked up at her mum's name. Kathy was looking at her.

"Yes, we might get to see your mum," said Kathy. "You'll like that."

They climbed the steps to the entrance of the building. What doors there might have been inside were destroyed. Within was a strange space: cavernous and made from shiny cream-coloured stone. There were escalators and glass frontages which looked as if they should belong to shops, but no shop signs. Human bodies littered the floor, dozens of them, as though everyone had been caught up in some instantaneous, deadly rampaging storm.

"What a waste," said Malcolm.

"A Hollywood film company was making a movie here," said Kathy.

"Then it's their fault for being here," he said, suddenly dismissive.

Kathy gave Captain Malcolm a peculiar look. "Foreign lives aren't as important as British ones?"

Malcolm gave it some thought. "Film people. Movies people. I never thought of them as real."

The soldiers were forming into groups in the clearest space in the giant hall, three groups of maybe eight or nine soldiers each, and a smaller group to one side.

Malcolm addressed the men at the front of each group. "This is operational HQ. You're going in with minimal planning, but it's strong planning. We are relying on momentum and effective covering fire. Each team commander will need to use his initiative, but run all communications through us here. We have no ability to regroup for a second attack. How long until *Yoth-Bilau* is scheduled to show, Dr Kaur?"

Kathy Kaur looked at her phone. "Forty-three minutes."

"Forty-three minutes before the Soulgate closes around our world and we're all truly doomed," said Malcolm. "Bravo team, get your marksmen on the roof." As a handful of men peeled off and hurried to emergency exit doors, Malcolm pointed at some further off escalators. "Up there are the shops, restaurants and the offices of the BBC. Beyond them are the wharf side bars and restaurants. There are two pedestrianised routes to the Cube. One at canalside, one at the storey above. Alpha team will accompany Dr Kaur and the package—" Malcolm looked at Prudence "—the package*s* to the Cube. Your primary mission is protecting them at all costs. Bravo is covering the approaches alongside the wharf side. Charlie team is going to set up positions to cover the bridge leading to Waterfront Walk and Commercial Street on the other side of the Cube building."

A pair of soldiers approached Kathy with the wire cage cylinder studded with blue john shards. It was held in a harness of canvas straps. They helped Kathy thread her arms through them so she could wear it like a backpack.

"Heavy?" said one, as she helped Kathy tighten the straps.

"Heavy enough," said Kathy. A set of wires was taped to Kathy's arm, and a chunky bracelet of electronics strapped to her wrist.

"There are no civilians out there," Malcolm continued. "Anything that moves is a viable target."

Another soldier came forward holding strips of black plastic. "Here, ma'am."

"Take my hand," Kathy told Prudence. Prudence did no such thing. Kathy grabbed it. The soldier stepped forward. With quick actions and a *zipzip* sound, he pulled a plastic loop around Prudence's wrists and attached it to one around Kathy's wrist.

"We're sticking together, Prudence," said Kathy and gave a jolly little laugh, as if it was all somehow funny. "You, me and—" She waggled the wrist with the electronics on it.

"That's a bomb," said Prudence, although she already knew the answer.

Kathy jiggled her shoulders to shift the bulk on her back. "Big enough to kill your dad."

"My dad was a man called Drew," said Prudence. "My mum told me that when I was in her belly."

"Is that what she said, eh?"

"He was a kind man and a funny man. She said that too. What you mean is *Yo-Morgantus*."

"I do," said Kathy.

"He will kill you."

"And that's what these are for," said Kathy, waggling both bomb controls and the straps holding Prudence to her. "I don't want him to kill me before I get a chance to tell him what we want." She tried to give Prudence a serious look. "We are the good guys. You do know that?"

Prudence remembered the soldiers shooting the living fish sculpture and dragging Yang away. She said nothing.

The court of *Yo-Morgantus* was conveniently thought of as occupying the top two floors of the Cube, but this was incorrect. The court of *Yo-Morgantus* occupied a space that might look like the upper floors of a modern tower block but which, even upon casual inspection, was obviously nothing of the sort. The hall in which the emissaries, ambassadors, hostages and hangers-on went about their foul daily existence was too tall and too wide to fit into the space it notionally occupied. Like a Mount Olympus for demonic pan-dimensional horrors, the Cube was less a home to the court and more of a gateway. To step into the dark and windowless court room was to put one foot into the reality of the Venislarn.

Dangling metal orbs and irregular mirrors on the walls reflected and amplified what little light there was. In the gloom, the walls rippled. Was reality here wavering like a sail in the wind, or were they floor length drapes: theatre curtains to conceal the things in the wings? Or were the walls as alive as the crowded floor?

Presz'lings moved about the floors and wall on their stilt-like legs, treating gravity as an option rather than a law. *Draybbea* squelched into, merged with, and separated from one another in a continuous flow. Chitinous, winged *croyi-takk* moved restlessly, like bees in a threatened hive. An inhumanly humanoid *Voor-D'yoi Lak* prowled through the crowd, its claws flexing, its circular wound mouth salivating.

Omar stepped forward, his mouth open like a dumb yokel. She couldn't tell if he was appalled, or as wonderstruck as a child in a sweet shop.

"This place—" he whispered.

Morag nodded. "It's something else. There used to be a big *Skrendul* thing over there. A stone giant. Never moved. Just waiting for the ending of the world." She grunted. "Huh! I never thought he'd actually move out."

"But this place—"

"Yeah."

"It's like—" Omar rubbed his finger together like he was feeling cloth, searching for something. "Doesn't the décor remind you of a really, truly tacky night club?"

"Yes!" said Morag. "*Thank* you. I've always thought that. *Yo-Morgantus* has very poor taste in interior design. And staff uniforms," she added, nodding towards the nearest people in the room.

Yo-Morgantus surrounded himself with human servants. Or rather, while his vast corpulent form dwelt in the ceiling space above – a cancerous fatberg big enough to block the channel tunnel – his retinue of naked redheads moved about the hall. They were his hands, his mouth, and his playthings. They serviced the godlings gathered about. They carried messages, or fought and fucked and danced for the entertainment of their master.

A stellated gastropod *royogthrap* rolled over and raised itself above Morag and Omar as though debating which to eat first.

"*Reh solesk-andu's!*" commanded a voice. The *royogthrap* wheeled away.

"Here's the queen bitch," Morag whispered to Omar. She straightened her aching back to stand tall and proud before Brigit.

Brigit – Morag didn't know her surname, or whether Brigit was even her real name – had been the preferred mouthpiece of *Yo-Morgantus* for almost as long as Morag had been in Birmingham. Morag despised her, spending a number of lonely drunken hours wondering quite why she hated Brigit so much. She had argued it was *Morgantus* she hated, not Brigit; but she knew that to be a lie. She hated them both.

She'd wondered if it was because Brigit seemed to enjoy her sordid role. Quietly, and uncomfortably, she'd considered if she hated Brigit because of her naked body, and the way she flaunted it. No, Morag wasn't simply jealous of Brigit's youthful and shapely figure, her pale unblemished skin, or how her bloody boobs seemed to defy gravity, (not that Morag wouldn't have swapped a month of her life to get any of those things). She had eventually admitted to herself (and it had taken a lot of alcohol to achieve this level of honesty) she hated Brigit for being beautiful and knowing it; for having the confidence to live her life as she saw fit, without hesitation or apology; for having no shame, no hang ups and no moments of doubt. Being the servant of a sadistic god-monster was just the frilly trimmings round the edges.

Brigit held her hand up high, her fingertips entwined with a fleshy streamer that hung from the ceiling – skin to skin contact with *Yo-Morgantus*.

"*San-shu chuman'n, Yo-Morgantus*," said Omar, bowing his head in reverent greeting.

Morag looked to the high ceiling. "Greetings, Lord *Morgantus*." She looked at Brigit. "Hey, Brigit."

Brigit treated them to a cold smile. All Brigit's smiles were cold. Or maybe Morag just chose to see them that way because she hated the smug cow.

"Morag. Professor Sheikh Omar. This is a…"

"Surprise?" suggested Morag.

"No," said Brigit. "A bit rude. You weren't invited. You weren't summoned."

"Lord *Morgantus*, we have come to negotiate."

"The consular mission's role is completed," said Brigit. "The ink on the contract is dried. The ship has sailed. *Axana-i adek hiif'ude*."

"We haven't come on behalf of the consular mission," said Morag. "Or, if we have, it's in our new role."

"New role, eh?"

"We've come on behalf of the other gods, lord," said Omar. "*Yoth Mammon, Yo Daganau-Pysh, Yo Kaxeos*. Others too," he lied.

Eyes, blind faces and pseudo-organic sensory appendages turned towards them. At that instant, it occurred to Morag that by coming as representatives of the *em-shadt* Venislarn in the city, they were usurping the role of some of the creatures in this room.

"What do they want?"

"They want assurances about their role in the world to come," said Omar.

"And I want to see my daughter," added Morag.

Brigit's expression turned from cold to playful to quizzical to consternation. Morag could read what those turns of expression meant.

"My daughter *is* here, isn't she?"

Brigit's slappably beautiful eyes widened. "You lost her?"

05:47AM

Chad had found the taxi driver, Hasnain, to be the most wonderful man to talk to. Sure, Chad had to get the ball rolling and, after reading Hasnain's name off the licence plaque on the dashboard, felt more than comfortable enough to talk to the man on first name terms. It was true Hasnain said little – in fact had said nothing at all to Chad – but there was a look in the driver's rheumy, tired and fire damaged eyes that spoke to Chad on a deep and personal level.

Given the situation, Chad had felt compelled to explain what his role was in relation to the critically important public perception of the Venislarn.

"True, it didn't happen quite as we expected," he admitted. "We had a whole slew of marketing and advertising campaigns which we were going to roll out in the weeks and months before the Venislarn revealed themselves. We had a movie – *Man of War*. It was going to be a lovely touching story. Bromance. Romance. An emotional piece bound to get you right in the feels. I was working up ideas for a manufactured rock band with a Venislarn angle. *Tentacular*. The idea came from a passing comment by a colleague, but I put a lot of work into it. I practically donated my creative kidney to it."

Hasnain's eyes stayed fixed on the road in front of them, not a flicker of emotion, but Chad could tell he had the man's sympathies. A puff of brick dust appeared from the building just beyond Chad's window. A puff of smoke and a sprinkling of dust fell from the wall. Which was odd.

Chad pressed his face closer to the window and tried to look around but saw no obvious cause. There were a number of distant pops, like firecrackers going off, but nothing of note.

"Oh, people often think that just because we're in Birmingham, we're on the periphery of things," he continued. "Hey, Chad, if you're such a big part of these end of the world projects, what are you doing in Birmingham? Why aren't you in … New York? Washington DC? Beijing? Who ever heard of the end of the world happening here?" He chuckled.

A tiny figure leapt up from the roadside and onto the bonnet of the car. It was a little cloth thing, a sort of gingerbread man creature executed in threadbare sack cloth for the top half and flowery patterned linen for the lower half. It swung a pencil around in its shapeless fist like it was Moses's staff. It looked up at a building across the road and shouted something, but its voice was too weak and high-pitched for Chad to hear through the glass. Then it turned, jumped off the bonnet, and ran towards the Cube building.

Chad watched it go. When it had vanished he tried to remember what he'd been saying.

"People don't know – and you probably can't tell from my accent," he said to Hasnain, "but I'm actually from round here. That's right, I know! You know St Chad's cathedral, the Roman Catholic place? Of course you do. You're a taxi driver. You've got the knowledge. My parents used to go there when I was a child. St Chad and yours truly. A pair of local boys. They've got his bones up on the altar there. I tell you, this is where it's happening. Right here."

Hasnain slipped the car into gear and reversed a short distance. A second later, a man in soldier's uniform fell from the sky and smacked into the road where the taxi had just been.

"Oh, my good God!" exclaimed Chad. "Someone call an ambulance! *I* should call a ... of course. There are no ambulances." Without further thought or words, he got out and went to the man. He was quite clearly dead. There was a series of ragged wounds in his chest. Because of the way he'd fallen, his helmet contained little more than a lump of red mush. He wore a little fist and castle insignia on his shoulder marked with the words 'Forward Company'.

There were further firecracker pops. Now, out of the car, Chad realised it was gunfire, and it was coming from above. He looked to the building directly above him. Another shot. A head appeared over the rooftop. The figure was slight, the rifle it carried too large in its hands. It looked for all the world like a schoolgirl.

Chad realised the girl was aiming at him. He felt a choking lump in his throat. She clearly decided he wasn't worth shooting and vanished again.

Vivian lifted her gaze and saw that Mrs Seth had entered the conference room once again, waddling behind the trolley. In fact it seemed to Vivian the trolley was now an extension of Mrs Seth, much in the same way that she had melded with her writing tools during the largest part of her past existence.

"Yes?" Vivian asked.

"You need more tea." It was a statement.

Vivian took the cup with raised eyebrows. Mrs Seth had not been briefed in the correct procedure for making Vivian's tea. It was therefore extremely irritating that she presumed to know how it should be prepared.

Vivian took a sip, and was forced to concede this was, in fact, excellent tea. "How interesting," she said.

"Interesting?"

"This is a ... good cup of tea. You know how to prepare it. A rare skill."

Mrs Seth laughed richly. "I think my methods might be a little bit different to yours."

"No. I doubt that they differ in any material way." Vivian had spent a great of time consuming tea. She knew what was required.

There was another knock at the conference room door. Deputy Council Leader Rahman entered, wheeling a sack truck laden with boxes of catering supplies. Surely he was one of the city's leaders? Vivian supposed he was grateful to be given a sense of purpose, even if it was to be some sort of errand boy for Mrs Seth.

"I was able to access the stores cupboard as you requested," he said to Mrs Seth. "Can you work with this?"

Mrs Seth peered at the boxes, examining labels and tutting loudly as she went. "You should know I can work with anything. Even these things."

Vivian made a show of not raising her gaze from the Bloody Big Book. "I do hope you have better tea than the stuff I can see on that trolley, or we shall all be in trouble," she said.

"What do you think you are drinking right now?"

Vivian looked up sharply. She regarded the cup of perfect tea, then she checked again to confirm that the tea on the trolley was indeed the cheapest of supermarket own-brand tea bags. Little more than floor sweepings. It was impossible for her to be drinking and enjoying tea made from such a low-grade source.

"Hah!" laughed Mrs Seth. "You'll be telling me next you don't approve of evaporated milk in tea." Mrs Seth had folded her arms across her ample chest. The woman was goading Vivian.

"I most certainly do not." Vivian did not want to enter into a debate, but some things could not go unchallenged.

"Well you're drinking that now, as well."

Vivian paused. Was Mrs Seth seriously saying this cup of tea was made from the worst possible teabags *and* evaporated milk? Two of the most serious horrors it was possible to inflict upon a cup of tea, yet it tasted wonderful. Vivian had been functionally all-knowing for most of her existence, yet this state of affairs was a staggering surprise.

"Oh yes, I've heard it all before." Mrs Seth was still going. "Warm the pot! As if we always have a pot! I even heard people who fuss if you make tea in the microwave."

Vivian dropped her pen. "What? No, no, you can't—"

"The microwave. A perfectly useful thing, and better than nothing at all, wouldn't you say?"

The thought was unconscionable to Vivian. Tea? From a microwave?

Mrs Seth harrumphed. "Are you one of these who insists it's all an important 'ritual'?" She mimed the air quotes. Vivian was reminded that this was Nina's mother, and saw a glimpse of where Nina's insufferable cheek had come from.

"Only in the sense that any practical task performed properly can be called a ritual," said Vivian. "The steps can be practised and learned."

"You cannot possibly believe that," said Mrs Seth scornfully. "It is, without any doubt, an art."

"Poppycock," said Vivian and turned back to her work.

"You and I both know this to be true," said Mrs Seth, not budging an inch. "Do you want to know how I am sure?"

"I'm sure you're about to tell me."

"If the steps can be learned, then my daughter Nina should be capable of making a decent cup of tea by now, wouldn't you say?"

"Obviously, a willingness to learn is paramount—"

"You have never tasted a decent cup of tea from her, have you?"

"...No."

Mrs Seth smiled with quiet triumph then turned around, wheeling her trolley from the room.

05:52AM

"I was told my daughter would be here," said Morag.

Brigit still had a surprised look on her face, either because she was surprised or because it suited *Yo-Morgantus*'s mood to make her wear that expression. "You lost her?"

"I was told the August Handmaidens of *Prein* had her."

"They took her from you?"

The rolling ball of knotted worry and anger in Morag's belly stopped her from replying with full fury. "No," she managed. "She … wandered off."

"Wandered off…" Brigit turned and walked away. Morag and Omar were expected to follow. Morag wasn't a big fan of following naked, lily-white arses, but follow they did. As they approached the furthest wall, heating vent covers popped from their housing and a tide of wobbling flesh flowed through. Morag couldn't help but be reminded of a sausage machine. Pink, grey, veiny blue and fat-marbled white, the body of *Yo-Morgantus* extruded itself through the building vents and into the hall, accompanied by the warm wet fug of unwashed flesh.

"My lord," whispered Omar and muttered a number of Venislarn spells that Morag hoped were meant to offer protection to the pair of them.

The continuous, unbroken loops of pulsing meat pooled on the floor, building one upon another to form a regular and ridged mound. Brigit stepped onto the first ridge and began to climb the wobbling steps. Only when Brigit sat on the top, and a rigid flap of flesh and skin folded up behind her back, did Morag realise it was a throne; one atop a dais of god-meat. Armrests rose to meet Brigit's arms. Tensing, questing folds of skin embraced and supported the human.

"Looking healthy there, lord," coughed Omar.

Brigit closed her eyes and breathed deeply, perhaps savouring the moment, perhaps communing with her god. "You gave birth to the *kaatbari* but five hours ago, ushering in this golden moment and you … you what? You let her wander off? A new-born?"

Gingers around the rooms laughed. Worse, they tittered, lightly and lovingly, as though Morag was some YouTube kitten tripping over her own feet, or a toddler saying 'pasketti' instead of 'spaghetti'. The Venislarn who felt they had some grasp of human modes of behaviour joined in with variously successful hoots, clacks, rasps and flatulent parps.

"I should think you would share my concerns," said Morag. "The *kaatbari* is missing and I want my daughter back. If the Handmaidens have—"

"If they have her," Brigit interrupted, "they will pay for their impudence, the offence they have caused."

"Pay, Lord *Morgantus*?" said the smooth female voice of a Handmaiden of *Prein*.

Seven of the creatures approached from the darkness, their shells ghostly in the dim reflected light. *Shara'naak Kye* was at the front. Some at the back had cracks in their plates, and seeping wounds. Seven Handmaidens remaining.

"What have you done with my daughter, bitch?" said Morag.

Shara'naak Kye's carapace tipped slightly as though considering, but the Handmaiden ignored her. "We not have come to pay but to collect, *Yo-Morgantus*," she said.

Brigit steepled her fingers. Strips of flesh ran from her underarms to the throne. She looked like the tensing wires of a suspension bridge. "Your gods are near and you think you can make demands of me."

"The armies of *Prein* approach with the fortress of *Hath-No*," said *Shara'naak Kye*. "And with them, the blind gods of *Suler'au Sukram*. You rule here and now, but who will rule hereafter?"

"*Morgantus* rules now and *Morgantus* will always—" Brigit hesitated. Her arm twitched. "Lord *Morgantus* knows there will be transition. Lord?" This last was spoken in a different tone. A query from Brigit herself, questioning things she had not previously known.

"Transition," Omar whispered to Morag.

"I heard," she replied.

Morgantus was playing his cards close to his chest.

Morag strode to meet the foremost Handmaiden. She should have been scared. The Venislarn were playing power politics in this very court; human lives would be secondary concerns. "What have you done with my daughter?"

Armoured plates ground together. "We do not answer to you, reviled one."

"You *adn-bhul* better, missus, or gods help me—"

Morag wasn't sure what the end of that sentence was going to be. It was cut off by a sudden buzz of noise from the *Croyyi-Takk* in the room. The desiccated insectoid flyers were abruptly agitated, wheeling to and fro in their dozens. A murmur set up among the Venislarn.

"*Fe horrh-a bas tito*?" said a *Presz'ling* near to Morag.

She whirled. "What? What kind of fruit makes a noise?"

. . .

Steve the Destroyer stood on the restaurant-lined pavement between the towering Cube building and the smaller but still massive Mailbox building. To his left was a drop to the lower level and the rippling canal. To his right, the bars and restaurants were all empty shells. A fire had ripped through them all at some point in the night, and now the only movement within was the coiling acrid smoke. The soldiers of Dr Kathy Kaur's Forward Company had to come this way to reach the Cube, and Yang had been quite insistent in her tactical analysis (before dashing off to merrily slaughter the soldiers in look-out positions on other buildings). If they were to have any hope of keeping Prudence alive, they should isolate and rescue her before Forward Company got into the building.

And so, without reinforcements, Steve stood in the middle of the rubble-strewn walkway and watched the soldiers moving towards him. They were big and well-armed and numerous, and he was but one outrider of *Prein* trapped in the body of a badly stitched doll, armed with only a pencil (albeit a sharp one). But Steve was ready for them.

He had adopted the pose: legs akimbo, arms out to make a spiky star of his body, the pencil held aloft. Tensing stomach muscles he didn't possess, he constricted his throat and let forth the high-pitched wails that were the call of the *tito* fruit. He even wiggled his body a little to produce the correct wavering ululations.

The lead soldier took up a position not three strides from Steve and hunkered down behind the cover of a charred floral planter. With one eye and his gun's sights on Steve, the man pressed a button on the side of his weapon and spoke.

"Alpha point. There's a thing here." He paused, listening. "A thing. A little man. Like a voodoo doll."

There was a brief burst of gunfire. It wasn't nearby, perhaps on the other side of the building or elsewhere. Somewhere down the path, Prudence called out. "Steve! Steve! I'm here." A child's hand momentarily appeared from behind the cover of a fire gutted building and waved, before being yanked back behind cover.

"What's he doing?" said the soldier. "Nothing. He's got his arms up and he's got a pencil and he's ... he's sort of wiggling his hips."

Steve did not react. He held his pose and continued with the *tito* fruit impression. Committing to the part was very important if it was to have any chance of success.

"It's sort of a bit like an Elvis hip wiggle," said the soldier. "But the pose... He's going for more of a Freddie Mercury type thing and—" He stopped, listening to the voices in his ear. "Threat assessment? Christ, I don't know. It's a rag doll doing a dance."

The soldiers further back were beginning to move forward, bunching towards this guy.

"No, no reason," said the soldier, adjusting his grip on his rifle as he aimed.

There was a crash from on high. Steve dared to angle his gaze upward. Windows had exploded outward high up on the side of the Cube and a swarm of *Croyyi-Takk* were pouring out into the sky. They spread out in a funnel as the mass corkscrewed round and down towards the ground and the soldiers.

"Dinner time, gobbet!" spat Steve triumphantly. Abandoning his artful and enticing *tito* fruit impression, he ran for cover.

05:58AM

Prudence stared as the Venislarn flying creatures dived on the troops: huge *Croyyi-Takk* with scissor-like jaws of bone and, darting among them, *Tud-burzu* with their flaming mouths and curling backs and little legs which clawed the air as they swooped.

"GLAMS," barked a soldier across from her and Kathy. He crouched behind a chunk of fallen masonry and slotted a fat grenade projectile into the launcher thing below his rifle. From the Mailbox building behind and along the walkway, other grenadiers were already firing theirs.

With dull thuds projectiles were launched upwards where, at a height, they unfolded rotor blade appendages and hovered. A *Croyyi-Takk* collided with one, and the hovering drone exploded, blasting a chunk from the creature's thorax.

"Aerial mines," said Kathy, grimly impressed.

But the flying Venislarn were crashing into the drone mines faster than new ones could be launched. The leading edge burst through. Soldiers opened fire and suddenly everything was noise.

Prudence tried to put her hands to her ears, but one was strapped to Kathy's.

A *Croyyi-Takk* landed heavily on the pavement by the Cube. Even as a soldier tried to get a decent shot at it, the creature knocked him back and pinned him to the ground with its skewering front legs.

Kathy was shouting into her headset. "What? What?"

A soldier came up behind, hooked his hand under Kathy's arm, lifting her bodily from her crouched position, and waved her forward.

Soldiers had to engage the defenders at close quarters now. Explosions stuttered, guns rattled. Invisible bullets whistled and shots sang out from the shooting positions on the buildings all around. There was smoke and the smell of something sharp that Prudence felt on her tongue, like the taste of blood.

Something – she didn't know what – drew her attention upward. She saw Venislarn creatures pouring down the side of the building. Climbers and creepers and things that moved with forms of locomotion that defied description.

Forward Company believed they could just walk her into the Venislarn's lair. It felt like they were all going to be slaughtered before they even reached the door. She looked around for Steve, wondering where he had run off to.

A CORNER WALL of *Yo-Morgantus*'s court room had been torn away as the *Croyyi-Takk* launched themselves through (in search of fruit or battle, Morag still couldn't fathom).

In the wake of the creatures teeming out of the hole after the *Croyyi-Takk*, Morag drifted inevitably towards the opening. The city spread out before them. The sky was a ruin of colours. The halted nuclear explosions had faded over the past hour to become a filigree of wild yellows among the swirling clouds. The shield that had held it back was a bruised purple and green. And now there was a growing hint on the blurred horizon that dawn was coming and the sun would rise on Earth's final day.

The gunfire and explosions from below were echoey and distant.

"The army?" suggested Morag.

Omar shook his head, unsure.

"Humanity's last stand," said Brigit.

Morag looked back at the woman on her throne of flesh.

With many of the Venislarn now gone to join the fray below, the hundred or more redheads in the room seemed to fill the space more. In the light of magic and fire and the dawn to come, stripped of the concealing shadows, the sea of nakedness was both horrifying and ridiculous.

"You guys picked the wrong side, you know," Morag said, the words bubbling up within her. "I don't know what you thought you'd get by giving yourself to him, but it wasn't worth it."

"Watch your tongue," said Brigit.

The Handmaiden *Shara'naak Kye* stepped swiftly across and raised a leg, held it above Morag's chest, to slash at her or to flick her backwards and out of the wall opening.

"Give her to us, *Morgantus. Yech an'hi idah*."

"You do not get to make demands, Handmaiden," said Brigit. "The true gods come and they will decide."

06:00AM

At some point, the stars over the black and silent lake went out and the barge sailed through total night, a rippling arrow between darkness above and darkness below. Even before Rod had noticed the stars were missing, silence had wrapped itself around him, and he sat on the cabin roof in a state of thought-free contemplation. The barge thrummed silently beneath him, a gentle rhythmic vibration, not an engine sound, but something more organic – like breathing, or the whooshing chambers of a glacially slow heart.

A light appeared ahead, a semi-circle of brightness on the horizon. Silver ripples of reflection dotted the water.

"What is that?" he wondered, thinking it might be a rising moon.

He tried to stand to get a better look. Before he'd even got to his knees, his hand touched something rough and solid above him, and he sat down hard in surprise. He put his hand up again and it brushed against cold and clammy stone.

The vanished stars. The cold ceiling. The semi-circle of light. "We're in a tunnel," he said.

Further back, Sven croaked with laughter.

"You'll need to be sharper than that if you are to last the day," said the King of Crimson in Rod's ear. Rod didn't realise how much he had been enjoying the deathly creature's silence until that moment.

They approached the opening. The light, as bright as the moon initially, found form and definition, fading into to a dusky grey. It was a canal tunnel (of course it was, he mentally chided himself). There was the light, and a towpath, and the hint of buildings beyond.

"Birmingham's still standing, then," he said.

The King had no comment on that.

Rod rapidly considered his plans: moor up, find Nina and Morag and whoever was still alive, and get up to a hundred human souls back on the barge and away to Sven's otherworldly port. It was not going to be much of a victory over the Venislarn, but it was something.

The view ahead expanded. There were puffs of smoke and strange shapes in the oddly coloured sky. He thought he heard the patter of distant gunfire and the flat bang of munitions.

Rod checked his pistol. "And you'll keep me alive until we're done," he said to the King.

"I do not have to do anything," the King replied.

"Until I punch out a god."

The King made a dismissive sing-song hum. "My powers are to use as I wish."

"Then stay out of my way, right?"

The black barge emerged into thin light. The sun was not yet risen, Rod blinked against the change in brightness. It took him two seconds to recognise where he was. He was unsure of the name of this particular stretch of canal – the names all blurred and merged in his mind – but it was the stretch which ran up from the south, past Birmingham University, and into the city centre.

Ahead there was a squat brick bridge, a hundred yard gap, a longer footbridge, and the big turn in front of the Cube before Gas Street Basin.

He looked behind him. The tunnel they had emerged from was no longer there. It had served its purpose, and was now gone. Rod wasn't keen on sneaky magic. Things really should stay as they were. Even weird Venislarn things should have the decency to maintain some consistency.

A battle was taking place over at the Cube, mostly on the far side, by the Mailbox. Venislarn things, none of which Rod could name, were crawling all over the artsy shaped cladding on the front of the Cube building, skittering madly like ants about their nest. In the sky, spikey flying things buzzed and soared and occasionally exploded as they tangled with robot drones peppering the area. There were some soldiers in position near the long footbridge at the corner of the cube, and in firing positions by the canalside. The focus of the aerial attackers suggested the bulk of the human forces were out of sight, round the other side of the building.

"Not good," said Sven as the barge heaved to the side of the canal, slowing. "Not good for business."

Rod stood and prepared to jump to the towpath. "You've got business with me. A hundred souls to the Port of Cellophane, or wherever."

"*Celephaïs*," said Sven. "And you've not even paid me."

"I'm working on that," he said and jumped ashore. He drew his pistol. "Just wait for us, yeah?"

Without waiting for confirmation, he scuttled forward to the relative shelter of the brick bridge. He took out his phone to check the time and to see if, by some miracle, there was a phone signal. It has just gone six a.m. and, no, there was no signal.

He'd have to go to the Library and hope to meet his colleagues there. The shortest route was along the left bank, round the corner, up along the canal basin, past the Tap and Spile pub, and then through the International Convention Centre and into the Library. The path ahead would take him right beneath the firefight and across some areas of exposed towpath with no cover. Longer, but possibly safer, would be to zig-zag anti-clockwise around the Cube, away from the fighting, and down past the Peace Gardens, the Keg and Grill, the Craven Arms and then back up to Centenary Square.

It was a solid enough plan although the fact his mental map had unnecessarily made use of pubs was perhaps a reflection of what he would really like to do if he (and the world) survived the day.

The King in Crimson loomed behind him, all tattered and bloodied bandages. "What are your intentions, patron?" he whispered, perhaps a note of condescension in his voice.

"Can you run?" said Rod. He looked at the trailing rags around the King's hidden feet and then shrugged. "Don't care, really."

He jogged up the steps to the side of the bridge. He kept close to the solid iron parapet as he crossed. He heard a shot ricochet off metal as he scurried but couldn't tell how close it was. Down the other side, now on the same bank as the Cube, he clung close to the apartment building which edged the canal, and moved onward. In the brick-paved alley between the apartments and the Cube he saw a body, twisted and bent. The soldier had either been thrown by an explosion or dropped from a considerable height.

Rod was tempted to inspect the body and pilfer the weapons, but whatever had killed the soldier might still be around. The entrance to the shopping arcade on the Cube's lower level was directly in front of him. Through the thick glass he could dimly see an empty open area. With a glance to the rooftops and the surrounding area, constantly reminding himself that urban warfare was a three-dimensional affair, he nipped from the shadows of one building and into the arcade doorway.

"I thought you might be trying to circumnavigate this battlefield," suggested the King in Crimson.

"Shut up," said Rod. "I'm just cutting through."

"I bow to the experience of a military man."

Rod pulled the glass door open. In a normal building he'd be clearing his path room by room, slicing the pie and checking his angles at every corner, but he was entering a world of glass partitions and open spaces. It was effectively a three-hundred-and-sixty-degree arena. The main passage, cutting a diagonal under the square footprint of the Cube, ran between restaurants, gyms, tanning salons and spas. A woman's face grinned from a teeth-whitening advert in a shop window. The incongruity of that smile was so grotesque it held his attention for a half-second too long; he almost failed to spot the soldier moving along the towpath outside.

They saw each other at the same moment. The soldier raised his rifle and fired on full auto. That was a mistake. There was a training gym between the two of them with plate glass walls, one at the shopfront, one of the canalside. The soldier's shots crazed the glass, ruining his vision for the second or more it took the glass to fall. Rod ducked forward, moving through a shattered pane and into the gym itself. A bank of cross-trainers was hardly ideal cover, but he could position himself by the bases of the machines.

Rod maintained a low position that would nonetheless allow him to move and react. Either the soldier would move on, or he would enter the gym through the smashed window. If he did that, once he was near enough, Rod would subdue him.

Glass crunched beneath a boot. Okay, it was the second option. Rod craned his neck to look through the uprights of the cross trainer. The man had his rifle slung low and held a grenade in his left hand.

Rod cursed silently. If that was a high explosive grenade then he was as good as dead. If it was a smoke grenade or a flash-bang then Rod might lose any advantage he currently had.

"I struggle to understand what you're doing sometimes," said the King of Crimson, leaning against a support column behind Rod.

The soldier didn't turn. It seemed the King was invisible to everyone but Rod. Maybe that meant the King didn't even exist. Perhaps Rod hadn't even been to Carcosa. Perhaps he'd spent the night madly digging his way out of the collapsed tunnel and squatting under bridges until he had emerged five minutes ago by the canal with a rich delusional world in his head. Perhaps.

"Can't you distract him for me?" Rod hissed.

"I am not your servant," the rotted creature hissed back. "I am a king, after all."

The soldier stepped over a treadmill, readying to pull the pin on the grenade.

Rod reached between the King's legs to the bank of power sockets in the support column. He flicked on as many of them as he could with one motion. Training machine consoles flickered, a TV screen came on and there was the whir of machinery.

The soldier gave an audible, "Wha'?" and looked around.

Rod came up and shot him twice – clean, measured shots. Both in the chest, striking body armour. The soldier stepped back in surprise. He must have trodden on the moving treadmill because his legs whipped from under him and he half-cartwheeled, half-rolled away, noisily colliding with a rack of weights.

Rod moved forward swiftly, both hands supporting his pistol, checking his peripherals as he approached.

The soldier shouted, "No! No!" but it wasn't at Rod. The urgency and tone were wrong.

The grenade, thought Rod. The bugger had dropped it,

perhaps pulled the pin as he fell. Rod spun about, hurrying back towards any cover.

The explosion was a sharp, ear-rattling crack. The light of the flash-bang was enough to disorientate Rod but, with his back turned, not enough to temporarily blind him. He doubled back again immediately. The soldier was still on the floor, on his back, breathing hard and blinking, his hands moving to his rifle as his training kicked in.

"Drop it! Drop it!" Rod yelled, pistol pointed. His voice was a wobbly muffle in his own ears. Either the soldier couldn't hear, or chose to ignore him – closing a hand around the trigger grip of his rifle. Rod shot him, in the face, one shot. The man fell still.

"Stupid bugger," said Rod as he swept the area for more hostiles.

Seeing none, he grabbed the soldier's body by his chest pack and dragged him out of the gym, into the arcade, and into a corner. One last check for combatants, then Rod hurriedly went through the soldier's things. He loosened the man's helmet, took the personal radio ear-piece from the man and put it in his own ear.

"*—team move up. Bravo team clearing the flyers. Launch all GLAMS. Get Dr Kaur and the Murray girl in there.*"

"Murray girl?" Rod said out loud. He set aside the man's SA80 rifle for his use. It was fitted with an underslung grenade launcher, which might be handy.

Another voice cut across the channel, screaming in pain and fear.

Rod grimaced and began to remove the body's body armour and combat webbing. Undressing a corpse was awkward and difficult, like undressing a drunk friend at the end of a long night out – the passivity of the limp body felt like deliberate obstructiveness.

"*Human hostile spotted,*" came another voice. Rod immediately stopped and picked up the rifle. *"Rooftop of buildings above Waterside Walk. Little dot of a thing. Shit—!"*

The voice went quiet. Once Rod was sure the hostile they were talking about wasn't him, he re-checked his surroundings and resumed stripping the corpse. He swapped his jacket for the body armour and webbing. There were spare ammo magazines. There was blue tape around some of them. He looked inside. The rounds were tipped with a dark shiny blue. Venislarn killers. The soldier had a half dozen grenades for the launcher. There were a couple of black striped grenades Rod didn't recognise. He read the designation on the side and thought of the hovering drones he'd glimpsed. GLAMS. Grenade Launched Aerial Mine System.

"Cool," he said, impressed in spite of himself.

The constant gunfire sounded nearer. He could mentally picture the team of soldiers on the path between the Mailbox and the Cube, pepper-potting their way along the restaurant fronts towards the Cube and Rod's current position.

"Charlie nine," called a voice over the radio. *"Charlie nine check in. Your current position?"*

Rod momentarily regarded the poor idiot sprawled beneath him.

"He looks so peaceful," said the King in Crimson.

"Shut up," said Rod. There was big bloody hole to the right of the dead man's nose, and his eye socket had been pretty much sucked into the wound. He didn't look anything like peaceful. Rod took his spoils and scurried on through the building.

06:01AM

Prudence Murray didn't have much use for being afraid. In her short life she'd seen a lot of death and destruction, and not enough of the flowers and stars she'd hoped for when she and Steve had set out. In the face of the random and senseless violence she'd witnessed, Prudence had felt more anger than fear. This was her world, and each part of it seemed to be falling apart even as she looked at it. How could she be anything but angry?

But the spluttering bang of the soldiers' guns, the explosions and the screams of both men and Venislarn surrounding her were too startling to be ignored. She recoiled from each new shocking noise, and found herself clinging to the horrible Kathy Kaur as they were dragged from one unsafe hiding hole to another.

A *Voor-D'yoi Lak* peeled one man apart, seemingly just to see what his insides looked like, then danced off on tumbling limbs to find another victim. Although Kathy and the nearby soldiers were talking loudly and tersely into their communicators, giving and receiving orders, it felt like all order had vanished from the world.

Prudence wished she knew where Steve was.

"Forward!" barked a soldier. Prudence was dragged with Kathy to the next position.

On the level below, a soldier tumbled into the canal in the grip of something shapeless and slimy. Prudence watched, but he didn't come up again. There was an explosion above, and little hard chunks of something rained down on them, brittle and sharp.

"To the door!" the soldier shouted.

In a dash that felt too long and dangerous, Prudence was pulled to the entrance of the big Cube building, soldiers all around her. There was an abrupt change in sound as they ran into a big lobby area, as though the fighting and the explosions all belonged outside and couldn't intrude here. The soldiers even stopped to regain their breath, check their weapons and evaluate their position.

A soldier whose face was grey with cement dust all down one side, apart from where it had mingled with blood from a small cut, put his hand to his ear and then nodded. "Bravo team have taken significant losses and are going to withdraw to the forming up point."

Kathy Kaur shook her head. "Doesn't matter. We're here."

She pressed the button for the lift on the wall. The little round button lit up when she pressed it. Prudence found herself thinking despite everything – what they'd done to Yang and the concrete fish and the way she was tied to Kathy by a plastic strap that hurt her wrist – despite all that, she thought a little round button that lit up was a beautiful little thing. It wasn't flowers, or stars, but it was something.

There was a ding, as befitted a little round light, and doors opened. The lift was empty, obviously empty, but the soldiers checked it anyway. Kathy stepped in, pulling Prudence with her. Kathy jiggled the heavy bomb device she wore on her back.

"Time?" she asked.

"Six oh-one," said a soldier.

"Twenty-two minutes until *Yoth-Bilau* appears and the Soulgate closes for good," she said without emotion.

"We'll maintain our position here."

Kathy pressed one of the buttons on the large panel of illuminated buttons. It lit up. Lots of shiny buttons on the lift wall. Prudence itched to touch them.

Rod's plan had been to cut through the lower level of the building, round to the far street and away round to the Library. Until the mention of the 'Murray girl' changed everything. Whether it was Morag or her baby girl, it meant either his colleague or the Venislarn anti-Christ was in the building, which meant something was afoot.

"The exit is that way," the King in Crimson pointed out.

Rod didn't bother to comment.

He now wore the dead soldier's armour and combat webbing over his shirt. His jacket was folded neatly and left in the doorway by the gym. It was only a cheap suit jacket from Burton's, but he was loath to leave it. He carried the SA80 rifle, a hi-ex grenade loaded in its underslung launcher.

Knowing he might regret it at any instant, he crept up the glass spiral stairs from the lower canalside arcade to the upper walkway entrance on the 'true' ground level. Progressing through three-dimensions in what was an essentially transparent environment made covering one's angle extremely difficult, but he progressed swiftly and purposefully.

When he rounded the corner to the final flight, he saw six men in the main lobby. All of them were turned to face closing lift doors. Rod caught a fleeting glimpse of two figures inside the lift: the curvaceous Kathy Kaur with some bulky snail shell thing on her back, and a shorter, slighter figure with a mass of untidy coppery hair. Too short to be Morag, but surely too tall to be Morag's girl.

"Dr Kaur and the girl in the lift," said one of the soldiers. Rod heard it both out loud and in his earpiece.

One of the soldiers turned. Rod was already aiming, having picked the three he was going to take down before he retreated out of shot, fired his grenade, and re-engaged.

"Give me the girl and no one gets hurt! Much!" screeched a high-pitched voice.

"Tiny hostile!" someone yelled. They began firing, off to the side.

It was a gift of a distraction. Rod shot one soldier, a three-round burst to the lower back. He switched to a second target and repeated it. Shouts or screams were lost in the gunfire.

Steve the Destroyer, the high-pitched screecher, bounced off a counter and pirouetted towards a soldier who had just discovered that shooting a high energy doll was a difficult thing. Steve slashed out with his pencil weapon but missed the man's shoulder by a good foot.

It didn't matter. The creature's antics had their attention. Rod put down a third soldier before any of them had spotted him. The one who did see him managed a single syllable before Rod put life limiting wounds in him. Steve bounced between the remaining two, and they nearly caught each other in their crossfire. They were both yelling, but Rod couldn't make out what over the noise and the cross-chatter in his ear.

He pressed forward. They were two to his one, but he had momentum and confusion on his side. They'd be wondering what had happened to their comrades, thoughts flying too quickly for analysis. Rod shot one in the gut and shoulder. The final one finally saw Rod, turning his gun toward him. The shots went wild. The soldier started running for cover, but too late. Three shots –

shoulder, rib and thigh – and he crashed down against a decorative pillar.

Rod climbed the final step into the lobby. Most of the men were dead; the others soon would be. He separated the dying from their weapons. There were no words of comfort he could offer them, no credible lies about help being on its way.

Only when he was sure the area was clear did Rod check himself. No wounds, no grazes.

Steve the Destroyer stood on a dead man's chest and repeatedly plunged his pencil spear into the man's eye. Rod picked a spot to kneel, check his ammo and consider the surrounding area.

"The man's dead," said Rod.

"He's dead when I say he's dead, fleshing!" crowed the blood-spattered imp.

06:03AM

Prudence pressed one of the buttons in the lift. It lit up and she felt a huge satisfaction. Kathy yanked her hand away.

"What are you doing?"

"I pressed a button."

"You don't press a button!"

Prudence glared at her. "You pressed a button."

"I'm in charge," said Kathy. "I know where we're going."

"I wanted to press a button."

"You do what you're told. Did no one ever teach you any manners?"

Prudence thought about the question. "No. My mummy taught me to stay safe and to not wander far, and to not poke things from other dimensions."

"You also shouldn't push buttons unless you're told you can."

Prudence looked at the woman intently. Kathy Kaur wasn't her mum. She quickly pressed another button on the panel just to see it light up.

"Jesus!" said Kathy and yanked her back again, hard. The strap around Prudence's wrist twisted into her flesh and burned.

"Ow!" squealed Prudence and the sound turned all by itself into a little cry.

Kathy sighed loudly. She turned Prudence round and inspected her wrist. "No permanent damage."

"You hurt me."

Kathy's expression became difficult to read. She brushed the shoulder of Prudence's T-shirt, and the short trousers she was wearing. Prudence had adjusted them several times in the night as they'd become tighter and tighter. Kathy looked at Prudence's grubby bare feet.

"What are you?"

Before Prudence could answer the lift dinged. Kathy drew the little pistol holstered at her belt. "This is your doing," she said.

The door opened. Kathy repeatedly tapped a button marked with double arrows and nervously watched the grey carpeted corridor outside.

There was a series of wet thumps coming from somewhere. The door closed.

"How many levels are there in hell?" Kathy said, but Prudence could tell she was talking to herself.

The doors closed again.

"That's what happens if you press buttons," said Kathy.

Prudence looked at the two lit floor buttons on the panel and wondered if she could get away with pressing more.

Soon enough, Steve tired of mutilating the man's face. Rod had switched out his ammo to a full clip of Venislarn killers and tried to make sense of the cross-chatter on his earpiece. There was a lot of confusion. As best as he could work out, Charlie team were holding their position, Bravo team was fighting off a *skrendul*, whatever that was, and it appeared Rod had wiped out most if not all of Alpha team. There was no mention of a Delta team, or an Echo or a Foxtrot. Rod decided to take that as a good sign.

The two voices on the chat that he recognised were Captain McKenna (who Rod knew as Malcolm: he used to work security detail for the consular mission before turning traitor) and Kathy Kaur. Her signal cut out intermittently from inside the rising lift.

"*—child pressed all the buttons,*" she said. "*We saw a shadow of* Yo Khazpapalanaka *on the fifteenth floor. Screwed with our perception of time for a ... felt like a week. Do not press another button, damn—!*" The chatter went quiet.

"Is Morag up there?" Rod asked Steve.

Steve stepped away from his stabby pencil fun. "I don't know, morsel! But I'm going up there to save the *kaatbari*. Who's the big guy?" He pointed with the bloody end of his pencil.

Rod glanced over his shoulder. The King in Crimson stood in his shadow, rot blackened limbs, weeping wounds on his chest and face, the stained mask quivering with the King's rattling breath.

"This is— Wait, you can see him?"

"Course I can see him, foolish lump! What other big guy would I be referring to?"

The outer doors to the lobby imploded. Something huge charged inwards. Girders popped, the ceiling actually rippled, ceiling tiles and light fittings burst from their housing as the monster powered into the building.

With a kick against the stair support, Rod propelled himself laterally across the floor away from the destruction. He scrabbled on hands and feet for an instant, slid into a firing position, and began shooting at the thing before it could clear itself from the rubble.

For a Venislarn it had a surprisingly regular appearance. It had two feet, two arms and a head, and no extra weird bits like tentacles or pollen sacs or fungoid frills. It was still definitely a monster. It was fifteen feet high at least, and its overall body shape was a round-topped cone. Crease lines marked its eyes, mouth, neck and groin, but it was otherwise featureless. It appeared to be made of stone: weathered and pocked stone. It was a fifteen feet high, walking, thrashing, concrete bollard.

It was also bullet proof, even to blue john Venislarn killers. Rod shifted his aim from chest to neck joint to eyes, but only struck stone.

"You could punch it," said the King in Crimson conversationally.

"And let you have my soul?" Rod grunted.

The creature marched forward. The top of its head was in the ceiling, but that offered no resistance. It carved through metal, plastic and glass like an upside-down icebreaker.

"*Skren-dul*!" cried Steve, as he hauled himself over the wreckage and charged the thing. It took Rod an instant to realise Steve was shouting its name, not a generic war cry (an instant during which Rod discovered the thing's groin was almost impervious to bullets – he was testing it out methodically, section by section – with no Achilles heel in the trouser department).

Steve scrambled up its leg. The thing actually noticed the tiny doll. The *skrendul* could have just sat down and pulverised Steve, but instead swept its stone arm round and scooped him up. The creature's mouth opened a crescent moon crack to eat Steve. Rod shot it in the mouth.

The *skrendul* roared in pain. It was a surprisingly dry and pathetic roar for a creature of such size, but the fact Rod could hurt it was the best news of the day. Its mouth widened, gagging at the shock. Rod slid his hand forward to the grenade launcher trigger. At this range, accuracy was not a problem. The grenade struck right in the tonsils (if the thing had tonsils) and the force of the initial impact and surprise caused the *skrendul* to snap its mouth shut around it.

The explosion, a hollow deep rumbling, did not escape through the *skrendul*'s tight lips. Its eyes bulged, showing the pond green pupils fully for a moment and then the eyes popped from their sockets, propelled on jets of pinky-white gore.

The *skrendul* rocked on its feet, then tumbled forward, one foot taking a final post-mortem step before it fell head first against the bank of lifts. Marble panelling splintered and more of the ceiling fell down. Steve the Destroyer bounced gracelessly on the floor and skidded to a stop just in front of Rod.

Rod kept his aim on the *skrendul* until he felt certain it wasn't going to move again. It lay against the wall, completely blocking the lift doors. Several of the dead soldiers were now buried under its bulk.

Steve coughed the dust away, even though Rod was sure the little thing didn't have any actual lungs. "I didn't need your help you know," he spat.

Rod held in a sharp reply. "Is that your general tactic?" he asked. "Fly in like an irritating distraction and expect others to clean up the mess you started?"

"I don't know what you mean," said Steve, wounded.

"I do," said the King in Crimson.

Rod stood and considered their lot. There were three of them. One who was useless in a fight, one who wouldn't fight unless it amused him, and Rod. Above them were twenty-five storeys with at least one god, Kathy Kaur and at least one Miss Murray waiting for them.

"Looks like we're taking the stairs," he said.

06:08AM

Vivian did not get distracted from her task of writing the Bloody Big Book. If she could continue to write through the devastating battle back in *Hath-No*, and the continuing destruction of the human world in her present situation, then the mundane comings and goings of the humans who shared her space were very easy to ignore. Normally. What had penetrated her consciousness was a smell. It was stronger than the sulphurous blasts of the Venislarn onslaught which shook the building and provided a muffled symphony of destruction here in the basement. It was stronger and very much more pleasant, like the baking of a cake.

Vivian sniffed the air. It *was* baking cake. Nothing else would create a smell like that. She got up from her seat, carrying her papers with her. Walking and writing was sub-optimal, but she had to see for herself. Of course she knew a cake was being baked, but the words flowing from her hand failed to adequately convey the delicious allure of the smell.

"This kitchen has no oven," she said to Mrs Seth, who was

busy in the small catering nook. "Yet you have created the smell of baking."

"This is not the first time I have been without an oven," said Mrs Seth, turning around and moving aside so Vivian could see her handiwork. "The gentleman from the council found me everything I needed to make one. A pity he could not be so dependable with the emptying of my bins."

The metal draining board accommodated a home-made oven. The metal box had previously housed a desktop computer, but now it lay on its side, propped up with tins of baked beans. The heat source underneath was an array of tea light candles. Vivian was mildly appalled at the sight of naked flames in an office, but it probably wasn't the riskiest thing happening in their current environment. Within the open slot of Mrs Seth's PC-based oven, Vivian could see a cake rising up out of a tin that looked as if it might once have held shortbread.

"Remarkable." Vivian nodded.

"Thank you," said Mrs Seth.

"That was not intended as a compliment, you understand, but rather as a comment upon the idea that this is the time for cake."

Mrs Seth scowled at Vivian, drawing herself up to her full height – which brought her roughly in line with Vivian's shoulder. "Who appointed you the expert on when it is time for cake? If I say it is time for cake, then I have my reasons."

"And in the face of an impending apocalypse, what could those reasons possibly be?"

"There are those of us, Mrs Grey, who would prefer to face the impending apocalypse with a piece of cake! I look around this place and I see a group of people who do not look as if they are having a good time. You, of course, have a better idea for fixing that, yes?"

Vivian shook her head at the notion she would even consider the mood of others a priority for her problem-solving skills. She returned to her seat in the conference room, but before she sat down, the doorway was blocked by a breathless Mr Seth.

"I return with pens!" he gasped.

"Very good. Put them down here, if you would."

"No, no, no. I need to show you a few things first." Mr Seth failed to notice Vivian's deliberate attempts to ignore him. She turned to her work, confident she could block out his chatter. She was dimly aware that he had taken a seat next to her and was somehow very busy with his stationery. She reasoned he would leave eventually.

"I shall walk you through some of the choices that I have made for you," said Mr Seth. "You should know I have always had a keen interest in fine penmanship. For many years I had the honour of filling out all of the certificates awarded to the Brownies and Rainbows in our area."

Vivian looked up at him. "Nina was in the Girl Guides?"

"Oh no. Well only for a few weeks. There was an ... incident. But they asked me to carry on writing the certificates after she left, once they saw how beautiful my writing was."

"Yes, I'm sure they did. Now, can we please hurry this along? I do have work to do."

"Yes you do, and may I compliment you on your work? To maintain such a meticulous style, and to write so quickly, is a skill to be much admired."

Vivian said nothing. He was correct.

Mr Seth coughed and continued. "Right, well I got the security guard to take me round all of the offices in this building. I searched the desks and the stationery cupboards. I can confidently say that I found the best pens available."

Vivian was mildly intrigued, so she turned to see what he had brought her. It was arguable that a few moments invested in securing better equipment would increase her productivity.

"I have written some small samples with each pen. Now, you

will see I have brought you some good quality ballpoint pens, because I found only two fountain pens. Let us look at the ballpoints first of all. Can I draw your attention to this vintage Paper Mate? I am not sure when they last made this sleek steel version, but it has a nice smooth action. I also found a Waterman, which is, of course, a premium brand, but I believe the Paper Mate contains a fresh refill." He looked up to check she was watching. He seemed satisfied he had her attention. "Now, I don't know if you're going to need to use colour in your work at all, but I brought you a couple of these."

He demonstrated a pen with sliders that could change from blue to black and red, making a little scribble with each colour. He glanced up at Vivian's face.

"No? No. Perhaps that is not for you. A little childish, I would imagine." He set those aside. "I brought you a total of six of these Parker ballpoints. I can only assume they were given out as a gift to employees at some point. They will serve as decent enough workhorses, although personally I find them a little pedestrian." Vivian permitted a small part of her mind to speculate on whether she herself had favourites when it came to pens. She concluded she probably did, but those memories were just a faint notion that she had once delighted in a nicely crafted tool, whatever it might have been.

Mr Seth grinned widely. "I have saved possibly the best for last. Two Schaeffer fountain pens. One of them is paired with a propelling pencil, which could be a pleasing alternative if you wanted a break from—"

"—The Bloody Big Book cannot be written in pencil," snapped Vivian. "That would invite disaster."

"I see." He set aside the pencil. "I made sure to bring you a bottle of ink as well, but let me assure you I filled the bladder on both of these pens, so they are ready to go."

Vivian picked up one of the pens. It was a marbled red and

black colour. Probably a good match for the sky outside by now. She removed the lid and it sat comfortably in her hand, much chunkier than the pens from the gift shop. She wondered why it felt familiar somehow.

"Where did you find this, exactly?" she asked.

"It was on the seventh floor. In a box with some other things."

"I see."

She was certain this was her own pen, put in a box but not discarded after her death. Foolish sentimentality, but at least it meant she had a dependable pen to work with. "Good work. Thank you," she said to Mr Seth.

Mrs Seth entered the room with a plate. "I have brought you a slice of cake."

"Did I say I was hungry?" said Vivian.

"No. The consumption of cake has little to do with hunger. You doubted the need for cake, but I challenge you to eat a slice and tell me it was time wasted."

"Time," said Vivian, looking around. "What time is it?"

"It is six ten," said Mr Seth, consulting his watch.

"Well, you should know this building is going to be reduced to rubble in just over an hour. You should both make your way out as quickly as possible."

Mrs Seth bustled forward, holding out the plate. "So, are you going to eat this cake or what?"

"I'm sure others would appreciate it more. Have you offered a slice to Mrs Fiddler?"

"Who?" said Mrs Seth.

Vivian grunted. "...The *Cha'dhu Forrikler* are here."

"Who?"

Vivian shook her head and returned to her work. She was aware of cake being placed by her elbow but did not touch it.

"This book seems strangely important to you," said Mr Seth eventually.

"This is everything," said Vivian.

"It can't be everything," said Mr Seth. "It's just a book."

"The pages are surprisingly thin. It is a recollection of everything that has happened, is happening and will happen in this reality."

"No," he said, shaking his head.

"I started from the edges," she explained. "It took me a while to realise what I was constructing. I thought I was writing a commentary on the Bloody Big Book. Then I realised the commentary *was* the book, and the book contained the world. Once I realised what I was doing, I started at the edges, like a jigsaw, and worked my way in towards these tricky final details: the moments in the here and now."

"You are writing what is happening now?"

"Nearly," she said. "I have covered the broader details. For example, the *Cha'dhu Forrikler* are descending. They are the arbiters of reality. Perhaps I am only transcribing what they already know. Portions of our world have already been consumed in their edit."

"That doesn't make sense, madam."

"Things become harder to explain when there are no human points of reference. I say that the *Forrikler* are descending but, in truth, they approach along a *velakh* plane – a flickering through the *the-agh* sheafs. *Hath-No*, the fortress which was once my home, comes through a much more conventional hole in the *lo-frax* membrane. It will be here in a few minutes in fact. The unfound *Esk'ehlad* brotherhood travel by the vocalisation of their choir. Do they sing their way here, or is this world the song they sing? There's no distinction for them. *Yo Chi'ented*, who consumes probabilities and causal events, is sieving his way to this juncture, winnowing worlds and gnawing his way around the thread of inedible truth."

"You speak in English, but it is all nonsense."

"Very well," said Vivian. "Or I could speak of what is happening in the mundane world which remains. Things become more concrete as I write them. Nina, your daughter, is alive by the way. She is less than a mile away. She is travelling with a *samakha* called Pupfish and my husband who is a donkey."

"You married a donkey?"

"He wasn't a donkey when I married him. But then he did something unforgiveable and so I transformed him into one. Now, Nina thinks I will lift the enchantment and allow him to perform the *kaat-bed sho* ritual. He thinks, and she thinks, that will drive the Venislarn back and save the world."

"Will it?"

She allowed herself a small, pained expression. "Death is inevitable. But people still expect to triumph over it, to find a final victory and a happy ending. The only victory is in avoiding an end, in keeping going. The next footstep is a victory. The next breath is a victory. But this world is doomed."

"We are in the Kali Yuga," said Mr Seth.

"The end times," nodded Vivian. "The bull of Dharma has only one leg."

"You know Hinduism?"

"I used to know everything," she said. "Sometimes I think I still do."

"Then you also know that the gods destroy this world so that it can be remade. As one book closes, another is opened."

Vivian was silent and even tried to keep her thoughts neutral. She did not know what beings, powerful beyond reckoning, might be observing this moment through unseen methods.

"Your daughter is doing her best to avert the end of the world," she said. "She will be here soon. Meanwhile, her former colleagues are trying to undo it all in their own way. Morag Murray thinks she can bargain our way out of hell, but she is going to be disappointed. Kathy Kaur thinks she can terrorise *Yo-*

Morgantus into calling off the invasion, which is just as ludicrous. And Rod Campbell—"

"Oh, we have met Rod," said Mr Seth. "Big chap. Always wears a tie. Very well presented."

"He's rushing in with a gun and no plan and thinks he can save some fraction of humanity from the final hell. A foolish endeavour."

Mrs Seth grunted, unimpressed. "You think he's a fool."

Vivian considered her answer before speaking. "No. He's not a fool. He's a good man. But it's almost impossible to tell the difference between the two." She bent to her work for a moment. "Having said that, he has found the lift doors on the ground floor to be blocked and so has decided to take the stairs to the twenty-fifth floor of the Cube building. If he thought about it for a moment, he could just go to the second floor and take the lift from there. So, who can say?"

06:11AM

It was not only the sky that was changing colour minute by minute. With the irregularity and untrustworthiness of a dream, the world immediately beyond the city centre was shifting out of true. As Morag watched, the distinction between the shield over the city, the distant suburbs and the horizon blurred and melded.

"The *Nid Cahaodril* are nearly here," said Brigit. "The fields of my parents."

"*Morgantus*'s secret gods," whispered Omar. "What we know about them…" He shook his head at his own ignorance.

Brigit stood on her fleshy dais to watch the slow but certain collapse of the world. *Morgantus* spoke through her. "The way has been made soft and edible. Feel them come. Feel their gratitude."

"Send them back!" commanded Kathy Kaur, pushing through the doors from the lobby.

Morag's emotions towards Kathy were complex, and had hardened recently. They came rushing back to her as she saw the woman enter. Kathy wore a heavy backpack that just screamed 'bomb'. Wires joined to a wrist unit only confirmed that impression. In one hand, she held a short pistol, possibly the same one with which she'd killed the August Handmaiden, *Shala'pinz Syu,* what felt like a lifetime ago, but was only yesterday. Tied to her other hand, was Morag's little girl, Prudence.

Morag's heart leapt and broke in one action. How Prudence had grown! A prepubescent slip of a thing, narrow legs poking out of those stupid adapted shorts Morag had dressed her in back she was a toddler, a few short hours ago. Her feet were filthy, her face smeared with dust and soot.

"Mummy!"

Prudence tried to pull forward, but Kathy held her in place. Morag dashed forward and Kathy raised the pistol.

"Don't!" she snarled.

Morag had to fight her almost overwhelming emotions to halt her charge. Monsters hissed and gurgled. A *Uriye Inai'e* wheeled through the rafters to drop on Kathy. She saw it and shifted her aim.

"*Cuda'nih, fnah-yo!*" Kathy called. "*Fa'slorvha pessh khol-kharid!*"

The many-tentacled *Uriye Inai'e* didn't quite back off, but heeded her warning enough to hold its position.

Red-haired courtiers jostled, some to get away from Kathy, others to get a better look. The remaining Venislarn shifted and repositioned themselves. The Handmaidens hovered close to Morag; their petty desire for revenge was not forgotten.

"Give me my daughter," said Morag. It was an obvious, trite and pointless thing to demand, but it was the only thought in Morag's head. It burned inside her.

Kathy raised the hand tied to Prudence's. "I have the *kaatbari!*" she announced to the court. She turned slightly to show them all the device on her back. The blue stone, formed from the toxic secretions of the renegade *Crippen-Ai,* shone faintly. "I have the means to kill every single being in this room. Enough explosive to rip the top off this building."

Omar placed a hand on Morag's shoulder as he hobbled forward. "Mad or brilliant. It's so hard to decide," he whispered.

Kathy gestured to the device on her wrist and turned so that all could see. "*Gue-am-bhun, yo cad yoth.* This is a dead man trigger. You kill me, the bomb explodes. You all die."

"Mad *and* brilliant?" suggested Omar quietly.

"I'm going to kill her," whispered Morag.

"She's going to kill herself."

Kathy turned so she was facing Brigit and *Yo-Morgantus*. She spoke with powerful confidence, but Morag was near enough to see the tremor of fear in her legs.

"I have the means to kill us all. I have the *kaatbari*, the key to the *kaat'zhedu*. We have—" she consulted her wrist "—thirteen minutes until *Yoth-Bilau* arrives and the Soulgate closes around us for good. You will hear my demands."

Brigit stepped forward from her throne. She hesitated. There was true fear on her face. A tassel of skin snaked out from Morgantus's mass and wrapped itself around her ankle. The fear vanished. "What are your demands?"

The Handmaiden *Shara'naak Kye* began a bitter complaint. Brigit silenced her with an upheld hand. "What are your demands?" she repeated.

Kathy adjusted her stance. Nervousness rippled through her. "You, *Morgantus*, leave. Take your retinue with you and abandon the Earth."

Kathy waited for a response, but Brigit gave none. A streamer of flesh was moving silently across the floor towards Kathy. One touch and she would belong to *Yo-Morgantus*.

"End this invasion. Leave this planet. Leave us alone to rebuild."

Brigit nodded slowly. "I see."

Kathy fired her gun at the strip of sneaking flesh. It recoiled like a stretched spring. The *Uriye Inai'e* dropped from the ceiling.

With luck more than skill, for she was no soldier, Kathy sidestepped and shot it. The creature clawed itself in a pitiful frantic circle as it died, a bubbling wound in its teeth-covered underside.

Prudence was crouched as much as her bonds would allow, her free hand pressed to her ear.

"Don't do this. Let her go," said Morag.

"My demands," said Kathy simply.

There was a flat roar from outside as a new shape appeared in the sky over Birmingham. Its massive curved underside was just about visible through the hole ripped in the wall. For an instant, Morag wondered if this was *Yoth-Bilau* and they were all now trapped in hell for eternity. But no. To look on *Yoth-Bilau* was to experience pain, and this new arrival, this crazy huge impossibly hovering moon thing was just a ball of hole-studded mud.

"*Hath-No* is here," sang *Shara'naak Kye*. "The hordes of *Prein* are here. *Morgantus*, relinquish your post and surrender the Murray women to us. Morag Murray is a murderer."

"That woman killed your sister, *Shala'pinz Syu*," said Morag, pointing at Kathy. "With that very weapon."

The Handmaiden whirled and shifted her plates furiously.

"Do not interfere!" Kathy retorted. "I am in charge!"

"No!" said Brigit with smooth magisterial authority. "No." She put her hands on her hips, legs akimbo in a Peter Pan pose that might have looked domineering and powerful, if she wasn't naked and her arms' position just drew all observers' eyes to her ginger pubis.

"I am prince of this city," *Morgantus* spoke through her. "I have kept the balance and my will is law. *Has been* law. The apocalypse has been ushered in with all the rituals and preparations. The way has been softened and made edible and the *Nid Cahaodril* are here and my role is complete."

"Oh, I don't like the sound of this," said Omar, but Morag had other things on her mind.

"I will abandon the Earth," said Brigit. Kathy gave a sudden and surely involuntary gasp of laughter. "I will abandon the Earth and follow the declining path. This earth with its rivers and mountains and motorway interchanges; its hair mascara, AstroTurf and labradoodles. Humanity crawls like a rash upon its surface, deluded in its presumption of mastery when it has failed at the most basic elements of housekeeping. I will wait the approval of my lords. My role is complete and I will walk the declining path."

"He's leaving?" said Morag.

"He's had enough of being in this colonial backwater," said Professor Omar. "Perhaps he feels the call of the Venislarn Home Counties, the sound of leather on willow, and the smell of linseed oil and cucumber sandwiches at four."

"What?"

"Forgive me," he said. "I am dying, you know."

Morgantus drew himself back into a tall bulk. At the sight of him, Morag was unaccountably put in mind of the pink blancmange served for school dinners at Avoch Primary School when she was a girl. The mental recollection did not improve her opinions of either blancmange or *Morgantus*.

Brigit gasped suddenly, her conscious will returned to her. "Lord? You are leaving us?"

"And take the rest of these *vangru* with you, too!" said Kathy.

"You cede the city to the *Prein* and the blind gods of *Suler'au Sukram*?" said *Shara'naak Kye*.

Ribbons of flesh flicked among *Yo-Morgantus's* human pets.

"—With my duties discharged," said a woman.

"—I will take the declining path," said another, whose red hair was streaked with grey.

"—The city does not need me to oversee it," said a man.

"Look!" cried another. A dozen fingers pointed to the window.

As a hundred forms, shapeless at such distance, began to drop from the moon-fortress of *Hath-No*, other shapes moved into sight. Tall fiery tornados – the children of *Kaxeos* – whipped across the city to the south. A shape surged in the canal waters, and the frilled limb of *Daganau-Pysh* appeared. The creaking, leaf-shedding army of *Yoth-Thorani* were just visible moving through the buildings around the National Indoor Arena.

"Gods come," spoke *Yo-Morgantus* through more than one voice. "Petty rivals with petty claims that you, Morag Murray, have stirred in them."

Something warm brushed Morag's neck. She was plunged into another state of consciousness. She was still here, but now she perceived her body as though through an intermediary, something seen on television or a movie screen, but not experienced. While she knew *Morgantus* had taken control of her, driving her body with his thoughts, she did not think that thought with her own mind; there was no mind belonging to her anymore. She perceived as a conduit: sight and sound passing through her to elsewhere.

Morag Murray approached the flesh mound of *Yo-Morgantus* and spoke, her voice in unison with many others.

"I will take the declining path. I relinquish this city. Morag Murray has set the gods against one another. And so she will receive them and she, the mother of gods, the kingmaker, will arbitrate between them and rule as my successor."

Morag stood on the first step, her feet sinking in the warm, sweaty flesh of her god. From on high, flayed from some portion of his body, *Morgantus* lowered a cloak of skin across her shoulders. It was coarse and gnarled, marked with sprouting hairs and goosebumps, and very much alive. The coronation robe folded itself over her. It insinuated itself inside her loose clothes, tore them away and wrapped her body in its pleats and layers. Cloak became robe became the dress and accoutrements of a queen.

"No!" yelled Kathy and the Handmaidens together.

"You mock us!" said *Shara'naak Kye*.

She was correct. *Morgantus* allowed the knowledge to flow through Morag. With his gods' approval, he was departing. And as a final joke (as much as he understood human humour), he was placing Morag on the metaphorical throne as his successor.

"The city is given to Morag Murray as long as it stands," she announced.

06:14AM

Rod stopped to catch his breath at the twenty-fifth floor. As he had stated many times to any who would listen, he was built for endurance running rather than sprinting, and even at a steady jog, twenty-five floors was too much of a sprint for his liking.

"Don't tarry, worm!" said Steve, dangling from his combat webbing. "Seize the moment and charge in."

"I'm checking the approaches," Rod gasped. He angled his rifle up the stairwell leading to the roof level, then checked the stairs below for any pursuers. He took his own sweet time about it. Yes, methodical operational practices were key, but he was also too knackered to seize anything at this very instant. He wasn't charging anywhere until he was good and ready.

"The way to the roof is clear, patron," said the King in Crimson. "And no one has followed us."

"Oh, you've finally decided to be helpful?" said Rod.

"I am keen to see what happens next," the ghoul offered.

Rod wasn't too clear on what should happen next. A hall full of individual humanoid hostiles he could handle – well, not exactly handle, but he would know what had to be done. There were few problems in life which couldn't be solved with explosives and high-speed projectiles. A hall full of weird god things and oddities from beyond doing unspeakable things in other dimensions ... that was trickier.

He moved through the swing doors into the lobby area. A wide window overlooked the city to the north. He couldn't begin to comprehend what was happening with the sky. Something was swimming powerfully down the canal, a great bow wave washing up over the towpath and crashing against the pubs and businesses along its length. There were puffs of explosions and the flutter of activity suggesting the battle between Kathy's renegade forces and the Venislarn was not yet concluded. The radio chatter was now more sporadic.

He moved to the large doors which led to the court of *Yo-Morgantus*. "No attacking anyone unless I say so," he told Steve.

"Steve makes promises to no one," the little creature replied.

There was no point trying to press the point further. He pushed the door open and slid in, gun raised.

Nothing attacked him. Nothing and no one even noticed him.

In a massive hall that was a fair bit emptier than he expected, all eyes and faces and weird blobby things were directed to a tall, pinky-grey platform at the centre of the room. Strutting insectoid shapes and shapeless sluglike forms were all focused on the woman on the throne-like dais. Maybe a hundred of *Morgantus's* naked slaves were also watching. And standing close by were Kathy, Omar and that red-haired girl who must be Prudence Murray (even though she *couldn't* be). And the woman on the stage, dressed in what looked like a wedding dress that had been rinsed in cow's blood, was Morag.

And still no one had noticed him.

He coughed politely. Finally some of them turned. "Ay up," he said in greeting.

There was a burbling complaint from some slimy beast.

"Rodney!" cried Omar, with a delight Rod had never elicited in the man before. Omar looked pale and hunched, as if old age had come upon him all at once.

Kathy Kaur, finally noticing, raised her compact Sig Sauer pistol.

"Don't," said Rod, his rifle already aimed for a headshot.

"Shoot and we all die," she said.

"Do it!" squeaked Steve from his shoulder.

Rod squinted at the device on her wrist. "Dead man trigger?"

"Yes," said Kathy.

"Stupid," he said. It was a heartfelt comment. Such devices, only favoured by desperate terrorists and their like, were as prone to killing friend as they were foe.

"Rod Campbell," said Morag. Instantly he knew it wasn't Morag – *his* Morag – speaking those words. "Put down your weapon. It is not needed. Our business here is almost concluded."

"It is not!" said one of the ghostly-white crab monster Handmaiden things. "We do not recognise your decision to give the city to the Murray woman."

"To Morag?" said Rod.

"*Yo-Morgantus*, having decided he's had enough of Earth and is going to ask his masters to return him to some other realm, is playing some last-minute shenanigans before he leaves," said Omar.

"You cannot leave us, lord," declared a young naked ginger. She flung herself at the wobbly bouncy castle that was her god. She pressed herself into its rolls of fat.

"If you're making last minute requests," Rod called, "then let these people go." He released his supporting hand from the rifle for a moment to wave at the ginger crowd.

"*Let* them go?" said Morag with imperial aloofness. "They are my willing servants."

"Aye, well I didn't say they weren't stupid." He stepped forward, eyes flicking to his peripheries. "You can do that thing, can't you? You can change their minds, put a bit of fear in them."

"This is a decision for your new regent – Morag." This was both a superficially and deeply odd thing to say, since it was Morag saying it. There was a twitch of emotion on Morag's face, an internal conversation between her and the god pulling her strings.

From the throne pile, tendrils of the god shot out and connected with the nearest redheads. Hands reached out, touching others. A rippling web of ginger interconnectedness spread out and – almost immediately – it collapsed in a series of groans, gasps and cries.

Those nearest to the towering mass of *Morgantus* tumbled away from him in sheer panic. Others clutched at their nakedness or stared at one another.

"Why are you naked? Hey, how come *I'm* naked?" said one.

"I told Mary I was just popping out for milk," said another.

"I think the drugs have worn off," said another.

And, in a tide that started in stutters but swiftly galvanised into a stampede, the mass of gingers ran for the door. Such was their haste they barely noticed Rod or his rifle. He was buffeted by them as they fled.

"Let them *all* go," he said.

The young woman who had thrown herself against Yo-Morgantus's side was still there. The fat body puffed out, like a belly stretching after a hearty meal, and ejected her from its embrace.

"Go, Brigit," said Morag. "You are released, your memories returned."

Brigit stood, frowning. She glanced about, seemed to be trying to shake something from her mind. "No, lord," she said. "You cannot do this to me."

"Go!" commanded Morag, but Brigit – Rod heard her sob, but could see no tears at this distance – stood her ground.

"All of them," repeated Rod and advanced on Kathy. He shouldered his rifle, taking out a combat knife. With firm gestures he made it clear he was going to cut Prudence Murray's straps.

"No fucking way, Campbell," Kathy said. She shook her pistol in case he'd forgotten about it.

Her sharp, beautiful face was screwed up in an ugly, unhappy frown, her eyebrows mashed together. Rod had once thought he could fall in love with that face, perhaps even had. Now it seemed out of place. She did not belong here. She should have known she could not stand among the Venislarn gods and bully them into submission.

"You will not derail this!" she said.

Omar gave a tired chuckle. "You've already lost, doctor."

Her gaze and aim shifted for a split second.

Rod stepped forward and to the side, a knight's move. The pistol was parallel with his waist, but off to the side. Kathy faltered, then fired anyway. He grabbed her wrist, twisted it, and snapped the Sig Sauer from her grip. He threw it behind him and brought his knife down to snip the plastic tie holding Prudence to Kathy's wrist. He stepped away cleanly, pushing Morag's girl behind him, and kicking the gun further away before Kathy even had chance to get over her surprise.

Something clattered on the floor behind Rod. He glanced back. Omar bent over, clutching himself. Snapping silver whelk things trickled from his shirt and bounced on the floor, like coins slipping from a cut purse.

"Shot," he said to Rod.

Rod's head swivelled from Omar to Kathy and back. Her one wild shot.

"Shot twice in one day," Omar grunted.

"Messing with my plans," said Kathy, finding her voice. "All you've done—" Her mouth froze around a syllable. She had become a statue. Rod saw the strip of *Morgantus*'s flesh which had slithered across and touched her lower leg.

Prudence pulled away from Rod and ran to Omar as the professor collapsed to his knees, then his side. Silver shellfish poured out in their dozens, abandoning him.

"Don't," said Prudence.

Rod looked round for the King in Crimson. "Do something!"

"Three wishes is all, patron," said the King.

Rod dropped to his knees next to Omar and opened the medic pack on his webbing. There was an Israeli combat bandage. Quick and easy to use.

"Hang on," said Rod and ripped Sheikh Omar's shirt open. The man's chest was a mass of wounds, nibbled away by the magical energy-giving whelks. White, gnawed rib bones broke the surface on both sides. There was so much blood that Rod couldn't even see where Kathy's shot had struck him.

"Could have been worse," Omar whispered. "There's this tribe in the Bay of Bengal—" He took a breath to continue, and died, to the sound of angry whelks clicking their shells.

Prudence looked at Rod, a wretched look on her face. "He gave me pink wafers. I think. It was a long time ago."

"He said I didn't have a mouth," added Steve.

"But we must scream," said Rod automatically.

The tap of bone claw on floor told him that the August Handmaidens of *Prein* were stepping closer. One had raised itself over Kathy Kaur, the pink wet mouth on its underside shuddering in anticipation.

"Don't do it," said Rod, simply. "You kill her. She explodes."

The Handmaiden hesitated. Rod looked at the backpack bomb Kathy wore and quickly calculated what kind of blast radius the thing might have. He stood, gently pulling Prudence to her feet beside him.

"Relinquish the woman and grant us the city," one of the Handmaidens said. "The *Nid Cahaodril* are not here. Your gods have forgotten you, *het Morgantus*. You are a seed on the wind, a *jezri pah ng'eyoll*."

Rod's Venislarn was almost non-existent, but he recognised a major diss when he heard one.

"You challenge me, *Shara'naak Kye*?" said Morag.

"*Hath-No* has brought our armies and the blind gods here," said the Handmaiden. "Yield to us."

Steve the Destroyer cackled in sudden glee. "Shows what you know, you foolish crones!" He swung onto Rod's shoulder and strutted (as much as a cloth doll can strut) along his upper arm.

"What are you doing?" said Rod.

"That's right!" Steve shouted to the hall. "It is I! Steve the Destroyer. Former outrider of the entourage of *Prein*!"

"It's a kind of postman," Prudence explained to Rod. She held an angry whelk in her hand and was stroking its shell.

"I was there at the battle of *Hath-No*!" Steve continued. "When the armies of *Suler'au Sukram* tried to take the fortress from *Sha-Datsei*. They lost. *Hath-No* crushed them, ejected them!"

"You lie!" said the Handmaiden.

Steve waved at the cloud of creatures dropping from the great moon blob hanging over the city. "Our brothers and sisters are not coming, *Kye*! They are dead! You and your—" He paused as he tried to count the Handmaidens. "Didn't there used to be more of you?"

The crab monster wheeled and stamped in uncontrolled fury. Her sisters pounded with equal despair. Shells clashed in violent grief. Kathy was caught in the confusion and knocked to the ground.

A trembling claw pointed at Morag. When the Handmaiden spoke, it was no longer in measured Received Pronunciation tones, but in a raw and bitter voice. "She did this! It is all her fault!"

It sounded unlikely, but Rod knew Morag and was prepared to believe if he followed the chain of cause and effect back through the days, weeks and months, all of this – literally all of it – might well be Morag's fault.

On the floor, Kathy groaned, grunted and slipped in a pool of her own blood. A stray claw had caught her on the back of her leg and opened it up.

"Bugger," said Rod and rushed to her, the opened Israeli bandage still in his hand. A dead Kathy was an exploding Kathy. Holding the bandage in his teeth for a moment, he widened the rip in the back of her trousers until the leg was fully exposed. The bandage pack had a pressure applicator which could staunch wounds and effectively stop bleeding for a while, but the injury had cut through an artery and Kathy was pumping blood out at an alarming speed.

"What's happening?" she murmured. Rod guessed that contact with *Morgantus* had been broken.

"We're making a mess of things, lass," he said.

"It's most entertaining," said the King in Crimson, close to Rod's shoulder.

"Take her outside," Morag commanded. The slimy, spindly and tentacled things in the hall did not rush forward to remove Kathy. If anything, they were retreating into the shadows. "Now!" she shouted.

A fleshy rope slapped onto Kathy's hand. She immediately tried to get to her feet, pulling away from Rod's ministrations.

"I've not finished!" he said.

Kathy slipped and struggled. Were there slashed tendons in that wound? Muscles that would no longer respond, regardless of what *Morgantus* commanded?

Rod saw one of the blob god's tendril sliding towards him. He rocked back up onto his feet and retreated swiftly. He pulled Prudence with him as more moved in from the side. There was no point trying to shoot the things. They were too numerous, and too hard a target.

"Back up, back up," he said urgently.

"Use your laser eyes, gobbet!" Steve shouted at Prudence.

Prudence stuttered and stumbled and cried out, "Mum!"

Brigit, not even physically attached to her god, rushed forward to try and haul Kathy away. But Kathy, plus her bomb pack, were heavy. Clearly years of being *Morgantus*'s plaything had not given Brigit the kind of muscles needed for the job.

"Help me, lord..." she grunted, failing to move Kathy more than a few inches.

In the once great hall, now half deserted and trashed, there were dozens of Venislarn creatures, poised to attack or flee, but only five humans. Rod was not sure if he gave two hoots about Kathy anymore – her fate was tied to that bomb – and that Brigit woman seemed hellbent on self-destruction, but he could still get Morag, Prudence, and himself out alive.

He glanced at Omar's corpse, and felt the weight of the man's death. Rod could hardly say he and Professor Sheikh Omar had been friends. The man had been a crook his entire career, always playing his own incomprehensible game with things best left untouched. And he'd rarely had a kind word for Rod that wasn't hidden behind sarcasm and class prejudice. On more than one occasion Omar had delighted in belittling Rod's northern heritage, his traditional outlook, and his skillset which undoubtedly stretched more towards the physical than the cerebral.

Rod unslung the rifle and fired a three round burst at the ceiling to get everyone's attention. "Listen!" he yelled.

A dead thing dropped from the darkness above. It was furry

and leathery, and its body and wings were peppered with bullet holes.

"Er, sorry about that," he said. "Everyone stop what they're doing."

A flesh ribbon trickled toward him. He stepped back.

"Stop it! I know … I know the, um, final word of unmaking." There was a lull as those listening took this in. "That's right," he said. "I do. The final word. Very dangerous. I discovered it while playing Venislarn Scrabble with the professor here. The late professor. Now, if you lot don't let us go – that's me, Prudence and Morag there – then I'll have no choice but to say it and, you know, unmake everything. And I don't think we want that, do we?"

Morag tilted her head, as though Morgantus was sifting through her mind in search of something. "He doesn't know it," she said. "He guessed some of the letters. He can't even speak Venislarn."

"That's not … incorrect," he said and winced. "Really making a dog's dinner of this," he muttered.

"Do you usually make such a damnable mess of things?" asked the King in Crimson.

Kathy gasped and floundered as she tried to crawl to the door, driven by whatever impulse Morgantus had put in her.

The mound of *Yo-Morgantus*'s flesh was shrinking and receding, folding itself away into conduits and vents in the back of the hall. It took Morag with it, riding a tide of flab that drew her in. The bloody god was fleeing!

"Lord!" shouted Brigit and ran to catch up with it.

Seeing the one-time prince of the city fleeing his throne room, the last of the court descended into pandemonium. *Yo-Morgantus* had been the axle of their crazy alien circus and, even before he had gone, the creatures reverted to their base natures. Several vanished into other dimensions with sharp snaps. Others hastened away via other more mundane exits. Old rivals, despite the bomb or in ignorance of it, set upon one another with suckers, hooks and acidic bile. Some of them leapt upon each other with unbound carnal desire. It was hard to distinguish which were which.

The lead Handmaiden angled her shell and claws at Rod. Her shells dialled round in constant agitation, screaming baby after screaming baby presented to him.

"You think you can take me, wench?" boasted Steve manically. "You think you can take me?"

Rod decided to give the little egotist the opportunity. He plucked Steve from his shoulder and flung him at the Handmaidens, giving him enough height to hopefully land on the Handmaiden's bony white shell.

"From hell's heart—!" screamed Steve, waving his blood-smeared pencil as he flew.

Rod didn't even watch him land. Not knowing, not daring to hope what distraction Steve offered, he grabbed Prudence and legged it for the door. Kathy mumbled something wordless as he passed. He knew he'd have long dark moments wondering what she meant if he survived, but he didn't hesitate.

Prudence yelled as Rod hauled her through the double doors and into the lobby. He paid no mind to the kaleidoscopic war taking place over the near formless ruin of the city – no longer a battle between humans and Venislarn, but between all manner of impossible other-worldly things, philosophically and physically incompatible beings, fighting over the strange spoils of this ravaged world.

Rod ran to the stair doors. August Handmaidens of *Prein*, two or three of them, smashed out of the hall and stumbled on their skittle legs as they came after him.

"Through here!" he shouted to Prudence. He hit the doors to the stairwell a second before the lead Handmaiden. The frame exploded behind Rod. He bodily hoisted Prudence under his arm and leapt the first three stairs up to avoid the creature crashing after him. He turned and fired at the corner of the stairs. The Handmaiden's shell cracked loudly, fatal fissures blasted by the blue john bullets. Her sister was already climbing over her corpse and he ran on, not wanting to meet one of them at close quarters.

Prudence shouted and yelled as he ran up the stairs. He ran and fired, ran and fired. He could not hear anything over the echoing gunshots and the clashing shells of the Handmaidens. Two flights, and the stairs came to stop at a plain white door. He dropped Prudence onto her feet and tried the door. It was locked. He brought his rifle round to aim.

"Shouldn't we have run down?" said Prudence.

Rod stared at the young girl.

"I *was* trying to tell you," she said.

Handmaidens scrabbled and crashed one flight below them.

"She was," said the King in Crimson, leaning nonchalantly against a wall.

"Bollocks," said Rod with feeling.

06:20AM

Chad had decided staying in the taxi with Hasnain the driver was the safest place to be. Hasnain, that silent and stoic knight of the city, seemed to know what was going on and how to stay out of harm's way.

"You must see a lot of things, being a taxi driver," said Chad.

Hasnain said nothing, but Chad knew he agreed and appreciated the insight.

"Probably not a lot of stuff like this," added Chad, gesturing at the world beyond the window. Outside, the air fizzed and crackled. The bangs and screams which had dominated the city all night were joined by strange vibrating tones, as if the whole city was being subjected to some sound-based healing.

"I once went to a spiritual retreat where they used brown noise to re-energise your chakras," said Chad. He frowned. "Was it brown noise? Could have been white noise. Purple noise? I don't know if I've made that one up. Anyway, it was the magical tone, five hundred and something hertz, corresponding to the mystical principle of light. Very healing. A lot of people in the creative industries swear by it. We do suffer for our art. Better than the naked birch whipping therapy I did in Dorset the year before with Leandra. I'm all for nakedness, but Leandra got a bit over-excited by the whipping part. Chased me through Whareham Forest with a branch. I've still got the marks somewhere."

Hasnain started the engine, pulled round in a semi-circle on the road and drove away from the Cube, round to the left and up a side road.

"Not waiting for Morag and the professor?" Chad asked.

YO-MORGANTUS FLOWED, and Morag flowed with him. Her body was wrapped entirely and snugly in his. His warm flesh pressed in on her from every side, a constant pressure. She could not move, except where he made room. She could not breathe except what he permitted her to breathe. He opened up air sacs and presented his orifices to her, expelling such air that she needed. He connected to her intimately, holding her safely in a grip that could not be broken.

She was blind and deaf in his embrace. She could see nothing. She could hear nothing – except the thump of his pounding organs and the whoosh of his blood and vital juices.

Morag did not panic. *Morgantus* touched her and told her not told panic, so she did not. He bent her and folded her as needed as they moved down through the Cube building at speed, a rolling wave of powerful flesh.

Morag swam in the body of *Yo-Morgantus,* and the part of her which still maintained some level of conscious thought exulted in the sensation. It would be so easy to merge with *Morgantus*, to not just reside in him but become one flesh. Others had done it before. On a non-conscious level, Morag knew the bulk of her lover and god was composed of such individuals. Men, women and children had touched the sacred flesh and been drawn into it. This skin was their skin. These quivering muscles and throbbing capillaries were gifts from them. They were part of him, still alive, components in the machine, praising him as they did his bidding.

Yo-Morgantus did not absorb her. They touched, but he did not make her part of him. He kept her, embraced her, but remained apart. He fed her feelings and perceptions. She knew Brigit was with them, wrapped in other folds, a bunk mate in this intimate vessel. She knew *Morgantus* was warping and flowing down through the Cube building. There was the sensation of depth, of a shaft where girder rungs flew past at speed.

There was a sense of urgency – a mundane and mortal feeling borrowed from all the bodies he'd consumed – that he might die here, on this alien world, and no one would mourn his passing.

PRUDENCE DIDN'T ALWAYS FIND the world an easy place to understand. She had been born only a few hours ago and suspected if she'd been given a longer period of time to grow up – a day or two or even a whole week! – then things might have made more sense. She even struggled to understand herself half the time. Knowledge and understanding popped up inside her, like little explosions of comprehension. She knew what hours and days and weeks were for one thing, even though no one had told her. She knew that this man on the roof beside her was called Rod Campbell and he was a friend of her mum. She knew this and trusted it as fact. She also knew that when he said everything was going to be all right, he was lying. He was lying because he was trying to be kind, but he was a rubbish liar and the more he repeated it, the less convincing he sounded.

"It's going to be all right," he said again. Prudence suspected he didn't even know he was saying it now.

He had blasted apart the door lock and, after pushing her through, fired something that had made a scary booming sound and filled the stairway with fire and smoke, for the moment stopping the August Handmaidens of *Prein* from following them. Now, he hurried frantically from one edge of the rooftop to another, constantly searching.

"We've just got to get down somehow," he said. "Another stair or..." He clearly didn't know what the 'or' was.

The rooftop was a square U shape around a deep drop through the centre of the building. The prongs of the U overlooked the canal and the fighting going on below. The fortress of *Hath-No* hung in the sky overhead, ominous and streaky brown, and still spitting out wave after wave of creatures. Over another section of the city, threads of light spread and split in a widening pattern, like an unravelling rainbow with a mad eye at its centre. Prudence knew this was the *Cha'dhu Forrikler*, just as she knew the crazy mud moon was *Hath-No*. The information simply came to her.

"There's *Sorod'leis Pah*," Prudence said, pointing at the Handmaiden which had finally pushed its way through the smoking, crumpled mess of the stair access on the other arm of the rooftop.

Rod brought his rifle to his shoulder, aimed for a long cool moment as the Handmaiden scuttled round, and fired. The Handmaiden crashed to the floor.

"Maybe there's a window cleaner's cradle somewhere," he said, looking over the edge of the building nearest him. "No. Maybe we can jump into the canal."

Prudence looked over the edge. The canal was a long way down. "How far is it?" she said.

"And how deep is it?" said Rod. "Hey! Hey!"

The shout wasn't for Prudence, and it wasn't elation at finding a new way down. It was aimed at the two creatures fighting in the canal at little further away. One was the Lord of the Deeps, *Yo Daganau-Pysh*, who was trying to throttle *Yoth-Qahake-Pysh*, Goddess of the Deep. His tentacles were fat and smooth and edged with fluted pink frills that were almost like leaves. She was countering by jabbing her long, bleached finger-claws into his body mass and attempting to impale him on the horny end of her head crest.

"That's our ride out of here!" yelled Rod.

"Where?" said Prudence.

"There!" he said. "The bloody canal boat it's got stuck on its head."

Prudence tried to understand what he was on about. "That *is* her head," she said.

It was true *Yoth-Qahake-Pysh*'s grey head crest did look a bit like one of the boats lining the canals. If Prudence focused really hard on the twisting gods as they fought, she thought she could see a couple of people trying to cling on to parts of that ridged skull.

Rod sighed bitterly. "Our way out of here. I thought I had a plan."

A bright light stung Prudence's eyes, and she looked round, across the city. It was bright, like the earlier explosions which had threatened to destroy the city, but this was confined to a solid orb of hot radiance, rising over the misty horizon, washing the world in yellow light.

"*Yoth-Bilau*," she said in recognition.

Rod grunted. "It's just the dawn. That's the sun. You've never seen the sun, have you?"

Prudence shook her head. "No, I haven't. It's *Yoth-Bilau*."

"No, it's just the sun—" Rod began. He stared at the rising orb. "To look upon *Yoth-Bilau* is pain itself," he said hollowly. "She causes mutations and tumours. She is accompanied by her stillborn children... Hell and buggeration! The planets?" He clenched his hands in anger. "Riddles! I hate this kind of riddle nonsense! Are you telling me that's *Yoth-Bilau*?"

"It is *Yoth-Bilau*," said Prudence.

"Bloody riddles! I had a whole argument with a door about it."

"Er, okay."

"And you're no help at all!" he said, directing this to an empty space behind his shoulder. "We're doomed now, aren't we?" he said to Prudence.

"Are we?" she said.

"*Yoth-Bilau* there means the Soulgate has closed. That's it. The trap is shut. Even if we kill ourselves, we can't escape. We can't die." He grunted and looked over the side of the building again. "We can't die."

There was a rolling thump, and two more Handmaidens forced their way through the smashed roof access door.

Rod put a hand on Prudence's back. He had big hands, like he could use them as shovels to dig up earth. "Do you trust me?" he said.

"Does it make a difference?" said Prudence.

"We're going to run and we're going to jump and we're going to try to hit the water."

"Try?"

The Handmaidens of *Prein* had rounded the second turn on the roof.

06:25AM

Kathy Kaur came groggily to herself as she was being dragged along a floor. It was not an unpleasant sensation. There was an enormous, throbbing pain in her leg and she could feel herself being dragged away from it, towards a better place. As her addled mind settled, she slipped from the grip of its nonsense and recognised what was actually happening. She was being pulled along the floor in the court of *Yo-Morgantus* by a *royogthrap* which had wrapped its mouth/stomach parts around the blue john bomb on her back and, perhaps unable to swallow her whole, was trying to haul her away to some shady lair to consume her.

Gasping against the pain, she searched for her pistol, before remembering Rod had taken it from her and thrown it away. She tried to sit up a little and look round. The hall was deserted, apart from the lifeless bodies of several Venislarn. She couldn't see her pistol.

She angled her head back to tell the worm-like *royogthrap* that eating a blue john bomb was the stupidest of all possible things for a Venislarn to do, but her voice came out as a weak croak. She coughed repeatedly, trying to clear it.

Despite her fogged thoughts, her doctor's training told her she was probably dying from her wounds. Her weakness and shallowness of breath indicated significant blood loss. She could feel little control over her limbs. The device on her wrist was monitoring her pulse. The moment it stopped, she would explode.

"I was going to kill thousands of you," she said to the *royogthrap,* or at least imagined herself saying it.

Something moved above her, a handful of thudding footsteps. There was a slicing sound, a watery cry, then the creature's grip on her was gone.

An August Handmaiden of *Prein* staggered into view. Her face plates trembled and tried to rotate, but she had suffered some sort of impact injury and the plates just ground against each other, oozing. There was *royogthrap* ichor on her claw.

"Did you murder our sister, *Shala'pinz Syu?*"

Kathy blinked.

"We will have our vengeance," said the Handmaiden. "On all who offend us."

It was doubtful the Handmaiden would make it out of the building with her wounds. Kathy tried to sit, but couldn't. With effort, she brought one hand over to the other.

The Handmaiden stumbled for a moment and raised a threatening claw. "Did you kill our sister?"

"Fuck this," said Kathy, and tore the pulse monitor from her wrist.

TAXI DRIVER HASNAIN had pulled over on a short bridge with views of the canal, the Cube, and the Mailbox beyond. In the canal, sea monsters thrashed about in a deadly embrace, while fish folk on the tow path cheered and chanted. Flying, fighting and falling creatures swarmed around the buildings.

"There was a lovely Thai restaurant down on the waterfront there," said Chad thoughtfully. "A lot of statues and wall carvings of nubile ladies with the bangles and headdresses and not much else, if you catch my drift. Could be off-putting at times, but the Pad Thai was absolutely to die for. I had a Groupon voucher for a Sunday banquet. Don't suppose I'll get to use it now."

There was an explosion. The ferocity and intensity took Chad by surprise, on a day where he thought he had exceeded his capacity for surprise. The top floors of the Cube puffed out in a blast of grey-blue smoke and misted fire. The sound reached him a half second later. It made the car rock and the windows creak. As Chad watched, clouds of rubble spun out, curving slowly downward. Small shapes dropped away from the building toward the canal.

"Those aren't people, are they?" said Chad.

Hasnain didn't offer an opinion.

Chad watched the descending fog of dust and debris. There was movement nearby and, from the towpath stairs, a tide of people suddenly appeared on the bridge. Men and women ran and scattered, some with hands held protectively over their heads, others flailing about in blind panic. Every single one of them had ginger hair and every one of them was stark balls-out naked. Chad watched their pasty white butts run off.

"Reminds me of Dorset," he said to himself.

06:54AM

Vivian Grey continued her efforts to finish the Bloody Big Book with the fountain pen Mr Seth had provided.

"I was talking to myself," lied Morag Murray, to cover the fact she had been conversing with the unborn kaatbari *inside her.*

She looked at the stack of petri dishes on the side in the laboratory. Each contained a sliver of brain-muscle mass snipped from the body of Polliqan Riti, *who resided in the circular tub at the centre of the room. It would be a further two days before Kathy Kaur sent him to the hell of Leng Space, a journey that would bring him back to Earth, only for him to be captured and entombed no more than two miles from this laboratory. While* Polliqan Riti *lolled about in the glass tank, his future self lay dormant in a container beneath the Mailbox, present and future selves co-existing in the city.*

"And it occurred to me, how are these artificial souls different from actual humans'?" Morag continued.

"Not at all, I hope," said Professor Sheikh Omar, "if we're to get the Venislarn to accept them as an offering."

Morag was uncertain about their plan to substitute these synthesised human souls with the real ones the Venislarn had been promised. "I mean, are we achieving anything? When we give these to the Handmaiden Shala'pinz Syu, they might be eaten – if they're lucky – or they might be subjected to tortures without end."

"And you are only now wondering if these off-cuts from another reality are capable of feeling pain, if they can suffer," said the professor.

"Yes. Precisely."

"What a lovely philosophical question." He smiled at this as though the question was a novel surprise. It was no such thing.

"It's not lovely," said Morag. "It's worrying."

Omar turned to the laboratory equipment, ostensibly to check on Kathy Kaur's progress in finding the next simulated person. It gave him time to consider how much of the truth – his understanding of the situation – he should share.

"If you create something so sophisticated and detailed that it becomes indistinguishable from the thing it is trying to mimic, does it become that thing?" he said eventually. "When does the map become the landscape it represents?"

"And?"

"And nothing. Like a zen Buddhist koan, the beauty is in the question, not the answer."

"Professor, please."

He set down the tool he was holding on the side of the tank and turned to her.

"In the Vault we have the Bloody Big Book or at least most of it. Have you ever read it?" he asked.

"Vivian told me I should," conceded Morag.

"And right she was. It is, in essence, a description of all creation. Every atom, every person, every moment. It is all reality in paper form."

"Is it?"

"In essence. And we must ask, is the universe contained within that book any less real or valid than the one we stand in? Are we, too, mere markings on a page, figuratively speaking?"

Vivian set the pen aside and closed the book. "It is time to leave," she said.

There was no one in the conference room with her and no one to say it to. Vivian was not in the habit of talking to herself, but she was, in a rather particular way, doing exactly that. She had written the passage in the Bloody Big Book which covered this moment some time ago, and she remembered it well.

Her spoken words were directed at the Vivian who had written them down. Past-Vivian had written *"It is time to leave"* a few lines before the Library began to collapse. Past-Vivian had noted them and the events which befell those people still in the Library. Now, present-Vivian spoke the words and knew the sequence of events which destroyed the Library were about to begin. She had spoken the words so she would write them down. She had written the words down so that she would speak them. An undergraduate philosopher might question if two events could cause each other and feel very smug about it, but Vivian had no time for amateur philosophers and their nonsense. The book and the spoken words existed, and the building was going to collapse.

She stood and tucked the best of the pens and the ink pot into her jacket pocket. She gathered the T-shirt and trousers she had asked Mrs Seth to fetch for her a short while ago. With the book and clothes under her arm, she left the room.

Mr and Mrs Seth were in the corridor with the two men from the council. Mrs Seth was pressing a slice of ginger and nutmeg spice cake into Councillor Rahman's hands and gently reminding him he must look into the matter of her refuse bin collections when he returned to the office.

"You are still here," said Vivian. It wasn't a question. It was a statement. Vivian no longer had any need to ask questions since, with effort, all was now known to her.

"The tea is brewing," said Mrs Seth. "Do you need another cup?"

"This building is about to be destroyed," said Vivian. "I warned you that you should leave."

The council CEO scoffed. "Madam. We're deep underground. What could possibly—"

She held up a finger to silence him. He stopped. She waited. Nothing immediately occurred.

He opened his mouth to speak, but she waggled her finger for him to keep silent. Put out, he closed his mouth and frowned at her.

There was a rumble from above, as of many tons of construction material caving in. Vivian upturned her hand in a 'see?' gesture.

"The *Cha'dhu Forrikler* are here," she said. "As their thoughts fluctuate, they are editing our existence to suit their needs."

The CEO's frown did not disappear. "What has that got to do with this building?"

"A brick here, a beam there. Molecules and memories are being torn from the world," said Vivian.

An alarm began to blare. A light flickered.

"Nonsense," said the councillor.

"Really?" said Vivian. "Tell me, where is Mrs Julie Fiddler?"

"Who?" said Mr Seth.

"Nina's primary school teacher. She was here in this bunker earlier. No one has seen her since two o'clock."

"I don't recall seeing any of Nina's old teachers here," said Mr Seth.

"No. She's been edited out. I am leaving this way. You will follow me."

The council CEO laughed. "I don't know who you are, madam, but this place is surely as safe as anywhere and you're not going to convince us with silly nonsense."

"You want convincing," she said. "Fine. What's your name?"

The CEO's frown returned. "What's that got to do with anything?"

"Everything. Tell me what your name is."

The CEO blinked and humphed in amusement, then huffed irritably. "It doesn't matter right now. And you're just trying to distract us."

"Your name," said Vivian.

"Well, it's—"

He looked to Councillor Rahman. Councillor Rahman looked back. "You don't remember?"

"Do you?"

A worried look passed over the councillor's face. "It's been a long and stressful night," he said.

The CEO started to quake violently. "Someone must remember! I mean, it's me! My name! My name is—"

"Edits," said Vivian simply. "The stairs are here. You will die if you try to take the lift." Vivian pushed through to the stairwell and began to climb.

"No, no, I'm bringing the cake," she heard Mrs Seth say to her husband.

"Wait!" shouted the CEO and ran to catch up with her. "Look! Here! My wallet!"

He fumbled in his panic to get the wallet from his inner pocket. He popped the clasp with a trembling thumb. The card slots inside the wallet were all empty. He opened the banknote pocket. It was empty.

He began to cry.

Vivian continued up the stairs. Mr and Mrs Seth and the two men from the council followed her, stunned. When, on a landing, they met a security guard who had had his face erased from existence by the *Cha'dhu Forrikler*, the CEO refused to go any further. He sat on a stair and stared at his empty wallet.

Vivian didn't wait while the others tried to persuade him. They wouldn't succeed and Vivian, who had not engaged in physical real-world exercise for millennia, was finding the stairs heavy going.

07:04AM

Poison rained down on *Yo-Morgantus* as he fled.

The congealed poison of the renegade *Polliqan Riti* drifted in clouds from the demolished Cube building and fell as crystalline droplets. They prickled and burned his skin as he rolled and galloped across the demolished buildings, along the canal and into the city. *Yo-Morgantus* fled from pain, searching for safety and his own gods.

Morag observed from within, her knowledge of the city as open to him as a map. Admittedly, it was a map with big gaps in it and not many names. They fled through the Mailbox, over the ruins of a French bistro where Morag had enjoyed a lukewarm dish of slop, shared three bottles of wine with her housemate Richard, then thrown up as she got into a taxi. On the mental map *Morgantus* followed, the restaurant, the vomit and the taxi rank were landmarks, and the only street she could actually name was Suffolk Street where they'd caught the taxi.

Morag saw without judgement – she could judge nothing as she was held in a state of thoughtless awareness – and knew *Yo-Morgantus* for what he truly was. *Yo-Morgantus*, who could rule over a human city, was nothing more than an intention. *Morgantus* was the first fork pressed into a banquet meal. *Morgantus* was a 'save the date' note for an impending wedding. *Morgantus* was a spoken word made real. He was a circling prayer, sent out into the cosmos.

Morag felt his pain and his furious indignation.

Morgantus powered through the entrance to New Street Station (past a Japanese restaurant where Morag had drunk too much *sake* and tried to leave without paying). Inside, a mass of *hort'ech* dolls circled the messy sacrificial offerings they had made in the concourse. Human and animal blood soaked into their fragile skin.

Morgantus tried to power his way through them. When the *hort'ech* dolls massed together and presented their shadow-sharp sides to him, he skirted round. The most insignificant of creatures were already starting to defy him.

He rolled away, upstairs to the balcony level in the shopping centre above. He thrust himself into the largest space he could find and ballooned to fill it. He was a soft-backed hermit crab in a shell made of bricks and mortar.

Outside, reality was being unspooled. *Tud-burzu* were distorting the sky with trails of fire. The unholy colours of *Ammi-Usub* melded earth flora and fauna and weaved new, tortured life forms. *Yoth-Mammon*, summoned forth at last from her place of holding, gorged her way across the land, swallowing buildings and minor gods with indifference. *Yoth-Thorani* had planted a forest of pain in the heart of the city and pinned living things onto thorn branches, where they could squirm for eternity. *Yo Khazpapalanaka* unbound the linkages between moments and shook them like peas in a sieve. *Em-shadt* gods who had slept inside the world, unnoticed, awoke. Geography buckled and turned in on itself.

Inside a shop above the railway station, *Yo-Morgantus* turned round in circles, like a dog flattening its bed, and sulked.

. . .

Vivian, Nina's parents and Councillor Rahman reached the ground floor of the Library. Mrs Seth came last, burdened by cake and fifty-odd years of bad diet and no exercise. She puffed like leaky bellows as she came through the glass door and into the lobby.

"What was..." She had to stop to catch her breath. "What was wrong with the lifts...?"

"Nothing. Unless you tried to use them."

The building around them protested as the forces outside battered it, and the *Cha'dhu Forrikler* unhelpfully rearranged physical matter across the world. Mr Seth stared through the high glass frontage. There was nothing out there that any of them would recognise. The Forward Management construction site at the centre of Centenary Square had been rolled flat. The buildings across the way, the old banks and institutions, had been demolished. Air and earth appeared to blend at the peripheries. It was impossible to tell if the swirling multicoloured vista above them was land or sky, or some towering liquid wave that would come crashing down on them.

Something fell from the high ceiling and smashed to one side.

"You two go out that way," Vivian told the Seths, pointing to the front doors. "Quickly. Before the façade falls down."

"You are coming too?" said Mr Seth.

Vivian tilted her head towards the rear exit past the children's library. "I'm going out the back."

"Why aren't we coming with you?" said Mrs Seth.

"Because that's how it's written," said Vivian.

Mrs Seth stepped forward meaningfully. She was a short woman, but she had bulk and she had a forceful nature. She clearly intended to give Vivian a piece of her mind.

Her husband put his hand on her arm. "We go," he said. "And then what?" he asked Vivian.

Vivian said nothing.

Mr Seth tugged at his wife's arm. She went reluctantly.

"Do not forget our bins, huh?" she called to the councillor.

"Do I not go with them?" said Councillor Rahman as the Seths left through the collapsed remnant of the revolving doors.

"I tell you not to," said Vivian.

The whole building shook.

"Is it safer coming with you?" he said.

"It makes no difference," she said, which was as simple and as generous an answer as she could give.

The councillor fingered the collar of his tracksuit nervously. "Yeah, no offence," he said and hurried to the front entrance.

"Don't go out that way," Vivian called after.

He stepped through the doors and shouted to the Seths, who were stepping uncertainly across the rubble of Centenary Square. "Hey! Wait a minute!"

There was a pervasive groan of tearing metal. The front of the Library of Birmingham was covered in a high façade of giant overlapping metal rings made from a tungsten-magnesium alloy with a selenium core, to keep Venislarn forces at bay. There had been little opportunity to put it to the test. With the bang of final support struts giving way, thirty feet of façade slipped from its position, sliding down like a portcullis to crash into pavement. Councillor Rahman never saw what hit him. Vivian knew this for a fact. She had written it that way.

She stepped briskly towards the rear exit. She had an appointment by the canal in less than twenty minutes.

07:24AM

"My butt hurts," said Nina.

"You could always get off and walk," said Pupfish.

Nina thought about it. "I was only passing comment. I'm fine really."

"Dunno if – *ggh!* – Donk likes it."

"It's a donkey. What's not to like?"

Nina had decided to try riding the lead donkey back at Moor Street. Walking donkeys were no faster than walking humans (or *samakha*), but they were more sure-footed, far less prone to tripping over on the rubble and ruin from the demolished Primark store. Donk led the group steadily through the mess while Nina had stumbled, teetered, and generally threatened to twist an ankle. Of course, Donk didn't have the additional distraction of looking out for clothing bargains amongst the ruins. Nina didn't mean to, but there was something about Primark's cut-price clothing that brought out her needy and greedy side. Even more so when it was free and lying around for anyone to take.

Nina had climbed on Donk and the beast hadn't objected. If he was Mr Grey, as she suspected, the old gent probably felt he was being chivalrous by giving her a lift. Donk wasn't quite so keen to go where directed, so Pupfish, rather than riding on Dink or Duncan, had to walk, leading the way.

Nina rolled her spent Chupa Chups stick from one side of her mouth to the other as they plodded up the pedestrianised New Street. Initially they had gone down the Moor Street link path, leading round to the Library via New Street Station, but the station building had looked unpleasantly busy. Flying *Tud-burzu* and vicious little *hort'ech* swarmed and battled inside. Something huge could be glimpsed moving in the upper levels. They had hurried through a covered shopping arcade onto New Street, and continued from there.

Nina rode with her wand resting in one hand, across the donkey's bristly mane, ready to blast anything that got too near. They had not seen another human since the train a couple of hours ago. A deserted city centre was a creepy city centre. It reminded Nina of Saturday or Sunday mornings, walking home from an all-nighter at a club or party, with the streets achingly empty and the buzz of drugs or alcohol still not yet worked out of her system.

"I could really go for a McDonalds breakfast," she said, tapping into those Sunday morning comedown cravings. "Sausage and Egg McMuffin. Double Sausage and Egg McMuffin."

"Never had a Maccy D," said Pupfish.

"When this is over..."

"I'd settle for a drink. This dust – *ggh!* – it's getting in me gills." His big fish eyes blinked suddenly. He looked back along the line of three donkeys.

"What?" said Nina, swivelling. "We being followed?"

"Nah. It occurred to me – *ggh!* – we should have checked out the donkeys back in the park."

"Checked out?"

"Mr Grey's a man, right?"

"Uh-huh."

"So we should have taken a look."

Nina let this sit for a few seconds, Donk rocking beneath her. "Are you looking at donkey dicks?" she asked.

"Trying to."

She thought about this some more. "I mean, it sort of makes sense."

"I thought they'd be easy to spot. Hung like a donkey and that."

"You saying none of our donkeys have dicks?"

"I haven't had a close-up look."

"You shouldn't have to."

"*Ggh!* That's what I'm saying."

Nina did not need this additional worry. They'd gone from twenty-eight donkeys to three and did not want to be bothered by the possibility that all she had left were dickless donkeys.

"I bet they do that thing where they suck their dicks inside their bodies," she said.

"They do what?" laughed Pupfish. It was a strange sound, laughter. Not just because it was *samakha* laughter. Laughter seemed to have gone from the world, and not just because the people had gone.

"Suck it into their bodies," said Nina.

"You been watching dirty DVDs?"

"Certainly none of yours. No, it's a thing. Animals don't go wandering around with their dicks out."

"Dogs do," he said. "I seen it. *Ggh!*"

"Cats!" said Nina. "You never see a cat dick."

"Never looked."

"Or birds. That pigeon you saw, bet it didn't have a dangling wang."

"Ggh! I don't think birds have dicks," said Pupfish.

"Then how to do they make baby birds, eh?"

He stroked his scaly chin and coughed a little. "It's eggs, innit."

Nina sighed. "I'm not going to start worrying about donkey dicks. He's either sucked it up inside him, or maybe he's even been turned into a girl donkey."

"You think the human man has been turned into a girl donkey?"

"Are you saying you don't believe in transgender donkeys?"

He shrugged. "No one's ever asked me to."

Winds howled down the canyon of ruined buildings as they climbed, only easing as the donkeys crested the pedestrianised hill into Victoria Square. They should have been able to see the Town Hall, the council building, and a statue of Queen Victoria standing regally above the Floozie in the Jacuzzi and the sphinx-like statues guarding the steps at the base of the square. The Town Hall and council buildings were gone, mashed together in a single pile by some passing titan. Victoria had been knocked askew and decapitated.

Halos of racing light circled the heads of the stone sphinx figures, their blank eyes glowed with an unnatural inner light. The statues were carved from stone. They had bald human heads and eagle wings. One had lion's paws, the other had bent hoofed feet. Nina had seen them many times, had even sat on their plinths when waiting for friends and lovers in the city centre. She had always assumed they were just statues – not some weird Venislarn shit.

"Er, hi!" she called to them. "I'm Nina." She slid gracelessly off Donk's back and spent an undignified few seconds trying to walk and stretch some feeling back into her bum. "*San-shu*, er, statues. *Ech kunir as sho' vei.*"

"You talking to the stone *shaska*?" said Pupfish.

"Shhh. They're sphinx things and they've got glowing eyes. Who knows what they can do? Didn't you ever watch *NeverEnding*

Story?" She stepped closer. "We just want to come past," she said, glancing from one statue to the other.

"We can go round," said Pupfish. "Don't have to bother with any of this *muda*."

"But the Library is only—" She waved her hand in the direction of Centenary Square. It was so near. The consular mission, her colleagues, her parents, maybe Mrs Grey and the means to undo this bloody mess.

The light above the nearest statue wavered and stuttered. Duncan the donkey made a nervous noise and tried to back away.

"It's going to speak," Nina whispered. "Or shoot us with its laser eyes."

"I hope it's the first one, man," said Pupfish.

The light scattered as a short figure stepped through onto the top of the statue's head. One side of its body was black and sooty. The stitching on the top of its head had come loose, looking like the hair of someone who had stuck their fingers in a plug socket. It leaned heavily on a charred pencil.

"You would not believe the day Steve has had."

07:33AM

Mr Seth opened his eyes, but it didn't help much. Thick grey dust swirled everywhere, like fog he could feel in his mouth, his nose and his eyes. He was standing, which was good. He wasn't all that sure where he was standing, because the landscape looked very unfamiliar. Like a spoil heap.

"Sheetal?" he called.

"I'm right here." She emerged from behind a statue on the pavement nearby. It had been a representation in gold, or highly polished bronze, of three posh old-timey men looking at a length of carpet. All that remained was the length of carpet, three sets of legs, and a steaming pool of melted metal running down to the gutter.

Mrs Seth tried to clean herself off, but in the billowing clouds of drifting smoke and dust it was impossible. "This is very unhygienic. I leaned on the cake. I think it's ruined."

"I believe it is all ruined," said Mr Seth. He looked across to where the Library of Birmingham had stood. There was nothing left but a concave depression in the earth, one that had also taken the REP Theatre and most of the International Convention Centre and Symphony Hall. "They're all gone. We saw that opera woman at the Symphony Hall."

"Katherine Jenkins."

"That's her. All gone."

There had been a noise going on for a long time. Or was it actually a noise? When the ground bounced up and down, and everything shook with unimaginable violence, that was more than just noise. He wondered if the earthquake, or whatever it was, had affected other parts of Birmingham. He looked around and across the city.

He blinked, realising he could see more than usual, even taking into account the nearby buildings which had been pulled down. In the distance, the world seemed to curve and ripple. Strands of landscape swirled up into the sky, like strips of orange peel. Tower blocks and railway lines, factory buildings and housing estates – all stretched upwards and away. He wondered if what he had thought of as the grey pink light of dawn in the sky was actually far-off lands, burned and smouldering, curled up to the height of clouds.

"I think perhaps we should get away from this place," he said, first clearing his throat to find his voice.

It was not clear where they should go. His wife took his hand and they stepped carefully through the dust and rubble, trying to move away from the worst of it.

"There will be no buses running," said Mrs Seth with a click of her tongue.

Mr Seth kept quiet. He knew no response was required, it was simply his wife's way of working through their situation. Neither of them were fond of change. It had taken her years to switch to a cordless vacuum cleaner, and it was only last month that he'd agreed to go to paperless bank statements. Well, he thought, that was a whole load of heartache and soul-searching for no good reason.

They trudged between smashed buildings. Some were folded slabs of concrete and others piles of red bricks. Pieces of grimy white marble littered the ground in front of them. Which building was made from marble? Mr Seth was unhappy to realise he had no idea. Would it be the same when he tried to recall the faces of his daughters? He pushed that thought firmly away. The girls would be fine. They had to be.

Were they moving downhill? It was hard to be sure when the horizon was just a few feet away and half of the country seemed to be up in the air. He looked to the orange sun and tried to orientate himself. He pointed in the opposite direction: at the floating landscape many miles up and above them.

"I think that might be Wales," he said.

"Do you think?" said his beloved.

A monster flew high overhead. It was roughly cone-shaped, all mouth and teeth at the fat end and trailing tentacles and weird outgrowths at the other.

"I don't know," he admitted.

She held him close. After a lifetime of being the man of the house, he realised this was one of those moments when she was offering him reassurance.

"How do we cope with this?" he said.

"It's like that hard quiz show on the telly," she said.

"*The Chase*?"

"No. We both like that one. I mean the *really* hard one with the four clues. That woman presenter. She likes a drink, you can tell, and she's married to that posh shouty comedian."

"*Only Connect*?"

"That's the one," said Mrs Seth. "We sit there watching it and neither you or I ever get the answers right. Even when they show the answer, we still don't understand it. It's so hard that we don't even know what the question means."

"Sometimes we get it."

"Exactly," she said. "And you feel so pleased with yourself when you do. Well, it's like that."

He nodded as they walked on. "Like that how?"

"We don't understand any of this, but we'll just keep going until we find something we do understand and we'll have to be happy with that."

They continued through the ruins.

07:49AM

Rod tried to shift his position and immediately regretted it. The upturned litter bin under his feet wobbled, and the noose cut sharply into his neck. He choked, gargled, and forced himself to be calm and still. Panic would lead to a stumble, a drop and slow strangulation.

The *samakha* pulled away the legless and lifeless corpse of the last contestant and moved along the line. The next contestant was Malcolm McKenna, the former consular mission guard turned Maccabee. Malcolm had a long cut across his brow and he blinked constantly to keep the blood out of his eye.

"Right," said the fat pale *samakha*, Hragra, wiping the last game off the glass door in the remains of the convention centre. "Who's up next? Fluke? *Chen di.*"

Rod couldn't be sure how long he had been floating in the canal before the *samakha* had found him. He had surfaced, groaning, by a towpath populated by silent, shellshocked ducks. Long powerful hands had closed around his arms and hauled him out.

He'd had no time to offer his thanks before the helping hands had grabbed him, bound him, and dragged him off. His situation, it clearly transpired, had not improved. The King in Crimson followed them silently. Rod couldn't see the ancient undead thing, but he could sense him. The King's presence was as solid as a favourite overcoat.

Rod had tried to pull away from his captors, to look round for Prudence in the water. He ached to spot her, have the *samakha* pull her out and know she was alive, but he couldn't see her.

The *samakha* were angry. Apparently, they had been betrayed in some way. The half-breeds who had taken him prisoner switched languages with little consideration for someone with no grasp of Venislarn beyond basic swearing and the equivalent of "My name is Rod. Can you tell me the way to the swimming pool?" As best as he could tell, someone had promised them all top quality apartments so they had followed their god *Yo Daganau-Pysh* here. There had been some sort of fight and *Daganau-Pysh* was gone, either dead or fighting elsewhere, and the *samakha* were left, battered and abandoned in this blazing hellscape, without either a god or a home.

Why this specifically meant the *samakha* were stringing up captured humans in the shadow of the demolished International Convention Centre and forcing them to play hangman for real was not clear.

Where a now collapsed footbridge had crossed the canal from Brindley Place to the ICC, there was a wide open space, once populated by a post-modern sculpture, a restaurant and the occasional waterfowl, now filled by a crowd of displaced *samakha* and their hangers-on. The air was thick with the smell of wet dust and fishy sweat.

A girder from the ICC, fallen across two towpath walls, formed a crossbeam. With rope and twine, and various boxes and oddments for their victims to stand on, four men were strung up, ready to drop. They were, in turn, a legless corpse, a soldier who had bled out before hanging, Malcolm and Rod.

Rod scanned the group for familiar faces. Apart from Pupfish's crew, Rod should have recognised a few of the women who had sold themselves to the fish-people, and therefore would have been registered with the consular mission. He recognised no one. Bitterly, he wondered if somehow this was all a punishment for his inability, even unwillingness, to socially interact with the Venislarn citizens of the city over the years. He could imagine Nina joking and charming her way out of this situation. Vivian would have had them cowering in fear, calling them out one by one, name by name.

When Fluke pushed himself out of the shadows and crossed to the glass pane they were using as a writing board, Rod called out to him in a half-strangled gurgle. "Fluke! Fluke! It's me! Rod!"

"Don't know you, G-man," said the youth. There was a dead and miserable tone in his voice, like he had seen things he shouldn't. Rod was not the best reader of emotions, and fish emotions were utterly beyond him, but there was something akin to social embarrassment and grief in the *samakha*'s voice. He dipped a finger in the corpse they were using as a paint pot and put smeared dashes on the glass. He turned to Malcolm. "Right. Five letters. This one is easy."

Malcolm, strung beside Rod, just in the edges of his vision, swayed in his noose, boots on tiptoe on a fire-blasted ornamental shrub planter. "Sod off! I'm not playing your sick games."

"Five letters," said Fluke and casually picked a Forward Company rifle off the ground.

"You can't do this," said Malcolm.

"*Ggh!* You've just got to guess a letter."

"I've got a son—"

Fluke took aim.

"E!" Malcolm spat. "Okay? E!"

Fluke grunted, put the rifle aside and daubed a sloppy lower case 'e' in the fourth space.

In the crowd, human and *samakha* eyes swung from the board to the dangling player.

"Guess a letter," Fluke said.

Malcolm stared and blinked and spat blood and snot away from his lips. "D or R," he muttered. "R!"

The crowd groaned as Fluke dipped his finger and sketched two 'r's in the first and fifth place.

"Hell, yeah," Malcolm panted.

"Keep going," grunted Rod. "R-blank-blank-E-R."

"What the hell d'you care?" Malcolm grunted back.

"Keep going," Rod insisted. "Stay alive."

"For what?"

The King in Crimson strolled up behind Rod and stood next to him. With the extra height the litter bin gave Rod, he was still only a couple of heads above the creature. Rod looked at the dried and crusted blood soaking the cowl. A fly buzzed about the King's head. Abstractedly, Rod wondered if it was a real earth fly, drawn to this mostly invisible entity, or if it too was apparition, a ghost-fly.

"River, raver, rover? Does he perhaps know someone called Roger?" the King mused.

"Not helping," Rod muttered. The cord was pressing up against his jaw, perhaps even his carotid artery. There was a greying at the edge of his vision and he could feel a headachey pressure building inside him.

"Letter, dog," said Fluke.

Malcolm gasped, swung precariously and managed to spit out, "A!"

"Lucky," said Fluke and drew the letter in the second space.

There were sounds of derision from the crowd: Venislarn curses and English shouts of "Too easy!"

"*Ggh!* One letter left," said Fluke.

Malcolm attempted a shrug but it wasn't possible in his position. "Could be anything."

"Guess, dog."

"Give him a clue at least," said Rod.

Fluke gave a display of gallant swagger. "Sure," he said. "It's what I'm gonna be one day."

"What?" said Malcolm.

"R-A-something-E-R," said the King in Crimson. "Rager? Raper?"

"P," blurted Rod. "It's P."

Malcolm tried to twist to look at him, but there wasn't enough give in the rope. "What? Being funny? C?" he called to Fluke. "Racer?"

Fluke picked up the rifle. Malcolm began to shout. Fluke fired in concentrated full auto. There was a dull thud. Malcolm's lower leg lay on the floor before them, flesh, bone and trousers roughly severed by gunfire.

Malcolm grunted, hopped, then slipped and swung free. Fluke watched him kick feebly before shooting him again. Malcolm jerked once and fell still, his corpse swinging with the momentum of his final moments.

"Well, G-man," said Fluke, turning to aim at Rod.

"It's P," said Rod and Fluke filled it in.

"Raper?" said the King in Crimson.

"Like Tupac, right?" said Rod.

"Bes' rapper there ever was," said Fluke, wiping the bloody letters from the glass with his hand.

Rod tried to take a breath and straighten himself up. He wasn't just up against random barbarity. There was a strong chance he was going to be killed by youth illiteracy.

07:53AM

Prudence trudged along the canal path, her arms wrapped around her wet body. Water trickled from her clothes and down her legs. The sensation made her twitch and shiver. She looked back and saw she was leaving a little trail of water droplets on the path behind her. She had goosebumps on her arms and an unpleasant tightness in her throat. She had swallowed a lot of canal water. She could feel *Yoth Bilau*'s warmth on her back, but it was not enough. She was cold. With so much of the world on fire, it seemed unfair that she should feel cold.

Ahead, where the path split to go both under and over a bridge, a grey-haired woman sat on a low wall. She waved at Prudence. "Young woman! Over here!"

Prudence did not wave back. Her arms were too busy hugging herself.

On the wall, to one side of the woman, was a big brown hardbacked book. On her other side was a small pile of folded clothes. Prudence saw the woman had only one arm, the sleeve of her jacket pinned back over the lost arm.

"You are Prudence Murray," said the woman.

Prudence abruptly recognised her. "You are the *Yoth-Kreylah ap Shallas*," she said.

"I was," said the woman. "I think I am Vivian Grey again."

"You were in *Hath-No*."

"I was brought back."

Prudence nodded. The woman looked very different from the last time Prudence had seen her, in the vision *Crippen Ai* had provided. Then, the *Yoth-Kreylah ap Shallas*, had been buried at the centre of a writing machine. Now— Prudence gave her a long look. Now she looked like an elderly aunt. Not a very nice one.

"What happened to your arm?" said Prudence.

"It was eaten by a carpet worm in a *jagrahad* forest," said Vivian Grey. "Most people would consider that a rude question."

"Was it a rude question?"

"I am not most people," said Vivian Grey. "I prefer honesty to politeness."

"Are you honest?"

"Yes."

"Are we going to die?"

"Everyone dies," said Vivian Grey.

Prudence nodded and couldn't help but think of what had recently happened. "We jumped off the top of the building. He was my mum's friend."

"Rod Campbell," said Vivian.

"I couldn't find him afterwards."

"No."

Prudence sniffed. It wasn't because she was sad, although she was. She had lost Steve the Destroyer, and Yang Mammon-Mammonson, and Rod, and had seen her mum for a short time but it hadn't really been her mum, not in the end. She sniffed because her throat and nose felt funny. It was probably something to do with all the canal water she had swallowed. But she *was* sad, all the same.

"Is that the book that has everything ever written in it?" she asked.

"The Book of Sand," said Vivian. "The Bloody Big Book."

"And it told you I would be here."

"It did."

Prudence pointed. "So are those clothes for me?"

"They are."

Without hesitation, Prudence stripped off her T-shirt and reached for the grey hoodie. "Is my mum dead?"

"No."

"Rod?"

"No."

"Steve?"

"No."

"Yang?"

Vivian paused to remember for a moment. "No."

Her skin was still wet, but the feel of the soft dry material against Prudence's body was wonderful. She tried to undo the wet string knot that kept her shorts on. "Will you help me find my mum?"

"No," said Vivian. "I need you to come with me."

"Where to?"

"A place where I can finish this book."

"Why?"

"Why what?" said Vivian. "Why do I need to finish the book? Or why do I need you to come with me? You should aim for clarity in all communication."

"Both," said Prudence. She gave up on the knot and forced the shorts down. They pinched her hips painfully, but she forced them off and picked up the elasticated jogging trousers.

"I must write the book because the world exists," said Vivian.

Prudence made an unimpressed noise. "You should aim for clarity in all communication."

"And you should be more respectful when talking to me."

"You prefer honesty to politeness."

"It is possible to possess both," said Vivian. "I can do it and so can you."

The trousers were baggy and long. Prudence pulled the drawstring at the waist tight and tried to tie a knot. Knots were not one of her strong points.

"Do not look to me for help," said Vivian. "Having only one hand has certain disadvantages."

"Is that why you need me?" said Prudence. "Because I've got two hands?"

"No. I need the *kaatbari*. I need a young woman with imagination." Vivian appraised Prudence at length. "You will need to roll the trouser bottoms up but, otherwise, the clothes are a good fit."

"I think I needed something smaller," said Prudence.

"You're nearly as big as Nina Seth and those are the smallest clothes I could find."

"Who is Nina Seth? I've met her, haven't I?"

"Yes. She is somewhere in the city. She has a donkey and is looking for you and me."

"I've never seen a donkey before," said Prudence.

Vivian's expression stiffened but she had nothing to say about that. "Come," she said, standing. "We have a bit of a walk ahead of us."

Carrying the book, Vivian led the way. Prudence followed her, down the lower fork of the path and into the darkness under the bridge.

07:58AM

A light appeared in front of Morag and, by the light, she saw a table.

She sat on a chair at the table. She looked at her surroundings as though waking from a dream. The walls, floor and low ceiling were a soft peachy pink. They were warm to the touch. The table was composed of the same stuff: a stiff extrusion of the same soft tissue, like a table-shaped subdermal implant. Brigit was sitting in the chair opposite. She had decided to put on some clothes for once. She wore an outfit of grey spongey material, as though an avantgarde clothes designer had decided to dress her in tripe.

Brigit had a sour look on her face. Brigit always had a sour look on her face.

Morag looked about the fleshy chamber which *Morgantus* had constructed inside himself. With chairs and tables and soft mood lighting, it was like he had tried to recreate a cosy café bar inside the chambers of a whale's heart. She understood *Morgantus* had created this space inside himself; she also understood he had done no such thing, that she was still firmly wrapped in his flesh, his orifices against hers, and he was merely creating a dream of a physical space.

"What kind of a game do you think you're playing here?" she said out loud. "This is well creepy. I'm not playing."

There was a bottle of wine and glasses on the table.

"But – there's a bottle of wine," she said and reached across. She looked at the label. She couldn't read it properly – this was a dream of sorts after all – but she got the impression it said something like *Chateau Vino Villa de Cote du Sol blah blah blah*, a general impression of a cheap and cheerful white wine. She poured a glass for herself and, as an afterthought, one for Brigit. When Brigit didn't respond, Morag slid it across the table to her.

"What is it with you?" said Morag. "Do you suffer from Resting Bitch Face, or are you actually a miserable cow?"

Brigit snatched up her wine and held it close to her chin. "Do you think I care what you think?"

"I don't know," said Morag. "I really don't know anything about you, do I? You're a name, a perfect body and a bloody pout, and that's it. I don't even know your surname."

Morag saw the miniscule movements around Brigit's eyes, micro-frowns. Maybe even Brigit didn't know her own surname. *Morgantus* liked to play with his pets, removing and inserting memories as he wished. It was quite possible Brigit wasn't even her real name.

"You think I have a perfect body?" said Brigit.

"Fishing for compliments, dear?"

"I'm wondering why you care."

"Who wouldn't want a great body?"

"You think men don't find you attractive?" said Brigit. "Was there a man you couldn't seduce with the body you've got?"

Morag snorted at the word 'seduce'. It felt stupidly old-fashioned. "Okay, in terms of pulling, snogging, shagging, I've not struggled to—" She shrugged. "Maybe I set a low bar. Maybe I'm lazy like that. But this is men we're talking about, right? That doesn't change the facts. You've got a stunning figure. Young and healthy and—"

Brigit smirked. It was a smile of sorts. "Because the young and healthy have got so much to live for, haven't they?"

"Can you not take a fucking compliment?" said Morag and laughed. She topped up her glass and saw that Brigit had barely touched hers. "I don't know if you're even into men?"

Brigit put her hand to the wall of their cosy booth. "*Yo-Morgantus* is the one I serve, the one I love."

"Did he make you say that? Are you under duress? Give me a sign. Blink once for yes, twice for no."

"I make my own choices."

"But he could have made you say that."

"Of my own free will."

"He might have made you think that."

"Are you just going to say that to everything I say?"

"But it's true."

"And you can't prove it one way or the other."

"Doesn't stop it being true," said Morag.

"Or irritating," said Brigit. "You want us to have an honest conversation?"

"I'd like you to drink up," said Morag. "You're falling behind."

With a spiteful look on her face, Brigit downed her glass and watched Morag refill it. "If you want the truth, this is it. I chose to serve Lord *Morgantus*."

"Why? He's an evil alien blob monster."

Morag expected a rumble of discontent to ripple through their little chamber but *Morgantus* was silent on the matter.

"He's a winner," said Brigit. "The truth is, when the end of the world comes, you want to be on the side that survives. If nuclear bombs are going to fall, do you care which nuclear bunker you climb inside? If the Earth is dying and there's just one SpaceX colonist ship going to Mars, do you care who's on it?"

Morag put her hand on her chest. "Me? Yeah. If it's the last ship to leave Earth, I'm going to take a long hard look at those weird Silicon Valley types I'm going to have to share it with. And when the bombs drop? You'll find me in the nearest field, bottle in hand, arms wide, shouting 'Bring it on, ya bastards!'"

"That's very principled of you."

"Bloody-minded, I think. *Yo-Morgantus* is a scumbag and I owe him nothing. You think he's your best ticket out of here, you're welcome to him." Morag laughed suddenly.

"What?" said Brigit.

"It's like that – oh, what do they call it? – Bedford Test? Bechford test. The one about women in movies."

Brigit shook her head. She didn't know and didn't care.

"Bechdel test!" said Morag. "That's it. My housemate, Richard, told me about it. Very aware of gender issues is Richard, despite being a shapeshifting Venislarn horror. He's clearly receptive to new ideas. He told me about the Bechdel test."

"You witter," said Brigit.

"Right. The Bechdel test is about whether women in movies talk to each other about something other than men. Cos that's what female characters do half the time in films. And here we are – look at us." She waved her glass between the two of them, nearly sloshing some over the side. She took a big gulp to make sure that didn't happen again. "We are two strong-willed women with drive and ambition. And what are we doing? We're talking about *Yo-Morgantus*." She nodded earnestly to drive the point home. "And we're doing it ... sat inside his *adn-bhul* brain! We're like thoughts in his head."

"Yeah? Is that your great insight?"

"Sorry. I forgot you were a source of scintillating topics of conversation." Morag swung her arm about to take in their cramped and foetid surroundings. "Here we are in Club Colonoscopy with only each other for company. You say something interesting."

Morag saw a finger of flesh emerge from the wall and reach for her. "Don't you dare," she said. "Don't mess with my mind."

"Why not?" said Brigit.

"*Morgantus* has me utterly in his power. He can touch me and erase my mind and insert memories. He could make me love him, fear him, make me think I'm a goldfish. Whatever. But the moment he does, he admits that he can't negotiate with me, person to … transdimensional individual. If he can't make me fear him by simply being who he is, if he can't make me love or respect him by showing me why he deserves to be loved or respected, if he has to resort to fucking with my mind … then the moment he touches me he has lost."

The finger extrusion wavered but moved no closer.

"That's the problem with gods," said Morag. "You just can't respect something that has that much power."

"What an interesting thought," said Brigit. "You've said it before though."

"Have I?"

The fleshy arm leapt out at her with viper speed and slapped on her wrist. Morag jerked back in surprise and screwed her eyes shut…

…When she opened her eyes, there was a light in front of her and, by the light, she saw a table.

She sat on a chair at the table. She looked at her surroundings as though waking from a dream. The walls, floor and low ceiling were a soft peachy pink. They were warm to the touch…

08:03AM

Mr Seth watched his feet as they progressed through the city. A viscous grey liquid seeped through the stones around them. It seemed to contain a large quantity of pigeon and rat corpses, flowing with purpose and against gravity. He looked away, and a familiar angle caught Mr Seth's eye. He realised where they were.

"Look at that. It's the Radisson!"

"The what?" said Mrs Seth.

"That big tall blue hotel – not so tall anymore," he said.

Everything was in ruins. Ahead of them, on the left, was a jagged mass of metal and glass: a skyscraper brought low. It was definitely the Radisson. That meant they were heading toward the markets and the Bull Ring.

"And there are people," said Mrs Seth.

In this landscape of confusion and noise, the savage roaring of monsters and the collapse of more buildings, they had not spotted any other people until now. She pointed into the distance. "Quickly."

A mouth formed in the nearest mass of grey goop. "Don't go that way," it wailed breathily.

"We must help the people," said Mrs Seth.

"Are you sure," said Mr Seth. "The face thing says we shouldn't."

She turned and fixed him with a familiar glare. "Listening to strange creatures now, are you? My father told you to invest in property. You didn't listen to him, but you think we should take advice from a talking mud pie?"

"I'm just saying—"

"No, no. I see how it is."

The feather strewn grey slop reached out. Mrs Seth stepped away quickly. "Come! We're going to see the people."

It seemed inordinately important to connect with the strangers at the end of the street. They were moving listlessly, a whole group of them.

"It is most peculiar, the way they all look alike," said Mr Seth as they got closer. He took off his glasses, giving them a polish on his sleeve before putting them back on. "And are they all naked?"

"We must help them, Vikas."

"Do we usually rush towards naked people?"

"Hello! Come here and let me see you!"

Mr Seth was nervous about his wife's demanding attention from a large group of strangers, but they did look vulnerable, there was no doubt. All of them were pale, red-haired and completely unclothed.

"Give me your cardigan!"

He slipped it off his shoulders. Mrs Seth immediately draped it around the shoulders of the nearest woman. The people had dirt smudged bodies and quite a few cuts. Their gazes were hollow and gaunt.

"You've given away my best cardigan," said Mr Seth. "One cardigan and there's how many of these?"

"Then we must find more clothes! Go and look."

Mr Seth turned around, wondering where to look, exactly. If they had been in this part of town before it was ruined, there would probably have been at least some clothes shops. He couldn't see a single place that so much as resembled a shop anymore. He paused and squinted into the middle distance. No, there was one place that looked a bit less damaged, up where the road crossed a bridge by the fish market. He did not want to go and check it out until he was certain the red-headed people did not pose a threat to his wife, but she saw his hesitation and made an angry shooing motion.

"Go on! Hurry up!"

Mr Seth walked up the road. In front of him, so close that he almost lost a foot, a private hire taxi shot out of a side road, swung about and slapped sideways into a concrete lane divider. The engine juddered and stopped.

Mr Seth approached cautiously. The driver was trying to restart the engine, without success.

The rear door opened and a man stepped out. "I think it's done for, Hasnain," he said. "You've flooded, it or something."

Mr Seth realised he knew the man. "Hello."

The man turned. Chad. His name was Chad. "Oh, hello! Nina's dad, isn't it?"

Mr Seth nodded. "You are the man who wanted to know what kind of yoghurt people were."

"I was! I am!"

Mr Seth patted his chest. "Ski. Tropical flavour. No bits. What are you doing?"

"Hasnain here has been driving me round and—" He bent to look through the open door to the driver. "You're flogging a dead horse, Hasnain. Give it a rest. Come out here and meet Mr Seth. And what are you doing, Mr Seth?"

"Finding clothes for naked people."

Chad was as dishevelled as the rest of them, but smiled with an unhinged zeal that Mr Seth found alarming. "Sounds wonderful." Chad saw the crowd of naked ginger people down the road. "That lot?"

"I wondered if it was a religious thing?" suggested Mr Seth.

"What? Some sort of Gingerfarianism type deal? No, I think they're *Yo-Morgantus's* cast-offs. Poor lambs. And where are we shopping today?"

Mr Seth gesture vaguely at the remains of the nearest shops.

"Splendid," said Chad. "I did a summer internship as a dresser at the Gershwin Theatre in Manhattan. You know it? No? I say internship. It was all a bit of blur. A lot of coke passed through a lot of nostrils, but never let it be said that I don't have an eye for fashion."

"I mean..." Mr Seth tugged at his sweaty and filthy shirt. "Jumpers and coats will be fine."

Chad clapped a hand on his shoulder. "Dream big, Mr Seth. Let's not limit ourselves. Come on, Hasnain!"

08:08AM

They left Malcolm hanging from the girder next to Rod. His dead body twisted and turned. Rod could feel the minute vibrations it sent through the metal and rope around his own neck.

There were mutters and arguments among the refugees from *Daganau Vei*. While some were content to sit around, moping and torturing captured enemies, some (mostly the human women) felt live hangman was not the best way to spend their time. There were shouts about food and accommodation. The arguments led nowhere. Fluke went to the window pane to mark up the dashes for another game.

"You don't have to do this," said Rod.

"You think someone's – *ggh!* – forcing me?" said Fluke.

"You know me."

There were burbled mutters of Venislarn from the *samakha*.

"You a G-man," said Fluke. "The Man. You spent years tryin' a put us down. No more."

Rod would have shaken his head, but his neck was in a delicate position. "This isn't right. What would your girlfriend think?" He racked his brain. He'd met her at least once. Fluke was dating Pupfish's mum and her name was— "Kirsten! Huh? Think of what she'd say. She here?"

Fluke's mouth curled cruelly, unhappily. Not the right choice of words Rod realised. She wasn't here. That could only mean a limited number of things, none of them good.

Fluke finished the dashes. Four short words. "For old times' sake, G-man. I'll make it easy. It's one of Tupac's albums."

"Great," said Rod, whose familiarity with rap music ended sometime in the mid-eighties. He looked at the letter spaces. "E?" he hazarded.

Before Fluke could write it in, there was a violent shout from a *samakha*. He was pointing towards the smoky ruins of the convention centre. Wending their way through the barely navigable mess came two figures. One was a *samakha*. The other was riding a donkey at the head of a small train of donkeys. Wind billowed her long coat in the morning haze.

"Nina," Rod whispered, surprised at the delight in his voice.

They approached unhurriedly, the donkey finding its own careful way through the rubble. Nina squinted ahead. She clenched something white between tight lips. Had she taken to smoking roll ups? thought Rod, then realised it was a lollipop stick.

"Who's this?" shouted a *samakha,* or words Rod guessed were broadly to that effect. Others yelled at Fluke to shoot. He didn't, but he hefted the rifle and held it ready.

"Morning folks," said Nina as they came down off the edge of the ruins.

"Pupfish," said Fluke.

"What are you doing, man?" said Pupfish. "He looked around. "*Ggh!* Where's Allana? And my mum?"

Fluke shook his head. "Everything's *adn-bhul* fubar, man."

"And Rod?" said Nina. "Cut him down."

There were hisses and jeers from the gathered *samakha*. A scrawny and pale fish boy picked up one of the other confiscated rifles.

Pupfish lifted his arm to show he was carrying a pistol. "We ain't doing this," he said. "*Ggh!* We need to stick together."

"You don't know what we've been through," said Fluke, raising his rifle, "I can shoot you before you point that thing."

"I'll kill you all if you don't surrender," cried Steve the Destroyer from atop a fallen stone column.

Nina slid from her donkey and shook out her dusty coat. "This isn't a day for fighting among ourselves."

"*Ggh!* You don't get to tell us what to do anymore," said Fluke. There was a wobble of emotion in his voice. "You ruined everything, *shaska*. All of you."

"I'm quicker 'an you," said Pupfish. "Don't do it."

Rod could see this was going to end poorly. Despite their words, Nina and Pupfish had done nothing to de-escalate the situation. Saying 'don't do it' in that tone, in that moment, Pupfish might just as well have yelled "Draw!"

Fluke levelled his rifle. There was a burst of gunfire. Fluke was thrown sideways and to the ground. The gun-toting scrawny *samakha* stared, realising he was now alone and probably wishing he'd never picked up the gun in the first place. "Muda," he said.

Another blast of gunfire hit him in the chest and he fell, dead.

Nina looked at Pupfish. This pistol in his hand hadn't moved a millimetre. "Dang, you're fast."

There was instant alarm and commotion among the crowd. Many wisely backed away. Those who'd made threatening moves eyed Pupfish's gun and the wand Nina now held, and made sure they didn't look any more threatening than the *samakha* to either side of them.

Nina stepped forward, scanning the buildings in the vicinity.

Rod was glad to see she recognised the gunshots had come from elsewhere. "Steve," she said. "Help Rod down."

Pupfish crouched beside Fluke, webbed hands on his dead friend's chest.

Steve scurried up Rod's leg. Rod swayed in his urgency to be freed and nearly hung himself in the process. "Quickly," he grunted.

"You threw me at a Handmaiden," said Steve.

"Spur of the moment."

"I stabbed her with such fury!" said Steve with a hint of glee.

Rod considered the thick white shells of the Handmaidens and the pencil weapon Steve carried. "Really?"

"I drew offensive pictures on her," said Steve. "With such fury."

Steve had worked through one of the knots above Rod's head and the rope suddenly sagged a little. Rod pulled free, feeling the energy go from his strained body. He jumped down before he fell.

"You could have helped him, you bag of bones," Steve said to the King in Crimson.

"I was enjoying things as they were," said the King.

Rod rolled onto his back, dragging his bound hands under his bent legs so they were in front of him. He stood and went over to Nina and Pupfish. He couldn't hug her with tied wrists, so gave her a shoulder bump of affectionate greeting.

"Wands and donkeys?" he said.

"A strange night." She took out a flick knife to cut through his bonds.

"We failed," he said. With a freed hand, he pointed at the Sun. "The Soulgate's closed. This is hell on Earth now."

He remembered Nina had set out from the library with Ricky Lee, and his absence spoke for itself. Maurice was gone, back in the mine under the university. Morag had been taken by *Morgantus*. Prudence was drowned or lost. There would be other losses, not yet reckoned.

Pupfish was still crouching silently over Fluke's body. Rod put a hand on the lad's shoulder.

"It's how he would've wanted to go," he said. "*Ggh!* Really. A hail of bullets. Like Tupac."

"And maybe this is his killer," said the King in Crimson.

A short figure approached along the towpath, rifle at shoulder height ready to fire. It was a girl, a schoolgirl, battered and injured, but moving with quiet confidence.

"I thought you'd deserted us," said Steve.

"Yang Mammon-Mammonson," said Nina in recognition.

The mammonite child eyed them with malevolent suspicion. Her rifle flicked between Rod and Nina. "You came to our school," she said. "You. You rode a bicycle into our sports hall and were chased by fish."

"That's actually true," said Rod. "You shot the fish."

"You picked a fight with our headteacher and beat her," Yang said to Nina.

"I did. I heard she was killed the next day."

"We don't tolerate weakness," said Yang.

Yang stepped to the side and looked at the crowd of Fish Town refugees. "The next one to give me a funny look gets shot," she said. The crowd shrank back further. She returned her attention to Nina and Rod. "Where's Prudence?"

Nina frowned. "What's it to you?"

"She was going to put in a good word for me," said Yang. "After the world had ended. Make sure we had KFC and Vans and Amazon and that. I'd kill for a KFC right now."

Pupfish stood and rooted around in his pockets. "Chupa Chups?" he said, offering Yang a lollipop.

"Freely given?" she said.

"What?" said Pupfish.

"You don't want anything in exchange?"

He shrugged and looked away. Yang unwrapped it.

"I'm going to find a pub," said Rod

"A pub?" squeaked Steve the Destroyer. "A pub? We did not rescue you from certain death so you could drown your sorrows in ale!"

"Didn't you hear," said Rod. "The world's ended. We lost. But they might just be serving last orders somewhere."

08:12AM

Mr Seth stepped over the debris-blasted pavement and into the shop, followed by Chad and the taxi driver Hasnain. The taxi driver appeared to be mute. Mr Seth wondered if that was because of the burns on the side of his face, all the while suspecting the reason was far more *mystical* and didn't like to ask.

To his dismay Mr Seth saw this was not a clothes shop, but that odd mixture of a place where his wife might buy cheap novels, and a young Nina once bought a unicorn to paint, declaring it would be perfect for her sister's birthday. To Mr Seth's certain knowledge the unicorn remained unpainted. He tried hard to imagine anything resembling clothes that might be inside the place , but his mind drew a blank.

"We need clothes but there is nothing here."

"Are you sure?" beamed Chad. "Thinking outside the box is a speciality of mine. Look closely, my good friend, and you will find clothes." Mr Seth stepped aside as Chad brushed by. "Love this place! It's a creative's paradise!"

Mr Seth gazed to the heavens, regretted seeing at the sky, then looked over to see what his wife was doing. She was fussing over the crowd of people gathered around her, while glancing in his direction to see what he was up to. He'd better look busy. He followed Chad inside the shop. The man was quite possibly an idiot, but it was impossible to ignore his energy.

"Grab some of these things!" Chad called, his arms already full. "We can use them."

It appeared Chad was applying the idea that if they grabbed enough items then something would be of use. Mr Seth plucked things from the display nearest to him.

"No. Not the red. You can't dress them in red! It will make their complexion look florid. Very unflattering. Those green colours will really pop for them, grab that."

Mr Seth dropped the packets he was holding and did as he was told. He saw some bags hanging near to the till and filled them with packets of – what was it? – green crepe paper.

"Great job!" said Chad as Mr Seth handed him some of the bags. "Now help me with these carpet tiles."

"Carpet tiles?" said Mr Seth.

"Oh, indeedy do. That's it. Rip them up."

"You want to dress people in carpet tiles?"

"Think creatively," said Chad.

Again Mr Seth did as he was told, but didn't feel certain about it. "One might have thought," he ventured, "that if the world is going to hell, then artistic creativity needs to step aside. Perhaps other, more practical skills, would be better applied?"

Chad threw him a look that wasn't so much wounded as mortally injured. "Mr Seth! When everything is falling apart and the soul cries out in anguish, that's when we need artists more than ever. Now, beads! I must have beads!"

08:19AM

Vivian walked along the Birmingham Fazeley Canal with swift, economic strides. The Murray girl had to scurry to keep up with her. Vivian was unconcerned. In fact, she made a conscious effort to walk just a little too fast for the girl's comfort. Vivian didn't dislike the girl, but she believed a realistic understanding of one's personal weaknesses was character building.

"Where are we going?" asked Prudence.

"St Chad's Cathedral," said Vivian.

"Why?"

"Because it's still standing."

"How do you know?" said Prudence.

"I don't. But I will when we see it from the canal, a little way ahead. We will see it, see that it's still standing, and decide to shelter in there while I write the remainder of the book."

"But you've not seen it yet?"

"No," said Vivian. "But I've read that I've seen it, so I know that I will see it and know it soon."

Prudence ran through that sentence a couple of times in her head. "Is it confusing to be you?" she asked.

"I am never confused," said Vivian with the certainty of a person who had addressed this question many times in her own mind. "The world may be confused. That's the world's problem. If you ever encounter confusion, be assured it is never your fault. If a book doesn't make sense, that's the fault of the writer, not the reader."

Prudence tapped Vivian's book. "Does this make sense?"

"If it doesn't that's not my fault," said Vivian. "I've described the universe as it is. Any confusion is with the universe, not the book."

Prudence giggled. Vivian wasn't sure what to make of giggling children. She wasn't sure what to make of children full stop. The girl was scruffy, wild and unafraid, and Vivian wasn't sure if she liked that. "What's funny?" she said.

"You," said Prudence. "I like you. You're never wrong, are you?"

"No, I'm not," said Vivian.

"I mean, you never think you're wrong. It must be very—" Prudence made dancing waves in the air with her hands while she thought "—very comforting to always think you're right. I'd like to be like that."

"Being right and thinking you're right are two different things."

"Yes. But you can't tell the difference."

"*I* can," said Vivian.

They walked through the cavernous Snow Hill tunnel. Brick dust pattered constantly into the canal from the arches high above, but Vivian knew the roof would hold. The sounds of the world being torn apart were mildly muffled down here and there was the illusory sense that this was a place of safety.

Vivian maintained her pace through the dark. "Don't trip," she said to Prudence.

"I won't," said Prudence and immediately did so, hissing as she stubbed her toe in a hole. She didn't cry and she didn't turn to Vivian for sympathy.

Vivian approved of this. "You're like your mother in many ways."

"What ways?" said Prudence.

"Physically. You look like her."

"Oh," said Prudence, uninterested.

"And you're stubborn. You don't complain. Your mum complained, but she directed that energy. Even in the face of the end of the world, she didn't fall to self-pity."

"Huh." The noise was non-committal, as though the girl needed to digest Vivian's words before she could comment.

They emerged from the tunnel into eye-wrenching, ever-changing daylight. The world was falling apart in ways that defied natural language. Distance and space and causality were fraying and whipping about. Very little beyond the immediate made sense anymore.

"What happens when we get to the cathedral?" Prudence asked.

"I'll finish the book. I have very little left to write."

"And then what?"

"Then what?"

"When the book's finished," said Prudence.

"I will stop and rest."

Prudence's feet pattered next to Vivian's in disjointed syncopation. "Do you know how it's going to end?" asked the girl.

"How would you end it?" said Vivian.

"If it was my story?"

"Yes."

Prudence Murray had never written or told a story before. "And then Prudence woke up. It was all a dream. And she and her mummy went out for KFC and Krushem milkshakes."

"That would be a deeply unconvincing ending," said Vivian.

"It's a great ending," said Prudence. "You could write it now and it would work."

Vivian shook her head stiffly. She considered explaining why it was the wrong ending, but her attention was arrested by something in the sky. A *bhaldis* traverser was climbing a thread between one portion of the sky and another. The iridescent shimmer of its green-purple wing casings was startling and beautiful.

"I rode one of those," Vivian said, unprompted.

"The big beetle thing?"

"It's even bigger than it looks. There are whole towns and communities living on its back. I rode it across *Leng* space to the fortress of *Hath-No*."

"Cool," said Prudence.

Vivian thought 'cool' was an empty and uncouth word, but did not correct Prudence. She was struck by the measureless length of experience between her old life on earth, her sojourn in hell, and this current existence.

"It was cool," she agreed. She began to look away and saw something else. "Look. There."

Across a landscape of demolished buildings she pointed out an imposing red brick building with two prominent spires.

"Is that the cathedral?" said Prudence.

"That's St Chad's. And it's still standing. As good a place as any to seek shelter. This way."

Vivian made for the steps leading up to the roadside.

08:39AM

The five of them (eight if one counted the donkeys, nine if one counted the unseen King in Crimson) must have made an unusual sight as they moved across the city. Rod walked as point. Pupfish and the schoolgirl Yang walked behind and to the sides, the three forming a loose triangle. All carried rifles taken from the dead of Forward Company.

Nina and Steve the Destroyer followed with the donkeys, the tail of a loose arrow. Nina had waved away the offer of a rifle, preferring the crooked wand she carried. Steve had demanded a rifle, but Rod firmly pointed out that even the ammo magazine was too big for Steve to carry. Steve's suggestions that a rifle be tied to a donkey's head where he could use it as a mounted weapon were roundly ignored.

Rod eyed Pupfish warily. The *samakha* lad carried the assault rifle like he was Arnold Schwarzenegger on a jungle mission, cocky and sloppy. By comparison, the mammonite girl carried hers like a true professional; her discipline regarding her lines of sight and firing arc was faultless.

Back at the canal, when they'd left the pathetic remnants of the Fish Town community, Rod had been foolish enough to check with Yang if she was familiar with the functions of her weapon. She'd given him a furious look from her one good eye and snapped, "What do you think they teach us at school?"

They had passed through the remains of Centenary Square and looked at the space where the Library had once been. No words were exchanged. No suggestion of searching the rubble was made. They moved on, across the city, exploring but aimless.

St Philip's cathedral had been reduced to an indentation in the middle of Pigeon Park as though a giant foot had come crashing down on it. Rod thought he could see car length claw marks at one end. Banks and businesses had been swept down like dominoes. Black cabs and city buses were buried under it all.

They worked their way down to Edmund Street. Segmented insectoid things the size of cows crawled in and out of the skeleton of an office block. Pupfish wasted a magazine on full auto shooting at the things. Yang picked off two with single shots, and the others vanished.

A Warrior personnel carrier half-blocked the road, its nose embedded in a wall. There were the pulverised remains of army soldiers here and there. How many was impossible to count; they were more of an undifferentiated ragù than individual bodies.

Rod stepped round the vehicle and gave an "Ah-ha!" of satisfaction.

"What is it?" said Nina, from behind.

It was the Old Contemptibles pub, mostly standing. Rod went straight for the door, found it was locked and immediately shoulder barged it with the determination of a man who had been denied alcoholic sustenance for too long. By the time the others entered (including the donkeys), Rod was behind the bar, wiping down the pumps and looking around for clean glasses.

"Is this where you were heading all along?" said Nina.

"I said as much," he replied, ignoring her deeply disappointed tone.

"I thought you were speaking, you know, figuratively."

"Flaming miracle this place is still standing. Now, what's everyone having? Only the manual pumps are still working. But that's fine. We've got some Beavertown Neck Oil. That's a lovely, no-fuss IPA. Real crisp. Beavertown Gamma Ray. That's a much fruitier pint. Something special. Got Victory Brewing's Dirtwolf. Powerful stuff. I personally fancy a pint of the American Sister. Anyone?" He looked to the others as he put a glass under the pump and drew a stream of golden pale ale.

Nina swore under her breath, making sure she was just loud enough for him to hear. "You can have one pint and then we're going," she said. "A swift one."

As the pint settled, Rod grabbed crisps and nuts from beneath the optics and tossed them onto the bar in the direction of Pupfish and Yang. He fished around in a dark fridge and pulled out a couple of bottles of J2o juice and snapped off the lids. He put them on the bar for Yang and whoever.

"Where would we go after this?" he said candidly. "Everyone's dead. They're all dead." He topped up his pint to a nice head. He was a drinker rather than a barman and was pleased with his first effort.

"They might still be alive," said Pupfish, after taking a big swig of juice. Rod knew the boy was talking about his girlfriend and mum, lost in the Fishtown tragedy. "And if they're dead – *ggh!* – I want some payback."

"On who?" said Rod. "On what? Revenge is a pointless business."

When no one seemed inclined to take him up on the offer of a drink, he took his pint round to a corner table, brushed the worst of the fallen plaster off a stool, and sat. A human, a *samakha*, a mammonite and three donkeys watched him take his first sip. He wasn't going to let them stop his enjoyment and he smacked his lips defiantly.

"You don't give up," said Nina. There was real surprise in her voice. "*You* don't give up."

"I'm not giving up," he said. "I'm just stopping."

"The man's a coward," jeered Steve.

One of the donkeys stretched out its neck and nibbled the edge of a packet of crisps on the bar.

"Our only half-baked plan," said Rod, "was to get that donkey – *one* of those donkeys – and maybe with the help of Vivian – who might still be in hell for all we know – perform some theoretical magic ritual which might, just might, turn back the clock and stop this thing."

"And we have the donkey – *one* of these donkeys! If we can find Vivian or Omar—"

"Omar's dead," said Rod. He said it bluntly. He meant it to hurt. He knew he was being a selfish, mardy bugger for saying it, but he was beyond caring. "Omar died in the Cube. And that ritual—" He laughed and took a gulp of beer. "I saw the play."

"What play?"

"*The* play. The King in Crimson. I spent an afternoon, or a day or a week, in Carcosa—"

"Bull-*muda*."

"I did. And I saw *the* play. I saw what happens. Your ritual involves killing the child. Morag's child."

"Oh, you picked up on that?" said the King in Crimson, sliding into the seat opposite Rod.

"Child sacrifice," said Rod. "Which, under the circumstances, you might think is a price worth paying. But Vivian didn't." He looked at the donkeys. He didn't know which one he was supposed to be looking at. The one eating crisps, the one doing a silent crap on the floor, or the one nudging Pupfish to have its ears scratched. "You never thought to ask who turned Mr Grey into a donkey?"

"Vivian?" said Nina.

"Shows what her opinion was of his ideas," said Rod.

"Then we find Vivian and we find Morag's girl—"

"She said she'd put in a good word for us," said Yang.

"Great," said Rod, throwing up his hands, irritated. He felt himself suddenly cast into the role of grumpy dad, trying to keep his cool in the face of this clan of short-sighted and self-centred individuals. "Great. Let's do that. You start. Where are they?"

Nina said nothing. She held a tight expression on her face. Rod couldn't tell if she was stumped or angry.

"None of it makes sense," he said, his voice softening. "The tools we'd normally rely on, even a basic sense of reality, is gone. I thought I could rescue some people, but even that plan sank. I have nothing." He contemplated his pint and drained it. "That's it."

08:51AM

Mr Seth and Chad went back to the naked crowd surrounding Mrs Seth. Hasnain followed obediently, his arms stacked with shop goods.

"I don't know what's the matter with these people, but they don't seem entirely right to me," said Mrs Seth. "I've handed out the last of my cake, but they looked half-starved."

"They are from the court of *Yo-Morgantus*," said Chad.

"And who's he when he's at home?" she asked.

"Oh, he's the mighty lord of this great city," said one of the ginger people with sudden and automatic enthusiasm.

"He's the only one deserving of our love," added another.

"Oh. And why's that?" asked Mrs Seth.

"Because—" The redhead instantly faltered. "Because—"

"There was a reason," said another, but didn't add any more.

"He said he would show me sights and experiences which no other human had known," offered a woman.

"Yes? And?" said Mrs Seth.

The woman gazed hollowly into the distance. "On reflection, I wish he hadn't…"

"He made me think I was a prime number for a whole month," said a man.

"And how was that?" asked Mrs Seth.

"Less fun than you'd think."

"They have been used as his personal playthings," said Chad. "They might need to adjust a little."

"They need to get some clothes on is what they need," said Mrs Seth, "so why have you brought art supplies?"

Mr Seth recognised the look his wife was giving Chad. It was one of such focused disappointment it would stop most people in their tracks, but Chad blundered on.

"We have the makings of some temporary outfits for these lovelies. They all have such gorgeous colouring, don't you think? It's like having a pre-Raphaelite painting brought to life. You'll have seen the paintings in the museum, of course?"

Mr Seth had no idea what he was on about.

"Hey sweetie, let's sort you out." Chad beckoned over one of the young women and pulled open a packet of crepe paper. "Now what I have in mind is we can make some outer garments from carpet tiles, but we don't want them to chafe. So I'm about to invent the crepe paper bikini. What do we all think?"

Mr Seth watched his wife give a grudging nod of approval. She and Chad worked as a team to create a bandeau top around the woman's breasts and then something like a loin cloth to match.

"How can we make carpet tiles wearable?" asked Mr Seth, thinking he should be contributing.

"Unwrap that ribbon and grab a stapler. We will make tabards."

Mr Seth had no idea what a tabard was, but he did as he was told. It turned out that a tabard was one carpet tile in front and one behind, suspended from the shoulders with lengths of ribbon. Mr Seth got busy with the stapler and added a skirt made from more crepe paper.

"Oh my dear, you look like a picture!" Chad cried as they finished work on the first woman. "You're like a pre-Raphaelite Amazon gladiator. Amazing! I must Instagram— Oh."

Mr Seth did not understand most of the words that came out of Chad's mouth, but he did understand someone who had been distracted from the fact the world has ended, but just remembered. He squeezed his arm gently.

"Good work, son. Let's get to the others."

It took some time to dress the entire group of redheads. It would have been a lot easier if they joined in and helped each other, but they remained mostly confused and passive, seemingly fixated on Mrs Seth. She nodded in approval at them all and turned to her husband.

"We need to get them all somewhere safe. They need feeding."

"Why is this suddenly our problem?" asked Mr Seth.

She gave him a sharp look "Where is your sense of charity, Vikas? Look how thin they all are."

He had been trying to count them, but there were too many. Together they herded the redheads onward, up the hill, away from the major conflagrations of the city centre. They scurried from one temporary shelter to another; watching the people in their makeshift garments, moving fearfully across the rocky landscape, Mr Seth was suddenly put in mind of that old cavemen and dinosaurs movie from his childhood. The only aspect of it he could remember clearly was the blonde heroine in her fur bikini.

An office block had slipped sideways, half-demolishing a combined Chinese supermarket and restaurant.

"Food!" Mrs Seth declared and led them all in. A kitchen was found. There was no electricity, but one of the cooking units had a separate gas cannister underneath. Soon there was a pan of water heating up. Packets of dried noodles were pulled from the shelves and Mrs Seth, with a serenity that seemed to come from the act of domesticity, began to whip up pan after pan of instant noodles.

Mr Seth formed the people into a line and, with some encouragement, got one of them to hand out bowls from the commercial catering aisle. As noodles were ladled out, Chad handed out chopsticks and tried to show them what to do.

"Like this," he said. "Gather and eat. Don't be afraid to slurp."

The orange-haired tribe looked confused, more by the act of eating than the use of chopsticks.

"But it's tasty!" said Mr Seth. He gave an exaggerated smile and rubbed his belly. "Come on, you must eat!"

"I think that *Yo-Morgantus* had some sort of umbilical cord that he fed them through," said Chad.

"Umbilical?" Mr Seth pulled a horrified face.

Eventually, a young man licked his lips and reached for a strand of noodles, as if it was a strange idea, but he was willing to try. Once he had put it into his mouth, he smiled. He made appreciative chomping noises and soon others joined in.

Mr Seth joined his wife in the dusty kitchen, boiling water, stirring, serving. Bowls flowed through their hands.

Mr Seth didn't notice when the line of people stopped being all redheads and other people joined. It was only when his hand met with that of a fishman as he passed over a bowl that Mr Seth realised they had gone from serving redheads to all manner of bedraggled people. Mr Seth froze for a moment and stared at the fishman.

"*Khol-khoya su'li?*" said the fishman.

"I met a ... one of your lot earlier," Mr Seth heard himself say. "Friend of my daughter's."

The fishman stared at him. He had big spherical eyes. His stare was unnerving.

"His name was Pupfish," said Mrs Seth. "He had a big appetite." She put an extra dollop of noodles in the creature's bowl and it moved on.

Fish creatures, ragged women and even children passed before them. A boy in Thomas the Tank Engine pyjamas hung close to his mother's side and stared at Mr and Mrs Seth. He waved when they left the counter.

Those with food sat in no particular place in the restaurant seating, almost entirely focused on their food: fish people and humans of all types bunched together. Chad walked among them, distributing colourful packs of biscuits and sweets, moving about with gay abandon like some sort of gift-giving elf.

The line continued, the Seths continued, and there was a certain rhythm and peace in their work which they knew couldn't last.

09:00AM

St Chad's Cathedral (Mrs Vivian Grey informed Prudence without being prompted) had been built in the Gothic Revival style and modelled on a German *hallenkirke*, a form which allowed for its impressive interior size despite it being constructed from brick rather than stone.

"You know a lot about churches," said Prudence politely as they entered.

"I know a lot about everything now," said Vivian.

The church was a high-ceilinged hall. Not as large as the throne room of *Yo-Morgantus,* but here, with the peculiar daylight pouring through the stained glass windows, you could actually see the size of the space.

"Why hasn't it fallen down?" said Prudence.

"Chance," said Vivian. She angled her head to one side. "During the Second World War, an incendiary bomb fell through the roof there. It would have burned the place to the ground, but it hit some central heating pipes as it fell and the water put out the incendiary. Chance."

Narrow columns held up the high ceiling. Near the front, the pillars were worked with stripes of gold spiralling around them. There was a lot of shiny gold, Prudence thought.

"This will do," said Vivian. She stopped by one of the long wooden pews lining the cathedral hall. "I'd like you to get that table and bring it over here."

Prudence went to a table by the wall. It was covered with little leaflets and a tiered metal thing with tiny candles on it. "Do you want the things on the table?" she asked.

"No," said Vivian. "Just the table."

Prudence brushed everything off with a swipe of her arm. It was very satisfying in its own way. She dragged the table across the floor to the seats Vivian had chosen. Vivian pushed the pew in front out of the way with her hip and the table was squeezed into the gap.

"Quite acceptable," said Vivian.

She let the book drop to the table and began extracting various pens from her pocket. Prudence watched her. There was a method to what she was doing, a ritual. Prudence suspected Vivian liked pens. Really liked them.

Vivian opened the book. It was big and its spine creaked as Vivian leafed through its pale yellow pages. There was lots and lots of writing. Vivian eventually stopped, not at an entirely blank page, but one where a gap had been left. She picked up a pen, paused only a moment, and began writing. Prudence watched her until she got bored. This did not take long.

"What shall I do?" she asked.

"Do?" said Vivian and gave a tiny sigh. "I don't need you to do anything at this moment. Just be prepared." She went back to her writing.

Prudence huffed and went for a wander. She went up and down the aisles of the church. She counted the columns. She looked at the pictures of the people in the stained glass windows. Most of them were wearing brightly coloured robes. Most of them were men. Most of them had serious looks on their faces. Very few seemed to be having a good time.

Prudence went to the front of the church and looked at the shiny gold decorations. It occurred to her that gold looked interesting from a distance, but up close, particularly when there was lots of it, it was very boring stuff.

She went back to Vivian. "Who's the person with his arms out above that table?"

Vivian half-looked up from her work. "I am busy."

"I know."

"I have barely a few thousand words left to write, some key punctuation to insert, and then I'm done."

"I know. But I'm bored and I'm asking."

Vivian looked across to where Prudence had pointed. "That's Jesus," she said. "And the table is an altar."

"He doesn't look very happy."

"It's a statue of him being crucified. Being killed. It's not surprising he looks unhappy."

"Is he in your book?" said Prudence.

"He is mentioned constantly. Usually when his name is used as a swear word."

"I wish my name was a swear word."

Vivian riffled through the pages of the book. "Here's ... the last time I wrote about him." She turned the book round. Prudence read. It was a section of text from a scene that had begun on the previous page.

"There's a Michael Moorcock story," said Julie Fiddler, looking at the half-eaten cupcake on the table between them.

"Sounds like a porn pseudonym," said Nina.

Mrs Fiddler wrinkled her nose. The action distracted her from the temptation to pick up and eat the rest of the cake.

"The main character goes back in time with the hope of meeting the historical Jesus but, discovering only a poor man with learning disabilities, finds himself stepping into the role, repeating Jesus's parables, faking his miracles. Of course, then we get into the problem of bootstrapping, which is another time-travel no-no."

"Wow. You're a nerd, Mrs Fiddler." Nina said it with a note of scorn, but she couldn't help but warm to the woman.

Mrs Fiddler smiled. "Which is only code for I like things and I've taken the time to learn about them. My point is, Nina, I believe most strongly that if you tried to change the past, this past we are seeing, you would only help to cement events into place."

"I don't buy that," said Nina with a shake of her head. "You're basically saying there's no free will, we have no control over our actions."

"Do you remember that time you were jealous of Zeinab Imran's fish display poster and ripped it off the wall?"

"You have no evidence I did that," said Nina, which was a lie but one that came easily to her.

"Such random acts of selfishness are easier to bear if you remember there's no free will. It wasn't your fault."

"That's what I'm saying,"

"What's written is written," said Mrs Fiddler. "You can't change a book if you don't like the ending."

"But you can always close the book."

"Not quite sure how that's relevant."

"Just saying."

"What's a porn p-suedonym?" said Prudence.

"It's a silent P," said Vivian. "And that's the question you want to ask?"

Prudence looked at the figure over the altar. "Why have they got a statue of the Jesus man being killed?"

"Christians believe he died to save the world."

"The whole world?"

"That's what they believe."

Prudence shrugged. "Huh. You'd think he'd look more pleased with himself then."

Vivian turned back to the page she'd been working on and continued writing.

09:30AM

Rod went to fetch himself another pint. It was his third. Nina was counting.

"You're going to drink yourself drunk?" she said, seething.

"I'm going to drink until the barrel is empty," Rod replied. "Not going to let good beer go to waste."

Nina had no illusions about craft beer. Like posh restaurants, folk music, camping holidays and anything on BBC4, there was no way anyone could actually like it. She had long ago concluded middle-aged people like Rod just pretended to like it in order to make themselves seem interesting. It was a midlife crisis in liquid form. It was piss on the way in and piss on the way out.

"You're not doing this," she said.

"I bloody well am." He pulled a pint and addressed the empty seat opposite his at the table. "You want one, your majesty?" He sniffed. "Suit yourself."

"He's gone mad," said Yang.

"He's being a twat," said Nina.

When Rod put his pint down, Nina grabbed his left shirt sleeve and yanked.

"Lay off," he said.

She yanked, pulled and pushed and, with a combination of moves, managed to half rip, half push his sleeve back to his upper arm.

"What the hell are you doin', lass?" he growled.

"Reminding you of … this!" With a final effort, she pushed his sleeve up to expose his bare shoulder.

He looked at her. She looked at his white, unblemished shoulder.

"What happened?" she said.

"What?"

"Did you get rid of it?"

He made a foul and unhappy sound and carefully, with angry little movements, rolled up his other sleeve. "You mean this?" he said.

"Ah-ha! That!" She prodded his tattoo. "*Carpe Diem*. Which is not foreign for 'fish of the day'," she said as an aside to Yang.

"I do speak Latin," said Yang. "*I* have an education, you know."

"Seize the cocking day," said Nina. "That's what it says." She gave Rod a victorious look. "That's what you're meant to do."

"There's no day left to seize," he said and tried to sit down. Nina blocked his way.

"Bollocks," she said. "You don't stop. You never give up. You know you died, right?"

He paused. "Yes. You told me."

"You fell from a helicopter and went splat on a rooftop."

"Yes, you told me," he repeated sullenly.

"Did I give up then? No I *adn-bhul* didn't. I went back in time through a hole this big and spent months with no Wi-Fi and no social media, and saved the world from a psycho-bitch just so I could come back again and save you."

He was momentarily thrown, mildly intimidated. "I ... know," he said. "And I'm grateful."

"Are you?"

"Yes," he said.

"Cos you don't act like it. I do all that for you cos you're the best man I know. You are! The best man I know in the whole wide world, and you act like a selfish prick who doesn't really love me—"

"Love you? Nina, I'm really, really—"

"Not like that!" she said. "Ugh! Christ, you're old enough to be my granddad."

"There's literally less than twenty years difference—"

"You act like you don't care."

"I'm tired!"

"We're all tired! It's Friday. It's been a long week and it's not over. But we cope!"

"I don't know what to do," said Rod. "I lost Prudence. *Morgantus* wrapped Morag up and ran off. The consular mission is gone and—"

"What's he like?" asked Pupfish.

"*Morgantus*?" said Rod.

"I've never seen him but I heard – *ggh!* – he's like a big pink blob."

"A big pus-filled bag of skin and flesh," nodded Rod.

"So," said Pupfish slowly, building up to a thought, "like that – *ggh!* – thing we saw in New Street Station?"

"What thing?" said Rod.

"We don't know what we saw in New Street," said Nina, then checked herself. "We *don't* know what we saw in New Street Station." She spread her hands. "Could be worth checking."

Rod looked at the pint on the table. There was clearly some tug of emotions going on inside that big fat head of his, but it still looked like a glass of cloudy piss to Nina.

"We could do that," he said finally. He nodded, reaffirming the thought, and turned to address them all. His eyes twitched with some swift thinking. "We go to New Street. We explore." He pointed at Yang and Pupfish's rifles. "We pepper *Morgantus*. He *can* be hurt, possibly even killed."

"Good," said Nina.

"We rescue Morag. Maybe she has some insight. Maybe we can even get answers out of him."

"What about the donkeys?" said Nina.

"You stay with them."

"*Bhul-zhu*. You need me. You think you can go in and face Venislarn without me? You'd drop at the first enchantment cast at you. And you don't even speak the language."

"I do," he said. "Mostly."

"*Kash ka, muda khi umlaq. Deha-kz'sa qhadau, neas hpar thu.*"

"I got the bit where you called me 'shit for brains'." His jaw worked as he reconsidered. "Okay. Steve – you and the King in Crimson are going to stay behind and tend the donkeys."

"The who?" said Nina.

"Steve does not do menial animal care when there are wars to be fought!" said the doll.

Rod turned to the empty seat. "You will do this one thing for me, please," he said, as though arguing with an unseen presence. "It doesn't count as a wish. And I promise, if I see *Morgantus*, I will punch his lights out for you. Deal?"

"I still think he's gone mad," said Yang.

Rod smiled. "Yang, I reckon you'll like this next bit." He made for the outer door, Nina and the others followed.

"Rod," she said. "Did you touch the *Azhur-Banipal shad Nekku*?"

"The red stone," he said. "Aye. But I had to."

"You traded your soul to the King in Crimson?" She failed to hide the worry in her voice.

"He's actually a pleasant chap once you've got to know him."

"But your soul…"

"One thing at a time." He walked up the pavement to where the armoured army vehicle had crashed into a wall. He climbed up to the driver's hatch and contemplated both the vehicle and the wall. He looked at the armaments and then down to Yang Mammon-Mammonson.

"If we can get this out, do you think you could learn how to operate it?" said Rod.

"Who says I haven't already?" said Yang.

Rod's eyes met Nina's. She grinned.

"I'm coming back for that pint after though," he said.

09:48AM

"Drink up," said Morag. "You're falling behind."

Brigit downed her glass and scowled at Morag as she did so. Scowling with your lips round the rim of a wine glass was a feat in itself. "You want the truth?" said Brigit when she'd finished.

"Please," said Morag.

Brigit looked at her levelly. "What happened to your sister?"

Morag recoiled.

"Think," said Brigit. "Think back to your earliest memories. When you came to the court of *Yo-Morgantus* on your first week here, you shared a memory with him. You and your parents at the Moray Firth. The dying otter on the beach. And on your mother's knee..."

"My baby sister..."

Brigit gestured at herself. "Did you just forget about me?"

Morag felt a leaping swell of emotion inside. Tears pricked her eyes.

"Our parents died within years of each other. You and I were left behind."

Morag gazed into Brigit's eyes. What physical similarities were there between them, apart from the hair, obviously?

"You were meant to look after me," said Brigit. "But you didn't. I came here, to this city. I fell in with ... a different crowd."

"I don't remember," said Morag softly, feeling she was on the cusp of having it all flood back to her.

"And when you heard what happened to me..." Brigit put her hand on Morag's. "Don't you remember? That was why you joined the consular mission."

It made sense. The pieces slotted together. Someone, somehow, had tampered with Morag's memories to make her forget. Maybe it was even *Yo-Morgantus* on that first meeting.

"What happened to your accent?" said Morag, the question coming to her out of nowhere.

"People change."

"No..." It didn't seem right. Morag thought furiously. "Our house in Fortrose. Which bedroom was yours?"

"Which bedroom? I—"

"What was the name of the cat?"

"The cat, yes."

"You must remember the cat."

"Of course, the cat," said Brigit. "His name was—"

"*Her* name."

"Her name was—"

"We didn't have a bloody cat," said Morag. "Our mum— My mum couldn't stand them. False memories. I never had a fucking sister."

A sob exploded from Brigit's lips. "How can you say that? Morag! After all this time—" Brigit's expression snapped from one thing to another, like a badly edited film. "Fine," she said, emotionlessly, wiping the tears from her cheeks. "Thought we had you, this time."

"This time?" said Morag.

A tendril of *Yo-Morgantus*'s being shot out and touched Morag's wrist. She jerked back in surprise.

BRIGIT DRANK HER WINE, down to the very last drop, a look of foul contempt on her face. "You want the truth?" she said.

"Yes," said Morag.

Brigit put her glass on the table and Morag refilled it. "I was given to *Yo-Morgantus* as a child."

"Who by?"

"My parents of course."

Morag shook her head. "Why?"

"They thought the world was ending."

Morag frowned.

Brigit toyed with the stem of her glass. "I was the *kaatbari*." She smiled at the surprise on Morag's face. "What? You thought your daughter was the first?" She laughed. "No. My parents conceived me so I could be used in a magical ritual to drive the Venislarn from this world. Start the apocalypse, then kill me. That was the plan. I was born purely so I could be sacrificed."

"That's..."

"Monstrous, I know. My mum was a cold, heartless calculating machine. My dad was just interested in *whether* it could be done. He never questioned whether it *should* be done."

"And they just handed you over?"

"It didn't work out quite like that," said Brigit. "This was a scam they were pulling, a confidence trick. The *kaat-bed sho* ritual that my dad, Giles Grey, had devised involved presenting me to the Venislarn as—"

"Wait wait wait! Giles Grey? As in Mr Grey?"

"Yes. Giles and Vivian Grey were my parents." There was a bitter smile on her face. "Did you never wonder what had happened to Vivian Grey to turn her into such a soulless bitch? Never wondered what drives her to *fix* the Venislarn threat?"

Morag was temporarily robbed of words. "That's ... that's..."

"Horrible," nodded Brigit.

Morag's mind reeled. "You don't look at all like her."

"I take after my dad."

"But ... you have blue eyes. Hers are brown, aren't they?"

"So?"

"Can brown-eyed people have blue-eyed babies? I thought that wasn't possible."

"I'm fairly certain it is," said Brigit.

Morag raised an eyebrow. "Only fairly certain?"

Brigit opened her mouth to speak, then realised she was on the back foot. "Damn," she said. "Thought we had you this time."

"This time?"

"You want the truth?" said Brigit.

"Yes," said Morag.

Brigit put her glass on the table and Morag obligingly refilled it. "There is no one called Brigit."

"Then who are you?"

Brigit smiled like a cat. "I'm Morag Murray."

"Um – and I can't emphasise this enough – what the fuck?"

Brigit spoke with slow patience. "This isn't happening. We're not really sitting here. We – that is *I* – am curled up inside *Yo-Morgantus*'s loving embrace. This is all illusion."

"I suspected as much," said Morag, "but this... There's still two of us."

"Morag was a member of the consular mission to the Venislarn," said Brigit, "but *Yo-Morgantus* decided to take her – me – for himself. We've concocted this notion of "Brigit" as a way of separating the past life from the present. Brigit lives with her god, while we pretend Morag still walks free in the city. Think about it. Have you ever seen Morag and Brigit in the same place at the same time?"

Morag thought about it far longer than it deserved. "Yes. Obviously, yes. I mean, literally, yes." She looked up at the glowing pink ceiling to address *Morgantus* directly. "Okay, this one's just stupid. Are you running out of mind games?"

An extrusion of flesh grabbed Morag. She jerked back instinctively.

Yo-Morgantus rifled through Morag's thoughts and memories. He plucked out ones that might entertain him and brought Morag out of consciousness to play with them. From the dull darkness of deep sleep within his grip, Morag began to build up a creeping awareness of what he was doing. He was sneaking into her library of memories to read them, but now she was beginning to notice things: a metaphorical bookmark in the wrong place, a figurative volume misplaced or left out in plain sight. His rummagings became more obvious and she was able to observe them.

But now, he was starting to take her library of memories more seriously. In his idle search for diversion from his abruptly altered status, he started to come across disquieting fragments. He compiled. He made a stack of books. He cross-referenced—

Brigit slammed her hand on the table in the imaginary wine bar. "What's going on?" she demanded.

Morag blinked wearily. "What's going on? I feel like I've had a herd of elephants trampling through my head."

"Something is going on," insisted Brigit.

"The end of the world?"

"I mean this…" Brigit touched Morag and Morag was plunged into a memory.

Morag was in the lobby of the Library with Vivian and Sheikh Omar, a few short hours ago.

"He stated that the objects might exist because they had been comprehensively described in the Bloody Big Book," said Vivian, "and the describing of them made them real."

Memory-Morag nodded, though she didn't know what Vivian was on about.

"The cosmologist, Max Tegmark," Vivian continued, "expressed the view that all structures which mathematically exist also exist as physical structures. The complexity of the concept is indistinguishable from the reality."

Omar gave a half-hearted chuckle. "Sounds like flimflam to me."

Vivian glared at him.

"Oh, I'm all in favour of flimflammery," said Omar.

Morag was back at the table, her hands held in Brigit's.

"What does it mean?" said Brigit.

"Flimflam?" suggested Morag.

Brigit's lip curled into snarl. "And this…"

Another memory. Morag was in the Think Tank with Omar, while Kathy explored a virtual reality Birmingham.

"—you are only now wondering if these off-cuts from another reality are capable of feeling pain, if they can suffer," Omar was saying.

Memory-Morag was preoccupied with the fake human souls in the petri dishes. "Yes. Precisely," she said.

"What a lovely philosophical question," said Omar genially.

"It's not lovely. It's worrying."

Omar briefly checked the computer equipment before looking at Morag. "If you create something so sophisticated and detailed that it becomes indistinguishable from the thing it is trying to mimic, does it become that thing? When does the map become the landscape it represents?"

M<small>ORAG LOOKED</small> across the table at Brigit. She fought a rising nausea within her. Leaping from one mental state to another felt not dissimilar to being thrown about on a rickety fairground ride. She wondered if she could get memory whiplash.

"They're up to something, aren't they?" said Brigit.

"Who?"

"Vivian Grey and Professor Omar."

"The professor is dead."

"Like that would stop him! And then this!"

"Wait—" she said, but it was too late. They flipped into another memory.

M<small>EMORY-</small>M<small>ORAG STOOD</small> beside Omar in a lift in the Cube.

"This," she said, pointing upwards. "A deal with Morgantus. Do we stand a chance?"

Professor Omar smiled and squeezed her hand. She had known few acts of physical affection from him. "Not a hope in hell, my dear," he said softly.

"Then why?" she said. "What was the point?"

"Misdirection."

"What?"

There was twinkle in Omar's eyes. "If Morgantus is watching us, then his eyes are not where they should be."

"You mean Mr Grey's ritual?"

"No. Not that either."

Brigit's hands were almost crushing Morag's with the urgency of her grip. "See? See!"

"I don't see," said Morag.

And they plunged under again.

In the laboratory *within the Think Tank, Professor Sheikh Omar looked Morag in the eye.*

"And we must ask, is the universe contained within that book any less real or valid than the one we stand in? Are we, too, mere markings on a page?"

Morag returned to pain. Her fingers were white and pink with the pressure on them.

"Let me go!" she said, hissing at the agony.

"They are doing something! With the book!" Brigit yelled.

"I don't know!" Morag yelled back.

Brigit roared, but it wasn't really Brigit. In a body without a mouth, *Yo-Morgantus* cried out in rage and alarm to any Venislarn who might hear him. He no longer wallowed in self-pity. A far greater emotion had taken over, and it took Morag a long moment to realise what it was.

Yo-Morgantus was afraid.

Prudence looked up as a great noise passed over the cathedral. It was not one of the usual explosive booms, fiery roars or huge throaty calls that she'd heard much of her life. This was a creaking, a stretching, a pulling apart of all things. Something outside was taking the world in its impossible claws and dragging it, finding weaknesses in its surface and ripping them open.

"Will they ever be happy?" she said.

"Happiness is a human concept," said Vivian. "It is the absence of things which give our life meaning: pain, loss and misery."

Prudence thought about this. "Do you get invited to many birthday parties?"

"Are you being deliberately insulting?"

"I don't think so," said Prudence. "Am I?"

Vivian put her pen aside. "We will have to draw a protective circle around ourselves. Venislarn creatures might find their way in soon. We can use those candles to draw it."

Prudence hurried to get the items. She collected some of the votive candles which had fallen on the floor. "Am I drawing it, or you?" she asked.

"Are you good at following instructions?"

"Depends if I like the instruction," said Prudence.

Vivian grunted, amused by her honesty.

"No, I do not get invited to many birthday parties," said Vivian. "But I don't particularly approve of birthday celebrations anyway. Mine especially."

"Don't like to think about getting old?"

"That does not bother me at all," she said. "Birthdays just seem to be an excuse for other people to interrupt my busy schedule with their nonsense. People can be so thoughtless."

"You can come to my next birthday party," said Prudence. "If I have one."

"Very well," said Vivian. "Now, I want you to draw a big circle around this pew and table. One line, uninterrupted…"

09:51AM

Rod had not been trained in driving the Warrior personnel carrier, but gave it his best go. He worked on the assumption that, having driven cars, trains and tractors, there would have to be some commonality between the controls of this vehicle and more familiar ones. The engine started and, with only mild gear-crunching, wall-demolishing consternation, he managed to reverse it out onto the road.

Among the supplies strapped to the vehicle's exterior, he found a box of personal radios. He set them up and handed them out, to Nina, Yang, Pupfish and Steve.

"*Ggh!* How am I meant to wear this?" said Pupfish, ably demonstrating that headsets were not built for *samakha* ears or skulls.

"You have to put it on one side," said Rod, angling it partly over Pupfish's head, so the earpiece was in an approximately correct position. "You look like you're DJing in a club."

"DJ Pupfish would be a remarkably cool name," agreed Nina.

"A little help, gobbet!" shouted Steve. The miniscule cloth

thing was trying to work out how to wear or carry the radio system.

"You've just got to stay back," said Rod. "Here." He attached it to the nearest donkey's bridle, speaking to both Steve and the King in Crimson. "You are the baggage train. Stay with the donkeys. Keep them safe."

"There is no glory in donkeys," said Steve.

"I was never happy including these beasts in the play," said the King.

Rod turned to the vehicle and banged the side, indicating to Yang she should man the thirty mil auto-cannon. She was already in position.

"Right," said Rod. "We proceed across Pigeon Park, across to—"

"Proceed?" said Nina.

"Aye?"

"Not just 'go' then? We're proceeding?"

"I'm just speaking ... formally. Are you going to give me lip, soldier?"

"No, sir."

"Right— Down to Corporation Street and then down the hill to the station. I'll be driving. Yang's in the turret." There was a bang from inside as confirmation.

"We're not going in the tank?" said Pupfish.

"It's not a tank and, no, we travel as a loose group. You're the eyes and ears, and if we get bogged down in battle, you and Nina can progress as a separate covert unit."

"Sneak ninja attack force, yeah," said Pupfish.

"I would make a superior ninja attack force," argued Steve.

"You're armed with a pencil," Nina pointed out.

"I had a knife earlier, but lost it," said Steve.

"And now you're on donkey duty," said Pupfish.

Rod climbed back to the Warrior's driver's hatch. "That's it. Stay close. Stay in constant communication. You see something, call out."

Rod settled into the seat, glanced over the simple controls arrayed before him, and started up the Rolls Royce engine.

Yo-Morgantus rolled through the spaces and halls inside the shopping centre above the train station. Preoccupied with a threat Morag did not yet understand, *Morgantus*'s thoughts were unfiltered and open to her.

He flowed down the escalators and through the dancing *hort'ech* dolls. He touched them and spread his message of alarm. They reeled and ran.

He pushed through along the pedestrian walkways and, finding a trio of *croyi-takk,* spread his message to them too: Find Vivian Grey. Stop her.

The *croyi-takk* flew out, chittering and screeching.

Tud-burzu swarmed about him. There came the cry of *Esk'ehlad* brethren as they picked up the message. A *Voor-D'yoi Lak* loped into view. The cry had gone out and was heard.

Yo-Morgantus emerged from the station on Stephenson Street, by the tramlines. He had been hiding, after losing his castle and throne. His gods, the *Nid Cahaodril*, had utterly ignored him. Now, he flowed out, the herald of a new battle.

Away in the sky, *Kaxeos* and his children boiled and twisted. The unholy colours of *Ammi-Usub* swam in, infecting all things. Flying down from an impossible distance and of monstrous size, *Yoth Mammon* descended in response to the call. A rustling roar of a thousand voices announced *Yoth Thorani*'s temporary halt in hostilities and the march of her army of trees. Even buried within *Yo-Morgantus*, Morag felt the editing gaze of the *Cha'dhu Forrikler* pass through her (disassembling her key parts, inspecting them, and reassembling her in microseconds). It left her undeleted for the time being. Slicing in from across the city, visible only to the eye as pencil-line thick tendrils of blackness, came the spiralling vortex of *Yo Khazpapalanaka*. Time itself had joined the search.

09:55AM

One moment, Mr Seth was collecting bowls to take to the kitchen for washing, then there was stutter: a whirlpool of spider-web lines passing across his vision. The next moment he was walking through a bombed-out street beneath a threatening sky that was no sky at all. Crazed patterns ran across it, like someone had smashed a colour television and all the images had poured out, spooling into crazy patterns.

"Don't look at it!" said Mrs Seth, pulling on his arm to yank his attention away. Her tone suggested it wasn't the first time she had said it.

"What are we doing here?" he asked, confused.

Behind them, stretching in a long line, maybe a hundred long, were the men, women and ... other things they had collected in their group. Most walked with heads bowed. Some, those who had looked up for perhaps too long, had separated themselves from the line and were starting to root themselves to the ground, taking on new and terrible forms.

"Keep your heads down!" Mrs Seth called back sternly to their followers.

Mr Seth stumbled on beside her. They seemed to be heading somewhere with a purpose, but he wasn't sure where. "I'm a little unsure what's going on," he admitted.

Mrs Seth pointed up without looking. "You said it was the unholy colours of something-something."

"Did I?" he said, impressed with himself.

"You were right about the building, so I assumed you knew something."

"What building?"

A frown passed across her face and she put her hand to his brow. "You shouldn't have looked up. It's affected your brain."

"Nice to know I've got one," he said, an automatic piece of silly humour.

Mr Seth was suddenly in the Chinese supermarket again. His arm was wheeling round, directing people towards the door. The people sitting around on the floor and restaurant seating were less than willing to move.

"Got to go. Got to leave," he said.

"But why?" said a large ginger woman whose green crepe sarong creased into folds around her ample frame.

"Um..." said Mr Seth, who didn't know.

"Fix her up good and proper," said one of the fishmen with the careful pronunciation of one who was reciting an unknown foreign phrase. "*Beph-al ng'ah,*"

"The roof's going to fall in," added a dust covered brunette.

"Is it?" said Mr Seth.

By the kitchen, Mrs Seth was gathering together the most useful utensils and food stuffs into a sturdy carrier bag. She gave him a frank look. "*You* said that!"

"I did?" He tried to remember what he'd been doing, and what he'd said. He found nothing.

"You certainly did," said Chad, encouraging people to stand. "You sounded very certain of the fact."

"Well, it must be the case then!" Mr Seth declared. "Everybody out!"

THEY FOUND THE CANAL.

Mr Seth had just been urging people to leave the shelter of the supermarket, and now, here they were beside the canal. The lack of landmarks made it nearly impossible to tell where they were, but the colour of the rubble and the split in the canal over there made Mr Seth think they were perhaps somewhere near where the National Indoor Arena had once stood.

He pointed across the water. "There used to be a pub there. Bill Clinton, the American president, dropped in for a pint."

"You already said," said Mrs Seth.

"Did I?"

"We're at the canal," she said. "Now what?"

"Now what what?" he said.

"You told us."

"Told you what?"

"That there was a way out. We were off to Selly Face or somewhere."

He shook his head. "I don't think— I'm not sure I'm feeling very well."

"You said there'd be a boat," said Chad, prompting him.

Mr Seth looked back along the water's edge. Most of the things in the water were not boats, they were parts of the surrounding buildings. The crowd of people who had followed them, arriving in dribs and drabs, were starting to fill out along the towpath. He couldn't recall how he and his wife had become the leaders of this wandering tribe. He wasn't sure he wanted the responsibility.

"Maybe this was a mistake," he suggested softly.

"No, you said," said Mrs Seth. She marched on along the canal and he walked with her.

"What is that?" He saw something up ahead. It was the right shape for a boat, but it was huge and dark, a little unsettling to look at. It listed heavily in the water as it drifted along the canal's edge.

"Hello!" called Mrs Seth.

Mrs Seth rapped the side of the boat as they approached.

A doughy man dressed in leather jumped down onto the towpath from the other end of the barge. He winced as he landed and rubbed his knee. He looked at the crowd of strangely-clad redheads and back at Mrs Seth.

"You the one hundred passengers for *Celephaïs*?" he asked.

"That's the place," said Mrs Seth.

"Is it?" said Mr Seth.

She shook her head, both concerned and disapproving. "Forgive my husband. I think he looked at the horrible swirly things in the sky."

"The unholy colours of *Ammi-Usub*," said the man.

"That's the one," said Mrs Seth. "That's the one you said," she told Mr Seth. "Yes. We are the one hundred passengers you're expecting, yes."

The man rubbed his chin regretfully. "I don't think we're going anywhere at the moment." He tapped the barge. "She's got a hull breach in her lower jaw. Had a run in with *Yo Daganau-Pysh*. She gave him as good as she got. Serves the bastard right. No offence," he said to one of the nearby fishmen.

"Fix her up good and proper," said the fishman, repeating his one phrase of English.

"Do you have food on board for all of these people?" asked Mrs Seth.

"That will be extra. But we're really not fit for travel, and we didn't agree a price with the English man."

"Great!" Chad held his hand up. "If there's negotiating to be done I can soon sort that out. Now tell me, who do we have the pleasure of meeting?"

"I am Sven."

"Lovely to meet you Sven," said Chad, shaking his hand.

Halfway up the hill, there was a roar of thunder and something unseen crushed the office block, the Chinese supermarket, and half the buildings on the road. The crowd of refugees bunched together in fear.

As they looked back, some began to stare at the sky.

"Don't look up!" Mr Seth shouted. "It's—" He tried to remember what the boatman, Sven, had said. "It's the unholy colours of *Ammi-Usub*. If you look at it, it will do strange things and kill you."

"How do you know that?" said Mrs Seth, trying not to sound impressed.

"Um. Someone told me," he said. "Not yet. I think. But they will."

"Are you okay?"

"It's been a confusing day. It will be, I think. Yes. Come on, everyone. This way."

He walked up the hill. He was not as fit a man as he once was. It was probably a good twenty or thirty years since he could have actually described himself as fit. But then one never expected to be hiking around a demolished city at the head of a group of homeless people.

Mrs Seth huffed and puffed as she walked beside him. She was shorter and probably even less fit than him, but she moved with dogged determination, as though a life of hard work had prepared her mentally for any exertions.

"Where are we going?" she said.

"The canal," he replied. "There's a boat waiting to take us to *Celephaïs*."

"How can you possibly know that?"

"I would really like to be able to explain," he said.

There was a scream from back along the line. They turned. A woman stood in the middle of the road, her face turned to the sky, her arms thrust out as though she was being electrocuted.

"Did you not hear my husband?" Mrs Seth snapped. "You look at the sky and you'll feel the back of my hand!"

"Well, what do you say?" Chad asked.

Mr Seth realised the question was being directed at him. He looked from Chad to Sven to Mrs Seth. They were back at the canal side.

"I really am struggling with what's going on," Mr Seth admitted. "Is no one else having a problem with time?"

"Time?" said Chad.

"Like everything's been chopped up into chunks and is in the wrong order."

Sven nodded sagely. "Is *Yo Khazpapalanaka*."

"That's easy for you to say," said Mrs Seth.

"He is, um, manifestation of time."

"I think I've heard of him," said Chad, sounding very much like someone who hadn't but wanted to feel involved.

"Time is not real," said Sven. "Time here is different to time there."

"Here and there?" said Mrs Seth.

Sven shrugged, sending a waft of stale sweat outward. "*Here* and *there* are different both here and there. Things aren't things all by themselves. Here, *Yo Khazpapalanaka* is the god of time. You can see him, like black spiderwebs in the air. He is playing the giddy goat, the fool." Sven prodded Mr Seth. "It's *Yo Khazpapalanaka*. You are not going mad."

"Oh," said Mr Seth. Sven's explanation made him feel much better. "That actually makes sense."

"Good," said Sven and adopted a more business-like manner again. "Now, price. A hundred people is a lot."

"Let's talk about how we can move this forward," said Chad. "I'm looking for things that are of value to you, my friend. Now, this is me just thinking off the top of my head, you understand, but I can't help noticing that your brand aesthetic is missing the mark. My friend, Vikas Seth here, says interior design doesn't count, but I can offer you an hour's consultancy as part of this deal. You either want to go spooky steampunk, and do it properly, or – and I'm saying this because I've had an inside view of next year's trending Pantone palette – we could deem that somewhat passé. Maybe it's time to bring you bang up to date with some zesty citrus accent colours, what do you say?"

Sven looked uninspired.

"Fix her up good and proper," said the fishman next to Mr Seth.

Mr Seth grinned. "Yes."

CHAD COLLECTED the bowls of finished noodles from the hungry people and brought them to the kitchen hatch. Mr Seth moved them from the hatch to the sink for Mrs Seth to wash, taking the washed ones from the draining board and putting them on the far counter to drip dry until he could get round to drying them manually.

He stopped, a bowl in each hands. He remembered. He put the

bowls down. "Back in a minute," he said to his wife and went out into the restaurant area.

It took him a short while to locate the fishman with the grubby brunette. He went up to them. "You," he said. "Am I right thinking you can fix boats?"

The fishman gurgled in his throat. "*Sheg'll pas beh rgn'pha*?"

"Boats. You can fix them. Hulls specifically."

The woman turned to her fishman boyfriend, or husband, or whatever he was, and spoke briefly in that throat strangling language.

"There's nothing Gill don't know about boats," she said.

"Right," said Mr Seth, feeling himself smile. "So if I showed him a boat, a canal boat, he could fix her up good and proper."

The woman began speaking in the language. The fishman watched Mr Seth.

"Fix her up good and proper," said Mr Seth.

"Fix her up good and proper," echoed the fishman slowly.

"Good man! Good man!" He dashed away.

On the way back to the kitchen, he nearly collided with Chad. "Chad," he said. "If you had to buy passage on a boat, paying only with your skills, what could you offer?"

"Fascinating icebreaker question," said the marketing man. "Now, I've always thought that I had an eye for—"

Mr Seth cut him off. "Interior design does not count."

"Oh. Oh, well. Well, in that case..." He paused in thought.

Mr Seth didn't wait for an answer, he hurried on. In the kitchen, he grabbed his wife from behind and placed a big kiss on her cheek.

"This is no time for messing about," she said.

"No, quite," he said. "Now, I have a question for you. Think quick. If we wanted to pay for a boat out of Birmingham but could only pay with the skills and abilities we possess – because we have nothing else – what do you have to offer?"

"I don't have time for nonsense neither," she said.

"Time is—" He tried to recall exactly what Sven had said and came up short. "—It's neither here nor there. I need you to think about it. And dry your hands because we've got to get out of here."

"Why?"

"Because the roof's about to fall in and crush anyone left inside." He went out into the seating area. He clapped his hands for attention. "Everyone! Gather up your things. We have to go. The building's about to collapse. No pushing, no shoving. Move in an orderly line and head out onto the pavement. And when you're out there, no looking up."

"What is going on?" demanded Mrs Seth, coming out of the kitchen and drying her hands on a tea towel.

"It's…" He contorted his face in thought. "It's like Only Connect. I've finally got one of the questions right. Everyone! Let's go!"

He swung his arm in a wheeling motion, directing them all towards the door.

Mr Seth guided the fishman towards the canal barge. "This is Gill," he said. "He can fix your boat."

"Good and proper," agreed Gill.

"That's a nice start," said Sven. "But, as I say, a hundred people is a lot. What else do you have?"

Mrs Seth started to root around in her handbag, then hesitated. She reached forward and, visibly fighting her own sense of revulsion, pulled at the edge of Sven's mouldering leather coat-tabard-thing. "This looks like it could do with cleaning. Or restitching. Possibly replacing."

Sven tilted his head, not quite convinced.

"Also, I do haircuts." She pulled a pair of scissors from her bag, followed a moment later by a hairbrush "I've cut all of my children's hair." She gave Sven's head a meaningful look.

He ran his fingers through his greasy strands of hair and looked, if not convinced, then definitely thoughtful.

Mrs Seth gestured back at the crowd behind her. "And I have a team ready to clean and cook and do light repairs."

"I think we could make this work," said Sven. He gestured for them to come aboard.

"But let's chat about those zesty citrus tones," said Chad, going below deck with the bargemaster.

Mr Seth waved the people onto the barge. The little boy in the train pyjamas was asleep on his mum's shoulder as she carried him on board. Mr Seth was the last of them all. He looked at the city before stepping down into the hold, but it was a city he no longer recognised. He went down the stairs. He could already hear his wife talking about the making of tea and cake.

09:57AM

Vivian pointed to the floor. "And another *jid-ap yoi* ward," she said.

Prudence drew one deftly. The girl's skills were impressive.

"And then I continue the pattern all the way round?"

"Quite. Your zahirs are accomplished."

"Are you mocking me?" said Prudence.

"No. Not at all," said Vivian. "I do not joke. I only know one joke. You do demonstrate a natural flair for sigils and wards."

"Thank you, Mrs Grey."

Vivian had confidence that the girl knew what she was doing, so she returned to her work in the book. The end was tantalisingly close. There were no great passages left to write. She had worked diligently on the book, her principle strategy to write from the outside in, from past and future and distant places to this point here and now.

It was akin to a jigsaw of limitless size. Despite its infinite scope, it had defined edges. There were beginning and ends. Vivian had resolutely sorted through the pieces and built those edges, boring and innocuous though they may have seemed. Working inward was relatively easy by comparison. It was a labour that could not have been achieved in this mortal world, constricted by time and logic. Vivian had sacrificed aeons of time and much of herself to lay down the many, many histories the book demanded.

As she flexed her aching hand and annotated this page and that, she tried to recall some of what it had been like to be the *Yoth-Kreylah ap Shallas* – the living black and white – the feel of her mechanical limbs, the automation of her writing processes, the acts of researching, scripting and filing as blindly unconscious as the beating of her heart, or the working of her liver. It was nearly all but gone from her now.

She had just enough residual comprehension to finish the book. In this jigsaw, all that was left were a dozen individual pieces. Their placement was obvious, and each, properly placed, would bring the true picture to life.

"So, can you tell me it?" said Prudence.

"Tell you what?" said Vivian.

"Your one joke."

"If you wish. When I was a child my parents gave me—"

She was interrupted by the smashing of glass. A *hort'ech* doll, mounted on a *Tud-burzu*, flew in and circled like a World War One spotter plane. Seeing Vivian and Prudence, the doll squealed in joy and spurred its mount to attack.

"Inside the circle, Prudence," said Vivian.

Prudence promptly obeyed.

Two yards from Vivian's face the *Tud-burzu* slammed into the edge of the circle's power and stopped, like a bird flying into a pane of glass. The *Tud-burzu* managed to stay airborne and wobbled back in a daze. The doll, thrown from its perch, slipped forward and in front of the flying creature's blowtorch mouth. It vanished into ash with a tiny scream. The *Tud-burzu* reeled away erratically, flew back up to the window and out.

"They know we're here," said Vivian.

"You say it like it was going to happen anyway."

"Indeed." Vivian collected her thoughts. "So, my parents gave me a huge pile of comics – you know what comics are, don't you? Good – but all of them had the last page of the story ripped out." Vivian paused for comedic effect. "I had to draw my own conclusions."

Prudence looked at her. Vivian mentally recounted what she said to check she'd got it right.

"That's the joke, is it?" said Prudence.

"Yes. The comics had had the last pages mysteriously removed, so I had to *draw* my own *conclusions*."

"Thank you," said the girl.

"No," said Vivian. "That's not the correct response to a joke."

Prudence touched the edge of the Bloody Big Book. "You've read everything in here, as you wrote it. You must have read every joke there's ever been."

"I suppose I have," said Vivian.

"But that's the one you picked as 'your' joke?"

Vivian sniffed. "I like it. It's clever."

Prudence tilted her head. "I don't know. I think I prefer funny to clever."

10:04AM

Nina found it hard enough to concentrate on a world being ripped apart at the seams by unfathomable demons. It was harder still doing so with the constant voice of Steve the Destroyer in her ear.

She and Pupfish were warily shadowing the battered tank vehicle that Rod insisted wasn't a real tank but sure looked like one (It had tracks! It had a big gun on top! Of course it was a tank!). With almost no buildings remaining in the city, only the curve of the landscape gave any sense of place. In this wind-whistling, smoky wasteland, Nina reckoned that this slope must be Corporation Street, and down there somewhere was the remnants of New Street Station and the Grand Central shopping centre.

A shadow whipped overheard. Pupfish tried to track it with his rifle sights but it was too fast.

"*So can I?*" said Steve over the comms.

"Can you what?" said Nina.

"*Give a donkey peanuts.*"

"Why would you give a donkey peanuts?" said Nina.

"Are you not listening, fleshling? The donkey has got behind the bar and pulled down a packet of the salted nuts."

"Can we keep comms for essential communications only?" said Rod.

"The King of Crimson, who is a chattering no-nothing, says donkeys do not eat peanuts," said Steve.

"Does the donkey have a nut allergy?" said Nina.

"How would I know, mortal? How would I know?"

Nina shrugged, even though the gesture was unseen. "Give the donkey the nuts. If Mr Grey has an allergy, he won't eat them."

"And if it is a regular donkey with an allergy?" demanded Steve.

The armoured vehicle lurched and almost stalled against a pile of white rubble.

"Essential communications only!" seethed Rod.

"Donkey deaths are not a priority matter to you, eh?" said Steve.

"Not right now," said Rod. "We're trying to sneak up on wherever Morgantus is hiding and you two are blathering about nuts!"

"Tell him, not me!" said Nina.

"Movement!" declared Yang in Nina's ear, a split-second before Nina saw it for herself.

A mass rolled up the hill towards them. It was white and pink. There were cuts in its flesh where it had scraped and gouged itself on the rough landscape. It was covered in stone dust which powdered its wounds. It looked like a mound of meat rolled in flour. It was rolling towards them.

"*Morgantus!*" Nina shouted and ducked sideways into the shadow of the nearest rock.

Pupfish froze in surprise and awe. The vehicle turret twisted, just before *Morgantus* struck it. No one had the presence of mind to fire.

The bulk of *Yo-Morgantus* momentarily swamped the vehicle before rolling on and away. There was a cry of disgust and alarm from Yang.

Pupfish remembered to fire as *Morgantus* streamed away up the hill. Nina couldn't see if he'd hit it.

"That's definitely him," said Rod.

"In a hurry to get somewhere," added Nina.

The armoured vehicle slowed and tried to turn in the space between rubble piles. The turret swung and the mounted cannon fired. It was an impressive boom.

"Did you hit it?" Nina called. There was no reply.

She had to scramble to be sure she was out of the way of the turning vehicle.

"We're pursuing," said Rod.

"All of us?" said Nina.

"Rear hatch," said Rod.

As the vehicle lurched to face the departing god, the square door in the rear of the vehicle popped open. Yang was there.

"Come on!" she yelled.

Pupfish was at the door first and held it as Nina stumbled after him.

Stonework shifted and a tangled bird's nest of black lines swept out. Nina held out a hand to ward it off.

"—IN LAST TIME," Nina said.

She was standing in a great big church. Stone columns, stained glass, a lot of shiny iconography over by the altar. Mrs Vivian Grey stood beside her, in the flesh. The woman looked like she had lost a lot of weight. And an arm. But the fiery glint in her eyes had not dimmed.

There was also a girl standing there. She was wearing a baggy tracksuit and holding Steve the Destroyer. Nina clocked the mass of ginger hair.

"This is Morag's baby girl?" she said, surprised.

The girl smiled. "I'm Prudence. You're Nina Seth. Vivian says I'm almost as big as you."

"I don't know about that," said Nina, bewildered. "Where are we?"

"St Chad's Cathedral," said Vivian.

"Rod's not here?"

"No."

The Venislarn that had touched her, *Yo Khazpapalanaka*, was a god of time, Nina thought. These were events that were yet to happen. She would be here at some point soon.

"Right," she said. "Um, I'm not Catholic, so where is this exactly? Like, I might need directions."

"But you're already here," said Prudence. "Surely, you know."

It sounded stupid, but Nina said, "I'm coming from the Old Contemptibles pub, on...?"

"Edmund Street," Vivian cut in. "You're really very close. You just need to walk away from the city centre towards the A38. Turn right, keep going. The cathedral is the huge red building on the other side of the road."

Nina nodded. "Thanks." She couldn't yet handle the feeling it would only be a matter of time before she'd find Vivian again. She fizzed with excitement. "That's great, I think we're—"

NINA CAME BACK to herself in the rubble-strewn street, halfway through a scream. The swirl of black lines tumbled up and away from her.

"Have you been hit?" Rod called. *"Have you been hit?"*

Nina held onto the edges of the door. "The cathedral."

"What?" said Rod.

"That was *Yo Khazpapalanaka*. Got to go to the cathedral."

"*Morgantus is just there! We're pursuing.*"

Nina shut the door in Yang's face. "We'll meet you there."

"*Where?*" said Rod.

"The cathedral." She slapped Pupfish's arm. "This way."

"We not going with them?"

"We're there before them," said Nina.

"What?"

She hurried along the road in what she guessed was the straightest route back to the pub. The armoured vehicle's throttle grumbled and Rod set forward at an angle, in pursuit of *Morgantus*.

Nina held her hand to her ear as she ran. "Steve. Ready the donkeys. We're going to St Chad's."

"*You hear that, you walking corpse?*" Steve said. "*We're moving out! I don't know if we're bringing the bag of nuts with us. I'll ask her.*"

"Just get outside," said Nina.

10:11AM

Rod noted that, for a mass of flesh, *Yo-Morgantus* had a surprisingly high turn of speed.

The Warrior had a powerful engine, and a four-speed automatic gearbox, so it could keep up with the fastest tanks on the battlefield. Yet Rod was having trouble maintaining pace with *Yo-Morgantus*. Rod had had experience of racing against blob monsters. He'd been pursued through abandoned railway tunnels by the monster, *Crippen-Ai*. But where *Crippen-Ai* was all brain and muscle, *Morgantus*, fatty, tumorous and scabby, had none of its sleekness.

The Warrior rode up and over piles of rubble and skidded through water, slime and alien tar stuff.

"I can't get – a decent shot if – you're bumping up and down all the – time," complained Yang from the turret gunner position.

"Keep three sixty vision," Rod replied. "We're making a target of ourselves."

"I'm watching," said Yang.

She let off a couple of rounds. The thirty-mil autocannon on the turret took six rounds in the magazine. Rounds of that calibre could pierce vehicle armour and concrete defences. These were UK Army rounds, not Forward Company's Venislarn killers, but a high-explosive shot at *Morgantus* should nonetheless rip a hole straight through him.

The remains of a statue told Rod they were at the top of New Street and heading towards Centenary Square. "He's definitely after something," he said.

He looked in his rear-view. The madness in the sky made him want to vomit. Fire tornadoes cut a curtain across the area behind them.

"Wind creatures behind us," he called to Yang.

"I can't shoot wind," Yang pointed out. "Crap. Trees."

"Where?"

A thing that might have been a mighty oak, stepped out from between rock piles. For a mighty English oak, it didn't look all that friendly. Fat roots shot through the ground beneath them, wriggling with the speed of water snakes. Something momentarily gripped the underside of their vehicle, then noisily broke away.

Smaller sapling trees came cascading down, planting themselves in the earth like fired arrows. They scored marks along the side of the vehicle, clawing at it with their leafy branches.

"I am not being killed by a living tree," said Rod. "I'd never live it down."

"All trees are alive," said Yang and blasted at the oak tree.

"You know what I mean," he grunted.

Morgantus was disappearing over the brow of the hill. Rod concentrated on giving chase.

STEVE WAITED on the pavement with the donkeys as instructed.

Nina ran toward him. "That way. That way," she said, pointing down to where the dual-carriageway had once stood.

Pupfish was bringing up the rear, sporadically firing.

"What's the urgency, gobbet?" said Steve, atop Donk's head.

"I know where Vivian is." She looked about them. "Is the King in Crimson here? Now?"

Steve pointed. "The creature likes to think he's a silent observer. But he prattles too much for that!" Steve slid a foil packet of peanuts to Nina across the donkey's brow. Donk shook his head irritably, but Steve held on with ease.

"I can't open them," he said. "I don't have the fingers."

Pupfish unleashed a final round and backed towards them. "*Ggh! Dendooshi* in the Snow Hill station building," he said. "Reckon it's that gang who followed us in Sutton."

"Why would it be the same *dendooshi*?" said Nina.

"Train station," said Pupfish.

"You think they caught the train? They're wolf creatures. They don't do public transport."

"You don't understand how gangs work."

"It's called a pack. They don't do trains."

Donk, Dink and Duncan moved warily out of the semi-shelter of the pub building.

When they reached the dual carriageway, Steve said, "This skeletal godling wants to know where Rod is," then snapped. "No, I am not your messenger boy! I will ram this pencil in what's left of your internal organs!"

Nina didn't have an answer, so said nothing.

Yo-Morgantus sprinted to the twisted ruin of the Library of Birmingham. He threw out pseudo-limbs and scraped at the buried steel and loose concrete.

Fear had focused him solely on the mission, and Morag felt his thoughts and senses without the filter of his conscious mind. She was pinned within him, unable to move, breathing only what he granted her. She would have screamed, but there was no space to scream into.

Morgantus pulled at the ruin, digging in search of answers. He wanted to unearth Vivian Grey and her Bloody Big Book. Morag didn't yet understand what threat they represented, but it was very real to *Morgantus*.

He had shared his fearful thoughts with any Venislarn who came near, and word had spread. Flying titans scoured from above. Scurrying earth creatures pored over the landscape. Things that could not be defined in relation to this physical world did … whatever it was they were doing.

The battered army vehicle that had followed them from New Street Station scrambled up into the civic square.

In all the chaos, a buzzing *Tud-burzu* wobbled in and latched itself onto *Morgantus*. *Morgantus* drank its memories. In a rush, Morag saw them.

A building, a smashed window and a large interior space. There were two figures (indistinguishable in the *Tud-burzu*'s mind but as clear as anything to Morag).

"Inside the circle, Prudence," instructed Vivian.

Morag felt a lurch of joy and anguish at the sight of her daughter, hastening inside the occult circle sketched on the ground.

The *Tud-burzu* dived at them but was deflected, losing its *hort'ech* rider in the process. It bounced away and fled to the window.

Morgantus disengaged and prodded Morag for information. She tried to hold back but it was not a matter of choice. Vivian and Prudence were in St Chad's Cathedral. Morag knew it, so *Morgantus* knew it.

Yo-Morgantus relinquished his fruitless search of the Library and set off in a new direction.

. . .

"Enemy is changing direction," shouted Rod and threw the Warrior into as hard a turn as it could manage. The tracked vehicle crunched through rubble and swung round the square to follow *Yo-Morgantus* as he set off in a new direction.

"Hostile at six o'clock," said Yang from her gunner position just behind Rod.

The girl was a fearless fighter and a canny marksman. He didn't know whether to be impressed or concerned about such skills in so innocent a body.

"Details?" he said and looked to his rear-view.

"We're being chased by my grandma."

Grandma? he thought. He looked momentarily at the young mammonite and rechecked his rear-view.

Yoth Mammon, a mouth of questing gums and razor-sharp teeth, so large it could block out the sun, was bearing down from behind. He floored the accelerator.

"Piss off, granny!" yelled Yang and fired a full magazine of six shells on full auto.

Rod followed *Yo-Morgantus* down a stony slope from the square and onto the old dual carriageway, hot in pursuit and hotly pursued.

10:24AM

Even after every human had been killed and all humanity's traffic had stopped, crossing the road was still difficult. Nina, Steve, the invisible King in Crimson and their tiny train of donkeys had to search for a break in the concrete divider running up the A38 dual carriageway so they could cross to St Chad's. A miserable pack of hungry *dendooshi* tried to attack them while they were crossing, but Nina's wand blasts and some wild firing from Pupfish sent them scattering.

Donk did not need any encouragement to get up the steps to the main doors. Nina pushed the door open with her back and the group passed through.

The interior of the Roman Catholic cathedral seemed remarkably unscathed. There were a few knocked over pews, and bits of fallen glass and masonry, but it was nothing that a good half hour with a broom couldn't sort out. Halfway down the aisle and off to the side, Vivian Grey had set out her space to sit in, surrounded by a circle of magical protection. Nina hurried forward.

"Steve!" yelled the pre-teen girl next to Vivian, and ran forward. She had a distinctive mop of red hair.

"Greetings, mortal!" yelled Steve in reply. He slid down Donk's nose and dashed to meet her.

Vivian reluctantly put down her pen and turned to face Nina.

"We did it!" said Nina. She couldn't help the manic grin on her face. "We got the donkey and we found you."

"Nina," acknowledged Vivian. "Michael," she said to Pupfish. "I was expecting you." She gestured to the Bloody Big Book on the table. "It was written."

Nina ignored the lacklustre greeting and wrapped her arms around the older woman's bony frame, hugging her tightly. "You were dead. And then you were in hell. And I knew we could bring you back somehow."

Vivian wriggled uncomfortably and extricated herself from the loving grip. "Yes. You missed me. It's understandable."

Nina should have been offended by Vivian's coldness, but she could only shake her head in delight and laugh. She turned to see the girl holding Steve up, the two of them hurriedly sharing stories. Prudence's mouth widened in a toothy smile when Steve told her that Yang was still alive.

"This is—" began Nina, then stopped herself. "Hang on. This is where I came in last time." She tried to remember what she'd seen and said in the future memory *Yo Khazpapalanaka* had dumped on her. "This is Morag's baby girl?" she recited, gesturing in her best approximation of surprise.

"I'm Prudence," said the girl. "You're Nina Seth. Vivian says I'm almost as big as you."

"I don't know about that." Nina held up her arms and looked round, making sure she gave herself (and her memories) a good look at the place. "Where are we?"

"St Chad's Cathedral," said Vivian.

"Rod's not here?"

"No."

"Right. Um, I'm not Catholic, so where is this exactly? Like, I might need directions."

"But you're already here," said Prudence. "Surely, you know."

Vivian waved the girl to be quiet.

"I'm coming from the Old Contemptibles pub," said Nina, "on...?"

"Edmund Street," said Vivian. "You're really very close. You just need to walk away from the city centre towards the A38. Turn right and keep going. The cathedral is the huge red building on the other side of the road."

Nina nodded. "Thanks." She gazed around, trying to recall how long the memory had lasted. "That's great. I think we're clear."

Prudence was looking at her like she was mad.

"I just had to send a message back in time to myself," explained Nina. She tugged at her Georgian coat. "I'm a time traveller, you know. Like Doctor Who?"

"Who?"

"That's the one. And—" she said with as much razzamatazz as she could muster, throwing in some jazz hands, "—I've brought you your donkey!"

She stepped aside to present Donk.

Vivian sighed heavily. It must have been an emotional moment for her. Here, at the end of the world, to be reunited with her husband. Donk batted his big donkey eyelashes and stepped side to side in nervous anticipation. Vivian cupped his white bristly chin in her one hand and brought her face close to look him in the eye. It was a love that transcended boundaries – Romeo and Juliet, Beauty and the Beast, Shrek and Fiona—

"This isn't him," said Vivian.

"What?"

"It's not Mr Grey."

This was not right. This was not how things should be. Rather than confusion, Nina felt anger. "Are you sure?"

"I think I know what my husband looks like."

"The *Hath-No* fury is married to a beast of burden!" laughed Steve.

"Okay, okay, okay," said Nina, determined to salvage the situation. "Then maybe it's this one..." She drew Vivian down the line to Dink.

"Definitely not," said Vivian. "Wrong colouring entirely."

"No. Okay, okay. Then, maybe our friend Duncan here..." Anger giving way to a frantic desperation, Nina pulled her towards the third donkey.

Vivian looked. "Ah."

"Ah? Ah, as in 'Ah, yes, that's him' or ah as in 'Ah, you've fucked up again, Nina'? Which is it?"

Vivian took his muzzle in her hand. Duncan the donkey snorted and pressed against her.

"This is him," she said, quietly.

"It is? Oh, that's an *adn-bhul* relief! Hoo!" She felt the sickening adrenaline rush through her. "Of course, it is. I was just building up the suspense!"

"Were you?" said Pupfish.

"Course I was! Now, Vivian, all you need to do is re-transform him, do the ritual thingy and we can all go back to—" she waved her hands and looked around, "—you know, not being at the end of the world and that."

"No," said Vivian.

Nina's brain wasn't ready to hear that. "What?"

"No. I'm not doing that." She relinquished Duncan AKA Mr Giles Grey and stepped back. "That's not what's going to happen."

"But the ritual..."

Vivian fixed her with a stare. It had been so long since Vivian had fixed her with one of her powerful stares, that Nina almost shivered.

"You know the ritual is only theoretical?"

"I kinda got that..."

"You know what the ritual entails?" Vivian turned to look at Prudence, the *kaatbari*. When Vivian looked back, Nina felt hot shame. "Shall I put the knife in your hand, Nina?"

"But this is the *world* we're talking about," said Nina. "I've heard you say many, many times that if you had to choose between one life and—"

"I know what I've said!" snapped Vivian, with more emotion than she ever usually let herself show. She walked back to her occult circle and the little writing table she'd set up for herself. Nina, stunned, had nothing to say.

"Shall I show you the statue of the Jesus man?" Prudence said to Steve and carried him down the aisle.

Pupfish slung his rifle casually over his shoulder and followed them. *"Ggh!* He's the one they parade round with a stick up his ass, right?"

Nina didn't know what to say or do. With numb fingers, she unknotted the ropes that bound the donkeys together and let them wander free.

Her radio earpiece crackled and warbled. *"Coming your way!"* said Rod's voice.

"Say again," said Nina. "Say again."

"Coming up to St Chad's cathedral. Pursuing Yo-Morgantus. *He's—"*

Nina ran down the aisle and shouted. "Get out of the way! He's coming! Get out of the way!"

10:26AM

A shadow fell across Prudence as she turned. A shape moved at a broken window high above.

Yo-Morgantus, monstrous and shapeless, poured through. He moved like liquid, but his brutish bulk pushed masonry inwards to crash onto the floor.

"Into the circle!" instructed Vivian, not shouting, but still loud and clear enough to be heard over the crunch of falling stone.

Gravity pulled the flesh-giant to the floor between Prudence and the safety of the circle. Strands of him still clung to the smashed window frame, pulling away reluctantly. Prudence tried not to think of her mother inside that thing, swallowed whole, held in its control.

Yo-Morgantus pooled on the floor, then launched himself towards Vivian. Pews exploded beneath his weight. Nina swung something and an invisible force rippled through the god's body, sending waves across the blubbery skin. Two of the donkeys brayed in high-pitched alarm and ran.

For a moment, Vivian and Nina were hidden from sight,

shrouded by *Yo-Morgantus*'s bulk, and Prudence feared they'd been swallowed too. Then he peeled back, a wave smashing against an invisible wall.

"The circle's holding," Prudence said to herself.

Pupfish put his big rifle to his soldier and started to fire.

"Blast him with your laser eyes, fleshling!" shouted Steve in her hands.

"I don't have laser eyes!" she shouted.

"I don't even see you trying!"

Patches of *Yo-Morgantus*, like individuals beneath the pink and wrinkled blanket of his skin, recoiled as they were shot, but Pupfish's attack had little overall effect on the god, except to draw his attention. *Morgantus*'s bulk swung round, turning to face them even though he had no face.

"Into the circle!" Vivian shouted again, like the only reason Prudence wasn't doing it was because she hadn't heard.

Morgantus flowed towards them. Prudence ran, across the aisle, between two pews on the other side of the cathedral. Pupfish began to follow her, too slowly, walking and firing, like he could hold the colossal thing back.

The entrance doors exploded inward. A big metal vehicle sped into the cathedral. Brickwork collapsed onto its roof then slid from its sleek back. There were several shouts, but the overall din was too huge for Prudence to make out any one voice.

Yo-Morgantus flopped and advanced across the aisle. At the sight of the tank-thing, Pupfish retreated faster than he had from the angry god. The tank pushed aside or flattened long pews, not slowing.

Prudence hurried, half-leaping, half-sprinting to the far wall to avoid being crushed between seats. Pupfish tried to run along pews to stay above the mess, but as the tank bore down on *Morgantus*, he fell and vanished amongst the piled-up wood.

Morgantus shifted to meet the tank. The vehicle plunged into him, head-diving into that gargantuan cushion. Fatty flaps of god flew round it. Blood and juices smeared under still-spinning caterpillar tracks. And then the shapeless arms of *Morgantus* folded over the tank completely, silencing it.

NINA WAITED for *Morgantus* to do something, but swallowing Rod, Yang and their vehicle seemed to have given him indigestion – or at least pause for thought.

"Come here, now!" Vivian called.

Prudence, who had been staring agog at *Morgantus*, came to her senses and began to run round the exterior of the seating area, circling back to them. Among the pews, there was a shift of splintered wood and the fishboy started to push his way free.

Small flying shapes battered at the stained glass windows. Even as Nina noticed them, larger ones smashed their way through. *Tud-burzu* carrying tracing paper thin *hort'ech* dolls swarmed in. A luminous *eyahl-cryd* flyer followed, sucker-like feeding tubes on the underside of wing-arms glistening. Nina let loose with her wand of *quirz'ir* binding. It was a powerful weapon, but the recoil was going to give her repetitive strain injury before the day was done. By the looks of things, the day might be done a bit sooner than any of them would like.

"We can stop this," she hissed to Vivian.

Vivian shook her head, but turned to her husband donkey anyway. She put her hand to the side of his head. He looked at her, patient and unjudging. *Tud-burzu* bounced off the walls of the circle around them.

Prudence squealed as one of the curly-spined flying creatures swooped in at her, ready to blast her with flame breath. Steve leapt from Prudence's shoulder and came down on the flyer's back, impaling the *hort'ech* rider with his pencil as he landed.

Prudence stumbled on and into the magic circle. The *Tud-*

burzu wheeled way overhead, with Steve cackling madly on its back.

Nina clutched Prudence to her and threw a blast of magic at the glowing *eyahl-cryd* as it swooped low.

"Once there was a time when I would have sacrificed a child, any child, to save the world," said Vivian.

Nina began to say something, but she realised the woman wasn't talking to her but to the donkey.

"If I could have pressed a button and put every human out of their misery, I would have." She worked her fingers through his fur. "Not anymore. *Shei at-al gha!*"

Duncan – Mr Grey – twisted in sudden agony. He fell to his knees, his back buckled in a way that surely did not conform to any donkey anatomy. Hide ripped bloodily.

"What's she doing to him?" said Prudence.

High above there was the crack of tiles and beams and support struts giving way as Venislarn beings ripped at the roof to force fresh entry.

There was gunfire in the aisle from Pupfish. *Yo-Morgantus* had got over his big meal and was now advancing towards him. Pupfish was trying to fight a three-hundred-and-sixty-degree skirmish all by himself. His tactic seemed to be swinging his rifle around and firing at random. Nina tried to fire at the flyers above without catching him in the blast cone of her wand.

There was a gasp from the floor. There was a man on hands and knees at the centre of what looked like an exploded donkey. He got to his feet uncertainly. His body was coated in blood and other donkey juices, but he was otherwise naked, sagging skin hanging off his narrow frame. He had a grey tufty beard and moustache. Nina couldn't decide if this was a hangover from being a bristly chinned donkey, or if Mr Grey had modelled his look on one of them oldy-timey Euro psychologists who thought everything was about sex.

He reached out for Vivian and spoke with difficulty, getting used to have a human mouth and voice box again. "Vivian, love, I've had many years to think about what I would say when this moment came and—"

"Yes, we don't have much time now though," she said curtly. "Can you fight?"

"But I've had time to reflect and I think it's important—"

"I'm sure it can wait until after we're done with the current crisis."

His brow creased with pained confusion. "But we might not survive."

"Then it won't matter, will it?" she said.

Panting, Pupfish stumbled into the circle, clattered round Vivian's writing desk and collided with Nina. "Assholes! *Ggh!* Everywhere!" Trying to get his breath back, gills fluttering, he looked at the naked Mr Grey. "See? *Ggh!* Hung like a donkey."

Nina did see. Well, that explained Vivian's attraction to him. She wondered what Mr Grey had seen in Vivian, immediately regretting the thought. Old people sex was disgusting. The end of the world was bad enough without that playing on her mind.

Prudence, also staring, tugged at Nina's hand. "Nina...?"

"I will take questions at the end," said Nina.

A fierce *Kaxid* tornado of fire imploded the remaining windows along one wall of the cathedral. From high above the building, a god roared in the sky. Through the cathedral doors, a tide of creatures, *dhuis* and *Voor-D'yoi Lak* and sinewy fungoid *mi'nasulu*, poured in to attack.

"Oh, we're popular today," said Nina, desperately unhappy with the situation.

Mr Grey picked up the largest scrap of bloody donkey hide on the floor and tied it around his waist as a loincloth. "Do we have weapons?" he asked.

A madness-inducing god of the *Ogdru Jahad* unfolded itself

into the church building. Above them, Steve hollered and whooped, apparently enjoying a buckaroo bronco ride while sowing chaos among the *Tud-burzu*.

10:29AM

The interior of the Warrior vehicle was dark, except for a single, dim interior light back in the infantry carrier section at the rear. The engines had died and the lights around the driver controls went out almost immediately.

The horrid flesh body of *Yo-Morgantus* was pushing its way through the three front observation hatches, coming through like massive rectangular blocks of sausage meat. Rod slammed and locked the panels as quickly as he could. Something burst as he shut the second and sprayed stinking pus across the tiny dashboard and his own legs. As he went to the third one, the god-flesh parted, and a human face looked through: a pale face, wide, terror-stricken eyes and a framing of ginger hair. In the rush, Rod couldn't see if it was Morag or Brigit. He slammed the panel, pinning and slicing flesh which poked around the edges.

"Turret won't move!" Yang called.

"Got us in a bear hug," said Rod, struggling to climb over his seatback and into the section behind.

The panels of the vehicle wailed mournfully as *Morgantus* tightened his grip. Rod squeezed past Yang's legs to get to the autocannon ammunition. He looked at her ankle length white socks and patent leather school shoes, and even in that moment of peril thinking they were odd things for someone to wear to face the end of the world.

Metal screamed under the pressure.

"Open the rear hatch and I'll knife the bastard!" said Yang.

"Here." Rod passed her a clip of three high explosive rounds. The clip was over five pounds in weight but Yang took it in a single hand.

"Mundane rounds have no permanent effect," she said, loading it into the magazine nonetheless.

"Full auto. Hi-ex rounds. Either we punch a hole through him or..."

Yang ducked from her turret position to stare at him. "Explosive. Point blank. Hot gases rapidly expanding. Won't that fucking kill us?"

Rod pulled a face. "A better end than trying to knife him. And don't swear."

"Don't stifle my freedom of speech. I could sue."

"No courts left to take me to," he said. Somewhere a rivet popped and the vehicle tilted alarmingly.

"The world has truly ended." She checked the ammo and prepared to fire.

GILES GREY CREATED complex gestures with dextrous fingers and bolts of energy shot out at surrounding Venislarn. Pupfish, recognising him as the powerful wizard he was, stayed beside the loincloth wearing mage, firing into the horde. Pupfish's focus appeared to be mostly on *dendooshi* and other creatures of the fur and teeth variety. Nina used her wand, but kept well clear of both man and fishboy. Her weapon was powerful but indiscriminate. Together, they kept a wall of firepower between the Venislarn and the circle where Vivian and Prudence stood close together.

There was one, two, then a third crumpled bang. Abruptly, *Yo-Morgantus* seemed to inflate to mountainous size before ripping apart like a bubblegum balloon. Meaty matter rained down across the cathedral and many Venislarn creatures. Skin, intestines, bulbous organs and gallons of sickly bile washed about.

Rod's tank thing slid out of the mess, on its side, sticky strands still attached to it.

Nina stood still and stared in amazement and hope.

With a loud wrenching sound, the rear access door fell open and two figures stumbled out, clinging to each other for support. Rod nearly slipped on a pool of something, but Yang kept him upright. For her tiny size, the mammonite schoolgirl was frighteningly strong. Nina hoped she'd never have to face her as an enemy.

Rod held back a moment, stopped to reach for something among the gutted god. Nina saw it was an arm. Yang argued. Rod resisted. Nina hurried forward. She blasted a *dhuis* to her left and a *Presz'ling* to her right, and slipped through the edge of the mess of *Morgantus* to reach them.

On the floor was Morag, dazed and reeling, but very much alive. Nina grabbed her other arm and helped pull her up.

Sections of *Morgantus* began to contract and pull together. The blob monster *Crippen Ai* which had threatened Birmingham, both in the past and the present, was a mass of brain and muscle. Every bit of that monster was capable of existing separately. *Yo-Morgantus* was a single creature, with a single brain in there somewhere. But he was as tough as cancer and nearly impossible to kill. A weeping, bleeding extension of *Morgantus* reared up to grab at Morag. Nina blasted it with the wand of *quirz'ir* binding, and neatly severed the limb.

Together, the three of them retreated to the circle. Pupfish and

Giles Grey were cutting a wedge into the Venislarn forces. The general situation was hopeless, but for now the last defenders of earth were making themselves felt.

Morag stumbled in the circle. Prudence grabbed for her. Morag fell on her knees, a full head shorter than her daughter. Nina thought the pair were the absolute spitting image of each other, or was that just because they were both gingers. Nina wondered if that made her a racist.

"Are you you?" said Prudence.

"I'm back," said Morag. "All me." She stretched up and put a kiss on Prudence's cheek. "How did you get so big?"

"I grew."

Morag shook her head. "I shouldn't have spent so much time at work. I missed it all."

"Can we go to KFC this weekend? I want a milkshake," said Prudence.

"Absolutely."

Vivian crouched over her desk, inexplicably trying to finish her book while all of hell was literally breaking loose around them. Rod, panting with exhaustion, threw a little wave at her.

"Nice to see you, Vivian."

"I'm trying to write, Rod. And I need more time. I'd appreciate no interruptions."

"Aye. Right you are." He looked around. Nina saw how his face focused.

"Is this the King in Crimson here?" She reached out.

"You've sort of put your hand in his kidneys," said Rod.

"I'll do worse if he tries to take your soul."

Rod's expression changed, but Nina couldn't read it.

"He heard you," he said.

10:32AM

The King in Crimson seemed more amused than frightened by Nina's words, but Rod appreciated the sentiment. In the current situation, losing one's soul to a chatty undead god was probably not the worst thing that could happen.

In an action so swift, there wasn't even time for sound, the roof of the cathedral vanished. A flying shape, bigger than a football stadium, whisked it away in its huge mouth. *Yoth Mammon*'s circular maw ground masonry and slate roofing down to nothing. A swirling disco light of mind-bending colours filled the open space above. It was no longer the sky. There was no longer enough of the world left to call that space the sky.

Gazing across the scene of monsters and magical misfires, Rod recognised it for the kind of snafu they had been in before, only on a larger, world-ending scale. A spiralling thing, like power cables in a hurricane, wormed its way into the building.

"*Yo Khazpapalanaka*," said Nina. "God of time. Don't let him touch you."

Weaving in amongst it all was Steve, riding some flying prawn thing. He appeared to have half a dozen paper doll corpses skewered on his pencil spear and he was now trying to prise apart the shell of the prawn thing, like it was a gourmet lobster dinner. The prawn thing was not best pleased.

"All the gods, all in one place," said Nina.

"Shit just got real," agreed Rod.

"Oh, you get to say it now, do you? That's my line."

"It is time our business was concluded, patron," said the King in Crimson, hands resting lightly on Rod's shoulders.

He shrugged. "YOLO."

Rod didn't have a weapon to join the firefight. He'd left his rifle in the Warrior and lost his handgun long before that. Yang had had the presence of mind to bring her rifle with her, but he wasn't going to try and take a weapon from that pre-teen sharpshooter.

Yang crouched at the edge of the circle and took patient individual headshots at some of the larger creatures, making every shot a kill. Rod hoped he'd never have to face her as an enemy.

Yo-Morgantus was moving, finding his feet, his metaphorical feet. The god had no feet except those he borrowed from other creatures. As the flattened deity brought himself together, he latched onto the Venislarn around him. Wolf things, corpse things, insectoid things, things Rod would have mistaken for furniture or abstract art if they weren't actually moving. Like an old man grasping for his Zimmer frame, *Yo-Morgantus* grasped for any being which might give him support. A tendril even grabbed the prawn thing Steve was flying, and he tumbled from its back to the cathedral tiles. As *Morgantus*'s presence spread, the wild menagerie of horrors gathered focus and more and more eyes – yellow reptilian eyes, compound eyes, weird antennae things, and unpleasantly human eyes – all turned to the small band of people inside the magic circle.

"It is over," said Brigit, walking towards the magic circle from the direction of the altar, through the chaos. Her naked body was covered in gore, but it didn't look like any had come from her. "This comes to an end."

Though there was fighting elsewhere, her voice rose clearly above it all. Rod realised the other creatures *Morgantus* controlled were lending their voices to hers. Every possible grunt, bark, whistle and click was modulated to enhance hers. She spoke with the power of a monster choir.

Brigit slowed as she neared the circle. "Magic spells? That's all you've got."

Yang swung her rifle round. The tentacled arms of a possessed starfish thing flew out. It grabbed the barrel of the rifle and yanked. Yang managed to fire before it was wrenched from her hands. The starfish monster died instantly, dangling from the end of *Morgantus*'s flesh arm. The rifle skittered on the floor.

As Brigit bent to pick it up. Nina raised her wand. Brigit twisted her fingers into some magic Mr Spock shape and the wand blast flowed harmlessly over her. Brigit held the rifle like a green recruit and aimed it underarm at Yang.

"Don't you even dare," said Yang. Brigit shot her in the chest.

Prudence yelled; Morag held her tightly. Rod dropped beside the girl, but she was dead, already gone.

Brigit tossed the rifle aside. She'd had her fun. The gun fell near where Steve had crash-landed.

Brigit surveyed the remaining humans slowly. "Nina, Morag, Vivian and, er, Rod, isn't it?" She smiled. "The consular mission's finest. Maiden, mother, crone." She waved her hand dismissively at Rod. "And the male one."

The King in Crimson leaned in behind Rod, so close that Rod could see his mask-covered face out of the corner of his eye and feel the corpse's breath on his cheek.

"Look what she did," said the King smoothly. "A young life snuffed out. Disgraceful." The King's skeletal hands massaged Rod's shoulders, trying to work the rage deeper into his body.

"Come outside your little circle now," said Brigit. "Have some dignity. We can tear it apart like paper if we wish."

"Keep talking," muttered Vivian, still busily scribbling away in that bloody book of hers.

Rod's fury swelled. He was holding the body of a stupid clever innocent murderous girl, swatted down without a thought, yet it was Vivian's incessant writing which brought his rage to the surface. The very notion that she could think a book was so bloody important, that all they had bought with their sacrifices was a little time!

"Flamin' ridiculous," he growled.

"That's right!" said the King. "Take your revenge. *Yo-Morgantus* is right there."

"The power to knock out any god?" said Rod between gritted teeth.

"Any god," the King hissed in encouragement.

Rod jumped up and forward, dropping Yang's body. He was never the fastest man. It wasn't his forte, but he only needed to be the fastest for a second. He moved towards Brigit and then ducked sideways. She wasn't expecting that. He stepped onto the back of some fat spider thing, leapt and punched.

It wasn't a great leap, but he could feel the King in Crimson at his back, lifting him. It was a weak punch, but it didn't need to be anything but a recognisable one.

Rod punched the tangled web of Bannakaffalatta, or whatever it was Nina had called it.

10:34AM

Something weird happened to time, before Morag's eyes. Outside the circle, figures leapt and jerked.

Rod had flung himself at the mass that was *Yo Khazpapalanaka*. He became a jerky series of images, like he'd been caught under an epilepsy-inducing strobe light. A figure had winked into existence behind Rod, a skeletal horror, seven feet high, its limbs and lower face wrapped in stained bandages, its body draped in the tattered remnants of regal red clothing. The creature's bony fingers were plunging, image by stuttering image, into Rod's back.

Nina shouted in anger, leaping from the normality of the circle into the slowing, sputtering time outside it. She swung her wand round to attack. As she moved into the strange realm of unconnected time, her shout became sliced into discrete chunks: shout, silence, shout, silence.

There was a puff of explosive smoke by the floor. Morag wouldn't have even seen it if the moments weren't being presented as separate tableaux. Steve the Destroyer had crawled, unseen, to the mammonite girl's dropped rifle and fired the grenade launcher device mounted below the barrel.

Time slowed further. Morag could see the grenade itself, unblurred. It was hard to judge where Steve was trying to aim it: Brigit or *Morgantus* or the skeleton. It struck none of them, hitting the chitinous back of a *zhadan* warrior spider.

Rod fell. Nina ran. Brigit leapt for the circle. The beginnings of an explosion, opened up in the *zhadan*'s side, a sphere of fire no bigger than a football.

And time stopped.

Inside the circle, Vivian continued with her work and Prudence struggled in Morag's arms, screaming at Yang's death. Outside, nothing moved.

Yoth Mammon was frozen amid the now still colours of *Ammi Usub*. *Yo-Morgantus* was a distended but solidly fixed mass of flesh. *Yo Khazpapalanaka* was a three-dimensional scribble of lines in the air, a sculpture. All the slathering creatures of the Venislarn apocalypse were caught, suspended in time. And there was silence.

It had been a long time since Morag had heard complete silence. Prudence slipped from her grip and dropped beside Yang.

"Don't leave the circle," Morag said automatically, but Prudence wasn't stupid.

Prudence held Yang's face and brushed the hair away from her eyes.

"We should have protected her," said Prudence, choking. She looked up at Vivian. "Your circle should have protected her."

"Magic circles are no protection against bullets," said Vivian.

"Then your magic circle is stupid!"

"Baby, don't..." Morag began.

"I should have saved her," said Prudence. "I'm the *kaatbari*. I'm the herald of the Soulgate. I have influence. I was going to make everything better. For everyone." She sobbed.

Morag went to her and held her. She didn't know what she was doing. She didn't know how to comfort her own child. It was still her first day of being a mum and she'd not been to any parenting classes or read any books or anything.

"I don't even have laser eyes," Prudence sobbed.

Morag wanted to wipe the tears from her daughter's eyes, but Morag had no tissues or cloth to hand. She was wearing a dress made from scabs of flesh and it was not ideal tear-dabbing material. She brushed Prudence's tears with her thumb and kissed the top of her head.

They stayed like that for a time, or at least a time within the timeless world that now surrounded them.

The scratching of Vivian's pen stopped. "It wasn't my circle anyway," she said.

Morag and Prudence looked at her. Vivian watched them over the open book.

"Do you think I can draw a magic circle which can hold back the massed gods of the Venislarn horde?" she asked. "Do you think I can conjure a circle which can hold back the flow of time itself?"

"Then..."

Vivian pointed her pen at Prudence. "I told you to draw, and you drew."

"You told me what to draw."

"I said words, but you created sigils I have never seen before. I said I needed a young woman with imagination."

Prudence blinked. "I did this?"

Vivian's expression stiffened and she tapped the book. "I'm doing the hard work, though."

Morag smoothed Prudence's hair and stood so she could look at the book on the table. "Why is that book so bloody important?" She tried to sound like she wasn't fucking annoyed, but she failed because she was really fucking annoyed.

Vivian wrote in an assured and speedy hand, filling in the gaps on a page that featured a complex diagram which looked like a medieval illustration of the cosmos.

"I once told you to read it and then you'd understand," Vivian said.

"It's a fucking infinite book," said Morag.

"Language, mum," said Prudence.

"We're all going to die," said Morag. "And then, because this is hell, we're going to be resurrected, reborn or rebooted into yet more fresh hell, and it's going to last forever. Why the fuck would I want to read that book?"

Vivian blew on the drying ink on the page and then turned over a gazillion pages to another section. "Don't you want to see how it ends?"

Morag resisted. She didn't want to give the annoying cow the satisfaction. But Morag couldn't resist forever, and there was nothing *but* forever inside this magic bubble. She stepped closer and looked.

"Final page," said Vivian. "I'm nearly done. A word here. Some arrows there."

10:38AM

Vivian watched Morag's face as she read. Vivian didn't need to watch her face – she had written this moment before, a long time ago – but she wanted to watch it, nonetheless.

Morag read it. She made a strange little noise, too surprised to be properly surprised. She read it again and then looked Vivian in the eye. "This is what happens?"

Vivian nodded.

Morag's mouth was open, like a slack-jawed ruminant. "All this time, you've been working on this?"

"Yes. I tried to tell you. The first week I met you."

"And Omar?"

"Him too."

"You two don't even like each other."

"Strange times make strange bedfellows."

Prudence stood beside Morag. Her lips moved as she silently read. "You've not finished," she said.

"Mere markings on the page," said Vivian. "But, um, ah…"

Outside the circle, *Yo Khazpapalanaka* stuttered and flexed, a sleeper about to awake.

"No time," said Morag.

The god of time itself moved a fraction. The massive freeze frame of the universe skipped a thousandth of a second. The grenade explosion expanded to a bright light. Brigit's fingers grazed the edge of the circle.

Time rushed in.

Rod died. Nina fired her wand. The explosion swallowed the *zhadan* spider, Nina and chunks of *Yo-Morgantus*. Brigit was flung forward like a doll. As was Steve, an actual doll. The blast picked up the desk and Vivian with it and tossed them back.

Vivian hit her head and blacked out.

She came to, maybe only a second later, with her ears ringing and a pain in her body that moved whenever she tried to locate it. She squirmed on the floor, briefly tried to support herself with a hand she hadn't had for millennia, then found her bearings.

The Bloody Big Book was open on the floor a couple of feet away. On hand and knees, Vivian lurched at it.

Only a few more markings to make.

"Pen, pen, pen," she muttered, looking round for something to write with.

There were booms from the heavens above. In the great play, tin sheets were being banged together to symbolise the tempest of immeasurable forces rallying against and with each other.

Light-blotting gods, bigger than cities, were falling toward the world. Vivian's vision was dimming by the second. There were no pens here though. She sat up, grunted at the pain, and looked round.

"Pen," she said.

There was the fizz and vacuum pop of offensive magic somewhere off to Vivian's left. Either Nina or her husband was still alive and fighting off the creatures. Elsewhere, creatures were tearing into each other. Alliances were falling apart at the end of things.

Vivian saw Morag, hunched with Prudence at her side, not five feet away.

Steve the Destroyer bounced over carcasses and rubble to reach Prudence. He appeared to be partly on fire.

"You're on fire," said Prudence.

"Pah!" he exclaimed, his voice warbling with a deranged tone. "You call this being on fire? Steve spits in the face of fire." He tried to put the fire out with his pencil spear. It was a poor effort.

Prudence suffocated Steve's fire by whacking him hard with a kneeler cushion.

"Picking a fight with me?" he said, dazed.

Brigit pushed herself up from where she had been thrown among the smashed pews, separated from her host god by the explosion. There was a ragged series of wounds in the side of her torso, a fistful of long wooden splinters embedded in her.

She hissed in pain. "Enough!"

"Ready to give in?" grunted Morag.

Brigit's face was untamed fury. She held her wounded side and staggered, framed against the shattered window. "The absolute and astonishing gall of it! You think that you can stand against us? It's preposterous. It's ... it's offensively stupid. Look at us! We're unstoppable. Infinite. Divine."

"And that's why we're better than you," Vivian coughed.

"Better?"

Prudence took the pencil from Steve and presented it to Vivian. Vivian blinking blood from her eyes, stared at it. Grimy and fire-blackened, it was barely more than a stick of charcoal, but it was a writing implement regardless.

"Infinite. All-powerful. You are those things," said Vivian. "You can do with us whatever you wish. And yet, in the face of the infinite and the divine, we can stand against you. We can say 'no' and know what saying 'no' means."

Prudence helped Vivian's shaking hand put pencil to paper. Vivian underlined a critical word.

Brigit laughed and the laugh became a painful cough. "And that makes you better than us?"

Prudence and Vivian moved as one. A comma. A question mark.

"We are better than you," said Vivian. "We are bigger than you. In every way that counts."

Yo-Morgantus reached out to his servants, the willing and the unwilling. *Yoth Mammon* curved downward to a final dive.

"Words!" Brigit snorted. "Finish your stupid story! See what good it does you!"

"It's not my story," said Vivian.

"What?" said Brigit.

The pencil made a final mark. A full stop.

"It's yours," said Vivian.

Yo-Morgantus connected with Brigit and comprehension immediately washed over her face.

"No," she whispered, horrified, but it was too late.

Demons reared and swooped to attack, but it was too late.

Streamers of pure light burst from the pages, shooting up and outwards. They split and curled away, a springtime of plant growth at a thousand times the speed. Golden light of revealing reality shone on the Venislarn throng. There was such an intense twinkling sunshine splendour that it might as well have been accompanied with the voices of a heavenly choir.

"Wow," said Prudence.

Morag looked up. "What's with the Disney special effects, Vivian?"

"It's the way I always imagined this moment," said Vivian. "And it's the way I decided to write it."

The light expanded until it swallowed everything.

FRIDAY

The Library of Birmingham was the largest public lending library in Europe. It had been designed by a Dutch architect and built with a façade of gold cladding overlaid with huge interlocking steel circles that made it look like a robot's birthday cake. The library was opened some years ago to great fanfare and then, due to local government funding cuts, almost immediately had its hours slashed. It was a bold and beautiful symbol of a city with grand aspirations and poor financial management.

On the third floor of the library, there was a large terrace garden. Visitors could step out of the building and into an area of sculpted flower beds and benches and look out across Centenary Square and the city centre beyond.

Morag stood at the railing and felt the stiff cool breeze on her face. The Birmingham skyline was not a notably impressive one. Bold and classical Victorian edifices stood among brutalist towers and ugly multi-storey car parks. And standing over it all were the cranes. Birmingham was a city that never seemed to stop reinventing itself. In Centenary Square below, people moved in all directions, to and from the convention centre, the canal basin, the theatres, the council buildings and the pedestrianised shopping areas. Traffic hummed somewhere, wherever it was that roadworks hadn't closed off the streets.

"What are you looking at?" said Prudence.

Prudence Murray, who was – what? Eleven years old? Twelve? – was actually wearing clothes that fitted her. The cuffs of her hoodie were frayed, and one of the neck tassels looked like it had been habitually chewed, as though Prudence had been wearing it every day for months.

"Blue sky," said Morag. "The city. People."

Mrs Vivian Grey put her hands on the rail and nodded at the vista before them, as though giving it her grudging approval. "This is a world where the Venislarn never came."

"Never?" said Nina.

Vivian's mouth turned down slightly. "We did finish the book in pencil. I wouldn't want to make concrete promises…"

Prudence took a step closer to Vivian and whispered, a whisper loud enough for anyone to hear. "So, the book we wrote…"

"*I* wrote. You helped in a minor capacity at the end."

"Are all the Venislarn in *that* book? Or is *this*—" she pointed two index fingers at the ground beneath them "—the book?"

The wind picked up for a moment and the rustling gust momentarily drowned out what Vivian said.

"…draw my own conclusions," said Prudence.

"So, none of it happened?" said Nina. "Are we all gonna get our memories retconned?"

"I do wish you would use real words, Miss Seth," said Vivian.

"It's like that Jumanji film," said Morag. "The game is finished and all the bits go back in the box. Everything restored."

"Shit!" said Nina, fighting with her tight jean pocket to get her phone out. Her ancient coat and dress had been lost in the revising of reality. Clumsy in her haste, she tapped at her phone.

"What's Jumanji?" said Prudence.

"Oh, it's a good film," said Morag. "Magical adventure. We should watch it. A movie afternoon sounds good." She frowned. "What day is it, anyway?"

Nina had managed to make her phone call. "Ricky? Ricky, it's me, Nina. Yeah. Nina. This is Chief Inspector Ricky Lee, right?"

"I don't care what day it is," said Rod, taking a deep, lung-filling breath. "There's a pint of American Sister waiting for me at the Old Contemptibles. You coming?" He looked to Morag and then Vivian. "Anyone? My round."

"I do not do pubs, Rod," said Vivian. "I think I might go for a walk. Perhaps the park."

"Oh, any particular park in mind?" said Morag lightly. "One with a donkey sanctuary, perhaps?"

"Your lack of subtlety is astonishing," said Vivian. "I wonder if it is a personal flaw or a generically Scottish one?"

"You didn't answer my question."

"And it is none of your business, Miss Murray," said Vivian and walked towards the library doors.

"Okay, so you don't know me in this reality," Nina said into her phone. "But maybe you would like to know me. I'm a complete sex kitten. Yes. Yes, I know you're married. Is that going to stop you?"

Rod shook his head. "So, Morag? Pub?" he said, trying again.

"Can't take a kid to a pub," she said.

"You said we could go for KFC this weekend," said Prudence.

Rod pulled a face. "No one wants to do that."

"We're having milkshakes," Prudence said, as though this would be the clincher.

"Okay," Nina was saying. "Six o'clock. The cocktail bar at the top of the Cube. Actually, no, I've never been there. Cool." She ended the call and looked at the others. "Well, that's my evening sorted. You?"

"Apparently, it's a toss-up between beer and milkshakes," said Rod.

Nina clicked her fingers. "Freakshakes. That's where it's at. I'm talking five thousand calories in a glass."

Prudence gasped. Morag was already shaking her head. "I don't think that's appropriate. Even for a growing a girl."

"My neighbour, Mr Chowdhry, owns this Freakshake Shack on the high street and, I swear – crap—!" She clutched her phone again. "I didn't even think to check where my parents had got to!"

As she tried to make her call, Morag felt the wind's chill get to her and steered Prudence towards the doors.

"So, we're agreed we're going for a drink," said Rod. "We just haven't decided what."

"We've got time," said Morag. "We can do them all."

They went into the library, which was just a library.

IZZY WU FOLLOWED the rest of the students through the lower level of the library. A study trip had sounded like a fun alternative to lectures, but she was already bored beyond belief. She thought it had looked cold out, but now her duffel coat was boiling hot and her knitted scarf was nearly strangling her.

The undergrads trudged in a line after Professor Omar of the Practical Theology department. The wander through the library's collections seemed a pointless excursion. Prints from two-hundred-year-old magazines. Scrapbooks of paintings of Shakespeare's plays. A mahoosive illustrated book of birds which the professor insisted everyone should be impressed by, but Izzy couldn't see why.

"Joe, Josh, this way. Maryam, if you and Kyra could actually bother to look," said the professor.

He urged them closer. Izzy kept a respectable distance. Professor Omar was a creepy guy and made her skin crawl. Everyone said he had a thing going on with the weird little man who worked in his office. Izzy wasn't homophobic, no way, but old folks should have put sex and stuff behind them years ago.

"So, what do you think this is?" said the professor.

"It's a bloody big book," said someone.

"Very good, Owen. It is. And, in truth, that's all we know about it. The leather binding is possibly eighteenth century – perhaps the work of Roedelius – but the ravages of time have made the interior pages inseparable and it is therefore, literally, a closed book to us. Some wag nicknamed it the Wittgenstein Volume because...?"

The professor let the questioning sentence hang in the hope one of his students would fill the silence. Izzy sighed and tugged at her scarf. On the wall opposite was a display shelf. Stuffed untidily between two archive boxes was a ragged doll. It was a foot high at most. Its top half was made from badly cut sack material. Its bottom half was made from neatly stitched cotton with a jaunty black and red floral pattern. The doll had a stitched-on smile, and two angry little wooden eyes. It looked like it had been scorched badly in a fire.

"Is this some sort of voodoo doll, professor?" she asked.

"I was talking about the Wittgenstein Volume," said the professor testily. "Ludwig Wittgenstein proposed a thought experiment, the notion that if you could describe the whole universe in a book – every single molecule and every single action – that book would not contain a single ethical judgement. This, to be clear, ladies and gentlemen, boys and girls, is not that book." He took a deep, nasally breath and adjusted his glasses. "But what a lovely thought though, eh? A universe without judgement."

The undergrads had no comment on the matter.

"No?" said the professor. "You're all Philistines, aren't you? And nothing would make you happier than if I said we should all go upstairs to the cafeteria for coffee and cake."

There was wordless but nonetheless audible approval for this notion.

"Philistines," repeated Professor Omar. "Cake it is."

Izzy waved her hand at the ugly doll. "Is it a voodoo doll then or what?"

"Gooey chocolate cake is calling, Miss Wu," said the professor. "We're moving on."

"But, sir..."

Izzy glanced back at the shelf but now there was just a space between the archive boxes and the doll had gone.

AUTHOR NOTES

YES – The Bella in the Wych Elm story is generally true as told here. A woman's skeletal body was found wedged inside an elm tree in Hagley Wood in 1943. Mysterious graffiti appeared on walls in the city, asking "Who put Bella in the Wych Elm?" and it still pops up from time to time. Go look.

NO – The body of Bella isn't that of a time-travelling Spanish sorceress. Theories have abounded, including suggestions that she was a German (or Dutch) spy, a local prostitute or even the victim of an occult murder linked to a 'Hand of Glory' ritual.

YES – The body, autopsy and other records all disappeared during the Second World War, adding to the mystery. One of the authors spent a wonderful afternoon in Hagley Woods and local area, exploring possible sites for that fateful elm.

YES – In 1949, a massive skull was discovered in a shop doorway on Broad Street. It was so big it damaged the back door of the police car they took it away in.

NO – It was not a Venislarn monster's skull. It was an elephant skull and the whole event was a surrealist joke engineered by the artist Desmond Morris.

YES – *That* Desmond Morris. Readers of a certain age will remember him as the maker and presenter of TV nature shows and as the author of *The Naked Ape*.

YES – The artist Conroy Maddox had a house overlooking Calthorpe Park in Birmingham. He wished it to become a house devoted to surrealism. Wild parties were commonplace. The jazz singer and art critic George Melly attended at least one of these parties. Poets, university communists and Windrush-era Caribbean immigrants were also often in attendance.

NO – These parties were not used for occult rituals. However, photographs and paintings from these parties featured Conroy Maddox in the company of a nun. A faked crucifixion of Conroy Maddox took place. The nun allegedly enjoyed a bottle of local Mitchell and Butler beer during the proceedings.

YES – As briefly mentioned in Oddjob 2, there is a mine underneath Birmingham University. It was excavated in 1905 by and for the undergraduates studying mining at the university. It's still there but, sadly, not accessible to members of the public.

NO – It's not in use as a magical storehouse. Nor is it illuminated by an eclectic array of kitsch lampshades. Which is a shame.

YES – The university clock tower is called Old Joe. It is the tallest free-standing clock tower in the world. According to some sources, it was the inspiration for the Eye of Sauron in Lord of the Rings.

YES – Spaghetti Junction (or to use its proper name, the Gravelly Hill Interchange) is a somewhat complicated looking road junction, opened in 1972. It has five levels of overlapping roads but is also a junction for rivers (the Tame and the Rea), railways (cross-city and Walsall) and canals (Tame Valley Canal and Birmingham and Fazeley Canal). Although there are other 'spaghetti junctions' around the world, the Birmingham one was the first to be given the name.

NO – Spaghetti Junction is in no apparent danger of becoming a loop-the-loop sushi conveyor belt for Venislarn diners.

YES – There are deer and donkeys in Sutton Park. At 2,400 acres, it is the second largest urban park in the UK. The park is a mixture of heathland, wetland and ancient woodland. Wild muntjac deer live in the park. The donkey sanctuary in the park is part of the nationwide Donkey Sanctuary charity.

NO – None of the donkeys in Sutton Park are magically transformed people.

NO – Carcosa is not our invention. It was first mentioned in Ambrose Bierce's story 'An inhabitant of Carcosa' published in 1886. It has been subsequently embellished upon by the likes of Robert W Chambers and August Derleth. It appears on the maps in the 'Song of Ice and Fire' books by George RR Martin's. It even appears in the TV shows True Detective and The Chilling Adventures of Sabrina.

YES – The Bridgeman playground sculptures were real things. They were constructed in the 1960s by Birmingham College of Arts sculptor John Bridgeman. There were several of them across the city and were meant to be both climbing frames and works of abstract sculpture.

NO – They're not really blood-drinking concrete monsters. And that's not the reason why all but one them have now been destroyed. The surviving 'fish' sculpture can be found in the park area near the tower blocks in what was once the grounds of Fox Hollies Hall in Acocks Green. The gateposts and gate are all that remains of the original manor house.

YES – There is an abandoned cinema forty feet underneath Holloway Circus roundabout in Birmingham city centre. The Smallbrook Queensway Odeon closed in 1988 and has been unused (and essentially unchanged) for over thirty years.

YES – Oscar Deutsch, a resident of Balsall Heath, created the Odeon cinema chain. He opened his first cinema in nearby

Brierley Hill. It was indeed later claimed that the word Odeon stood for "Oscar Deutsch Entertains Our Nation."

NO – The abandoned Odeon cinema hasn't been used a secret base by armed militia, as far as we know.

YES – St Chad was a local boy, relatively speaking. In the seventh century AD he was installed as bishop to the Mercians, and Lichfield (north of Birmingham) became the centre of his diocese. Several of his bones now rest in St Chad's Cathedral in Birmingham city centre.

YES – The statues of Queen Victoria, the sphinx-like Guardians and the Floozie in the Jacuzzi are as described in the book. The Floozie's proper name is 'River' but no one in Birmingham calls it that. The Floozie and the Guardians were designed by the Indian sculptor, Dhruva Mistry.

NO – The Guardians are not, as Nina supposes, "some weird Venislarn shit".

YES – The statue Mr and Mrs Seth cower behind is real. It is a gilded bronze statue of Matthew Boulton, James Watt and William Murdoch.

NO – Despite it gaining the nickname of 'The Carpet Salesmen', Boulton, Watt and Murdoch are not looking at a carpet but a plan of a steam engine. The three men worked together on developing steam engine designs in the late eighteenth and early nineteenth centuries.

YES – St Chad's Cathedral was struck by an incendiary bomb in World War Two but the church building was saved because the bomb had smashed heating pipes on the way down and the water extinguished the incendiary device.

YES – In 1998, while attending a G8 summit, US President Bill Clinton made a spur-of-the-moment decision to go for a drink and visited the Malt House pub. He had a pint and shared a plate of chips with Bill and June Scott from Hall Green.

NO – The use of both 'mom' and 'mum' is not a series of typos, or a desperate attempt to play to a US audience. Native residents of Birmingham use 'mom' routinely, so Nina talks about her mom. Elsewhere in the UK, it is more usual to say 'mum' so Morag talks about her mum.

ACKNOWLEDGMENTS

Writers often thank people who helped them during the writing process of the book and the people they often thank are other writers and editors and other people in the writing and publishing biz. We'd like to start by thanking our readers. Yeah, you. Whether it's by leaving reviews, or responding to our newsletters or by chatting to us directly on Facebook groups, readers have supported us through the writing of these books and many others.

Those readers have also been keen to help us with research and nuggets of personal and technical knowledge that have rounded out the narrative.

Among those readers, we would like to single out Sgt Mark Smith for being our informal military advisor and for providing sterling input regarding Rod's armaments and modus operandi. Mark provided us with a battle plan for storming the Cube that was so wonderfully comprehensive that we didn't have opportunity to include even a quarter of it in this book. Any omissions or mistakes in this area are definitely ours, not his.

We also would like to thank our friend and all-round good egg,

James Brogden, who was an invaluable source of information on Bella in the Wych Elm. Brogden's folk-horror novel, The Hollow Tree, tackles the Bella myth with far greater depth and sympathy than we do here.

ABOUT THE AUTHORS

Heide and Iain are married but not to each other.

Heide lives in North Warwickshire. Iain lives in South Birmingham.

It's a forty minute car drive door-to-door.

They do meet up in real life but far less than people imagine.

Website:

www.pigeonparkpress.com

Facebook:

The Comedy Kitchen

Clovenhoof Books

The Oddjobs Books Discussion Page

ALSO BY HEIDE GOODY AND IAIN GRANT

Clovenhoof

Charged with gross incompetence, Satan is fired from his job as Prince of Hell and exiled to that most terrible of places: English suburbia. Forced to live as a human under the name of Jeremy Clovenhoof, the dark lord not only has to contend with the fact that no one recognises him or gives him the credit he deserves but also has to put up with the bookish wargamer next door and the voracious man-eater upstairs.

Heaven, Hell and the city of Birmingham collide in a story that features murder, heavy metal, cannibalism, armed robbers, devious old ladies, Satanists who live with their mums, gentlemen of limited stature, dead vicars, petty archangels, flamethrowers, sex dolls, a blood-soaked school assembly and way too much alcohol.

Clovenhoof is outrageous and irreverent (and laugh out loud funny!) but it is also filled with huge warmth and humanity. Written by first-time collaborators Heide Goody and Iain Grant, Clovenhoof will have you rooting for the bad guy like never before.

F. Paul Wilson: "Clovenhoof is a delight. A funny, often hilarious romp with a dethroned Satan as he tries to adjust to modern suburbia. The breezy, ironic prose sets a perfect tone. If you need some laughs, here's the remedy."

Clovenhoof

Jaffle Inc

Alice works for Jaffle Tech incorporated, the world's biggest technology company and the creator of the Jaffle Port, the brain implant that gives users direct access to global communications, social networks and every knowledge source on the planet.

Alice is on Jaffle Standard, the free service offered to all people. All she has to do in return is let Jaffle use a bit of her brain's processing power. Maybe it's being used to control satellites. Maybe it's being used to further space exploration. Maybe it's helping control self-driving cars on the freeway. Her brain is helping Jaffle help the world. And Jaffle are only using the bits of her brain she doesn't need…

But when a kind deed goes wrong, Alice gains unauthorised access to her entire brain and discovers what she has been missing out on her entire life: music, art, laughter, love…

Now that she has discovered what her mind is truly capable of, how long will the company bosses let her keep it?

Jaffle Inc

Printed in Great Britain
by Amazon